WORLDS IN COLLISION

BOOK 2 OF THE *GEMINI GATE* SERIES
STEVEN E. WILDE

Worlds in Collision (The Gemini Gate series, Book 2)
Steven E. Wilde
Hardcover edition 978-1-77342-086-8
Paperback edition 978-1-77342-085-1

Produced by IndieBookLauncher.com
www.IndieBookLauncher.com
Editing: Nassau Hedron
Cover Design: Saul Bottcher
Interior Design and Typesetting: Saul Bottcher

The body text of this book is set in Adobe Caslon.

Also Available
Ebook edition, ISBN 978-1-77342-087-5

Other Books in the Gemini Gate series
Omega Crisis
World in Chaos
Battle for Aspen Valley
Door Between Twin Worlds

Dedicated to my five children.
Thank you for your support and encouragement. I love you all.

"And I beheld when he had opened the sixth seal, and, lo, there was a great earthquake; and the sun became black as sackcloth of hair, and the moon became as blood; And the stars of heaven fell unto the earth, even as a fig tree casteth her untimely figs, when she is shaken of a mighty wind."

—Revelation 6:12–13

"A man shall have in the skin of his flesh a rising, a scab, or bright spot, and it be in the skin of his flesh like the plague of leprosy."

—Leviticus 13:2

Prologue

The Mayfield home, Washington, D.C., 4 July

"*Mom!*" Levi called, as the front door slammed and two sets of young feet stomped across the linoleum floor.

"In my bedroom, Levi," she replied, without looking up from her packing. She closed the suitcase and laid it on the pile at the side of the dresser, then moved to the bathroom to see what was left.

"Mom!" Levi said from the bathroom doorway, causing Brianne to look up and see the reflections of her twins' faces in the mirror. Levi and Rebekah were thirteen, with Bekka about two inches taller than Levi, a result of her having started puberty. "Nick's family just left. Is it time for us to go, too?"

"Will you two take these suitcases, and the ones from your bedrooms, down to the front door? Then your dad can load them in the trailer when he gets here."

Bekka, named after her aunt, was calm and deliberate, in contrast to her younger brother's impulsiveness. When Levi turned and hurried to the stack of luggage, Bekka stayed at the door, looking at her mom.

"Are we going to die?" she asked. Her mother stopped, the bottle of lotion in her hand halfway to the bag she was filling with cosmetics.

"No, dear," she replied with a forced smile, trying to hide her own fear. "As soon as your dad arrives, we're leaving, and we'll be far away before the deadline."

"The news said all the roads are bottlenecked, because everyone waited too long before they decided to leave."

Bri went to her daughter, smiling reassuringly, and bent over slightly, so their faces were on the same level. *She's getting so tall,* Bri thought. *She'll be a woman soon.*

"We'll be fine," she said, putting an arm around Bekka's shoulders.

"Bekka, come and help," Levi called from the hallway. "I'm on my second load already, and you haven't done anything yet."

"Com-ming," Bekka said, rolling her eyes. Bri patted her shoulder as she backed away and turned toward the bedroom door.

"Dad's here," Levi called up the stairs a few minutes later.

Bri hurried down the stairs and met her husband as he was entering the house. After a quick hug and kiss, she backed up and looked into his tired eyes.

"You're late, Brady," she said, worriedly. "What happened?"

"Traffic," he said. "Drivers are ignoring traffic signals and blocking intersections. The police are trying to direct traffic at the major intersections, but everyone's just ignoring them. And what are they going to do? They're not going to hold up traffic by taking the time to write a ticket."

"Okay, well, we're packed and ready to go. You can check the bedroom while we start loading the trailer."

"Forget the trailer. We'll never get it through traffic. Put what you can in the car."

"It won't all fit in the car," Bri complained.

"Then I'll tie some to the ski rack. Or, we can have the twins sit on it."

They loaded the car quickly and pulled into the street. Almost immediately, Bri discovered what Brady had meant. Trying to merge into traffic at Mt. Vernon Square, one impatient driver came within inches of hitting their car rather than let them in. When Brady hit his brakes to avoid a collision, several cars behind him started honking.

She noticed a policeman looking their way, but he seemed more concerned with keeping traffic moving than crossing through traffic to straighten out one driver. He even sent cars driving down the wrong side of the road, just to keep the stream of vehicles flowing, but it was still bumper-to-bumper.

While they inched forward, Bri couldn't resist reminding Brady that they could have avoided this situation.

"I wish we'd accepted Terry's offer to let us stay with them for a few days," she said quietly.

"We've been over this," Brady said through clenched teeth. "My workload was too heavy to take the time off."

"You know that was only an excuse. You just didn't want to accept the possibility that Terry and his friends knew something you didn't."

"They only *suspected* the terrorists had a bomb. They believed what that idiot, President McCormick, told the UN, then tried to convince you that they were right." Brady's comment attracted the attention of the twins.

"Were they right, Dad?" Levi asked. "Do the terrorists have a bomb?"

"We don't know, son, but the president's decision to evacuate the city created this traffic nightmare."

"So, they *might* have a bomb. Then, why did we wait so long to leave? They closed the schools right after the president threatened Russia at the UN, and the government's been bussing people out of the city ever since."

Brady made eye contact with his wife before answering, wondering if she had prompted him to say that.

"There's no proof that they have a bomb, Levi, and I had a lot of work. You can see that a lot of other people believed the same way we did."

"The same way *you* did," Bri said quietly, so that only Brady could hear her bitter correction. "Well, we're about to find out."

The twins played on their tablets while Brady and Bri listened to the radio, which played quietly in the background, giving them reports of traffic jams for miles on every road out of the city. Each time they were about to merge onto a new street, Brady would claim that this was where traffic would start moving faster—then he'd get quiet again, as they continued to creep along.

"A snail could move faster than this," he finally complained, knowing his comment gave Bri one more opportunity to accuse him, and fully expecting it.

"Where are we going?" Bekka asked. "Mom?" she added when neither parent answered.

"First objective is to get at least twenty miles away from the National Mall," Bri finally said. "We're almost across the city. Once we cross the Potomac River, we'll be able to get on the Interstate, then traffic should move faster. We'll figure out where to go . . . after that. Probably toward the southwest."

When they merged onto the Potomac Highway, traffic did, in fact, move faster. *Finally*, Brady thought. Then they were over the river and onto the Interstate, where it accelerated quickly. He found himself releasing a breath he'd been holding, as he pressed down on the gas pedal to keep up with the cars ahead of them.

On the radio, the announcer said that military forces had been ordered to leave the downtown area.

"Dad!" Levi called excitedly. "There's a helicopter. Look! Out your window."

Brady took a quick look and confirmed that a military heli-copter appeared to be leaving the downtown area, flying parallel to them into Virginia at high speed. He wished they were moving that fast.

"Mom," Bekka said, her fear evident in her voice, "It's ten min-utes to three. Have we gone far enough?"

"We're fine, dear," Bri said.

Brady looked at her out of the corner of his eye and noticed her concerned expression. They hadn't gone nearly far enough to avoid damage from a nuclear explosion—if there *was* an explosion. He clenched his jaw and thought furiously about how and where they could find shelter.

His anxiety level increased quickly as they continued for sev-eral more minutes at freeway speed. He realized how close they were to the deadline, and that if he was wrong, if there really was a bomb, he had put his greatest treasure—his family—in deadly danger.

He wondered why he had let his pride get in the way. They could have taken that trip to Utah to be with Bri's family for a few days. His mind was reeling and he was losing hope, until their high-speed race to safety reminded him of a TV program he'd seen of storm chasers, who'd hidden under an overpass to avoid the worst of a tornado as it passed overhead. Was it possible that they could do the same thing? He realized that the thought had been prompted by a highway sign that identified an off-ramp just ahead. He could see that there was little cross-traffic passing un-der the freeway on the two-lane road. He checked his side-view mirror and plunged into the right-hand lane, cutting off a car that was in his blind spot and continued onto the off-ramp. At the bottom of the ramp, he cut through the lighter traffic, not bother-ing to use a turn signal, and slammed on his brakes, stopping on the side of the road under the bridge.

"Everyone, get down," he said, "and cover your head." Bri lay down across the center console without removing her seatbelt, then Brady threw himself on top of her, just as the earth shook beneath their feet.

"Dad!" Levi said.

"Get down! Stay down until I tell you to get up!"

It was as if the world around them had come to life, as if a giant had picked up everything in its path and thrown it at them—trees, fences, chunks of houses and garages, even cars filled with people crushed almost beyond recognition—flew past them, and into them, while the wind shrieked.

The ground bucked, picking up their car and throwing it against the concrete underside of the bridge, smashing it and dropping it back into the jumble of rubble. The last thing Brady remembered was the car being thrown backward and smashed by heavy objects, then rolling, over and over.

Two thousand miles away, in a hidden bunker near Logan, Utah, Terry Stephens thought about his sister, Bri, and prayed that she and her family had gotten away in time.

1

It would be madness

"I still can't believe they actually did it."

President Gregory McCormick had just finished watching a live helicopter news report of the nuclear explosion in Washington, D.C., from his small office in the Prime bunker.

The report had shown a fireball, two thousand feet in diameter, exploding from the National Mall, and forming a mushroom cloud over the great city. Within moments, the cloud had risen a thousand feet into the air. A shock wave had swept furiously across the landscape, destroying everything in its path and creating a boiling debris cloud that spread across the landscape in all directions.

The Washington monument had been struck by the shock wave and toppled, shattering into pieces as it fell. The Capitol building, at the other end of the Mall, had exploded violently at almost the same time. The Smithsonian buildings, on either side of the Mall, had been blown apart and carried away on the nuclear wind, adding millions of high-speed projectiles to the cloud.

Everything within a mile of the National Mall had been obliterated within seconds—not a building or monument was left standing—and structures had suffered major damage for miles.

"The United States adopted a nuclear deterrence policy during the Cold War," his secretary of defense, General James Seymour had explained weeks earlier, "which held that the threat of using strong weapons against the enemy, prevented the enemy's use of those same weapons." He knew that the United States and Soviet Union had built stockpiles of nuclear weapons, along with delivery systems, back in the fifties and sixties, and that by the time the Cold War had ended, there were enough nuclear weapons in the world to annihilate civilization several times over. Eighteen countries had signed the *Treaty on the Non-Proliferation of Nuclear Weapons* by 1970, and 191 countries had eventually agreed to adhere to the *NPT*. But despite the treaty, more than twenty-two thousand nuclear weapons still existed in the world at last count.

"The U.S. position," Jim had continued, "was that, once armed, neither side had any incentive to initiate a conflict, or to disarm. It created a stalemate, neither side willing to risk starting a war that would cause the complete annihilation of both the attacker and the attacked—what we call mutually assured destruction, or MAD."

"How appropriate," McCormick had replied sarcastically. "It would be *madness* to start a nuclear war."

"Exactly," Jim had said. "But Soviet policy during the same period was that a nuclear war *could* be fought and won. Maybe they still think that way, and that's why their Siloviki—former KGB, turned mafia, turned industrialists—are willing to supply nuclear technology to madmen."

"Should we let them destroy the capital and not retaliate?" the president had asked, testing Jim's resolve.

"Greg," Jim had said, "I'm glad we're finally willing to take the war to the terrorists, and the countries complicit with them. If we knew where the Al-Qaeda strongholds were, I would obviously have recommended an attack on them. Since we don't, attacking

Russia and North Korea will have to do—and it'll send the same message."

Greg couldn't deny the fact that each terrorist attack seemed bolder than the last. If Al-Qaeda had found a willing partner among the Siloviki, the United States and her allies could expect to see more nuclear attacks in the future. It framed a dismal picture.

He had reluctantly agreed that they should respond to a nuclear attack with nuclear weapons—exactly what he had told the United Nations General Assembly.

Now he wondered what the freedom-loving people of the world thought as they watched the report. *If they see that we can't even protect ourselves, how can they possibly hope that we'll protect them?*

NSC meeting, Prime bunker situation room
4 July, 3:15 p.m. eastern time

President McCormick walked slowly into the room, focused on an internal debate about how to handle this meeting of his National Security Council. He needed to tell his people that he had authorized a nuclear retaliation, and he knew there were some folks on the council who didn't support that decision. In fact, he was convinced that there was at least one traitor in this group, someone who'd been leaking information to their enemies, though his security people had yet to identify that person or persons.

The room was filled to capacity, with an assortment of presidential advisers, NSC members and staff, Congressional and Senate leaders, and Supreme Court justices. The eight monitors on the wall showed him the situation rooms of the other underground government bunkers, similarly occupied and spread across the continent.

All eyes turned toward him as he moved to the midpoint of the conference table and sat facing the wall of monitors.

Currently, the SEC DEF monitor was tuned to the news broadcast from the Washington, D.C. station that he and Jim had been watching earlier. The only sound in the room was the voice of the reporter, and the president could see from the expressions on people's faces—shock, anger, or fear—and the bowed heads, that they were as horrified as he was. The scene changed suddenly to show SecDef Seymour, who was just settling into his seat. The president made eye contact with him and nodded, hoping that his face masked his inner feelings.

"As you can see," McCormick began, "Al-Qaeda followed through on their threat, with the help of unprincipled co-conspirators. North Korea has also launched a missile, aimed at Seattle, Washington. In response, I just authorized the military to fire three missiles, as I promised—no, as I threatened—in the United Nations General Assembly meeting a few days ago. A conventional weapon will intercept the North Korean missile, a nuclear missile will retaliate against North Korea, and the third—also nuclear—is targeted on Moscow for their part in supplying the nuclear technology to the terrorists."

The response in the room was sudden and loud—some voicing support for his action and some questioning—which caused the president to raise a hand for silence.

"I would have preferred to strike directly at Al-Qaeda," he continued, "but contrary to what some believe, we still don't know where the terrorist leaders are hiding."

"Tom?" McCormick turned to his director of National Intelligence, Thomas Mitchell, who was seated at the table in the DNI bunker's situation room.

"Yes sir?"

"Did we determine how the Los Zetas drug cartel smuggled the bomb into the country?"

"Our best guess is the low-profile submarines we heard about."

"So, that wasn't just a rumor? Has the Coast Guard confirmed their existence?"

"It's no rumor. I was notified this morning that they found one, scuttled, off the coast of North Carolina."

"A million-dollar submarine, used once and discarded?"

"That's what it looks like. They're raising it now. We'll test it for trace radioactivity, which should tell us if it was the one that was used."

"Did we find the terrorist that was working with the cartel to assemble the bomb?"

"No, sir. It's possible he was the one who carried it into the city and detonated it, in which case we won't find him."

"You think he was the one who detonated it?" the president asked.

"No, not really. Al-Qaeda generally uses sleepers to do their dirty work. Then they can walk away to plan their next attack. I suspect the terrorist handed the bomb off to some brainwashed young man, who was ready to make the ultimate sacrifice for the cause and receive his great reward."

"Mr. President," Jim interrupted. "You should see this recording. It shows what happened after the explosion."

Greg nodded, and Jim's face was replaced by a view of the mushroom cloud and destruction of Washington, D.C., taken from the same helicopter they had been watching earlier. As he watched, the force of the explosion began to shake the news helicopter, which tilted forward, knocking the reporter and camera to the floor. The reporter's flailing legs were the only visible sign that he had been there at all. Screaming and cursing screeched through the reporter's microphone just before a loud explosion filled the air. Then the video failed altogether. The scene changed abruptly to a temporary newsroom in a school classroom, where a distraught anchor was watching his co-anchor run off-stage with her hand over her mouth.

The recording disappeared and Jim's face returned to the SEC DEF screen. In the quiet of the room, the president thought of the dead and dying, of the earlier reports of looting and violence in major cities across the country, which had become deadly, but the scene they had just watched felt much more personal. McCormick's stomach churned. Looking around the room, it was clear that many others had been similarly affected.

As everyone sat silently, an aide brought a report to the SecDef, detailing what had happened, and Jim knew immediately that he needed to tell the president.

"Mr. President?" Jim said, almost in a whisper. He was sure his face reflected the shock he felt.

"What is it Jim?"

"China . . . " he started, then had to swallow before starting again. "The Cheyenne Mountain control center in Colorado reports that China just launched ninety-nine missiles at the United States."

He looked up to see the president's reaction before continuing.

McCormick stared at him for several moments before responding.

"What?" he finally asked.

"It says, 'China just . . .' "

"I heard what you said," McCormick cut him off, becoming

agitated. "I'm just having trouble understanding. Are you saying China launched *a hundred* missiles, in response to the *one* we launched at North Korea?"

Jim wasn't sure it was wise to correct Greg in his current frame of mind, but he wanted the recording of this discussion to be accurate.

"Actually, sir, we launched two missiles in the direction of . . . "

"One, two, what's the difference?" Greg interrupted again, his voice rising in pitch as he squirmed in his seat and pounded the table in front of him. *"A hundred missiles? What message are they trying to send us?"* He swore, which was unusual for him. Suddenly he paused, tilted his head to one side, and stared at Jim.

"You said ninety-nine. Why not an even hundred?"

Jim studied Greg for a few moments, wondering if his good friend was having difficulty handling the stress.

"We're not sure. Perhaps they tried to launch a hundred and one failed." He paused before continuing, wondering if he should go on. "One of my analysts suggested that it might have been intentional." At Greg's questioning look, he sighed. "To the Chinese, the number nine is considered lucky. It means everlasting, long-lived, eternal. The analyst thought it might mean that China was using an overwhelming show of force at the beginning of the conflict to try to convince us to stand down and let them win."

"What, they think we won't respond to ninety-nine missiles being thrown at us?"

Jim had no response to that, so he looked down, then continued reading.

"They also reported that, of the ninety-nine missiles—they can't tell how many of them are nuclear—some are targeted at missile batteries across North America, particularly those in Montana, North Dakota, and around Cheyenne, Wyoming, two on Cheyenne Mountain, in Colorado, and others at major cities in the West and Midwest.

"*This* is disturbing," he continued without looking up. "Some of the missiles are targeted at previously unacknowledged missile batteries." Jim looked up. "They shouldn't have known those silos existed."

"How *did* they know?" the president asked.

"My best guess is that either they somehow broke into our classified databases, or we have sleepers in our military who compromised the information." As he expected, there was murmuring in his bunker—and probably the others—as people looked around, instinctively trying to determine whether a spy was right there among them. He hoped the security personnel were making note of any unusual reactions.

He paused to see if there would be any more questions, but the president just stared at him, so he moved on.

"A breakdown of the reported targets has been sent to each of the bunkers."

A military aide quickly placed a document in front of the president, then fled out of view at Greg's stern look.

"Russia also launched forty-five missiles . . . "

"Russia, too?" The president interrupted and swore again.

"Again," Jim continued, "we don't know how many of them are nuclear. Some are aimed at our eastern cities, and others at our allies in Europe and Israel."

Despite the overwhelming response from China and Russia, Jim had little doubt that the military could intercept all the missiles. He was surprised at how satisfying it was to be at war, and to be in charge of the offense.

The look of deep concentration on McCormick's face made him think Greg was too tired to understand what he was hearing.

This could be bad, he thought. If Greg couldn't handle the stress, someone might argue that he was unfit to lead and should be relieved of duty, and that would put the vice president in charge. Then where would they be?

"We had your prior authorization as to how to respond," Jim continued, "if Russia did more than intercept the missile fired at them, and if China launched any missiles: we would return fire with three times the number of missiles launched by China and Russia. Our primary objective would be to intercept the Chinese missiles with conventional weapons, and attack all of their known and suspected missile batteries, storage, and production facilities—and a few major cities, excluding Hong Kong. The westbound Russian missiles would be countered by our weapons batteries in England and France."

"And you did that?" The president asked.

"We did, including three nuclear missiles sent to the site in North Korea where their missile originated. The list of sites in China, Russia, and North Korea should be in front of you."

McCormick hesitated, as if confused by Jim's comment, then rifled through the pages in front of him until he found what he was looking for.

"It is. Okay, Jim." He set it down without reviewing it.

"Perhaps, sir," Jim said, "you'd like to review the reports before we proceed. I suggest we take a break and resume in, say, half an hour."

"Good idea," McCormick said distractedly, then looked at his watch.

"Back here at . . . 4:30, alright?"

Chantilly Shopping Center, Chantilly, Virginia
3:20 p.m. eastern time

Saleh drove around the area for over an hour watching for signs of a tail. Finally, satisfied that he wasn't being followed, he parked the rental car, walked into the shopping center, and approached the UPS Store. He used his key to open post office box 125 and retrieved two letters. One was addressed to Samuel Smith and the other to Andrew Jones. The family names meant nothing and the first names were code names. He was Samuel, the name he had used in England. He would learn who Andrew was if and when he needed to know—a brother from one of the Al-Qaeda cells in the U.S., he suspected—but he wouldn't open Andrew's letter. He returned it, closed and relocked the box, and placed the key in his pocket.

The letter for him would likely be from Ahmed, in Damascus, Syria, since he was Saleh's handler. It had been mailed before the explosion in Washington, D.C., so it was probably new instructions. His last communication to Ahmed had been to inform him that the bomb had been successfully assembled and was ready to smuggle into the U.S. He had intentionally neglected to tell Ahmed about the attack by armed soldiers—probably Americans—at the Los Zetas cartel plantation and the attempt to sabotage the bomb. It was better that Ahmed believe all was well. If he had failed, Ahmed would know because Saleh would be dead and in paradise, and there would be no explosion in Washington, D.C.

The drug lord, Jose Mendoza, had surprised Saleh by playing what he had called a *shell game*, moving the bomb from one location to another, using multiple trucks as decoys. He had said that it was to confuse the American spy satellites—assuming it was the Americans who had infiltrated the plantation—and a tactic that they had used successfully on numerous occasions to move drugs to the border.

When Mendoza had stopped at a dock on the Gulf of Mexico, Saleh couldn't tell why they were there, until Mendoza pointed out a small platform leading to the access hatch of a mostly sub-merged submarine. Saleh hadn't known the depth of the water at the dock, or the dimensions of the sub, but he'd had trouble believing that so little of the boat had been exposed.

"This will be your transportation to the United States," Mendoza had said with a sly smile.

Two of Mendoza's men had lifted the crate containing the bomb and carried it onto the sub, stuffing it through the hatch, one leading and the other following it down. Then Mendoza had made a hand gesture, indicating that Saleh should follow. Mendoza didn't offer to shake hands, or give words of encouragement or congratulations, nor did he thank Saleh for the rifles and bul-let-proof vests he'd received in exchange for his help and which had saved his life at least once already.

Saleh had hoped for a chance to kill Mendoza, and that had been his last opportunity. He'd considered how he could do it, but Mendoza's bodyguards were never more than a few feet away from him. Saleh was willing to sacrifice his own life, but he would have had to kill at least three men before he was subdued or, more likely, shot. That would have caused him to fail in his primary mis-sion and he hadn't been willing to displease Allah and his brothers in Syria.

So, he'd followed the bomb into the hatch and down the ladder to a dimly lit passageway that ran in both directions. The guard who had followed him pointed aft—the direction they had taken the bomb—and he'd had to stoop to avoid bumping his head, which had given him a better idea of the boat's size.

The guard had stopped him at an open hatch on his right and

pointed inside. He'd paused to watch the guards ahead of him carry the bomb through a similar opening about ten feet farther down the passageway, until the guard behind him nudged him in the back. He'd turned, prepared to curse the guard in Arabic. But seeing the sour expression on the guard's face and the automatic pistol in his hand had changed Saleh's mind, and he'd entered the small room. The only furnishings were a cot attached to the wall, a toilet and sink in one corner, and a cooler, which he'd confirmed contained an assortment of simple food and bottled water.

As soon as the sub had started to move, rocking from side to side, he'd become seasick, and had remained so the entire time he was onboard. He found he could neither eat nor drink, and everything he'd had in his stomach, he'd lost over the next few hours. When he wasn't bent over the toilet, he tried to rest on the cot or pace his tiny room for exercise. He tried to leave the room once, but the armed guard outside his door motioned for him to remain in his room. He remained in his room for the four-plus days that it took to reach their destination.

He hadn't been aware that the boat had stopped until someone knocked on the door, entered, and started speaking to him in rapid Spanish, pointing toward the door. He hadn't understood a word of it, but it had been clear that the guard wanted him to follow. The entire room swam before his eyes, and he'd considered lying back down, but when he'd noticed the bomb crate pass the open hatch, he'd decided that no matter how he felt, he needed to follow it. So, he'd struggled to his feet, making a final stop at the toilet to dry heave, before following.

It had been dark outside, but he could tell they were in open water, with a small fishing boat tied off to the little bathtub-shaped enclosure that kept seawater out of the hatch. The crate had been lifted into the fishing boat and taken immediately into the cabin, and he'd followed. No one had said a word and no one had smiled.

He hadn't known that the people on the fishing boat were Americans until they were well away from the sub and the sky had begun to lighten toward sunrise. The men had become light-hearted, drinking beer and talking about the night's catch, as if fishing was all they'd been doing that night.

"Hi. I'm Tim," one of the men had said as he'd entered the cabin. "We're at our destination. Your crate is being loaded into the trunk of your rental car. Time for you to go."

Saleh had been told that the cartel would set up transportation for him, but he'd expected to be driven to someplace where he could rent a car.

"The paperwork . . . " he started to say, but was cut off by Tim, if that was his real name.

"No problem. The car is rented to Samuel Smith, the name we found on your passport while you were asleep," Tim said with a sly smile.

Saleh's hand went automatically to his inside jacket pocket, where he'd kept his faked passport. It was there, but he pulled it out anyway and checked that it was the right one, which it was. When he looked back up, Tim was turning away, the smile still in place.

At first offended that they'd searched him, he'd realized after a moment that it didn't matter. He would never see them again, and they wouldn't turn him in because they had much to lose if they contacted the authorities. Besides, he'd been pleased to know that he'd actually been able to sleep on the fishing boat.

He'd found a map of South Carolina in the glove compartment of the car, which he'd used to get away from the coast. He'd driven around until he'd been satisfied that he wasn't being followed, then had found an internet café where he'd bought a coffee and pastry—he hadn't thought his stomach would handle anything heavier yet—then placed an innocuous post on a specific website, letting his contact in the U.S. know that he had arrived, and that he was en route to their prearranged meeting site in Nashville, Tennessee, and providing his estimated arrival date and time.

"Hi, the name's Adam," his contact had said when they'd finally met. Adam had looked like he could be a middle easterner, but with his flawless American English, Saleh hadn't been sure.

"Here are the keys and address for your apartment," Adam had said, handing him a set of keys and a folded piece of paper. "The apartment's close by," he'd added, handing him a folded map. "The location's marked on the map. It was rented in the name of Samuel Smith six months ago. The person who rented it paid for a one-year lease, saying that you'd be in and out a lot. Finally," he'd continued, handing Saleh a fat manila envelope, padded and still sealed, "here's a package I was told to deliver to you with instructions not to open it until you get to the apartment. I don't know what's in it and you won't see me again. Good luck with whatever it is you're doing."

Saleh had been focused on what might be in the envelope, not paying particular attention, when Adam had surprised him.

"Allahu akbar," Adam had said. *God is great.* Then he'd turned and walked away, lost in a crowd of people.

"Allahu akbar," Saleh had replied, finally confirming that Adam was a sleeper, and that per procedure, he had been activated for this specific assignment and may, or may not, ever be used again.

At the apartment, Saleh had opened the package, finding cash and several prepaid phones. There were the keys for, and directions to, another apartment in Virginia, and instructions for his mission, including how to contact the sleeper who would carry the bomb into Washington, D.C. What he hadn't expected to find was a loaded 9mm handgun, with a spare, loaded clip and a box of ammo. *What do they expect me to do with these?* he'd wondered then, and still wondered, since he hadn't needed to use them.

He'd contacted his sleeper, Austin, who lived in a rundown apartment building north of Washington, D.C., and activated him with a few key words that Austin had been given years earlier when he'd traveled to Islamabad and been recruited. To satisfy himself that Austin hadn't had second thoughts and reported the contact from Al-Qaeda, Saleh had hung up and called back with instructions after Austin had had time to inform authorities. He had Austin get in his car and go from one location to another, waiting until he arrived at each destination before telling him the next. Then Saleh followed him to see if they would pick up a tail.

Finally, Saleh had met Austin in a park. But before making himself known to the young man, he'd watched him for another thirty minutes, instructing him by phone to move from one part of the park to another, so Saleh could see if he was being followed on foot.

When he'd walked up to Austin and spoken in his Queen's English, he'd watched to see Austin's reaction. Would he be upset at the runaround, or patient and understanding of the need for confirmation.

"Hello Austin," he'd said, sitting down by him.

"Are you Samuel?" Austin had replied excitedly.

"I am. Can we go somewhere quiet to talk?"

"Anywhere you'd like. I can't believe you've finally contacted me."

They'd walked down a wooded path and arranged to meet again at a library. Saleh had arrived early to watch, one more time, to be sure Austin wasn't being followed. Austin had said all the right things and seemed ready to make the ultimate sacrifice for Allah.

In the course of their discussions, Saleh had discovered that Austin worked in the National Gallery of Art on Constitution Avenue in Washington, D.C., just blocks from the Capitol and the White House, plainly the reason that he'd been selected for this mission. It was a perfect hiding place for the bomb.

He had given Austin instructions on how to detonate the bomb, then delivered it in its crate to the rear of the building, immediately following the delivery of a shipment of crated artwork that was to be displayed in a few days. Austin had confirmed later that all of the delivered crates had been moved to the basement storeroom and the bomb crate hidden in a corner, as instructed.

When the curator of the Gallery had notified everyone that the building was being closed and everyone evacuated because of the bomb threat, Austin had contacted Saleh on a disposable cell phone and told him he was going to the storeroom. He would lock himself in and detonate the bomb at the appointed time. But Austin had been nervous, so they had prayed together and gone over the instructions several times. At 3:00 pm exactly, with Saleh on the phone praying with him, Austin had detonated the bomb. The phone line had gone dead, along with Austin and thousands of others who were still in the area.

Saleh had found the key and directions to P.O. Box 125 in Chantilly, Virginia, in his Virginia apartment, with instructions to get there as soon as he was finished in Washington, D.C. Now, here he was, in Chantilly, holding a letter that he knew had been sent from Syria and routed through at least two cities in the United States, by existing cells. The routine had been explained to him before starting this mission. Each cell, at each location, would open the envelope addressed to them, to find another envelope inside with another name and address on the outside. His envelope would be the final one, with his instructions inside.

What he didn't know, and wouldn't have cared if he did, was that, by coincidence, he was standing within a stone's throw of the elementary school where a TV news team was reporting on the explosion of a nuclear weapon in Washington, D.C.

Las Vegas, Nevada, 12:33 p.m. pacific time

The nighttime pedestrian bustle and lights of the Las Vegas Strip had transitioned into the hectic traffic of daytime business. The freeways were packed with locals going about their business, intermixed with tens of thousands of tourists trying to get to their hotels, or just passing through the Southern Nevada bottleneck to reach destinations in California, to the west, or Utah, to the east. Anyone getting off the freeway for gas or lunch, soon discovered that it took as much as thirty minutes just to get back on again. The streets were still crowded with tourists, but not nearly as many as the night before.

Few people, besides those at Nellis Air Force base, north of the city, were aware of the inbound Chinese missile.

The base had been notified as soon as NORAD had identified the missile's destination, twenty-seven minutes earlier. The Air Force, accustomed to emergency exercises, scrambled jets and other aircraft immediately, emptying the hangers, aprons, and taxiways. Whether the threat was real or a drill they didn't know, but either way they were getting the planes off the ground. The few military personnel left behind at the base—mainly communications and traffic control—headed for emergency underground bunkers.

The FBI, and other government agencies, along with police and emergency units in the area, had also been notified, but the civilian leadership was not as disciplined as the military. The bureaucrats who led the various agencies questioned the seriousness of the threat, then argued about what to do about it. Heated phone calls, from the mayor of Las Vegas to the chief of police, started the ball rolling to get local emergency units mobilized. Unfortunately, there was no alert system to warn the civilian population. The Las Vegas Police Department and the FBI finally started calling casinos, businesses, and homes, but only minutes before the missile arrived.

It was lunchtime, and people from around the world filled the restaurants and streets. While it was nothing new to locals, those visiting the city heard the sound of the aircraft passing overhead and craned their necks upward, pointing in awe as their formations headed in various directions at high speed. A few actually saw the missile as it grew in size, appearing to descend from directly overhead. They speculated excitedly that it might be a flying saucer or some other mysterious craft from Area 51. A few wondered if it was somehow related to the aircraft from the air force base. The few who knew what it was were already headed for shelter. Having done all they could, they abandoned the city and its citizens to their fate.

When the missile struck, the massive explosion left a deep crater where the base had been. Buildings and equipment, along with the men and women hidden in underground bunkers, were disintegrated in the first second, their fragments mixing with the desert sand and melting into fine glass particles, to become part of the radioactive fireball that spread out in every direction. The crater in the sand became a solid sheet of glass, many feet thick.

The shock wave spread out from the base, travelling at over five hundred miles per hour, vaporizing buildings. The heat wave—hotter than the sun—followed less than a second behind, melting flesh off the bones of people in its path, their bones disintegrating to ash, to be blown away on the wind.

Within seconds, the radioactive fireball extended over a mile from ground zero. At the Las Vegas Motor Speedway, where a race was in progress, the blast picked up speeding cars, fences, and stands full of spectators, and tumbled them together with the cars, RVs, and buses in the parking lot, then crushed and melted the combination into unrecognizable heaps of exploding and burning rubble.

On the highways, the blast crushed cars like accordions and blew them off the road. Farther away, the wind blew traffic to a standstill in every direction, then pushed it back, creating massive pileups of cars and trucks. Police and emergency vehicles, attempting to get into position to redirect traffic, became casualties. People who weren't killed instantly were trapped in their cars and survived for only a few seconds before their cars caught fire or exploded. Even the asphalt on the roads was melted and swept horizontally into rough waves. The accompanying heat and wind covered an ever-larger area, reducing slightly in their intensity.

North Las Vegas became a debris field. Residential buildings were flattened for several miles and high-rise buildings suffered major structural damage. Fires started and consumed large sections of the city. People inside the doomed buildings were crushed by collapsing walls, ceilings, and structural steel, dying long before the radiation could poison them. People in the open suffered horrible deaths. Nothing on wheels or legs could move fast enough to get out of the way.

As the giant mushroom cloud rose into the air, the winds at ground zero died, then reversed direction, being sucked into the vacuum left by the cloud. Anything on the ground light enough to become airborne was sucked back toward ground zero—toward what had been a powerful and important military installation.

Only minutes had passed.

Honolulu, Hawaii, 9:34 a.m. Hawaii-Aleutian time

When NORAD contacted the Pearl Harbor Naval Base, on the Island of Oahu, the military scrambled their aircraft as they had been trained to do. Most of the ships—except those in dry dock—had enough warning to get out of range of the expected explosion.

Notified of the emergency, the Hawaii Emergency Management Agency, HI-EMA, sent a push alert to smartphone users, which read: BALLISTIC MISSILE THREAT INBOUND TO HAWAII. SEEK IMMEDIATE SHELTER. THIS IS NOT A DRILL.

Television and radio broadcasts were interrupted by an audio message and scrolling banner, that stated:

> BALLISTIC MISSILE THREAT ALERT: If you are outdoors, seek immediate shelter in a building. Remain indoors well away from windows. If you are driving, pull safely to the side of the road and seek shelter in a nearby building or lie on the floor. We will announce when the threat has ended.

Hawaiian government officials, concerned over escalating tensions between North Korea and the United States, and recent North Korean ICBM tests, had been working for some time to refresh the state's emergency plans in case North Korea actually launched a nuclear attack. The government had started monthly tests of the alert system in late 2017, based on estimates that a missile launched from North Korea would leave Hawaiian residents only twenty to thirty minutes to prepare, once the warning was sent.

When the push alerts were received, people all over the islands stopped to look at their smartphone screens. Many thoughtfully considered whether this was a false alert, like one they had received in January 2018. But those who'd received Alert System test alerts after the false alarm understood that this was not a test or a mistake. They immediately hurried to the nearest public shelter, or to a nearby building to shelter in place. Tourists and locals who didn't have their cell phones with them observed the scene of urgency—even panic—and wondered what it was all about. Shouts of warning encouraged them to rush to nearby buildings to find out.

Twenty-three minutes after the first notification to the local populace, the missile scored a direct hit on the naval base, vaporizing that portion of the island, including the airport, and destroying most of downtown Honolulu. The ocean boiled, the water joining the vaporized rock, structures, vegetation, and bodies that exploded into the air.

The shock and heat waves spread outward from Honolulu. Funneled northward by the east and west mountain ranges, fires burned through the central valley, destroying buildings, pineapple plantations, and everything else between Pearl Harbor and the North Shore. People who thought to find shelter inside the Tetsuo Harano Tunnels, east of Honolulu, were caught by a five hundred mile-per-hour nuclear wind that tore through the tunnels, pushing and crushing everything ahead of it. Those protected from the explosion by the mountains were endangered by fires that raged across the mountains and down to the oceans. Of those who managed to avoid the fires, many braved the turbulent waters of the Pacific, and some of those were rescued by boats from the nearest island, Molokai, to the east, during a frantic rescue mission.

2

I was hoping we got everyone out

NSC meeting, SEC DEF bunker, 4 July, 4:30 pm eastern time

SecDef Jim Seymour sat in his situation room in the SEC DEF bunker, in Maryland, surrounded by the usual participants—military and government leaders and advisers—and all of the video screens were lit up.

The president looked refreshed, and a smile lit his face.

"We stopped all their missiles, right?" McCormick asked, optimistically.

Jim cringed and took a deep breath, hesitant to start his report, and watched the president's smile turn to a frown. Jim was frustrated—no, embarrassed—that his people had failed to intercept all of the inbound missiles. There had never been a real test of the missile defense system, but the failure was totally unacceptable. This was not the news he wanted to give his commander-in-chief, and the answer must have been obvious from the look on his face. Finally, he pulled himself together, accepting the failure as his responsibility, and began.

"Of the ninety-nine missiles fired by China, we succeeded in intercepting ninety-two, most of them over the Pacific."

"And the other seven?" McCormick asked, his frown deepening and his brow furrowing.

"Near-direct hits on the naval bases at Pearl Harbor and Everett, Washington, near Seattle; the Columbia Nuclear Plant

34

near Richland, Washington; the Lawrence Livermore National Laboratory at San Francisco; Nellis Air Force Base in Las Vegas; Naval Base Point Loma in San Diego; and one on the city of Los Angeles. All of that in addition to the nuclear bomb detonated in Washington D.C."

President McCormick returned to the meeting, refreshed from a power nap and in better spirits, convinced that the military superiority of the United States would handle the situation. But he was totally unprepared for Jim's report.

"Repeat that," he said.

Jim listed the seven locations again.

He cringed and swore again, thinking about the targets. Worse than he'd thought possible, and that was just the first volley.

"All of them in the western states, except the capital. Is that a coincidence?" Greg thought about people he knew in those cities—personal friends, acquaintances, and political supporters.

"We don't think so. The missiles that reached their targets were the first to pass their apogee and start back down. We had direct hits on the missiles, but the warheads had already separated, and one or more warheads from each missile survived the impact."

Greg thought about a family of five he knew in San Diego—good friends, a young couple and three small children—and said a quick prayer for them.

"How could that happen?" he asked no one in particular. He thought Jim looked like he'd been slugged in the stomach. The man was a good friend, and he hadn't meant his comment to sound like an accusation—he'd been surprised and frustrated by the military's failure to stop the missiles. "Sorry, Jim. Not your fault."

"With all due respect, sir . . . "

"Drop it, Jim. I won't shoot the messenger. We've never tested the missile defense system. Never needed to, thankfully . . . until now. We're probably lucky we stopped as many as we did."

"Yes, sir," Jim said, contritely.

"What about the missiles from Russia?"

"We got them all, sir," he said flatly.

Greg thought he was holding back. "But?"

Jim took a deep breath.

"Those that were destroyed over Europe resulted in massive EMPs, blacking out most of the EU. I'm afraid they're in for some tough times."

"An unintended consequence," Greg said, wincing and shaking his head. "What damage did our missiles do?"

"I'm still waiting for that report, sir. We know the Chinese launched an additional 199 missiles to counter ours. The Russians countered, as well. Here's the report now, sir," Jim continued, as a military aide placed a report in front of him and spoke in his ear. "A copy is on its way to you. Of the 297 locations we targeted in China, it looks like we hit 136. They're included in the report."

"Why didn't China stop more of our missiles?"

As Jim explained, Greg thought about the 1.4 billion people in China and wondered how many had already died.

"I can think of two possible reasons, sir. Like us, they've never tested their missile defense system. Or, if they used a large portion of their stockpile of weapons in the first volley, they might have decided to keep something in reserve."

"Clarify that for me."

"Yes, sir. They launched ninety-nine in the first volley . . . "

"Forget the numbers," Greg said angrily. "Why did they hold

back?"

Jim looked embarrassed. Greg assumed it was because of the military's failure, but another idea occurred to him. *Maybe he's embarrassed for me.* He was struggling to control his emotions, not handling this well.

"I think," Jim said, "that China overestimated their success or underestimated our resolve. They must understand by now how serious we are, and that they can't win. They're probably keeping missiles in reserve to protect their government bunkers. As far as we know, they only had about 450 nuclear missiles to begin with. We don't know how many of the missiles they've already launched were nuclear and how many were conventional, but they've already used almost 300 missiles. They may be out of the war, unless Russia decides to try to even the playing field further. But, if you're asking why China's government would hold back, and allow us to hit 136 targets?" Jim paused and Greg nodded for him to proceed. "I asked myself the same question. It's possible they aren't as worried about protecting some of the civilian sites."

Greg frowned and Jim shrugged.

"They're a large country, with a large population and relatively few defensive weapons."

Greg shook his head in disbelief. The Chinese had to be more concerned about their population than that, but he let it go.

"Okay. What about the missiles we fired at Russia?"

"With the 135 missiles launched from England and France," Jim looked at the report again, "we were able to destroy all of the missiles Russia launched. We hit twenty-three targets in the Russian provinces, but they intercepted the rest."

"Did we hit the Kremlin?"

"No sir, sorry."

"Send me the list."

"Yes sir."

"Any follow up from China or Russia?"

"None so far."

"What about India, Pakistan, and Israel? Or Iran?"

"No," Jim said and shook his head.

"Okay," Greg sighed, dreading the answer to the next question. "Who has a casualty report on the eight cities that were hit?"

"I've got what we have so far, sir," Director of Homeland Security Chuck Dickson said quietly.

Greg looked at the HOME SEC screen and could tell from Chuck's expression that he didn't want to share his report any more than Greg wanted to hear it.

"Go ahead Chuck," he said, trying to concentrate.

"Each of the eight explosions resulted in a large crater at the epicenter, surrounded by total destruction for a half mile to a mile in every direction. Farther out, the damage to the infrastructure was lower, but there are fires everywhere, many of them still burning. The only places on the island of Oahu that weren't devastated by fire were along the east and west coasts, where there was some protection provided by the mountains."

"Can it get any worse?" Greg asked morosely, as he stared at the table top, shaking his head.

"Do you want the worst, sir?"

Greg looked up and stared at Chuck, seeing the pain and sadness in his eyes.

"I better hear it," he said.

Chuck started slowly, likely debating how much detail needed to be shared.

"We've been gathering data from traffic cams in each of the cities and their suburbs. Before the cameras went out, they recorded a lot of the damage in progress, including the impact on the civilian populations."

"I was hoping we got everyone out of the big cities."

"That would be mostly true for the capital, but not the West Coast. They didn't have sufficient warning, or didn't take the warnings seriously."

"And that's my fault, dammit." He realized that he had a headache when it spiked, nearly immobilizing him. He folded his shaking hands on the table and looked straight ahead, seeing nothing but bombs exploding and people dying.

"Sir, the decision to delay communicating to the public . . . "

"Was my decision!" he yelled, his heart pounding in his chest and his head throbbing. *"Don't you dare* say it was a group decision. We talked about the possible impacts, but it was *my call.* I'm not going to put that on you or anyone else. Is that understood?" He jabbed a shaky finger at the monitor and looked around the room, breathing heavily, daring anyone to disagree. No one said a word. He moved his hands to his lap, under the table, so no one could see how badly they trembled. He tried to calm himself, breathing deeply a few times, then continued more calmly.

"Do we have any idea on numbers of casualties?" he asked, his voice uneven.

"Not yet," Chuck said. "We're working on estimates based on satellite images and analysis of the lead time given to the civilian population."

Greg thought about the death and destruction and wondered if he would go to hell for his part in this disaster. Would he be remembered, along with Hitler and Mussolini, for the millions of deaths on his hands? He shook himself out of his funk.

"What's being done for the capital and the other seven locations?"

"Sir," Chuck said, "Gary Monroe is the director of FEMA—

the Federal Emergency Management Agency. Their historical role has been to coordinate the federal response to floods, hurricanes, tornadoes, and wildfires—disasters that overwhelm the resources of local and state authorities. Since FEMA is part of Homeland Security, I've invited Gary to join us at the table."

"You're thinking that FEMA is in the best position to help us deal with the current emergency?" Greg asked.

"I am, sir," Chuck replied. He nodded toward a fiftyish man with a marine haircut who was sitting on his right in the HOME SEC situation room. "This is Director Monroe."

Monroe raised a hand.

"Welcome Director," Greg said.

"As you know," Chuck continued, "the current emergency is a little outside FEMA's normal remit. We've asked the military to assist us in delivering aid to the impacted locations as soon as we have direction on what to do. As a former marine, Director Monroe should have no difficulty coordinating the effort. Jim?"

"I've asked General Robert Peatross, chairman of the Joint Chiefs, to head up our side and work with Director Monroe," SecDef Jim Seymour said. "General Peatross?"

"I met with my staff after the first explosion," General Peatross said from his JCS bunker situation room. "They're already organizing first responder and hazmat teams for all eight areas as we speak. I've been on the phone with Director Monroe and we should have a progress report later today or first thing in the morning."

"Good," the president said. "Please contact my chief of staff, Eric Epstein, as soon as you have something, so he can set up a status meeting. Anything else ladies and gentlemen?"

"Actually, yes," the SecDef said.

"What is it, Jim?" The president was so exhausted, he didn't know how much more he could handle.

"The few Chinese missiles that were destroyed near or over land emitted EMPs that affected several western states. We're still assessing the extent of the problem, but it looks like most of the infrastructure in California, Oregon, Washington, Nevada, and the western portions of Arizona, Utah, Idaho and Montana, are shut down."

"Like Europe, you're talking about communications, transportation, water distribution, everything, right?"

"Yes, sir, including the electric power grid. FEMA and the military will organize to move food and water west. We'll also put together a plan to distribute hardened communications and transportation equipment to the distressed areas."

"Good. Anything I need to do?" Greg knew that it was the right question to ask, but his heart wasn't in it.

"It might be a good idea if you went on the air to tell the public that the government is still functioning," Chuck said.

"Good idea, Chuck. Eric," the president said tiredly.

"Yes sir?" Eric Epstein, the president's chief of staff, replied quickly from behind him.

"You're in the room. Good. Let's get our heads together right after this meeting and draft a message. Go see who's still on the air that can send it out."

"Right away, sir." Eric said and rushed out of the room.

"Is there anything else?" Greg asked, looking across the monitors again.

"Unfortunately, there is, sir." FEMA Director Monroe said.

"Yes, Director?"

"The explosions from the Chinese bombs created radioactive clouds, which are headed northeast along the entire West Coast, from San Diego to Alaska. With all communications now out on the West Coast, we're planning to use the Emergency Broadcasting System to broadcast instructions over the air, in case anyone still has the means to receive a signal. We'll also use mobile units, as soon as we can get them in place, to go through neighborhoods telling people to seek shelter."

"That's going to take some time to put in place, isn't it? What about the nuclear fallout?"

"Yes, sir, and it's a lot of territory to cover. We're more used to dealing with localized, and less urgent, emergencies. We'll have to have treatment facilities set up to deal with the cases of radiation sickness. We'll also prepare fliers on medical self-treatment that we can hand out."

"Hand out, as opposed to sending electronically," the president muttered, shaking his head. "Back to twentieth century technology. Anything else?" He looked around one more time. "Okay then. That's it for now. NSC meets again at six." He turned to see that Eric had returned to the room, but spoke so everyone could hear. "No one sleeps until we have this under control. Contact me if someone needs me."

He stood up, staggered, and placed a steadying hand on the back of his chair, then straightened and walked out, followed by his chief of staff.

"Sir?" Eric asked, as they walked down the corridor to Greg's office.

"Yes, Eric? What is it?" Greg asked tiredly.

"Excuse me saying so sir, but you look like you could fall asleep, standing. I think it would be a good idea for you to rest before your next meeting."

President McCormick's teeth clenched as he looked over his shoulder. *A lot of good the last power nap did me,* he thought. The intensity of his expression caused his chief of staff to stop walking.

"Eric, you heard what I said. We're going to get ahead of this, and I'm not going to be the weak link." He walked away, leaving Eric standing in the hallway.

Vice President Art Klemp watched the president's awkward exit and smirked, but quickly hid his expression.

This might be the opportunity he'd been waiting for. If he could successfully claim that Greg was unfit for duty, he could step in as next in line and take control.

He needed to talk to someone. As everyone stood and filed out of the room, he spotted Senator Robert Stenger, met him at the door, and asked him to walk with him to his office.

Art had found the senator to be a willing listener who shared his concerns, over drinks, about how Greg was managing—or mismanaging—the office of president of the United States. Art suspected that he might have shared too much information with the senator in the past, since some of what they had discussed had ended up reported on the evening news.

Art had believed that most of the shared information was non-essential, but *juicy*, until Greg had accused him of being the leak that resulted in the death of several soldiers. *Overseas somewhere,* he thought to himself. Art had denied being the leak—after all, he couldn't control the senator—but Greg had cut him out of all classified discussions since then. In fact, Greg had rarely spoken to Art after that.

Art's security detail, led by Perry, his head of security, followed closely behind, ever vigilant.

Colonel Johnson, the senior military officer in the VEEP bunker, sat down in the chair Art had just vacated—in front of the camera—and nodded to SecDef Jim Seymour.

"Senator Stenger walked out with the vice president and his security detail," he said. "Anything you want me to do?"

"Just continue to keep an eye on them," Jim replied.

"Art," Senator Stenger said, "what can I do for you?" So far, the senator had been able to stay below the president's radar, but being seen as closely associated with Art could attract the wrong kind of attention. He'd made a lot of money off the classified information Art had given him in the past, and Art had made a lot of money on Wall Street from the insider information Stenger had provided in return. It was the way Washington worked. But that could all change if they got arrested for selling government secrets. And who knew what this war was going to do to the economy and their portfolios.

"Bob, we've got to get Greg declared unfit for duty. You've got to help me."

"What can *I* do?" Stenger asked, surprised by the suggestion. Sure, the president was under a lot of stress and not handling it well, but he'd hate to put the fate of the world in Art's hands. Art was irrational and easily influenced even in the best of circumstances. He would come completely unglued under the pressure the president was facing. He didn't want to encourage Art, but decided he'd have to at least hear him out.

"I don't know," Art said. "Talk to people. Express your concern about Greg's mental stability under stress. People will see what we're seeing and agree. Once everyone's talking about it privately, someone will make a comment in a meeting and it will all come out."

"And if no one makes a comment in a meeting?"

"You can talk someone into doing it, or do it yourself."

"Let me see what I can do," Stenger said, but he thought to himself that if Art were in charge, they'd have to do the same thing to him—sooner rather than later.

Art smiled conspiratorially, so Stenger smiled back, except that his smile was artificial, meant only for Art.

3

We'll try to calm the public

Chantilly, Virginia, 5:18 p.m. eastern time

Saleh was sitting in a motel room, reading though the letter he'd picked up at the UPS Store earlier, trying to memorize his instructions before destroying it. He had the TV on mute, waiting for the announcement. The letter—from Ahmed, as he'd expected—said that Ahmed had been given the privilege of recording the next broadcast, that it would be televised on Al Jazeera television at 5:00 p.m. eastern time, and likely rebroadcast on U.S. network television within minutes after that. Ahmed wanted Saleh to see it, because it related to Saleh's next mission. He was already packed and would be ready to move as soon as the broadcast was over.

Prime bunker, 5:25 p.m. eastern time

A military aide knocked on the open door of the president's office, where he and Eric were working on the message he would give to the country in a few minutes.

"Sir," the aide said, "I was instructed to suggest you turn on your video monitor. Al-Qaeda just broadcast a statement on Al Jazeera TV, and we have a recording of it. We'll pipe it through to you."

Greg groaned and waved at Eric to turn it on.

A few seconds later the recording started. A man in traditional Arab garb stared into the camera, his face covered except for his eyes, which were dark and intense, and shook his fist at the camera. His bold voice was full of challenge. Although he spoke in his native tongue, an English translation had been added at the bottom of the screen.

"We, the children of the great God, Allah be praised, have struck a blow and brought the United States of America to its knees. We are preparing a second and final strike, which will at long last cut the head off the great Satan and her minions in Europe and Israel. The wheels are already in motion and there is nothing you can do to prevent this attack, which will occur at three p.m. eastern time on July eighth. We are Al-Qaeda, the sword of God."

The recording ended and Greg looked at Eric, seeing fear and insecurity in his eyes. Greg could feel the heat in his flushed face, and his jaw flexed in concentration.

"That's enough!" he said. "We'll try to calm the public. Then we take the offensive."

Despite his fatigue, Greg was suddenly focused like he hadn't been all day. Although, as far as he knew, Al-Qaeda was only responsible for the one bomb in Washington, D.C., the fact that they appeared to be taking credit for more, and continued to threaten the United States, angered him nearly as much as the bombings themselves.

"If it's the last thing I do," he said through gritted teeth, "this will be their last act of terrorism, and the last time they boast of their *pathetic* strength."

The concern Eric had been feeling, just moments before, fled in the face of the president's renewed energy. He'd worried that Greg would exhaust himself and leave the country at the mercy of people like Vice President Art Klemp. He was opposed to war, but with all the needless death and destruction, he longed for a demonstration of U.S. strength and resolve. He hadn't been alive in 1941, when Japan had bombed Pearl Harbor, but he wanted to see the U.S. show the same backbone it had then. He believed President Gregory McCormick was the right man to lead the country to victory, as long as he didn't wear himself out first.

"Get with Cy Hutchison and set up a conference call with the Prime Ministers of the UK, France, and Israel, as soon as possible," the president told him.

"You have the public statement at a quarter to six and the NSC at six," Eric reminded the president. "Do you want the conference call before or after? It's getting late in Europe and the Middle East."

The president took a deep breath and shook his head.

"We better make the public statement first. But the NSC can wait. Better yet," he corrected, "it would be good for my advisers to sit in on the conference call. So, get Jim, Tom, Chuck, and Cy to their situation rooms and pipe it in whenever Cy is ready. The rest of the NSC will have to wait until we're finished."

Eric looked down at the incomplete draft of the president's public statement, thinking about everything that needed to be done.

"Why don't you go set up the conference call and I'll finish up the statement," the president said.

"Are you sure?"

"I'm sure," the president said, smiling kindly.

As Eric hurried away, he sighed, remembering the first time the president had smiled at him like that. He'd been hired by an aide to work on Mr. McCormick's first Senate campaign, writing speeches, fifteen years earlier. After months of intense effort, he had still had little feedback to indicate that Mr. McCormick liked, or had even noticed, his work. That changed late on election night, after a particularly long and tiring day of campaigning, with few breaks, and little time to eat. The other candidate had just conceded the Senate race and Mr. McCormick had given his acceptance speech, drafted by Eric and revised by others in a few places. Family and key advisers surrounded Mr. McCormick to celebrate, amid congratulations and camera flashes.

Suddenly, Mr. McCormick had looked right at Eric, then excused himself and walked over. He placed an arm around Eric's shoulders, led him to the side of the room, through throngs of well-wishers, gave Eric the same smile he was seeing now, and thanked him.

Eric still remembered the compliment Mr. McCormick had paid him.

"Eric," he'd said, "you have a unique ability to understand what the public wants to hear. I know sometimes I've changed what you've written, and I'll probably continue to do that, because the words have to be my own, but I want you to know that I'm convinced your speechwriting is among the primary reasons why I won this election."

Eric had been speechless. Mr. McCormick had continued, still smiling.

"Bill told me this week that he's got other things to do, so I'd like you to stay on and be the head of my speechwriting team. What do you say?"

Eric hadn't known what to say, so he'd just nodded dumbly.

"Great," newly minted Senator McCormick had said, slapping Eric on the back. "See you tomorrow."

The Preserve, Logan Canyon, 3:18 p.m. mountain time

Terry and Amos returned to the office to listen to the remainder of the news report on the explosion in Washington, D.C., while Mike helped with dinner preparation.

Terry turned on the recording to what they had been watching earlier in the day, where the Washington, D.C. news anchors had just handed off coverage of the explosion to their Boston affiliate after watching their associates in the Skycam helicopter crash.

The camera was focused on a woman's serious face.

" . . . estimated wind velocities in excess of five hundred miles per hour before the equipment quit working. We still can't get close enough to identify where, exactly, the bomb was located, but aircraft flying at forty thousand feet, before being forced to leave the area due to the rising mushroom cloud, report the entire Washington, D.C. area is a huge debris field with nothing identifiable standing, not even the Washington Monument. The overpressure zone, the area where physical damage to the infrastructure is apparent, encompasses at least a four-mile radius around the Mall. Beyond that, we can't tell. There are numerous fires throughout the area."

The camera backed away from the woman to show a modern newsroom, with both the woman and a male co-anchor sitting behind a desk. The man broke into the report.

"We're being told that the radioactive mushroom cloud is headed our way. We've been instructed to leave the area immediately. This is Brent Close and Holly Stark in the Channel 4 newsroom in Boston, signing off. We are handing you off to our affiliate in Seattle, Washington. Stay safe."

Both reporters were out of their seats, removing their microphones and moving off-screen, before the camera even stopped. Shouting could be heard off-screen.

The scene on the TV changed to show a man entering the set and moving toward the news desk. He sat nervously on the edge of a desk and looked down at some papers in his hand. A woman started to enter the set, but the man looked up, waved her away, and began to speak.

"Hello, this is Gene Joiner, with Channel 2 News in Seattle, Washington. We have new information on the missile launched from North Korea that was targeted at Seattle. The government confirmed that the military has launched a missile to intercept and destroy the North Korean missile. However, the danger is not past. The destruction of a nuclear warhead over the Pacific may cause an electromagnetic pulse, or EMP, which could knock out all communications in the city, maybe the entire northwest. It depends on how close the missile is to the coast when it's intercepted.

"Our studio is being evacuated to shelters immediately. Everyone within the sound of my voice: if you haven't already gone to shelter, you should go immediately. South is your best choice, but north, south, or east, it doesn't matter. The government will get to us as soon as they can. Get out, now. Goodbye and God bless."

He was up and moving before he finished talking. He didn't bother signing off—the camera just turned off.

The TV screen was blank for about a minute, and then the two reporters they'd been watching earlier, in their temporary newsroom, appeared again.

"Hi again," the woman said. "Melanie Kearns and Dennis Spaulding here." A dry chuckle. "That was rather abrupt. Those poor people. What else is happening Dennis?" She sounded nervous, maybe a little scared. She shuddered involuntarily, then licked her lips, as though she still had a nasty taste in her mouth from vomiting after the helicopter crash.

Dennis looked at his co-anchor, a worried expression creasing his forehead.

"So, um, it appears we have been selected to be one of the official reporting stations for the government until the Emergency Broadcasting System takes over," he said, looking at Melanie, who was staring at the camera. "Don't they test that system every once in a while? Melanie?"

Melanie turned toward Dennis abruptly, as if she had just realized he was talking to her.

"Oh. All the time, Dennis."

"Okay," Dennis continued. "We're told the government thinks we're safe enough here in Chantilly, Virginia, for now, and we're getting updates from the government as we speak." Someone handed a couple of sheets of paper to Melanie as Dennis spoke to the camera.

"Here's a summary of what the government knows at this time," Melanie said, then started reading. "A nuclear device, estimated size, one hundred and fifty kilotons, was detonated near the National Mall, at three o'clock today, eastern daylight time. At the same time, North Korea launched a missile at Seattle, Washington, nuclear capability unknown. At 3:02 p.m., the United States launched three ICBM missiles, one to intercept the North Korean missile, and the other two, with multiple nuclear warheads, directed at Pyongyang, North Korea and Moscow, Russia.

"Um . . . at 3:07 pm, China launched multiple missiles at the United States. At 3:08 pm, Russia also launched missiles at the U.S. and our allies in Europe. Numbers, nuclear capability, and destinations have not yet been reported." Melanie stopped again and wiped her brow with a tissue. She looked at Dennis, who's face betrayed the same concern she appeared to have.

"The government," Melanie continued, "will take action to stop all inbound missiles. The intercepts should occur in the next fifteen to twenty minutes." She glanced at Dennis again, nervously, then continued.

"If the missiles are intercepted over the ocean, there should be little impact to the infrastructure. If intercepted over land or near the coast, an electromagnetic pulse, or EMP, may knock out regional communications and transportation.

"Worst case is that one or more warheads will survive the intercept and reach land. In that case, you have thirty to forty minutes to seek shelter." She stopped reading and turned to look at Dennis. "Does that mean thirty minutes from now, or thirty minutes from when the missiles were launched?"

He shrugged, but the fear in his eyes was evident. She started reading again, her voice cracking as she began.

"The g-government advises all citizens to remain calm and seek shelter immediately. They recommend that if you don't have an underground bunker—" She turned to Dennis again. "Do you have one Dennis?"

"Not many of those around," he replied, shaking his head slowly.

"You should get out of the open," she said, turning back to the camera. "It says the greatest risk will be from high winds, which will knock down buildings, and from high temperature, which will travel on the winds. So, the best place to be is below ground, in an underground shelter or basement. If you have a nuclear-qualified shelter in the area, private or public, go there. If you don't, go to the innermost portion of a building, but get out of the open. Wow!"

"They said to seek shelter immediately," Dennis said. "Did they mean, like, right now?"

"And get there in thirty to forty minutes." She said, then stared at Dennis without speaking, so Dennis jumped in again.

"It says that there is a list of public shelters online. Or you can call the number scrolling at the bottom of the screen for shelter information." A phone number and website address began scrolling across the bottom of the screen.

"Okay, we'll get you more information as it's given to us. We're going to find out what we need to do. In the meantime, we'll rerun some of the footage we showed earlier. Stay safe. We'll be right back."

Terry began flipping channels to see if there were updates from the government. On one channel, the presidential seal filled the screen and a banner ran continuously under the image, which read: **PRESIDENT GREGORY MCCORMICK WILL SPEAK TO THE NATION IN 2:24 MINUTES. PLEASE STAND BY.**

"What do you think that is?" Terry asked.

"Let's find out," Amos replied.

They waited patiently as the timer ran down, finally reaching **0:03, 0:02, 0:01, 0:00.**

"Please hold for President Gregory McCormick, president of the United States of America," a voice said. This announcement was followed by the voice of President McCormick.

Prime bunker, 5:45 p.m. eastern time

"This is President Gregory McCormick," Greg said in a sad, serious tone. "You know my voice. I'm speaking to you from a bunker near Washington, D.C. I am saddened to inform you that, despite our attempts at peaceful dialogue, and our warnings to our enemies, we were unable to prevent a nuclear attack on our country, earlier today. You probably saw TV footage of the explosion in our nation's capital. In addition, several dozen missiles were launched at our country from North Korea, China, and Russia. We retaliated in an effort to intercept the missiles and prevent further attacks. While many of our weapons struck true, unfortunately, some of our enemies' missiles also hit their marks.

"Significantly, despite our best efforts and our success at blocking nearly all of the weapons launched at our country, seven nuclear weapons, launched by China, struck communities here, primarily along our west coast and in Honolulu, Hawaii. Communications have been disrupted by interference from the explosions, so much of the western part of our country can't hear this broadcast.

"To those of you who *can* hear me, let me say that I am truly sorry that your government was unable to protect you from the needless destruction and misery that has been caused by the actions of selfish people who place little value on human life.

"Rest assured that your government is still functioning and is, as we speak, mobilizing to minister to the needs of those who have been affected. We are currently rushing aide to the impacted areas and will continue to do so until we are on our feet again.

"You may be asking what you can do to help. Please remember the famous words of President John F. Kennedy, who said, 'Ask not what your country can do for you—ask what you can do for your country'. What I ask you to do, first and foremost, is to take care of each other until we can get to you. If you have food, water, and shelter to spare, share it.

"Those who've been exposed to nuclear fallout will need care. Don't go looking for them and risk becoming contaminated yourselves. The best place to be now is indoors, away from the fallout. However, if those affected should come to you, please, please take them in. They need to be bathed, to remove the contamination from their skin, and given fresh clothing to wear. Destroy their contaminated clothing.

"Don't worry about casual contact with them. The cause of their suffering is not contagious. But they will need medical care. And if you or someone in your household needs care, we suggest you hang out a bright cloth—red or yellow will be most noticeable. Hang it in a window, or outside your door, where we can see it quickly and get medical assistance to you.

"The most important thing you can do to help others is to make them comfortable. But above all, keep yourselves safe. I will now turn the microphone over to our medical experts, who will give you additional precautions that you should take to prevent contamination to air, water, and food.

"Always remember: we are a great people. Together we have faced and overcome other disasters. We will face the current crisis with courage, and overcome it with the same resiliency we have shown in times past. I have faith in you, my fellow Americans. God bless America."

Eric watched the president, flanked by technicians, back away from the microphone on his desk and bow his head. One of the technicians turned off the president's microphone while the other listened through his headset, counting off on his fingers—three, two, one—then nodded. Eric knew that the technician's signal meant medical personnel, waiting at other microphones, in Prime and other bunkers, had begun a quickly-coordinated broadcast of additional instructions.

Eric looked at the president with compassion. This was a good man caught in an impossible situation. He hoped the president was listening to his own advice. He would need that courage to get through the current crisis . . . and the next election, he thought optimistically.

4

It's a good plan

Prime bunker, 6:00 p.m. eastern time

President McCormick arrived in the Prime situation room to find his advisors already in their places. Each was alone in his respective situation room. They waited for Greg to speak.

"Any change in the international situation?" Greg asked.

"Everyone seems to be waiting," Jim said.

"All of our intelligence sources have gone quiet," Tom added.

"What about the domestic situation?"

"There's a lot of chaos around the capital, in the western states, and other major cities, of course," Chuck said. "We're still getting organized to help."

"Any idea on casualties?"

Cy, who had a desk phone to his ear, placed a hand over the receiver and nodded to the president. Greg held up two fingers and mouthed, "two minutes," letting Cy know to give him two minutes before sending the call through. Cy spoke briefly into the phone, likely giving instructions to an operator, then hung up. The president then gave his advisers a brief summary of what he was going to do.

The phone rang and the president pushed the button to put the conference call on speaker.

"President McCormick here," he said.

An operator's voice came over the speaker.

"Mr. President, we have Prime Minister Theresa May of the United Kingdom, Prime Minister Édouard Philippe of France, and Prime Minister Benjamin Netanyahu of Israel waiting."

"Please connect them," the president said.

"When I hang up, they'll be on the line."

"Thank you." There was a click on the line as the operator hung up.

Brief greetings were exchanged. The president acknowledged the late hour and thanked them for making themselves available.

"Under the circumstances, Greg," Prime Minister May said, "none of us is getting much sleep. What news do you have?"

Greg had always enjoyed Theresa May's charming British accent. He thought it reflected her strength and education. He had fond memories of the weekend he and his wife, Liz, had stayed in London so Theresa could cook dinner for them. Her husband Philip had told Greg that Theresa was a very good cook, and she'd proved it.

Greg brought them up to date on events since their most recent discussion, a few days earlier, then addressed his current thinking.

"This latest statement from Al-Qaeda has me concerned for all of us. Even though it sounds like typical terrorist rhetoric, I'm now convinced that the Russian government, or their industrialists, are selling weapons to Al-Qaeda. We're prepared to take the offensive to try to stop them. We want to know how each of you feels about a nuclear war in the Middle East."

Prime Ministers May and Philippe waited for Prime Minister Netanyahu to speak, since Israel would be most directly affected.

"The Israeli people have been preparing shelters for just such an exchange for years," he said determinedly. "We're prepared for an offensive, if necessary. What do you propose?"

They spoke for a few minutes about options, and the potential impacts of nuclear explosions and EMPs on their countries and regions. They agreed that the terrorists had to be stopped, regardless of the cost. They compared lists, prepared by their advisers, of suspected Al-Qaeda strongholds and weapons stashes, and came up with a list of thirty-two probable sites in Iran, Syria, Libya, Algeria, Afghanistan, and Pakistan. They discussed the activity at ports on the Caspian and Black Seas, adding four more sites in the Russian provinces to their list. Minister Netanyahu identified another thirteen suspected ISIS hideouts, which they all agreed should be added to the list.

They debated the most likely reaction from Russia and other countries with nuclear weapons, then considered whether to warn the governments of the world that they were preparing to take the offensive.

"Not bloody likely," Minister May said emphatically. "Let's hope we catch them all napping."

When they finished talking, Greg summarized their plan.

"We'll begin bombing all forty-nine sites at six a.m. eastern on July eighth, three and a half days from now. That will make it the middle of a warm Sunday afternoon in northern Africa and the Middle East, and should catch most of the terrorists in their hiding places. Each of us will prepare our populations, but without showing our hand to Al-Qaeda or the rest of the world. We'll begin announcing publicly that we're preparing our citizens for the announced attack from Al-Qaeda, though our offensive will preempt the terrorist attack by about nine hours."

"Good," Minister Philippe responded. "I will recommend that other concerned European Union states also prepare shelters to protect their people from the terrorist threat, without tipping our hand."

While Minister Philippe was speaking, the president raised his eyebrows at his advisers, in effect asking for their agreement. He got thumbs up and nods of agreement across the board.

When Minister Philippe was finished, Greg asked the three world leaders if there was anything else they needed to consider.

"Do we believe that our offensive will prevent whatever it is that Al-Qaeda has planned?" Minister May asked. "What if they have sleepers in each of our countries, already in place, to carry out their threat with more nuclear weapons?"

"Good questions, Theresa. We need to keep looking and coordinate our intelligence, just in case."

"Agreed. It's a good plan. Let's hope it's good enough."

"I also agree," Minister Netanyahu said.

The president soberly thanked the leaders and bid them Godspeed, then ended the call and turned back to the screens in front of him.

"Anything else before we invite the rest of the NSC into the meeting?" Greg asked. After receiving only shaking heads in response, he added, "Where were we?"

Chuck raised his hand.

"Right," the president said. "I was asking Chuck about casualties. Let's wait for the others. Tom, will you give the word?"

Tom picked up his desk phone and spoke quietly for a moment. Within a couple of minutes, the other four screens lit up and the door to Prime opened. As the NSC members entered their respective situation rooms, side conversations were quickly concluded and everyone took their seats.

"Thank you all for your patience," Greg said, "while I completed a strategy session with our allies."

"What was the direction and outcome of the conversation?" Vice President Art Klemp asked.

It was, of course, the question the president expected to hear, even though he was not going to divulge the plan to take the offensive, but it irked him that it was Art who asked it first.

"We shared information about casualties in each other's countries and exchanged intelligence on Al-Qaeda activities."

Art was about to ask another question, a suspicious look on his face, so Greg hurried on. "Chuck has prepared an estimate of casualties. Go ahead Chuck."

"We can only guess at the number of casualties at this point," Chuck said. "I've sent you a quick estimate, based on the current population of each of the affected regions and the amount of warning people were given. We also factored in the number of foreign nationals we think left the Washington, D.C. area before the explosion.

"In summary, there are about thirty million people in the eight affected metropolitan areas. This table shows our figures for each metropolitan area." A table replaced Chuck's face on the HOME SEC screen in each of the bunkers, listing the eight locations, along with the estimated size of the nuclear warhead, the population of the area, and the estimated immediate death toll and injuries. "As you can see, with just a few days warning in the western states, we estimate maybe three million deaths and over four million additional injuries."

"These are just estimates, right?" Greg asked, surprised at how high they were. "The actual numbers could be much lower?"

"Or much higher," Chuck said. "There's no way to get better data at this time."

Greg tried to absorb the enormity of the disaster, while Chuck waited patiently.

"Do you want us to try to mobilize medical professionals from the unaffected areas," Chuck finally asked, "and send them in to help?"

"What's your recommendation?"

"Well, I'm worried that medical professionals might be needed where they are if Al-Qaeda follows through on their threat of further attacks," Chuck said. By the time he was finished, Greg was nodding his head in agreement.

"Everyone," Greg said, pleadingly, "we need all of you focused on your areas of specialty. If you see or hear anything that needs my attention, especially regarding the affected areas, or if you have any ideas on how we can help our people, please, pass them up your chain of command."

There were murmurs of agreement all around him.

Vice President Art Klemp sighed as he watched Greg. Instead of the tired, clumsy oaf from earlier in the day, Greg now seemed very presidential. Art had started asking questions as soon as the meeting had started in order to show that he could be a *take-charge* kind of president, but Greg had cut him off. He made eye contact now with Senator Stenger, who shook his head once and looked away, further disappointing Art.

The Preserve, Logan Canyon, 5:35 p.m. mountain time

Terry retrieved the Geiger counter from where he'd left it, just inside the lab, and tested the air. The radiation that had entered the lab through the portal during their test of the Observer earlier had dissipated enough that he no longer felt threatened by just being in the lab.

"The radiation has dispersed," he said. "It's still hard to imagine. Have we really created a portal to some other time or place?"

Amos remembered his excitement and confusion from earlier in the day, when they'd tested the Observer with two different control panels, and thought they'd discovered a portal.

"I'm still having trouble getting my head around the possibility, Terry. Have you thought any more about where the radiation that entered the lab might have come from?"

"Well, the explosion in Las Vegas was about two hours before the radiation sensors hit their low consumption threshold. If we make a couple of assumptions—like what we were seeing in the portal was our valley, and the winds from the explosion averaged about two hundred miles an hour between Las Vegas and here—then it could be radiation from that explosion."

"How likely is a two hundred mile an hour wind over that distance?"

"Well, it's less than four hundred miles from Las Vegas to here as the crow flies. If the nuclear winds started out at five hundred miles an hour in Las Vegas, I would think their velocity would decrease too fast to get here in two hours, but we have no basis for comparison. Maybe I could find some facts on the nuclear testing in Nevada in the fifties that affected Southern Utah. You want me to try?"

"I don't know if it's worth your time. Besides, I don't know how applicable those tests results would be. St. George is under two hundred miles from the Nevada test site, isn't it?"

"Yeah, something like that."

Prime bunker, 7:50 pm eastern time

President McCormick sat at the desk in his small office, looking at the reports he'd been given. It wasn't as comfortable as his personal office in Washington, D.C. or as nice as the Oval Office, but it was comfortable enough. He had a padded swivel chair that didn't squeak and an oak desk with drawers. He sat facing the open door and could see the elbow of one of his security guards standing just outside. Besides the notes he was reading, the only thing on the desk was a picture of his family which had been taken on the podium in the ballroom of the Crowne Plaza Hotel in Columbus, Ohio on election night, when he'd given his acceptance speech.

Eric knocked on the door frame and entered the room excitedly.

"Mr. President," Eric began, "it's Secretary Hutchison. The Russian president is on the line. He wants to talk to you."

"Has the NSC gathered?"

"They're just sitting down now for the eight o'clock meeting."

"Okay, get my advisers in there. Tell the remainder of the NSC that there's a delay. We'll let them know when we're ready for them. Give me five minutes to brief my advisers, then put President Putin through, voice only."

"Yes, sir." Eric walked briskly away, the rapid clicking of his heels on the linoleum floor dying away. Greg rose, collected his notes, and hurried to Prime, followed by his security detail. Tom, Jim, Chuck, and Cy had already arrived. They all looked up expectantly as he hurried to his seat and acknowledged them with a nod.

"President Putin is calling. What do I need to know before I talk to him?"

"They continue to mobilize their nuclear arsenal and activate their military," Jim said.

"We believe they're selling weapons systems to Iran and Syria," Tom added. "As you know, Iran wants nuclear weapons capability,

Syria wants to be rid of Israel, and Russia just wants to destabilize the West. These are long held positions, so we don't know how any of them tie into the current situation."

"Anything new Tom?"

"Traffic on the Caspian Sea between Russia and Iran is about the same as before. Nothing new."

"Movement of Russian troops into the southern satellite states," Jim said. "Could be normal military exercises, but I doubt it."

"Okay, thanks. I want you all to hear this conversation, but don't say anything unless I ask."

He pushed a button on the phone in front of him and told the operator to put the call through.

"President Putin's office," a male voice said in Russian-accented English.

"President McCormick is on the line now." A click and the operator had dropped off the line.

Vladimir Putin's voice came on the line. He spoke excellent English from his years as a KGB officer.

"Mr. President. So good to talk to you."

"This is early for you, President Putin. What time is it, five a.m.?"

"Yes, there's a lot to keep track of these days."

I bet there is, Greg thought, cynically.

"What can I do for you?"

"Ah. Straight to business. I like that. I called to clear the air with you, to be certain that there are no less-than-friendly intentions between our two countries."

"You have a strange way of showing your *friendly intentions.*"

"You refer to the unfortunate missile exchange. You have seen that our defenses are set on automatic response mode. You sent missiles at us, so our system responded. All of our actions have been defensive, not offensive, in nature. We have no stomach for an ongoing conflict."

Several possible responses ran through Greg's mind, like, "forty-five missiles to stop our one." He considered and rejected each one—none would be helpful in the current situation. He was certain that Russia would love to have some hawkish comment from the leader of the free world to put on the airwaves. His mind finally settled on something.

"So, we have your assurance that you're not providing offensive weapons to Eastern or Middle Eastern states that have less-than-friendly intentions toward their neighbors on the world stage."

"Absolutely. We have no dealings whatsoever with that sort. You can rest assured."

"So, if we find that you *are* selling tactical or strategic weapons to, say, Iran or Syria, we can take it that you have not been forth-coming, that your true intentions are far from friendly, and that we should prepare to defend ourselves and our allies? Is that a fair assessment of the situation?"

"Mr. President, you offend my honor." Putin sounded genu-inely hurt.

Greg paused before responding.

"Why did you call, President Putin?"

"As I said, we want to know that you are not preparing to initi-ate another offensive missile exchange."

Putin didn't emphasize the word, *another,* but Greg clearly understood Putin was accusing the U.S. of starting the nuclear exchange. Greg wanted to set the record straight but decided that would be a distraction from the real issue.

"And you ask for this assurance at the same time that your military is readying your nuclear arsenal and your industrialists are selling weapons to Iran and Syria." Greg didn't really know Russia was selling weapons to Iran or Syria, but he decided to try a bluff to see Putin's reaction. He wasn't disappointed.

Putin hesitated, just briefly, but it was enough.

"Mr. President, I assure you, we are not supplying offensive weapons to any of the countries that concern you."

"That's not what our sources say, Mr. President."

"Then I'm afraid your sources are mistaken."

Liar! Greg thought and decided to push this to the limit.

"And if we discover that they are not mistaken?"

"Then I suppose you will have to do whatever you think is fair."

"Sounds like we understand each other. Goodbye Mr. President. Please call again when you have *more* enlightening news." When Putin didn't respond, Greg hung up.

Moscow, Russia

Putin sat at his desk in his hardened bunker. He was not happy about the way his conversation with the American president had gone. He had hoped to disarm the United States with platitudes, but McCormick had shown more backbone than he'd expected, which was consistent with his launching of the three missiles following his threat at the UN.

He hadn't invited others to listen in, since he wasn't certain of the outcome of this meeting and didn't want to be embarrassed later when it was brought up in a Politburo meeting. Still, he was certain it had been recorded, and could yet become a problem for him. But Russia could still win this war—it was what he'd believed for many years.

Prime bunker

"Well, what do you think?" Greg asked his advisors.

"I'd say you hit the nail on the head," Tom said, a tight smile on his lips.

Greg returned the smile, but it was filled with concern.

"Tom, get in touch with your counterpart in Israeli intelligence, again. Bring him up to speed and see what he'll tell you."

"How much should *I* tell *him?*"

"You can tell him what we suspect about Russia's intentions. You can also try to determine if Prime Minister Netanyahu informed him of our plans. If he wants details, tell him you know that I spoke to the Prime Minister."

"Will do." Tom said as he stood up to leave.

"Tom," Greg said, making Tom stop and look at him. "You heard Theresa May's questions. Can we be sure that our offensive will prevent the next terrorist attack?"

"I've been thinking about that. The terrorist must have left tracks. We'll try to find them, starting with the submarine."

"Have you raised it?"

"Yes. It's an amazing piece of workmanship. So small that it can enter shallow waters, yet big enough to carry a huge payload of drugs—or a nuclear weapon."

"Could there have been two bombs on board?"

"No idea, but we'll begin there and look for clues."

"Okay, Tom. Thanks." Tom shut down his monitor, presumably to make the call to his counterpart in Israeli intelligence from another room. The others sat quietly, while Greg rested his chin on his hand and stared into space.

"What are you going to tell the NSC, Greg?" Jim finally asked.

Greg looked at Jim and smiled.

"We're going to give them just enough information to pique their interest. Then we're going to monitor transmissions out of the bunkers to see if we have a leak. China has too much information about our military capabilities. I've already set it up with

Tom. We'll be able to listen, and we may be able to intercept and block anything we don't want to get out before it's sent."

Finally, Greg hit a button on his phone. When an operator answered, he asked her to set up the room for the NSC meeting, then he returned his chin to his hand, staring into the corner of the room, thinking about his conversation with Vladimir Putin.

"Good evening ladies and gentlemen," Greg said when the full NSC was assembled. "I have news for you. But first, anything new for me?"

Chuck spoke up first, giving his analysts' estimates of the casualties in China and elsewhere. Then Jim reported on the status of the remaining missiles.

"We've retargeted enough missiles to cover the Al-Qaeda strongholds and reloaded the missile silos that were used this morning," he said.

Several in the room perked up at the mention of Al-Qaeda strongholds.

"What did Israel say?" Greg asked Tom.

"It didn't take long for the Prime Minister to talk to his people," Tom said. "They're already verifying the status of their shelters and setting up teams to evacuate the population." Now everyone's interest was piqued, and their full attention was on the president.

"Medical teams will be headed west, from Boise, Salt Lake City, Denver, and Phoenix, by morning," Chuck said.

When no one else spoke up, Greg wondered why no one, in particular Vice President Klemp, had asked for more information.

"I take back what I said earlier," he said. "You all look as tired as I feel. Take a break. We'll touch base one more time before the end of the day."

Art spoke up quickly then.

"Wait. *Wait!* What was all that about targeting Al-Qaeda strongholds and Israel sending everyone to shelters?"

"Ah, you *were* awake," Greg said. "Thanks for asking. Others may be curious, too. Cy and I have been on the phone with our allies and decided that, in light of the latest Al-Qaeda threat, we need to be prepared to defend our citizens in the event of another attack." He knew he was misleading them with this twist of the facts, but that was part of his strategy. "That includes being prepared to retaliate, if necessary. So, besides sending aid to the attacked sites and preparing thousands of shelters across the country, we're redirecting our missiles to known Al-Qaeda locations."

"You know where Al-Qaeda is hiding?" Art asked, surprised.

"We didn't until a little while ago," Greg said, "but we think we do now." He thought Art would ask where the hideouts were, and was prepared to give just enough information to make it irresistible for any traitor. But Art surprised him by changing the subject. Maybe he was getting used to being left out of sensitive conversations.

"And Israel?" Art asked.

"You heard what he said. If we get information of an imminent attack on Israel, they're prepared to put their entire population into shelters."

Art got very quiet.

Greg looked around the Prime situation room, as if to see if there were other questions. In reality, he was looking for certain types of reactions. He was good at reading faces, and saw a couple that concerned him, not just Art's.

"Okay," he said, "let's take a break. Make sure you have an aide on duty to call us back together if anything comes up. Good evening, ladies and gentlemen."

As everyone was filing out of Prime, Greg motioned one of his security guards over and gave him the names of two people, besides Art, who needed to be watched or questioned. The agent nodded and left the room to notify the bunker security team, who would pass the names on to Tom.

"What is it, Jim?" Greg asked after the others had left and only Jim's monitor was still active.

"Colonel Johnson recorded a conversation between Art and Senator Stenger. I thought you should hear it."

"Go ahead."

Jim looked down at the paper in his hand.

"Art said, 'Contrary to what Greg thinks, I'm not the leak to China. Greg hates me. If a missile is aimed at my bunker, I don't think he'll try to stop it. I think he wants me dead.' There was no response from the Senator." Jim looked up from the paper and waited.

Greg stared at Jim for a few moments, lost in thought.

"What do you think?" Greg finally asked.

"If not Art, then who? Stenger?"

Stenger got an error message on his phone again. He'd tried both calling and texting, multiple times, to no avail. He'd been told that his calls would be routed through multiple exchanges, so no one would know where they originated, and this was the first time he'd had a problem. He didn't know if it was on his end—a problem in the bunker—or on his contact's end. Maybe one of the bombs the U.S. had launched at China had taken out his contact's communications. Or, maybe, security was on to him. If so, this could be the end of a lucrative relationship.

The Western United States

Tremors shook the earth along the San Andreas fault, from Mexico to Cape Mendocino north of San Francisco, along the Hayward fault east of San Francisco, and along the Denali fault system in Alaska.

The seismology station in Hawaii had been destroyed in the explosion on July fourth. The ones at Berkeley and Caltech in California had been seriously damaged. Even the recording stations in Seattle, at the University of Nevada, in Reno, and others in the west, had no way to communicate their findings because communications were out. However, the earthquakes were large enough to be recorded on seismographs hundreds—even thousands—of miles away. At the University of Utah, in Salt Lake City, seismologists began recording and reporting to the NEIC in Denver, precursor shockwaves coming from the West Coast after midnight on July fifth, and the NEIC confirmed the reports on their own equipment.

When the day shift supervisor at the NEIC walked in and saw the board, he immediately alerted Homeland Security. It was 6:45 am, mountain daylight time.

5

I don't know what we've created

The Preserve, 5 July

After breakfast and chores were completed, Amos Blund asked his wife, Lillie, and their children, Michael, who was twenty-three, and Emily, two years younger, to join him in the office. He asked his partner, Terry Stephens, to invite his wife, Becca, and their daughter, Katie, who was the same age as Emily.

He thanked them all for coming, but before he could say more, Emily asked what was going on outside.

He didn't want to distress anyone with the images that were now stuck in his head, or the report of explosions on the West Coast, but he believed Emily wouldn't be satisfied until he gave her—the most sensitive among them—some indication of what was happening. He just hadn't figured out what to tell her. He'd become so upset when Jason had stirred up the family the previous day, with his taunting about what Amos was keeping from them, that he'd actually hit Jason and knocked him down—but not in time to stop Jason from upsetting Emily.

"Emily, it's ugly," he began slowly. "If you really want to know, there's no reason not to let you see for yourself. But that's not why we're meeting this morning, and I'd rather not get into it right now. Is it alright if we postpone that discussion until later?"

"Okay, Dad. But I really would like to know what's going on."

"Fine." He paused to bury the images in his head, as deeply as

74

he could, then composed himself and faced the group. "Some of you may not know this, but you've all been nominated to become directors of our corporation."

"We have a corporation?" Mike asked, with a laugh. "When did this happen?" As an engineer, he was goal oriented and focused on facts, rather than feelings, a trait that sometimes expressed itself in asking questions instead of waiting patiently.

"Your mother, Terry, and I set it up a few years ago, anticipating certain legal needs. We recently approved an amendment to the Articles of Incorporation, which added the rest of you as additional directors. Together, we form the executive board of the Aspen Valley Corporation. We don't know how long we'll be here," Amos continued. "We need some form of government, to keep order, make decisions, resolve disputes, take care of legal issues, and so on." Mike started to ask another question, but Amos held up a hand, palm toward Mike, to prevent the interruption.

"Let your dad finish," Lillie said quietly, taking Mike's hand in hers.

"Michael—all of you—I'm going to try to anticipate, and answer, all of your questions," Amos said. "If I don't, feel free to ask when I'm done. Okay?" Mike nodded, but he looked unhappy about it.

"Aspen Valley, including the Preserve and all of the supplies we filled it with, was bought with funds from the sale of patents that Terry and I legally owned and legally sold, through the corporation. When we designed the Preserve, we tried to anticipate every need and provide for it. We've only been here a few days, but I have yet to hear anyone complain that there was something we didn't plan for.

"We're going to encounter situations where it will be important for someone to be in charge. The seven of us are now *the board.* The corporation can survive after us. When I fail to function as the president of the corporation, the board will elect a new president. When a board member fails to function, the rest of the board will select a new board member, if necessary. Now, any questions?"

"So, Aspen Valley was purchased by the Aspen Valley Corporation?" Mike asked.

"Actually, the property is in the name of a shell company. We didn't know if the government would try to track us through the corporation, so it's in another name, one that's difficult to trace back to us. Besides, it's not called Aspen Valley on any map—we named it that after we bought it."

"Really?" Mike asked, laughing. "I never bothered to look."

"What are our duties as board members?" Lillie asked.

"Excellent question, honey. We need to divide up the functions of the Preserve, so that each of us is responsible for what we do best. Failing that, we'll divide them up so everyone has an equal burden. Agreed?" There were nods all around. "Then, as chairman, I call this meeting of the board of the Aspen Valley Corporation to order. Lillie, please take meeting minutes. Now, let's talk about our duties."

After some discussion, they finally agreed on roles.

"Lillie, can you please review the assignments," Amos said.

"Becca has food preparation," Lillie read from her meeting minutes, then added with a smile at Becca. "She's a natural. She's the best cook in the family, and she's already taking care of it now. Katie, our experienced teacher and former gymnast, has education and physical exercise. That's a lot of responsibility, but Rachel,"— Lillie was referring to her eighteen-year-old daughter— "with her almost-degree, will help with education. Michael has care of the gardens and food production. That's a waste of his engineering degree, unless he begins engineering new strains of vegetables."

Mike snorted a laugh, which started the others laughing.

"Sorry," he said, embarrassed.

"Terry has mechanical and electrical maintenance, in addition to lab equipment and experiments," Lillie continued. "I have day-to-day house management, babysitting, nose wiping, and other household disasters."

Amos started to laugh. Lillie always knew just what Amos needed, and right now she was trying to help him keep his mind off the war.

"Is that written in the minutes?" he asked.

"Do I need to erase it?" she asked seriously, turning her pencil end for end and laying the eraser on the paper. Then a smile crept onto her face, letting Amos know that she was teasing.

"No. I'm just wondering what the next board will think when they read the minutes from our very first board meeting."

"Well, it's not in the minutes. I just wanted everyone to know how important my job is."

"We'll never forget," Amos said, giving her a hug. "Not now. What else?"

"Emily has pet care—" Lillie started to say.

"What?" Mike interrupted. "We didn't say that, and we don't have any pets."

"Well, if we did, I would take care of them," Emily said, defensively.

"You didn't let me finish, Michael," Lillie said. "Emily has pet care, if we ever have pets, since she was studying to be a veterinarian, and has a love of animals, plants, and other living things. She'll also back me as assistant house manager. Amos will have the hospital, overall administration of the Preserve, and support and backup for all areas." She looked up from her notes and smiled smugly.

"Anyone want to change the assignments or add anything?" Amos asked.

"I move that we accept the assignments as read," Terry said.

"I second it," Mike said, "including Mom's unwritten additions."

"The motion has been seconded," Amos said. "All in favor raise your hand." They all raised their hands except Lillie. "Oh-oh, we have a dissenter. What's your concern, honey?"

"You know," Lillie said, "the rest of the family will be upset if the Board members don't share in the routine tasks around the Preserve, like meal preparation and cleanup."

"Do you want to change the motion?" Amos asked.

"I'd like the board members to share in the routine tasks around the Preserve."

"Okay, the motion is amended to include the caveat that board members will share in the routine tasks around the Preserve. All in favor?" They all raised their hands except Becca.

"What's wrong dear?" Terry asked. Becca didn't answer, but she was frowning.

"Oh Becca," Lillie said. "That's so insensitive of me. Meal preparation is already a full-time job. I want to change my change. I want Becca to be exempted from the routine tasks. Is that okay, Amos?"

Amos looked down and shook his head. It took effort not to laugh out loud. "Okay," he finally said, when he could talk without laughing, "the original motion—"

"What was the original motion?" Terry asked, which started everyone laughing.

"The original motion, to accept the board assignments, is amended to include a caveat that all board members, except Becca, will share in the routine tasks around the Preserve. All in favor?" Everyone raised their hands. "It's unanimous. Good. Did you get that into the minutes?" Amos asked Lillie.

"Oh, yes," Lillie replied. "I like taking the minutes."

Amos looked over her shoulder at what she was writing.

"Are you doodling all over the meeting minutes?" he asked in surprise. Emily, sitting on the other side of her mother, looked over at her notes and started to laugh.

"You drew flowers in the margins," she said.

"They're just flowers. I think they're pretty. They add personality. Don't you think?"

"Yes, honey," Amos said, laughing. "I do."

"Is that it, then?" Mike asked. "We can go?" He took Katie's hand and started to get up.

"Actually, Michael, I'd like to take a few minutes to discuss how we determine priorities, resolve disputes, administer discipline, and a few other concerns. Anything we can't resolve immediately, we'll note in the minutes and table until the next meeting." Mike rolled his eyes and Amos looked at his watch. "We'll limit it to thirty minutes, then end the meeting, no matter what. Is that okay?"

Mike nodded reluctantly, releasing Katie's hand and dropping back into his chair.

Amos called everyone together for a meeting, just before lunch, in the community center. Chairs had been set up in rows at one end of the forty-foot-long room, so everyone could sit together and hear. But despite being carpeted, the noise echoed off the metal shell of the room.

They had to wait for Jason, who sauntered in a few minutes late and made an ugly face at Amos on his way to a chair.

"As I've said before," Amos said when everyone was seated, "although we'll treat each other as if we're one big, happy family, my goal is to run the Preserve as a business. We have a corporation, the Aspen Valley Corporation."

Amos had asked Lillie to let this be his idea, so that he would take the brunt of any complaints about how the Preserve was run. His confrontation with Jason the previous day had convinced him that he was right, despite the fact that Lillie had insisted, smiling at him, that she could have handled Jason without all the fuss.

Now, Amos introduced the board and explained their responsibilities. Everyone was receptive except Nathan, who was indifferent and said nothing, and Jason, who looked like he wanted to interrupt—but didn't—when Amos explained Lillie's role as house manager. He was certain Jason was thinking about the previous day's *fuss*.

Emily and Matt Green, instead of paying attention, sat off to one side, holding hands and gazing into each other's eyes. Lillie had asked Amos not to be too hard on Emily for distracting Matthew constantly, since they had agreed to let him join them.

"Any questions?" Amos asked when he'd finished his explanation. "Yes, Chris?"

Chris Stephens had raised his hand politely and waited to be recognized. He may have been afraid that Amos was going to jump on him, like he had Jason.

"Is there any way we can get new computer games?" Chris asked quietly.

Was it possible they didn't have the games the children wanted?

"Have you gone through all the games on the system already?" Amos asked.

Chris looked a little embarrassed.

"Well, no. I was just wondering, in case it ever came up."

"Okay, Chris," Amos said with a sigh of relief. "Your first task after lunch will be to go through the video library and see if there are any games or movies that you want, that we don't have. Anyone else who's interested, can help. Give your list to Mike before the end of the day and we'll see if we can get them."

"New virtual reality games are coming to market almost daily now," Mike said. "There are probably some that we don't have. I'll check."

Jason stormed out of the community center as soon as it became apparent that this meeting was just another of Amos's attempts to *pacify the dumb beasts* so they wouldn't rebel against the established order in this *prison*. He didn't bother to look at anyone. He had nothing in common with any of them, not even Brittany.

He went to his room and changed into workout clothes, then went to the exercise room to work off some stress, a routine that he needed almost daily now. As he pumped iron, he rehashed his argument that Brittany had ruined his life by insisting that they stay in Logan for the children's sake. He'd been offered a promotion several years before, but only if he would move to Chicago, and he'd thought at the time that his family was more important than the job. He didn't believe that any more. Everyone knew that if you turned down a promotion, there wouldn't be another offer—you had hit your ceiling.

"I should have taken the promotion and moved, even if I'd had to go alone," he thought aloud.

Jason switched from bench presses to squats. He was working

up a good sweat, which always made him feel better. But he realized he was still angry and needed more. He would never forgive Brittany for systematically undermining him with the boys: making them go to bed instead of staying up late with him after a long work day, insisting that they do their homework when he wanted to watch a ballgame on TV with them, and so many other things.

At one point, when Aaron had been about twelve and had stayed up to "be with Dad," he'd thought Aaron might want to emulate him, find a good job and become a productive member of society. He'd even taken him to the office in the hopes of impressing him with what his dad had accomplished, but Aaron had thumbed his nose at the working world, and Jason had realized that for Aaron it had just been an excuse to get out of school.

After that, Aaron had started staying out late with strange friends, listening to weird music, and getting tattoos. Brittany had asked Jason to try to straighten Aaron out, but he had just laughed. It was her fault that Aaron had turned out the way he had. *If she'd only* . . . he thought, shaking his head.

Jason moved to one of the stationary bikes, feeling like he was finally working the stress out of his system. Then he thought about his decision to come to this hellhole and his anxiety level jumped back up again. Coming here had been a knee-jerk reaction to Aaron's violent death, and he'd regretted it every day since. Instead of wasting his time on menial chores like stirring noodles in a pot, sweeping floors, and cleaning toilets, he could have been in Logan, or Las Vegas, enjoying life.

Sure, he'd felt the earthquakes and believed the California Faults had let loose, but all the other garbage Amos and Terry were feeding them—about nuclear explosions and five-hundred-mile-an-hour winds—was just that: garbage.

There was nothing that needed to be done in the Preserve that he couldn't do or manage. He was sure of it. He didn't know what Amos and Terry were doing in their lab, probably manufacturing the videos they were showing him, but he would either figure out their game, or he would find a way to leave the Preserve.

After lunch, while Becca and her current food preparation team worked on cleaning up, Amos, Terry, and Mike returned to the lab.

"Mike, will you take notes and project them on the monitor so we can see if there's anything we're leaving out?" Amos asked.

"Sure thing," Mike replied, quickly connecting his tablet to the wall monitor and making two lists, one for *Observations* and one for *Possible Hypotheses*.

"That's good, Mike—just what I would have done," Amos said.

"I know, Dad."

"Okay," Amos continued, thinking about their discovery the previous day. "With the original panel, the one we used in Logan that doesn't match the schematic—let's call that one Panel A—we were able to see the hillside in Ogden, over forty miles away."

"But we don't know if it was the correct hillside," Terry added, "because the new medical building wasn't where it was supposed to be."

"Yeah," Amos said pensively, "it just looked like the right hillside. And we know that building is there, because we've driven past the construction site. So, what does that tell us about Panel A?"

"Dad, we need to weigh into the equation our observations here in the lab, yesterday," Mike said.

"Good point, Mike," Amos replied. "We had basically the same experience here. We could see what looked like Aspen

Valley, above us, but there were trees where there shouldn't have been—in the area we cleared to build the Preserve. Now, what do the two experiences tell us?"

"Well," Mike said, "we thought it meant we were looking at the correct locations, but either in the past—before we cut the trees down—or in the future."

"The distant future," Terry corrected.

"Right," Mike continued, nodding his head in agreement, "because the trees over the Preserve, and in the rest of the valley, were all the same size. Is that still what we think?"

"Are you asking if there are other possibilities?" Amos asked, and Mike nodded. "I have no idea, Mike. Even entertaining the idea that we've invented a time machine is mind-boggling. I get a headache thinking about it. And when I think too long on it, I have nightmares about aliens coming out of the portal to kidnap me."

"Seeing Martians now, are you, Amos?" Terry chuckled.

"Or body snatchers. It's disturbing, Terry."

"Sorry, Amos. I don't mean to make light of it. I'm having my own nightmares."

Amos stared at Terry, lost in thought, while Terry stared back.

Mike looked back and forth between them until it made him nervous, then broke the silence.

"Uh . . . what can we say about the new panel?" he asked.

Amos and Terry turned simultaneously to look at Mike, making a scene from *Invasion of the Body Snatchers* come to mind. *I wish Dad hadn't mentioned body snatchers,* he thought as he shivered.

"Let's move on," he added quickly, looking down at his tablet. "With the new panel, the one that matches the schematic—I suppose you want to call it Panel B—we were able to see the valley above us in its present condition."

"That's what it looked like," Terry said. "We can't say for sure because we had to cut the test short on account of the radiation coming into the lab."

"Doesn't the radiation leak yesterday tell us for sure that we were looking at our valley?" Mike asked.

"I don't know, Mike," Amos said. "We considered the source of the radiation and decided that we couldn't be sure it was from one of the explosions, so it may be coincidental. I don't have a better explanation, but if that's right, it would mean . . . " Amos got pensive. "How could that be? It would mean, that with Panel B, we have what? A portal? A door or gate from the lab into the valley directly above us?"

"Isn't that what we decided?" Mike said. "Isn't it the radiation in the valley that entered the lab?"

"I don't know, Mike," Amos said. "It's such a radical idea that I'm having a hard time accepting it."

Terry stared at him.

"Oookay," Terry said slowly. "I get it. So, using Panel B, we learned that the portal isn't just an image or picture. It's a door or gate." He laughed self-consciously. "Can we say anything else about it, other than, *that's impossible?*"

They thought about that for a few minutes.

"If it wasn't our valley that we were seeing, with Panel B," Amos finally said, "I can't imagine what it was, but nothing would surprise me now."

"You and me both." Terry said.

"Well," Mike said, "we still have questions left that we couldn't answer yesterday. I wrote them down." Mike quickly pulled up a file on his tablet with a list of questions.

"One: We wondered if Panel A was also a portal, not just an image, or, if not, could we build a third panel that had the features of both Panels A and B. Two: We wondered if we could travel through a portal into another time or place."

"You mean, would it be safe for people to travel through the portal, right?" his dad asked.

"Right. Three: We also wondered if the portal was directional, which would mean we could manipulate it to look this way or that way. And four: we wondered if we could jump from one location, or time, to another."

The three men looked at each other without speaking, and Amos shook his head.

When Lillie opened the door and looked into the lab, the three men were laughing.

"I don't know what we've created, Amos," she heard Terry say, "but I'm convinced we've found a door of some kind. And to a real place. The past? The future? I don't know. But I know how we can find out."

"It's either that," Mike added, "or we're all having the same hallucination!"

"Something doesn't add up," Amos said, as he concentrated on Mike's notes on the wall monitor.

"What is it?" Terry asked.

"It's dinner time," Lillie said from the doorway, interrupting the conversation and making all of them jump a little. "And Becca will be upset if you're late."

Mike placed a hand on his chest and pretended to be in pain, then started to chuckle.

"Great timing, Mom. That adds up to cold leftovers if we don't go now."

Mike shut down his tablet and the TV monitor as Amos and Terry stood and followed Lillie out.

"If I knew what it was, Terry, it would add up," Amos said, still deep in thought.

"This might be a first," Terry said. "I don't know when I've ever seen you this perplexed. I don't know what's buggin' you, Amos, but I'm burned out just thinking about it."

"Mike," Amos said, turning back toward him as he followed Amos, "print out those notes and post them on the wall, where I can review them when I'm in the lab, will you?"

"Sure thing, Dad." Mike said, laughing along with Terry at his dad's frustration.

After dinner, Amos, Terry, and Mike started to leave the dining room, when Lillie asked Amos to stay. Most of the women were still seated, so the men sat back down.

"What's up?" Amos asked.

"They've been asking me what's going on outside, Amos, and I don't know what to tell them."

"We need to know what's happening out there, Amos," Becca said.

"Mr. Blund, you can't keep us in the dark," Katie added.

"I understand. Please call me Amos, Katie. What are you telling them?" he asked Lillie, unconsciously tensing up.

"Was Jason telling the truth about innocent people being shot and trampled to death?" Emily asked.

"Amos, they need to have a general idea of what's happening," Lillie said. "It will help them appreciate what we have here."

"It's not fair, Daddy," Rachel said.

Amos knew his daughter only used the word "daddy" when she wanted something—badly.

Maybe they're right, he thought. Maybe he'd feel better if he didn't try to keep everything inside. He released a breath he'd been holding and rested his elbows on the table.

"Does Brittany want to know as well?" Terry asked.

"She just left," Becca said. "Should I go get her?"

"Feel free to invite whoever you want," Amos said. "We'll wait until you get back."

"We're all here." Becca said, closing the door, when everyone eighteen and older, except Jason, had gathered around them in the Dining Room.

Amos summarized what they'd seen and heard in the news reports the previous day. He spoke generally, hoping to say just enough to satisfy their curiosity, at the same time hoping to avoid too many questions.

"There were soldiers involved in protecting buildings and property, not just the police. And yes, there was shooting. I imagine bystanders were killed. The military calls that *collateral damage.* It was hard to watch. It was all really hard to sit through.

"At the airports, there was pushing and shoving and general panic as people tried to get out of cities they thought might be targeted. People were hurt, and some were trampled.

"There were nuclear explosions in Washington, D.C. and seven western cities. It was just like watching the newsreels of the bombs dropped on Japan and the tests in Nevada during the Cold War."

"What cities?" Emily asked.

"I wasn't alive then," Rachel said at the same time, "and I haven't seen the newsreels."

"Be grateful," Amos said, then told them about the seven western cities, and described what a nuclear bomb looks like when it explodes—the high winds and destruction, the fires, and the mushroom cloud.

"Do you think there were people still in the cities when the bombs exploded?" Rachel asked.

"I'm sure there were, Rachel. The government had some warning, so they tried to evacuate those areas, but I'm sure there were still people there. I'm also sure they didn't feel a thing. It would be the people farther out—one to five miles away from the explosions—who would have suffered most. They had to endure fires, flying debris, collapsing buildings—it would be terrible. I'm certain there was, and still is, a lot of suffering."

"Those poor people," Emily said, a quiver in her voice and tears in her eyes.

"What's going to happen to us here?" Katie Stephens asked, her voice so quiet that Amos barely heard it.

"We'll be fine, Katie," Amos said. "The Preserve can survive anything except a direct hit, and I can't imagine any combination of events where a bomb would be dropped here."

Her mother, Becca, placed an arm around her shoulders and hugged her. Everyone was quiet for a minute.

"Is it the end of the world?" Brittany Carlsen asked. The others looked at her questioningly. "I started reading the Bible," she said by way of explanation. "People say the Bible will tell us the signs of the times. I want to know if this is it—one of those signs."

"I don't know, Brittany," Amos replied, with the calm sensitivity he'd developed as a doctor. "If you figure it out, please tell us."

Amos looked around to see if there were any more questions. He noticed that Brittany had lowered her head. As he watched, a tear dropped off the end of her nose. She didn't move, even to wipe it away. He caught Lillie's attention and nodded in Brittany's direction.

Lillie got up and went over to Brittany, kneeling beside her chair.

"Are you okay?" she asked.

Brittany shook her head without looking up, then suddenly looked at Amos and blurted out an apology.

"I'm sorry about Jason . . . what Jason . . . " She couldn't go on. She broke down and sobbed into her hands.

Lillie looked at Amos pleadingly as she pulled a tissue from a nearby box on the table and handed it to Brittany.

"Brittany," he said quietly, "it's okay. Yesterday wasn't one of my better days."

"That's an understatement." Lillie said. It had the desired effect. Several of the others started to laugh, discretely. Even Brittany was affected by Lillie's humor. Amos, accustomed to Lillie's sometimes sarcastic method of easing tensions, chuckled along with them.

"Alright," Amos said, "it was one of my worst days, and that's saying something." His admission got everyone laughing, including Brittany, but especially his children.

"I tried to talk to Jason about respecting your authority," Brittany said, more soberly, "but he won't talk about it. He said you're hiding something, then he wouldn't say any more. That confrontation really bruised his ego."

"I'm sor—" Amos started to say, but Brittany interrupted him.

"No, don't misunderstand me. I blame Jason completely for what happened. He was totally wrong. I just don't know what's gotten into him—why he's acting this way. We've drifted apart over the years, but I've never seen him act like this before."

Maybe we have two bulls in the herd and there's only room for one, Amos thought, as some of the group began to stand and stretch.

"Thank you, Brittany," Amos said. "Now, that's really all we know about what's going on outside. Terry's monitoring TV, radio, and internet, and he'll tell us when he finds out anything new."

6

Are we going to die?

The Western United States, 6 July, Morning

In California, those who had just survived nuclear explosions re-located from damaged homes and offices to hundreds of schools, churches, and other public buildings. Overworked public and private medical personnel treated the displaced in these hastily-organized shelters, where cots had been set up in rows, filling up available space. In some shelters, hundreds of injured children sought comfort from their parents, many of whom were injured themselves.

The tremors along the West Coast faults—what seismologists call precursor shocks—had continued sporadically, throughout July fifth and into the sixth. Authorities feared that some of the temporary shelters, already weakened by nuclear explosions, might not survive a major earthquake, but there was nowhere else to place the injured.

The first major earthquake—along the San Andreas fault, just outside of San Francisco—measured 7.8 on the Richter scale. It was recorded at the University of Utah at 10:14 a.m. Mountain Time, 9:14 local time. When the earthquake hit, it split the bay area down the middle, part of the city moving north and part moving south. Many of the temporary medical shelters failed structurally. Ceilings and walls collapsed, crushing victims where they lay. Medical personnel were trapped alongside their patients.

Floating bridges broke apart. Elevated bridges collapsed, their steel frames swaying and twisting until enough cables broke, or beams failed, that the remainder couldn't hold the weight of the structure. The only escape was to the south, but few from the city made it any farther than a few blocks from their homes or shelters before the destruction halted their progress.

Over the next twenty-four hours, the fault continued to shift laterally, eventually moving more than twelve feet.

Seventy-two minutes after the San Andreas quake, the Hayward fault, running predominantly north and south through Oakland, parallel to the San Andreas, slipped during a 7.4 magnitude quake. Many structures that had survived the San Andreas quake collapsed.

The seismographs in Salt Lake City recorded a third major earthquake at 1:27 p.m. Mountain Time. This one, along the Denali fault system in Alaska, registered at a staggering 8.5 magnitude, over thirty times more powerful than the earthquake in San Francisco. The Denali quake created wide cracks in the ground and a vertical shift of more than four feet. Because of the remoteness of the Denali system, there were few casualties from the actual earthquake, but structures miles away were damaged and fires caused by broken gas lines burned out of control.

The shaking from the three earthquakes caused shock waves that traveled across the Pacific Ocean and along the coast.

The report that NEIC officials in Denver sent to HomeSec

read in part:

> . . . expect aftershocks and devastating tsunamis to hit the west coast of the U.S., as well as the rest of the Pacific rim, within hours. Please advise all relief agencies and government personnel within the affected regions to move citizens away from coastal areas and toward higher ground as quickly as possible.

By the time word reached Director of Homeland Security Chuck Dickson, the tsunamis were already building in the Pacific.

A footnote in the NEIC report read:

> NOTE: Earthquakes have also occurred in Pakistan, India, Nepal, China, Russia, and around the Pacific Rim. The extent of tectonic movement globally is unprecedented; anticipate additional earthquakes in unexpected locations, along with other natural disasters, such as landslides and tsunamis.

The Preserve

Lillie was sitting on a couch in the community center, watching Rylee Parker and Sydney Carlsen play Monopoly on a card table, when they felt the shaking from the earthquakes in California. During the first quake, the game pieces moved more than an inch across the game board, the table shook, and lightweight objects slid off shelves.

Lillie had been staying close to the girls to keep an eye on Rylee, whom she now thought of as, and was trying to love as if she were, her own daughter. She was pleased to see Rylee enjoying a quiet morning with Sydney instead of suffering from emotional fits over the deaths of her parents and brother or watching for Nathan.

"What was that?" Rylee asked loudly, holding on to her chair

as the table shook and the game pieces rattled. Sydney looked at Rylee with concern as she did the same.

"It's alright," Lillie said, as she waited for the shaking to stop. Then she went to the girls and put an arm around each of them.

"Are we going to die?" Rylee asked with wide, fearful eyes, her raised eyebrows forming wrinkles on her forehead.

"No Rylee," Lillie responded in her calmest, sweetest voice, with her most reassuring smile. She was sure Rylee was thinking about the tragic loss of her parents and younger brother, just days before. "It was just an earthquake. You've never been through an earthquake before, have you?"

Rylee shook her head, her eyes welling up with tears.

Lillie heard someone enter the room, likely to check on them, but she stayed focused on Rylee. When she finally looked up, whoever had come in had left again.

When the room shook for a second time, moving game pieces across the board, Lillie suggested that maybe the girls would prefer to go to the library and read a book or to the exercise room to work out. When Lillie felt a third quake in less than four hours, she went looking for the girls, finding them tumbling on the floor mats in the exercise room.

"Is everything okay?" Lillie asked, sticking her head through the doorway, but not entering.

"We're fine, Lillie," Sydney said, finishing her roundoff.

"Nicely done, Sydney," Lillie said. "Is that something you learned at home or did Katie help you with it?"

"Mostly with Katie's help," she said.

"What are you working on, Rylee?" she asked.

"I'm way behind Sydney," Rylee said. "Was that another earthquake?"

"I'm sure it was. Either it was a little one or it was far away, like the other two. Nothing to worry about."

"I don't like them," Rylee said.

"We'll be fine, honey. Amos is keeping a watchful eye on the Preserve. If there's a problem, he'll take care of it."

"I've had enough exercise," Rylee said. "Let's go back to the community center." Sydney agreed, so Lillie walked back with them.

Chris Stephens and Rachel Blund entered the room holding hands, followed by Mike Blund and Katie Stephens. Jason Carlsen entered, wiping his forehead with the towel around his neck, probably coming from the exercise area.

"That's the third one in the last four hours," Chris said, "but they don't appear to be getting any stronger. If it's the Wasatch Fault, the big one's still coming."

Rachel smacked Chris on the arm.

"Don't upset anyone, Chris," she whispered. "Most of us have never been through an earthquake."

"Neither have I," Chris griped. "But you don't see it bothering me, do you?"

"Maybe it *is* bothering you and that's why you're being so obnoxious."

"Am not!" Chris said, but he was smiling.

Terry entered from the office tunnel with a Geiger counter in each hand and met Mike and Katie halfway across the room.

"Mike, will you give me a hand, please?" he asked, handing one of the small machines to Mike. The two men headed off in different directions, and Lillie explained to the girls that the men would verify that no leaks had developed as a result of the earthquakes.

When they returned—Mike from the direction of the hospital and Terry from the direction of the bedrooms—nearly everyone else had gathered, their continued unease a physical presence in the room.

"Well?" Chris asked Mike.

"Everything's okay at this end of the Preserve," Mike said, looking at Terry.

"Same here," Terry said, taking Mike's Geiger counter.

"How do we know there are no leaks?" Jason asked. "How do we know your equipment's working properly?"

Terry looked at Amos, who had closed his lips tightly. Lillie, holding on to Amos's arm, jabbed him in the ribs to distract him.

"Just a minute, Jason," Terry said. "Don't go anywhere." Terry set down one of the Geiger counters and walked away toward the office, winking at Amos as he passed.

"Can't he answer my question?" Jason complained, staring at Amos, who turned away and sat down without responding.

Terry returned a few minutes later, carrying a small metal box in his gloved hands and wearing a vest similar to the kind that a dentist places over patients when taking x-rays, with straps to hold it in place around his neck and behind his back. He picked up the Geiger counter and walked to a table away from the family. Jason started to follow, until Terry warned him off.

"Stay back, Jason," Terry said. "I have a small amount of radioactive material in this box and it could affect your health."

"Hmmph," Jason said doubtfully. But he stopped walking and looked on with interest at what Terry was doing.

"By the way," Terry said, "the earthquakes were along the west coast, from Mexico to Alaska, in case you're wondering. Three major earthquakes and several smaller ones. With that much tectonic activity occurring over such a short period of time, I wouldn't be surprised if we feel more of them."

Rylee looked at Lillie with fear in her eyes. Lillie, sitting next to Amos on a nearby couch, smiled reassuringly at her.

Terry turned on the Geiger counter and held it near the box. Nothing happened until he unclasped the lid of the box with his other hand, and opened it just a crack. As the Geiger counter began to chatter, Terry closed the lid and re-latched it. The chatter slowed perceptibly but continued.

"I suggest everyone find somewhere else to be for the next couple of hours, until dinner," Terry said. The girls jumped up and hurried out of the room, the others following more slowly.

"How do I know that's radioactive?" Jason asked, without getting closer, but not backing away.

Lillie could tell, from Amos's squirming, that he wanted to say something, but Terry beat him to it. "The Geiger counter went off, didn't it?" Terry asked.

Lillie thought Jason looked a little foolish and hoped he would let it go, but he didn't.

"What are you doing with radioactive material, anyway? Isn't that illegal?"

"Jason," Amos said in exasperation, "let it go. We have radioactive material, and we have a license to have it."

Jason didn't reply, but he stared at Amos for a few moments. Lillie held firmly to Amos's arm and hoped Jason wouldn't say anything that gave Amos an excuse for another confrontation. Finally, Jason turned and stormed off.

"Thank you for not saying anything else," Lillie said.

"I'll leave him in your capable hands," Amos said.

"Your sarcasm isn't helpful."

Amos took a deep breath, smiled, and pulled Lillie into an embrace.

"I'm sorry, honey. I didn't mean to take it out on you. I just can't believe how easily he upsets me."

"I know. I've never seen you react this way to anyone. Your

normal bedside manner is lacking some polish."

"If it were his bedside, I might dance a jig."

"You don't need to wish him ill. You know he doesn't want to be here," Lillie said, frowning.

"I don't want him here either. Should we let him out?"

"You know that won't work out well, for all the reasons we explained to him before we came. By the way," Lillie changed the subject to get Amos's mind off Jason, "what was bothering you, Terry, and Mike earlier, in the office?"

"Well, you remember our theories about the Observer being a portal to another time or place?"

"Yes, I remember your crazy theory—but I don't think any less of you for it," Lillie replied, flippantly.

"Thanks. I guess. Anyway, I'm missing something—something that would help us understand what we're seeing. It seems so implausible, even impossible. But the evidence of something strange is right there in front of us. A door? I don't know, but I can't imagine what else it could be."

"Well, whatever it is you're missing, you'll think of it," she said, patting him on the knee and standing.

"Yeah, probably. I think we're done for today. I'm reluctant to turn the Observer on again until we have a better idea about what's going on."

"That's going to be hard on you." She fought to keep the smile off her face. She knew he couldn't sit still when he had an unsolved mystery.

"Yeah," he replied, obviously frustrated, "my curiosity is tearing me up inside, almost literally."

She couldn't resist a laugh, knowing he'd have trouble sleeping until he'd figured it out, the image of a door to another time or place invading his dreams.

"Lies to cover the lies," Jason said, as he ran on the treadmill. Alone in the exercise room, he'd worked up a sweat, which always helped him think. His mind wandered back to the conversation with Terry and Amos. He'd tried all day to figure out why they had radioactive material, let alone a license to have it, if, in fact, they *did* have a license for it. It must have something to do with whatever they were hiding in their lab. How could he find out what it was?

The Prime Situation Room

In an emergency NSC meeting—though it seemed to Greg that they were all emergency meetings now—HomeSec Chuck Dickson notified the president that he was directing his people to evacuate from coastal areas and to take as many people with them as they could.

"The rescue workers have been hampered by the damage from the explosions and fallout," Chuck said. "Their hazmat suits are bulky and awkward to work in for any length of time, limiting how much they can help. With primary communication systems out, their coordination efforts have nearly stalled. They're working in small teams at this point."

"The military has been trying to assist," SecDef Jim Seymour broke in. "They have portable radios and military hazmat suits that are more formfitting. Because they're better outfitted, they've been asked to coordinate the rescue efforts in many areas."

"And now, with the earthquakes," Chuck said, "there are very few structures near the fault zones that are safe to enter."

"The goal right now," Jim added, "is to get as many people as possible over the faults and headed east. But trying to cross an active fault zone is hazardous."

"More than staying where they are?" Greg asked.

"We've commandeered all the helicopters we can locate—that weren't damaged by collapsed hangars or EMPs—to help in shuttling people safely. We're also bulldozing paths across the faults, in places where that makes sense. We need to minimize the risk to the rescuers."

"Okay," Greg said, deciding it was more important to hear what was being done than to question their reports.

"Now tsunamis are building in the Pacific," Chuck said. "We're trying to determine the timing of their arrival, so we can notify the rescue teams. We want to reduce distractions from their efforts to help the earthquake victims."

"It appears that nuclear fallout may be the least of our concerns," Greg said quietly, then stared into a corner of the room, thinking about what he'd just been told.

"Greg," Tom said, causing Greg to turn back and look at Tom's monitor. "We think we've found the terrorist's trail."

Greg motioned for him to continue.

"We had the NSA search auto rental agencies along the South Carolina coast for cars rented during the months prior to the Washington attack. They were able to eliminate most of the rentals from consideration by comparing names and addresses against known U.S. citizens living in other parts of the country, who might have been travelling. Assuming that our terrorist came into the country with the bomb, they compared the remaining list against international flight manifests. We were able to eliminate all but nine names, down from a huge list at the start. We're holding the list of car rentals, in case the list of nine doesn't pan out and we have to start over with a different set of assumptions."

"Okay, so what's next?"

"Now we're looking at motel and hotel reservations between South Carolina and Washington, D.C. to see if any of the names pop up somewhere else."

"There has to be thousands of places he could have stayed overnight. Or maybe he slept in his car. Or maybe he traded cars. Or maybe he changed names. This sounds impossible."

"We had to make some assumptions, Greg, and one of them was that he hasn't been to the U.S. before, so he thinks he can use the same name everywhere. That's easier for him. We also sent the list of nine to our allies, including Israel, to see if a name pops up somewhere else."

"Okay," Greg said in frustration, "keep me posted."

7

What about the TV control

The Preserve, 6 July, Afternoon

Terry entered the lab and found Amos sitting at the table, twirling a pencil with his fingers, between making notes on a pad of paper. Amos had told Terry that he was prepared to short-circuit their research on the Observer—something he had never done before on an experiment—until he could figure out what he was missing.

"Have you remembered what was bugging you about the portal?" Terry asked.

"No, and I'm not sleeping well."

"Want to try something?" Terry asked, approaching the Observer.

"I'm ready to listen. Anything to help me get a good night's sleep."

"Great," Terry said, laughing. "I don't see how we'll know what's going on if we don't experiment with it."

Amos didn't answer.

"You remember that with Panel B, radiation entered the lab from the valley—our valley," Terry said.

"That's what we think, so far. Yes."

"But with Panel A, no radiation entered the lab. What if we play with Panel A and see what else we can learn?"

"And if the radiation sensors go off again?"

"Well, it'll tell us *something*."

"That isn't the correct way to run an experiment," Amos

growled quietly, "but I'll go along if we take careful notes."

Terry nodded toward the notepad on the table in front of his partner as he loaded Panel A into the Observer. Then he turned it on to open a view to the valley.

The vegetation is green with life, Amos thought wistfully as he watched. *What a contrast to the videos of fires and destruction we've been watching.*

Terry kept his hand close to the *off* button and waited.

"No radiation alarm," he said after a couple of minutes. "What are you thinking?"

"How beautiful the valley is. It looks so much like our valley."

"That's what I thought. You have a look of longing on your face."

"That obvious, huh? Makes me wish we could go through the portal—just to enjoy it again."

"Why can't we?" Terry asked with a sly smile.

"Well, for one thing, we don't know if Panel A is a portal, like Panel B seems to be. And we don't know enough about what we're looking at, what kind of harm we could cause."

"Or what kind of damage it could cause us?" Terry asked, making Amos frown.

"I'd love to find out what we've discovered," Amos said. "Is this really our valley? In the past or the future? If it's in the past, is it the near past or distant past? Or is it something altogether different—something we haven't thought of? And what kind of dangers are there?" He sighed. "Okay, Terry. What next?" Amos started making notes on a pad of paper, which he would ask Mike to convert to a digital record.

"Well, it's certainly the twin of our valley," Terry said, making Amos stop and wonder at his choice of words, but before he could ask, he was distracted as Terry continued.

"What's blowing your hair, right now, Amos?"

"Huh," Amos said, looking up. It only took a moment before he realized his hair was being ruffled by a wind. He turned to the image generated by Panel A. It was impossible, but he was certain he could feel a breeze on his face. He turned back to Terry, grinning ear to ear. "Really? It's a portal, like Panel B?"

"I think that answers *that*. Amazing! What's over there? Amos, I think we need to go through and see."

"More than amazing, Terry. It's unbelievable! I . . . " Amos stopped, before committing himself. "Maybe we should calm down a bit and think this through."

"Fine," Terry said, looking like a child who'd just been sent to his room. "Should we continue?"

Amos ran his hand through his hair, a little chagrinned at possibly insulting his good friend. He nodded, looking back at the portal, and started grinning again.

"We've seen the image pass through stationary, inanimate objects," Terry said calmly, possibly embarrassed by Amos's sudden lack of enthusiasm, "like the building on the university campus. But, since it really seems to be a door or gate, shouldn't we be able to get something to come through it into the lab?"

Amos looked back at Terry.

"You mean an animal, or blowing leaves, or something like that?"

"Well, so far nothing stationary has entered the lab, so maybe we need to find something that moves on its own power."

"We don't know what kind of animals live in this valley. What if they're dangerous? Or what if we unknowingly allow some kind of environmental hazard to pass from one side to the other?"

"You mean, like radiation."

"Or a virus or bacteria."

"That's a risk," Terry said without apology. "But we've had the portal open for almost ten minutes now and I don't feel any contamination."

"Now you're making fun of me," Amos said, but he felt energized by the questions and possibilities. He stared at the portal, fidgeting with his pencil and weighing the pros and cons of risking cross-contamination. Terry waited patiently.

"Okay, let's look for an animal," he finally said, his curiosity overcoming his caution.

Terry smiled: Amos was hooked. Terry began moving the image around the valley, passing through trees and bushes. Amos sighed, as he felt the breeze several more times, and he thought he could smell the trees and the other familiar odors of summer. Maybe it was his imagination.

They searched for more than two hours. Each time they saw movement in the bushes, they guided the portal toward it cautiously. Amos held his breath every time, until they confirmed that what they'd seen was only a small—or at least harmless—animal, or something else that couldn't hurt them. It was curious, but the animals must have sensed the portal's presence. Invariably, each one of them moved away when the portal got close. But in one instance, the portal went right through a startled deer, showing them its internal organs, before the animal ran away, apparently unharmed.

"Well, we know we can see internal organs without obvious harm to the host," Terry said. "That's one positive outcome."

"Yeah, but what about more subtle damage, like at the cellular level?" Amos asked pensively. "I just wish we had a way to run some tests."

"Well, I don't think you're gonna' get a deer to stand still while you look around at its insides."

As the portal passed through a tree, Amos made a note on his pad. He wanted Mike to figure out a way to digitally record what they were seeing through the portal. And he hadn't forgotten their original goal: they needed to figure out a way to diagnose internal injuries without the use of conventional, intrusive methods.

Suddenly, Amos remembered that he'd called a board meeting, and the others would be arriving soon.

"Let's give it up for today," he said.

"Just a sec," Terry whispered.

Amos turned to look at Terry, who nodded toward the portal. Turning back, he saw a small rabbit sitting about two feet from the portal, looking the other way. It was chewing on something. Terry held a finger to his lips, then winked at Amos. He picked up a TV control from the table and tossed it through the portal so that it landed just beyond the rabbit.

The rabbit turned and ran away from the sound—straight toward them. It jumped right through the portal and into the lab, startling Amos and making Terry laugh. The rabbit froze at the sound and stared at Amos, who reached out, intending to touch it, to prove to himself that it was real. His movement caused the rabbit to turn and jump back through the portal and away, out of sight. Terry laughed even harder.

"Wouldn't that have been something to show Mike?" Amos said, laughing along with Terry now. "But what about the TV control?"

Terry moved the portal right up to the control.

"Reach through and pick it up."

Amos stared at him for a moment, his laughter dying, as he thought about possible effects at the cellular level.

"Why not?" he finally said. "We've ignored just about every other scientific protocol. Why not contaminate the experiment with personal interaction?" He turned around, reached through the portal, and picked up the control, then started to laugh again.

"What did it feel like?" Terry asked.

"Wow! It was a little tingly," he replied through his laughter.

"Tingly," Terry teased. "That sounds very scientific."

"Can you believe it? I just reached into the past . . . or the future . . . or something. Holy cow!"

Just then, the door opened and Mike stuck his head in.

"What's so funny?" he asked.

"Hang around after the board meeting and we'll show you," Amos said. "We just saw something incredible, but you have to see it for yourself."

The West Coast and Pacific Rim, 6 July, Afternoon

The tsunamis reached the west coast late in the afternoon.

A fifty-foot wall of water slammed into the shoreline near Los Angeles. Slowing imperceptibly as it swept over and around Catalina Island, it continued building until it reached the coast. Once on land, the massive wave slowed again as it washed across the missile impact zone in downtown Los Angeles, picking up thousands of tons of debris and pushing it farther inland. The rapidly moving flood of seawater extinguished fires, eventually reducing the amount of smoke billowing into the skies, but it also swept injured survivors off their feet, trapping many in underwater snags.

By the time the floodwater reached San Bernardino, where rescue workers were shuttling survivors over the fault, it had been reduced to a gentle wave a few inches deep. Thousands of people stared in disbelief as salt water lapped at their feet and fish flopped around in the receding tide—eighty miles inland.

Elsewhere along the coast, buildings damaged by earthquakes and homes overlooking the ocean were washed away. Hundreds of thousands of people, still trying to get away from the coast, were trapped on crowded freeways, where many drowned.

On the island of Oahu, devastated by the warhead that struck the naval base, there were few survivors. With no one to sound the tsunami sirens, once the twenty-five-foot wave was visible it was far too late to get to safety.

Similar scenes occurred all around the Pacific Rim, with ten- to sixty-foot waves crashing into the coasts of China, Japan, and the Pacific islands. Low-lying islands in the Philippines, Indonesia, and elsewhere were buried in the waves. The people who hadn't already left the islands, or moved to higher ground, were washed away and lost.

The Preserve

"I'll catch up with you in a few minutes," Mike told Katie as the other board members left the office. "I need to speak with Dad."

"Let's go to the lab," Amos said, motioning for Mike to follow.

"What's up?" Mike asked, as he watched Terry turn on the Observer.

"Take a seat and watch," Terry said, his face neutral as he maneuvered the Portal around and between the bushes and trees in Aspen Valley.

"I thought you weren't going to try this again until you learned more about what we were seeing," Mike said. He sat impatiently, his mind wandering to Katie and the emotions he'd been feeling recently. Every time she took his hand, or placed her hand on his leg, or rubbed up against him, he felt things he'd never felt before.

"Well, we had no choice really," Amos said. "It was driving me nuts. And we've come to some conclusions."

"Are you watching, Mike?" Terry asked quietly.

Mike realized that he'd been distracted by his thoughts and looked up at the image again. He didn't see whatever it was Terry wanted him to see.

"You see that mouse?" Terry whispered.

"Where? Oh, there. Looks like it's eating something." He didn't understand. "What about it?"

"Watch," Terry said as he moved the portal right up behind the mouse.

Mike focused on the mouse, and didn't notice the TV control Terry lobbed through the portal, until it whizzed past his head, making him jerk reflexively. It landed just beyond the mouse. The mouse turned and scurried through the image into the lab.

"Yikes," Mike yelped in surprise, lifting his feet off the floor as the mouse ran under his chair, then scrabbling onto the table next to him. "It really *is* a portal?" He couldn't believe what he was seeing. He knew they had previously theorized that one of the panels might have created a portal, but he hadn't realized that his dad and Terry had confirmed it.

The two older men started laughing. Mike breathed heavily, and his eyes darted from them, to the portal, to the mouse, which was running around the room, apparently looking for a hiding place.

"How did you . . . ? When did you . . . ? What the heck's going on?" Mike sputtered. Then he began to laugh along with them.

"Your dad knew you'd be surprised," Terry said, entertained by Mike's reaction.

"Tell me!" Mike said, shaking with excitement.

"First," Amos said, when he could stop laughing for a moment, "we need to catch the mouse and send him home. We don't want to start breeding mice in the Preserve. Grab the garbage can and help me."

They each put on gloves and then found something they might be able to use to trap the tiny creature. They chased the mouse around the lab until Mike finally got the garbage can over it. They gathered around and slowly raised the can until the mouse tried to escape. Terry caught it in is gloved hands and sent it back through the portal, where it scampered away, running for its life.

"Do you want to get the TV control back, please?" Terry asked Mike.

"Can I stick my hand though that thing? Is it safe?"

"I've done it," Amos said. "Nothing appears to be wrong with my hand. I think you're safe to try it."

Mike was skeptical, but he took the two steps to the portal anyway and knelt down, breathing heavily and grinning broadly. He looked one last time at his dad, who was smiling at him, then reached through and picked up the control.

"Wow! I mean . . . Wow! That's a strange feeling. And you're sure there's no harm?"

"I'll run tests on our hands later."

"Does this mean we're safe to go though there and look around? It's a portal, right? Dad, what have you discovered?"

"Not yet," Amos said, turning serious. "We need to do more testing. But it appears that casual exposure to the portal doesn't have a negative effect."

"When can we . . . ?" Mike started to say, thinking about the adventure of going into the past or future, but Amos interrupted him.

"Mike. Stop. There's a lot we need to learn about what's on the other side of the portal before we risk sending a person through. We didn't appear to damage our hands, but what about internal organs? Or, if it's the past, what if we contaminate it with something we take with us? Or what if someone sees us and it affects a decision they make in the future? Or what if we have an emergency? How do we retrieve someone if they can't move on their own power?"

"But that looks like the twin of our valley," Mike said in frustration. "We can't do too much damage."

Startled, Amos looked back and forth between Mike and Terry, waiting for one of them to explain.

"What?" Mike asked.

"Why did you use the word *twin?* That's the same word Terry used earlier. Have you guys been sharing ideas without me?" When both men looked surprised, Amos explained. "I thought you might have had some new insight about what's on the other side of the portal—something you hadn't shared with me," he said. Terry raised his eyebrows and shook his head, so Amos looked at Mike.

"Sorry, Dad. I didn't mean anything by it. Katie's been looking at my astrological sign—Gemini—trying to 'understand me better,' she said. Gemini is the sign of the twins, you know? So twins have been on my mind lately. I guess it just popped out."

"A Gemini gate," Amos said pensively, "a door between twin worlds. What does it mean, Terry? Mike?"

"Nothing comes to mind," Terry said, shaking his head.

Mike's face was blank.

"Okay," Amos said, "something to think about. In the meantime, let's agree that no one goes through the *Gemini gate* until we know more."

Mike could see the wisdom in what his dad had just said, but it frustrated him to know that the portal—this Gemini gate, as his dad had called it—was right here. It seemed to be safe, but he wasn't allowed to go through it. He knew his dad wouldn't budge, and it would be foolhardy to ignore his instructions. What if he got in trouble and they didn't know where to find him? He gritted his teeth and took several deep breaths to calm himself.

"Let's do things in the proper order, okay?" Amos said as he watched Mike's expressions and body language, but he could see that his son wasn't convinced. "Mike, I'm as anxious as you are to try it, but you need to promise me that you won't go through the portal on your own. Promise?"

Mike's eyes stopped darting around the room and his breathing calmed. Finally, he nodded his head.

"Yeah, okay," he said with obvious reluctance.

"Isn't there a young lady waiting for you in the gardens?" Amos asked with a smile.

Mike's eyes lit up and he headed toward the door.

"I better get back to Katie," he said. With his hand on the doorknob, he looked over his shoulder with a smile. "Thanks for the demonstration, Terry."

"You're welcome, Mike."

8

We nailed it

"We received a report from the UK on our list of nine," Tom told the president. "One of the names, Samuel Smith, is wanted for questioning in a New Years' Eve terrorist attack in London. They have a video of him in conversation with a suspect from the attack. We have the video and we're sharing it with police, the FBI, CIA, and other agencies all across the east and as far west as the Mississippi River.

"And we've already received a response from an unlikely source," he continued. "A little motel in Chantilly, Virginia. An FBI agent, travelling through on a different assignment, stayed there overnight and struck up a conversation with the clerk. Apparently, the clerk is a conspiracy theorist and is particularly suspicious of anyone who looks like they might be from the Middle East." Tom started to chuckle as he continued.

"The clerk set up a hidden camera in the lobby months ago, hoping for a chance to catch a terrorist. He took a snapshot of a man calling himself Samuel Smith, who rented a room for the night of the bombing, then disappeared without sleeping in the bed. The face matches the one in the video from the UK."

"I don't suppose he knew where Mr. Smith was going in such a hurry?" Greg asked.

"No, he didn't, but he gave us a good description of his car, which matches a car on the list from the auto rental agency. I've put out an APB"—an All-Points Bulletin— "to all agencies, including transportation departments that might have traffic cameras in the area. We'll try to determine which way he's travelling and catch up with him."

Across the United States, 7 July

"Al-Qaeda has threatened further bombing. Seek shelter immediately." This message was broadcast every few minutes—by radio, television, satellite, cable, and the Internet—to all parts of the country. Where there were no electronic communications, the message began to appear in printed format, whether stapled to telephone poles or taped to front doors, and it came with a toll-free number for those who wanted additional information, such as shelter locations or shelter-in-place instructions.

Many of those who received the message, and who had working transportation—a car, truck, trailer, or mobile home—loaded up as much as they could of food, water, clothing, and other emergency supplies. While some blindly assumed that they were safe, most took the warning seriously and headed toward the places they believed to be the safest—usually the mountains or the center of the continent beyond. Many thought they would be safer in Mexico and headed south. Where before only the west and the northeast had been in turmoil, now the entire nation became a mass of moving bodies, resulting in huge traffic jams. Left behind were chaos, vandalism, and violence.

Martial Law, which had previously been declared in a few cities—those hard hit by violence and crime—was extended to the entire country, but it did little good. The police, national guard, and military—those who hadn't gone AWOL to care for their loved ones—were forced to divide their attention between relief efforts, evacuations, and now crowd control.

Following the strategy developed with his advisors and allies—to lull the terrorists into thinking they were afraid of another terrorist attack—the president made a public plea to Al-Qaeda to stop the madness and come to the negotiating table. After a couple of hours, long enough for Al-Qaeda to receive the message and put together a response, a reply appeared on Al Jazeera TV and radio, laughing at the miserable plight of the crippled Satan and her minions.

"It will be our pleasure," the response said, "to put the United States of America out of its misery."

Russia

Based on his recent conversation with President McCormick, Russian President Vladimir Putin suspected that McCormick was playing Al-Qaeda for fools—that he had no intention of negotiating with them—and he issued a warning to the United States and her allies that Russia would not tolerate, and would immediately respond in kind to, the launching of any further long-range missiles.

The Preserve, 7 July

"Mike, you're no more anxious than I am," Amos said, once again concerned about Mike's persistent interest in going to the twin world.

"But we've already been through the gate and it didn't hurt us," Mike insisted.

"Only our hands. And I've already said we could experiment with the gate. There's a lot we need to learn about how it works and how to control it, but we can't go through it until we know more about it *and* the twin world."

"There are some things we could learn about both without going through the gate," Terry said quietly, but it was enough to capture the other men's attention.

"What? How?" Mike asked, impatiently.

"Well, we've been playing with the original control panel," Terry said, "the one we called Panel A, and we've answered one of the questions we had—we've discovered that it's also a door, like Panel B. But we can't experiment with Panel B because of the radiation."

"Right," Mike said.

"But," Terry continued, "even with Panel A, we don't know if the *twin* world is *our* world, in the past or future, or something else altogether different. We need to find a man-made structure that will help us pin that down. We can practice controlling the gate while we look around Aspen Valley, and maybe work our way down the canyon toward Logan."

Mike's eyes lit up.

"Yeah! Is there a road in the canyon, Dad?"

"I don't know," Amos said. "I didn't think to look."

"If there is, is it paved or gravel or dirt?" Terry asked. "That should narrow down the time frame."

"Are there farms and towns in the canyon?" Mike asked.

"We could take time to do some online research, to find out when the canyon was settled," Amos said. When he saw Mike's sour expression, likely because that would delay their experimenting with the gate, he added. "Or, we could just go to Logan and find the date on a newspaper or calendar."

"I vote for that," Mike said, as his face lit up again.

"Of course," Terry said. "That would be the most direct route to take."

Amos insisted that they take time to make a list of things to try with the gate—like changing direction, controlling movement, things to look for on the way, and things to avoid. Mike took notes and kept the other two on track, so they could keep moving forward. They practiced maneuvering the gate. They saw animals as they crossed the valley, but nothing unusual, then found a paved road exactly where they would have expected it in their own, familiar world. Amos was at the controls as they followed the road down the canyon.

"What's that noise?" Mike asked from his front row seat, directly in front of the gate.

"Sounds like a car," Terry said. "Amos, do you hear it?"

It took a moment for the sound to register with Amos, who was busy trying to remember how each of the controls worked.

"I don't see anything in front of us," he said, then rotated the portal 180 degrees so that they could see *up* the canyon instead.

A car was barreling down the canyon, on a collision course with the gate, and Amos had a terrible vision of it crashing right into the interior of the lab at sixty or more miles per hour.

Mike dove to his right, and Terry, standing next to him, dove to the left.

Amos knew he had to try to prevent a collision, but not being as familiar with the operation of the gate as Mike or Terry, took precious moments to determine the best course of action. He gritted his teeth and stood his ground.

Just as the vehicle was about to smash into Amos, standing in the Preserve, the portal's opening winked out and the car disappeared from view. The car had approached so close that Amos could see the shocked look on the driver's face, as he registered the obstacle in his path.

When it was apparent that the disaster had been successfully averted, Amos collapsed into a chair, shaking, his heart pounding. Beads of sweat broke out on his forehead and upper lip. Mike and Terry stood slowly on either side of where the portal had just disappeared and looked around, finally focusing on Amos. Mike's eyes were as big as saucers.

"That was too close," Mike said. "What would have happened if we hadn't noticed that car?"

"I don't know," Terry said, "and I don't want to find out."

"Would it have entered the lab at high speed?"

"Would have been a disaster, if it had," Terry said. "Hey Amos, you okay?"

"I will be if my heart ever slows down," Amos said. He had two fingers on his throat and was looking at his watch, taking his pulse. "Let's not do that again, okay?"

"Did you see the driver's expression?" Mike asked and started chuckling nervously.

"You mean, just before you abandoned ship and left me to face that monster by myself?" Amos asked.

"I hope he's okay," Terry said. "I heard his brakes."

"So did I," Amos agreed, "and he started to swerve, like he was losing control, or maybe trying to veer around the gate. He could have left the road if he lost control of his car."

That sobered them up quickly.

"Do you think we should check on him?" Terry asked.

"Michael," Amos said, running his fingers through his hair, "Why don't you take over and bring the portal back up in the same location. But keep the opening small while we look around."

Mike took the controls and opened the portal. Thankfully, it opened back up right where it had closed. Within seconds they saw skid marks on the road, which continued for thirty feet in a wavy pattern. The marks ran to the edge of the road and stopped, but the car wasn't there. It seemed that the driver had managed to stop before leaving the highway.

"Thank goodness," Amos said.

"What do you think he thought he saw?" Mike asked, then mimicked a drunk. "I'm gonna' hafta lay off 'da booze when I'm drivin'!" That got them laughing again, more from relief than anything else.

"I was just thinking about that," Amos finally said. "A minute ago, you asked what would've happened if we hadn't noticed that car."

"Right," Mike said.

"Remember when you showed me how the Observer was working, shortly after we arrived at the Preserve?"

"Yeah," Mike said, laughing. "You were really surprised that it was a portal, not a projection on the wall."

"Right. Looking through one side of the portal, or gate, I was looking *away* from the cliff. Looking through the other side, I was looking *at* it."

"That's right," Mike said, excitedly, "which means that the driver would have been looking at the inside of the lab to begin with, at that wall," he said, pointing to the blank metal wall at the end of the lab, behind the gate. "But when you rotated the gate, so we could see him, then he could also see *us*, including all of the equipment in the lab."

"Exactly," Terry said somberly. "So, if we hadn't rotated the gate, he would have come crashing into the lab and smashed into the lab wall—a solid wall—at high speed."

"And if I hadn't figured out how to shut down the gate in time," Amos said, "that collision would have been with the Observer *and me.*"

"Well, I'd hate to lose the Observer," Terry said with mock seriousness, then chuckled at his own humor.

By the time the men maneuvered the gate to the mouth of

Logan Canyon, they'd already passed several small communities and farms in the canyon. Everything looked late twentieth century. Even the cars they passed looked normal to them, although they had to admit that none of them knew much about the makes, models, and years of automobiles.

Mike stopped the gate at the mouth of Logan Canyon and raised it a hundred and fifty feet above the roadway to get a broad aerial view of Cache Valley. From the air, Logan looked about the same as they remembered it. The university campus was off to the right, and the community spread out almost a hundred and eighty degrees in front of them.

"What do you want to do first?" Amos asked.

"Let's find a newspaper," Terry said.

Lillie opened the door to the lab and stuck her head in.

"Lunch time, boys," she said.

"Sorry, honey," Amos said, looking at his watch. "Let's shut it down for now, guys."

"How's it going?" she asked as Mike closed the gate and shut down the Observer.

"I'll show you after lunch, if you want," Amos said. He took her hand and walked out with her, followed by Terry and Mike.

"That looks like *our* Logan," Lillie said as she sat in front of the lab table while Amos worked the Observer. "This is incredible! I can't believe I'm really seeing this. It's like I'm looking down from an airplane, but I'm sitting underground in your lab. Really amazing!"

"It is," Amos agreed. "We still haven't determined what time period we're looking at. We were just trying to decide what to do next when you called us to lunch."

"It makes me want to go see our house."

Her comment startled him, and he thought about the possible ramifications. When he didn't respond, Lillie turned and looked at him.

"You didn't plan on that, did you?" she asked. "Or you didn't consider it."

"Didn't even occur to me. What if . . ." his thoughts were suddenly flying a hundred miles an hour.

"What if we're there?" she asked.

"What a paradox that would be. I'm convinced we're looking at the past or the future, but I thought we'd be looking at the distant past."

"That doesn't look like the distant past to me. Might even be the near future. Have you looked at a newspaper to find the date?"

"We'll do that next."

"Why not do it right now? I'd love to see it."

Amos opened his mouth but nothing came out. It wouldn't be fair to go ahead without Mike and Terry. Mike, especially, would be so disappointed.

"You don't want to do anything without Michael, do you?" she said, as if reading his mind. At his surprised look, she added. "I know how important this it to him."

"Of course you do."

"Let Mike play, then show me later."

"Okay, let's find a newspaper," Amos said.

"You said Lillie wants to see our neighborhood, to see if we're there?" Terry asked with a grin, as Mike opened the gate above the mouth of Logan canyon.

"Let's keep the gate small and stay above the traffic," Amos said, ignoring Terry. Finding their doppelgängers wasn't what Amos wanted to be thinking about right now.

Mike manipulated the gate down Fourth, then south on Main.

"Where should we look for a newspaper?" Mike finally asked. So far, his dad and Terry had commented on several stores they knew, none of which looked different from when they'd left Logan, but apparently, they weren't thinking about a newspaper.

"There's an international market just ahead," Amos said.

"I think there's a news stand inside the Smith's store on Fourth," Terry said.

"We just went past Smith's," Amos said. "Let's keep going."

"What if," Mike thought aloud, "we just send the gate to Smith's?"

"Can we do that?" Amos asked.

"That's one of the questions on the list we made, and I've been thinking about how long it takes to get anywhere, even moving quickly," Mike said. "What if we turn it off, then reset the coordinates to a new location and turn it on again."

"We don't know the exact coordinates of the store. We could end up inside a wall or some other obstacle," Terry said.

"Like a body?" Amos asked.

"That's a possibility, isn't it?" Terry asked.

"Do we have any idea what would happen to a body if we went through it?" Mike asked.

"We designed it for that purpose, and we did go through that deer," Terry replied.

"Mike and I have both put a hand through it without any detrimental results, but no, we don't know if it might have the potential to harm someone."

"Okay, but how do we know where to send it?" Terry asked.

"I have a suggestion," Mike said, interrupting. "We've just been there. The coordinates are in memory. I should be able to figure out where to send it."

"Okay, Mike," Amos said, "but I suggest we set it for fifty feet above the parking lot and see where we end up. That would even help us calibrate the gate. You know, like setting surveying markers as reference points for future location searches."

Mike knew what his dad was talking about. The U.S. Bureau of Land Management, or BLM, had created a public lands survey system—the Township and Range System—that divided the country's public lands into six-mile squares, and placed surveying markers at each corner of each square, as a reference point for future land surveys. Amos was suggesting that they teach the portal to set virtual markers, as reference points for future searches.

"Great idea," Terry said. "Try it, Mike."

Mike grinned and opened the Observer's memory to search for the coordinates. Terry joined him, just to consult, letting Mike work the controls and enter the coordinates. Amos watched while thinking about the problems of time and location.

"Woo-hee," Mike yelled as they looked down on the Smith's grocery store a few minutes later. They were over the parking lot, looking down at the front of the store. "We nailed it."

Terry and Amos laughed at Mike's enthusiasm.

"*You* nailed it, Mike," Terry said, slapping him on the shoulder. "Your calculations were right on the money."

Amos studied the front of the store.

"Mike, make the opening smaller. If anyone looks up here, they might see a small image of people, or whatever's visible, floating in the air. We need to be more inconspicuous."

Mike closed the portal so that the image in front of them was no more than six inches across.

"That better?"

"Yeah, that's good."

They watched as people moved through the doors of the shop.

"Do you know where the newspapers are located inside the store?" Amos asked.

"Yeah. Let me try this," Mike replied. He reduced the gate to an inch in diameter, moved it down to the front of the store, through the wall, and up to the side of the courtesy desk. He was about six feet above a stack of newspapers. He focused on the front page of the paper, carefully avoiding the people moving around in the store. When he saw the date on the newspaper, he backed up and let the others have a look. Then they stared at each other in shocked surprise.

"That's today's date," Amos said.

"What does it mean?" Mike asked.

Suddenly, all the assumptions they'd made about the gate showing them the past or future, were invalidated—all their conclusions turned upside down and inside out.

"Amos?" Terry asked, fear and amazement in his voice.

"Terry?" Amos asked in return, looking at his friend.

"We're not looking at the past," Terry said. "Or the future."

"We're looking at today," Mike reminded them. "What does that mean?"

"Is it possible? Amos?" Terry asked.

"I . . . I really don't know," Amos stuttered.

"Amos," Terry said, becoming agitated. "If we're not looking at the past or the future then . . . what?"

"Dad, what does it mean?" Mike asked at the same time.

"Okay, okay," Amos said, anxious and excited at the same time. "We need to think this through."

The alarm on Amos's watch went off, startling all of them.

"Great timing," Amos said. "We need to go to dinner. After Lillie had to call us to lunch, she made me promise she wouldn't have to call us again."

The three men stared at each other for another few moments, each lost in his own thoughts, and then they reluctantly shut down the Observer and left the lab.

After dinner, Amos and Terry returned to the lab. Mike needed to go to the gardens, but he slipped a note to his dad on his way out of the dining room.

Amos had noticed, during dinner, that Mike had paid more attention to the note he'd been writing, than to his dinner—or to Katie, which he might pay for later. Amos had watched him write something, think about it, then erase it and write something else. He'd done it several times, and by the time the meal was finished Katie had looked frustrated with him.

Amos read the note aloud, through the erasures.

"'Parallel world—only logical possibility.'"

"A parallel world," Terry repeated, chuckling nervously and shaking his head. "A twin world in an alternate universe? It was hard enough accepting the idea that we were looking at the past or the future. Now I have to rethink everything."

"A parallel world," Amos said, pensively. "Is it possible, Terry? Really? We asked ourselves before if we were hallucinating. Now I have to ask it again. Is this real?"

"Maybe we *should* go see if we can find ourselves," Terry laughed self-consciously. "That would be interesting. Hello Terry, I'm you."

Amos looked at Terry, then ran his fingers through his hair.

"Sorry to disappoint you. I have no idea what to think. We're in uncharted territory."

"Pioneers of the twenty-first century," Terry said when Amos paused.

Amos looked at Terry, a question in his expression.

"*Should we?* I mean . . . go look for ourselves? I don't know. Is it possible we exist in this alternate universe? I don't know that, either. We can sit here and consider options, or we can make a decision and move forward. What do you want to do?"

"Let's think about it overnight."

9

No-win situation

Meeting of the president and his advisers
8 July, 5:30 a.m. eastern time

"Greg," HomeSec Chuck Dickson said, "are you sure that we've given people enough time to find shelter? You realize that as soon as we start launching missiles, there'll be a response from Russia—possibly China, too."

"Thanks for your concern, Chuck," the president said. "Unfortunately, we're in a no-win situation. If we continue as planned, we put citizens at risk. If we delay, we put the world at risk of another Al-Qaeda attack. We didn't ask for this war, just like we didn't ask for World War I or World War II. The fate of the world hinges on our eliminating the enemies of peace and freedom. We have to do this."

Chuck nodded unhappily. Greg turned to SecDef Jim Seymour.

"Are we ready?"

"Yes, Mr. President. At your command," Jim replied, a little more enthusiastically than Greg would have liked.

"Anything else we need to consider, gentlemen?" He saw only shaking of heads. "Okay, let's open the lines to our allies and see if they're ready to proceed."

Greg touched a button on his control panel and the voice of the operator said, "Yes, Mr. President?"

"Please send the call through."

"Ready, Mr. President," the operator said a few seconds later as the conference call connected.

The president greeted Prime Ministers Theresa May, Édouard Philippe, and Benjamin Netanyahu, before confirming that their respective governments were ready to proceed.

"General Seymour will coordinate with your designated military leaders," Greg said, "as soon as we complete this call and give the word."

"What's the latest on our terrorist, Mr. Smith?" Minister May asked before Greg could close the call.

"Thank you for asking, Theresa. Tom?"

"We've tracked him as far as the outskirts of Atlanta. If he's part of the terrorist plot, and with the deadline this afternoon, he has to be close to his destination. We're sending a team to stake out the CDC just north of Atlanta, in case that's his target."

"Is that the most likely target?"

"Well, there are several stadiums, historic sites, and places of worship, including a synagogue, but there's nothing extraordinary going on at any of them this afternoon. There's a Coca Cola bottling plant . . . "

"I think we can rule that one out," Greg said, interrupting.

"Then, I think it's the CDC. It houses samples of several deadly viruses."

"Well, we all hope you get him. We've rounded up several suspected terrorists and are interrogating them. Nothing yet."

"Anything else," Greg asked. "No? Then I'll wish Godspeed to all."

The call ended, and Jim took a call from his counterparts in the UK, France, and Israel, leaving his speaker on so the others could listen.

At the same time, Chuck was on another line giving directions to his staff to have all the relief workers stop whatever they were doing and get themselves, and anyone else they could, to the nearest shelters.

United States, France, Israel, and the United Kingdom, Sunday, 6:00 a.m. eastern time

At exactly six a.m., eastern daylight time, Jim gave the word, and close to two hundred and fifty missiles—land-based, and in submarines and aircraft, around the world—were launched at the forty-nine suspected Al-Qaeda and ISIS sites, ports on the Caspian and Black Seas, and cities in southern Russian provinces. Enough of the missiles were nuclear to ensure that none of the people responsible for the threats and attacks survived.

They look like fireworks, the president thought, as he sat in his underground bunker, watching satellite images of the coordinated offensive. *An appropriate response to Al-Qaeda's fourth of July terror attack.*

Moscow, 6:03 a.m. Eastern time (3:03 pm local)

Russian President Vladimir Putin wasn't surprised when his aide reported that American missiles were in the air. He'd underestimated President McCormick's resolve in the beginning, but had come to believe that McCormick would retaliate, as he'd said. He chuckled, then noticed the surprised look on the face of the aide.

"How ironic that the United States will be remembered as pursuing nuclear war while Russia sat back with clean hands and watched. They bombed the Al-Qaeda sites, as I thought they would, didn't they? Even after claiming they didn't know where they were."

"I'm sorry, sir," the aide said, handing a report to his president. "Here's a list of the targets, which includes locations in our southern provinces."

Putin's initial good humor evaporated instantly.

"Stop those missiles!"

"Yes, sir," the aide said, then saluted and left hurriedly. By the time Russia launched its defensive missiles, it was too late to intercept many of those coming from the United States and its allies. Each of the forty-nine locations received at least one hit.

As the reality of the situation became clear, Putin stormed around his office, cursing the American president for having the nerve to attack Russia. As an afterthought, an hour later, he ordered an aide to talk to the Siloviki. He learned later that the Siloviki, despite repeated attempts over several hours, had been unable to contact their Al-Qaeda customers. Although not surprised, Putin was nevertheless frustrated that McCormick's attack on the terrorists seemed to have succeeded.

Islamabad, Pakistan, 6:09 a.m. eastern time (4:09 p.m. local)

Leaders at all levels of the government in Islamabad were shocked and enraged. It was unfathomable that America and her allies had targeted sites within their borders. They immediately launched their own missiles, first to intercept those that were incoming, then to retaliate on the nearest U.S. ally, which was Israel. Then, fearing a coordinated attack from India—their on-again, off-again unfriendly neighbor to the east, and a country that had recently been courting favor with the United States—they fired missiles at India, too, in a preemptive offensive attack.

New Delhi, India, 6:14 a.m. eastern time (4:44 p.m. local)

In India, government leaders and the general populace alike were surprised by the unprovoked attack from Pakistan. The Indian government responded by returning fire on several major cities and known weapons sites in Pakistan. Then, fearing a retaliatory attack from China, they launched missiles east and north, at the neighbor with whom they'd argued over borders for years.

Beijing, China, 6:18 a.m. eastern time (7:18 p.m. local)

In the early evening, while attempting to enjoy a meal with his family, China's President, Xi Jinping, was notified by a military aide that missiles were headed toward China. He immediately contacted his office, where three generals were meeting with military analysts, assessing the death toll and destruction from the first volley of U.S. missiles, the earthquakes, and the tsunamis. He'd demanded hourly reports from the various regions where there were problems, but there were so many reports, detailing so much damage, that he was inundated with information. Now his generals were summarizing the reports and sending him only the most significant data.

"Who launched the missiles?" Jinping demanded from the general who answered the phone.

"We have missiles in the air from India, the U.S., Russia, Israel, Pakistan, and countries in Europe," the general said.

Misunderstanding the general's response, Jinping believed his country was under attack from multiple directions.

"Well, counter the missiles and retaliate!" he bellowed, exploding in frustration at this latest insult.

Northern Africa, the Middle East, and Pakistan
6:28 a.m. eastern time

The Allied missiles struck the targeted terrorist strongholds minutes apart. Most of the locations had little warning—some had none. The destruction was swift and total. After reviewing satellite images of the attacks, President McCormick requested a follow-up meeting with the Prime Ministers of Israel, France, and the United Kingdom.

"It appears that the offensive was successful," Prime Minister Netanyahu said. "We detect no movement and no outgoing communications from any of the sites."

"Our intelligence people report the same," Prime Minister May said. "I know there are huge Muslim populations in the United Kingdom and around the world. We can only hope that the most radical—the Al-Qaeda and ISIS terrorists—have been eradicated from the face of the earth."

"I'll second that sentiment," Prime Minister Philippe said.

"I'm certain you've all seen or heard about the reaction to our offensive," President McCormick said. "Russia, China, Pakistan, and India—that's the list so far—have started launching their own nuclear arsenals. So, while our offensive was successful, unfortunately it appears to have stirred a hornet's nest. The next few days will tell if the leaders of the world's nations accept our actions against the terrorists or throw the world into chaos. It might be useful to get back together in a couple of days to see if there's anything we can do—or should do—to reestablish relationships."

Atlanta, Georgia, Sunday, 7:00 a.m. eastern time

Saleh had memorized his instructions, and was waiting outside the apartment building where he'd been told his contact lived. He was early, but within half an hour he would be accompanying his contact to retrieve the explosives. The contact had already been checked out and cleared, so he didn't have to go through that whole routine—they could get right to the point.

The explosives were in a suicide vest this time—nonnuclear— and he'd been assured in the letter that the vest held enough explosives to breach the protective barriers and release the agents locked deep inside the CDC, but only if he followed his instructions explicitly. They explained which door to use, the path to follow inside the facility, and how long it should take to get there. He knew he might need to use his gun in order to get to his destination, but the knowledge failed to stir any emotion in him. It was important to meet the timetable, and that was his only concern.

While he waited for the appointed time to call his contact, he listened to an all-news radio broadcast. It amused him how the Americans could become so obsessed with trivial things, like political divisions, when such acts as he was committing certainly crossed party lines. Suddenly the program was interrupted by a breaking story.

"We've just received a report that the United States and her allies launched more missiles at six a.m. eastern this morning. The report said the missiles, some of which were nuclear, were aimed at known and suspected Al-Qaeda and ISIS terrorist sites in the Middle East and Northern Africa. We're waiting for more information and will share it as soon as it's available."

The program returned to a panel of alleged experts, who began discussing the latest breaking news. Saleh stared at the radio dial, noting the station, so he could check back for follow up reports. He wondered at the timing of the attack by the infidels. As sad as it made him to think of all the brothers who would suffer in this attack, he would follow through with his mission. If anything, it was even more important now.

"Allahu akbar," he said when his contact answered the phone.

"Allahu akbar, I've been expecting your call."

"I'm waiting outside. Let's go."

A few moments later, a young American male exited the apartment building, walking quickly while pushing his arm into the sleeve of a light jacket. Saleh reached across the seat and opened the door. The young man slid into the seat and held out his hand.

"I'm Jackson," he said.

"Samuel," Saleh said, taking the offered hand and shaking it the way he'd been taught in England. "Where's the package?"

Jackson gave him directions to a nearby self-storage facility as they talked quietly. Saleh tried to assess Jackson's frame of mind as they conversed. He had to assess whether Jackson was ready to make the required sacrifice—if not, he was to eliminate Jackson and wear the vest himself.

When they arrived, Jackson unlocked his storage unit and raised the overhead door, while checking his surroundings to make sure there was no one around. Everything was laid out neatly on shelves. He went to a shelf holding a bulky backpack, opened the pack, and showed Saleh the vest, wrapped with sticks of explosives linked together.

"What have you been told about the mission?" Saleh asked.

"I use my power company panel truck to get close to the building. Then I walk in wearing the vest and set off the explosives. You'll tell me where I need to be for maximum impact." He opened a pocket in the backpack and brought out a radio and Bluetooth earpiece. "You get the radio and I get the earpiece. You talk to me all the way in and tell me when it's time."

"Are you prepared to do that?"

"That's what I committed to do."

"But that's not what I asked."

Jackson appeared to think about the question for a few moments before answering.

"I have an okay life. No family, not many friends, a dumb job. I have a girlfriend, and we could have a family one day; but yes, I'm ready."

Judging by his experience with sleepers in London, Saleh decided that if Jackson got a little reinforcement to his training, he would be fine. So, Saleh would help him prepare.

"Let's go back to your apartment. We can read the prophet's words and pray."

Jackson nodded, picked up the backpack, and followed Saleh to the car.

"Report," Agent Scott said quietly into his headset. As the most senior agent currently in the FBI's Atlanta office, he was in charge of the team tasked with the CDC stakeout. He'd been itching for this type of assignment for years, but had always been beaten out by more senior agents. But right now the most experienced agents were still on their way back from the capital, where they'd been helping with the search for the nuclear weapon. If he could wrap this up quickly, it would be a big feather in his cap.

"James, in place," he heard.

"Fredericks, in place. Nothing to report."

"Kearney, in place. All clear."

"Wright, in place. Nothing in sight but a utility truck."

"Okay," Scott said, "report anything, I mean *anything*, that looks unusual."

"Uh . . . Wright here. I took a look at the driver of the utility truck . . ."

He didn't have to specify that he'd used binoculars—it was procedure.

"And?" Scott asked impatiently.

"Maybe it's nothing."

"What *is it?*"

"Well, he's not wearing the usual company shirt. You know, the one with a logo on it?"

"What's he wearing?"

"That's the thing. He's got on a light jacket, but it looks bulky, like he's got something on underneath it."

"Fredericks, get a second set of eyes over there," Scott said as he started to move to the front of the building to see for himself.

"On it," Fredericks said.

"The rest of you, stay put," Scott added, "but keep your eyes open."

"I see him," Fredericks said. "I agree it looks suspicious, and he's headed for the front door of the building."

"Stop him!"

"On it."

"Wait!" Wright said. "His lips are moving. Either he's talking to himself or he has an accomplice."

"He has a Bluetooth earpiece," Fredericks said.

"He must have an accomplice," Scott said. "Stay under cover and look around for possible . . . "

"Got one," Kearney said, interrupting. "My ten o'clock. In a car"

"I see him," James replied. "He's talking into a radio."

"Okay," Scott said, thinking quickly. "Wright, approach the utility guy. Don't let him get inside the building. Kearns and James, close in on the car—without being seen, if possible."

Jackson had pulled into the parking lot, but all the parking spaces close to the door had been occupied.

"I'll park in the closest space available," he'd said.

"Not good enough," Saleh had replied. "Park right in front of the door if you have to."

"That will be too suspicious."

"I don't care. You need to get inside quickly."

Jackson had ignored Saleh's instructions and parked in an open stall about six spaces from the front door. He'd casually listened to Saleh's tirade, not always in English, and, he'd suspected, not all complimentary.

"Look, I'm here now and ready to go in. Do you want to argue, or do you want me to get started?"

"Okay, get going," Saleh had said after he'd fumed a bit more.

Jackson had stepped out of the truck, straightened his jacket, and headed for the front door.

"There's someone in the parking lot," Saleh said. "You have to hurry."

"Where?" Jackson asked, looking around.

"Don't stop. Don't look around. Run!"

"Hey, buddy!" a man called as he hurried across the parking lot toward Jackson. "I have a question."

"Don't stop!" Saleh yelled in his ear. Jackson debated taking the earpiece out so he wouldn't have to listen to Saleh. He started moving toward the door again.

"Hey, wait," the man called. He was much closer and looked like someone with authority.

"Shoot him and get inside!" Saleh yelled. He sounded like he was afraid. The thought crossed Jackson's mind that if he failed in this mission, Al-Qaeda would not let him live. He thought about the gun. If he pulled it out, he could get shot if this guy was some kind of security. If he didn't do what Saleh said, Saleh might shoot him. If he went inside and set off the bomb, he would be dead for sure. In the end, his indecision decided the outcome.

Suddenly, the man was right beside him, his gun pointed at Jackson's chest. "Keep your hands where I can see them. What are you wearing under your jacket?"

Saleh's whole world was collapsing before his eyes. Jackson had failed him by not following directions, and now he didn't have time to get the explosives and take them inside himself. He could shoot Jackson and the man standing next to him, or he could drive away. Then he realized Jackson knew too much—he had to die. He pulled out his gun and opened the car door.

"The accomplice is getting out of his car," Kearney said, making Fredericks stop and look in that direction. He caught the reflection of the gun barrel as it pointed in his direction, so he pushed Jackson one way and dropped the other way, just as bullets started flying. He kept his head down, listening to gunfire from at least three sources. Then a car engine started and tires squealed as a car sped away.

"He's getting away," James said.

"I think I hit him at least once," Kearney added.

"I'm calling in an APB to watch for him," Scott said. "Any injuries? What about the utility guy, Fredericks?"

Fredericks had gone to the utility worker as soon as he'd heard the car leave. He still had his gun out and pointed at the downed man, just in case, as he approached. Everyone reported that they were fine. Fredericks was the last to report.

"I'm fine. Just a few scrapes. The utility guy was shot in the head. His pulse is weak. I'm checking to see what he was carrying before I try to stabilize him."

"Good idea," Scott said. "I've called for an ambulance and I'm on my way. James and Kearney, get the car and try to follow the accomplice."

Saleh fumed as he sped away from the CDC, taking corners at dangerous speeds. He was following a preplanned escape route, but figured he would have to adapt since he hadn't planned on the shattered window and bullet holes in the sides of the car, and he didn't want to draw too much attention to himself. The left side of his face stung in several places and he could feel what he assumed to be blood running down his face and neck. He knew there must be pieces of safety glass embedded in his skin from the shattered window, so he decided not to touch his cheek until he could stop and look in a mirror. The rest of his body felt fine, so he couldn't tell if he'd been hit by a bullet, but maybe he had and adrenaline was keeping the pain at bay. If so, he'd feel it soon. He had to find a place to stop and check himself over.

He thought he'd hit Jackson while he was lying on the ground. He hoped so, but couldn't be sure. He also thought that this response couldn't have come from routine security at the CDC. It was more like an ambush. If it was the FBI, his cover had been blown. He needed to get out of the area before they brought in reinforcements and cut off all escape routes. His motel room would be a good place to check the damage to his face, but if the FBI knew it was him, they might also know where he was staying and they'd have the motel under surveillance. If they'd called in reinforcements, he didn't know how quickly they could have the area blocked off—it might already be too late.

He saw a sign for a mechanic's shop and slowed, pulling into the lot. It looked like the shop was closed, as he'd hoped it would be on a Sunday afternoon. He parked between two cars, as far back in the lot as he could, hoping his license plate would be difficult to read from the street. He turned the rearview mirror so he could see himself and delicately plucked glass from his face and neck. Then he poured water onto a tissue and wiped his face and neck. There were two spots on his neck that were still bleeding, so he kept a dry tissue on them as he periodically checked the street and planned his next steps.

He got out of the car and looked it over. There were bullet holes in both side door panels. He thanked Allah that none of the bullets had struck him, a sure sign that Allah approved of his actions.

"Then why didn't Allah help me in the attack on the CDC?" he wondered aloud, telling himself immediately that his question was one of curiosity, not doubt. The failure was obviously Jackson's fault. *The infidels corrupted Jackson's faith*, he decided, satisfied that he would be given another opportunity to prove himself faithful.

He grabbed his backpack from the back seat and walked down the row of cars, checking doors. He finally found one that was unlocked, threw his pack into the back seat, then reached under the dash and hotwired the car. After it started, but before he could put the car in gear, a man came around the back of shop waving and yelling for him to stop.

This was a complication Saleh didn't want or need, so he powered down the window and shot the man. He aimed for the chest, but the man must have seen the gun and moved, so the bullet hit him in the arm. Saleh debated quickly about trying to kill him, but decided it was more important to get some distance between him and the shop.

Besides, the man had turned and run, and he didn't want to waste more time. The FBI would know shortly where he was, either way. He drove out of the lot and away, obeying traffic laws so as not to attract attention.

"He's been spotted."

Agent Scott addressed his team, who were spread out around the neighborhood, looking for the terrorist. They had discovered the suicide vest—the wearer had died of the gunshot wound—and now knew that it had been a failed attack on the CDC by terrorists.

"He shot a mechanic in a parking lot on Gibson," he continued. "That's less than ten minutes from the CDC, so it's got to be our guy. A team is on its way to investigate."

"I bet he switched cars if it was in a parking lot," Kearney said.

"The investigators have been told to find out if he took another car and get us a description. We'll know as soon as they find someone to open the shop and figure out if a car's missing."

"Maybe whatever he stole will break down on him," Fredericks said sarcastically.

"Our instructions are to move our search in that direction," Scott said.

The car Saleh had stolen started making noise. *Engine trouble,* he thought and started looking for a replacement. He drove into an older neighborhood to continue his search. After a few minutes, the car started jerking, and the engine noises increased in volume and frequency. Afraid that the car was about to stall on him, he pulled to the side of the street in front of an older home, with a single, detached garage that stood to one side of the house and slightly farther back on the lot.

He looked around at the nearby houses, to see if anyone was watching. Seeing no one, he stuffed his gun into his belt and covered it with his shirttail. Then he got out, grabbed his pack and walked confidently to the garage, watching the front windows of the house for any activity.

He looked quickly at the back of the house, but could see no movement through the windows. Looking back at the street, he could tell that the only way neighbors would see what he was doing was to walk out to the street and look between the house and the garage.

The side door was locked, and it opened noisily when he kicked it in, so he looked back at the house to see if he had attracted any attention. No one appeared. Inside, he found a late-model, bright blue, four-door sedan. He hotwired the car, which was a bit more difficult than the previous one since it was newer. Then he used a remote attached to the visor to open the garage door. As he backed the car into the street, a well-dressed, older man walked by on the sidewalk. He stared at Saleh, arched his eyebrows, then lowered his head and moved on. Saleh debated shooting the old man to prevent his calling the authorities, then decided this car should get him out of the area before anyone could catch him. Besides, he thought, these Americans are so trusting, I can always get another car later.

"You were right, Fredericks," Agent Scott said. "The car broke down, but he stole another one." He gave them the location and description of the car. "Nobody hurt this time, but the car's a newer one, so it's probably more reliable. We're not likely to find him hitchhiking on the side of the road."

Around the World, 8-9 July

Over a period of approximately thirty hours, the nuclear and conventional arsenals of the world's nuclear powers were nearly depleted. Each country had attempted to stop the missiles launched at them and had returned fire. The Israelis ran out of missiles quickly, the military joining the civilian population in their bunkers, to try to outlast the war, while the U.S. defended them remotely.

Pakistan and India, then China, ran out next. Their infrastructures and populations suffering heavy casualties.

The U.S. and Russia fought on, inflicting EMPs and nuclear destruction on each other and their neighbors. There were so many missiles in the air at one time, it was impossible to track and defeat all of them. In addition to strategic military sites, missiles were fired at the known and suspected 'secret' government bunkers, financial centers, power plants, hydroelectric dams, and other sites essential to maintaining the government, military, and infrastructure.

There was no clear battlefront. The missile exchange was managed from secret bunkers by generals taking orders from political leaders. When the war had begun, all U.S. military units had been ordered to deploy, to minimize the number of fixed targets for the enemy. While the army backed up national guard units in the cities, the navy, marines, and air force played active roles in targeting and delivering missiles to strategic enemy sites, then standing off to observe and report.

Battleships, aircraft carriers, and other naval vessels were targeted, but few were actually hit. However, many were knocked out of service by EMPs and lay dead in the water, with no one to rescue them.

One U.S. submarine was caught on the surface, early in the exchange, while responding to a mayday call, and an EMP fried all of its circuitry. The captain wasn't worried about it sinking, but they couldn't move, and they were too far from shore to attempt life rafts.

On both sides of the war, aircraft hit by EMPs fell out of the sky, their pilots and crewmen ejecting, if they could. The rescue of stranded military personnel was just one more item on General Seymour's action list.

Missiles that got past the U.S. defenses destroyed military bases and supply depots, power plants, hydroelectric dams, and other critical resources. The explosions were followed by secondary blasts at fuel storage sites and refineries. Fires raged, and radioactive fallout and smoke contaminated the air. The sun was hidden behind thick clouds of smoke and airborne contamination over much of the country.

A few non-nuclear countries had joined the war with conventional weapons, using the confusion of the war to attack neighbor states, usually to settle long-held grudges and disputes or to grab at resources they might desperately need in the postwar world.

Unhardened communications were knocked out around the world. Transportation and commerce were at a standstill.

The Glen Canyon Dam, on the Colorado River in Arizona, took a direct hit, destroying the dam and hydroelectric plant, and allowing millions of gallons of debris-filled water to cascade down the gorge. The flood struck the Hoover Dam on the Arizona-Nevada border, overflowing the top of the dam. The additional stress caused it to break apart and add more concrete, debris, and water to the flood.

The flood continued all the way to the Gulf of California, destroying dams, homes, and farmland, and carrying away anything that wasn't bolted down, including people.

Around the globe, in response to the onslaught from thousands of explosions, and the resultant earthquakes, tsunamis, and volcanic eruptions, the earth experienced incredible change. The rocky foundation of Manhattan Island collapsed, sinking New York City, so that only the tallest of the damaged buildings marked the location of the once-bustling city. Mountains of rock crashed down on valleys, burying hundreds of thousands of people in their homes and shelters.

Weather patterns began to change in unpredictable ways. Large sections of polar ice caps broke off and flowed into warm currents, where they began to melt. Huge clouds of dust and airborne debris caused temperatures to begin to drop, signaling the likelihood of an early and record-cold winter. U.S. cities along the Atlantic and Gulf coasts from Boston to Biloxi, and coastal cities around the world, were swamped by tidal waves and rising oceans.

Satellites recorded the horrific scenes of destruction around the world. The incredible and terrible exchange of July eighth devastated the infrastructure, environment, and citizenry of nearly every country in the Northern Hemisphere, and many in the south as well. Hundreds of millions of people died or were critically injured within the first forty-eight hours.

Those who lived through the global destruction were mostly unsheltered, hungry, desperate, and angry. Few people in the countries most affected by the storms of war or the storms of nature had sufficient clean food and water to survive for long. Most didn't know where to direct their anger and took it out on each other. If there had been any working video communications in the streets, they would have shown images of desperate survivors breaking into stores and fighting each other over the scant food and drink still available. The average citizens of the world, those who hadn't started, perpetuated, or encouraged the hostilities, were the real losers in this war.

10

It's like a different world

"Dad," Mike said, looking around the office at the other board members, "trying to sanitize the news for the rest of the group isn't working."

"I really believe that the actual news reports are too disturbing to share," Amos replied.

"Jason thinks we're lying to him," Terry said, "keeping the truth to ourselves."

"I know," Amos said, "but Jason's an idiot."

He sighed, getting a scowl from Lillie and a snicker from Mike.

"Okay Terry, feel free to share some of the reports with Jason and Brittany. They've already seen the looting and rioting, the mass migrations, and the death of the reporters in Washington, D.C. I'm reluctant to show anyone the latest footage, with the military crackdown and the missile attack. Everyone felt the earthquakes. I'm actually grateful we haven't been able to see what damage the earthquakes are causing. Maybe we should let the adults watch some raw footage, so they can see how bad it is. Then they can decide what their families should see."

"What's going on outside now?" Mike asked Terry.

"I stopped monitoring the news myself because reports have become so sporadic. I don't know what we'll find."

Terry shrugged as he turned on the television.

The first three stations he tried showed static. The next one showed a mushroom cloud rising into the air while a thick, debris-filled dust cloud spread quickly across the ground. The view held steady, as if the camera were on a tripod, but the image expanded and contracted, as if the cameraman were trying to get the big picture, as well as the detail. A time stamp in the bottom right corner was dated 4 July 12:33 p.m. It appeared to have been taken from several stories above ground level. Three voices could be heard: a man, who was trying to describe what he was recording, and two others—a man and a woman—in the background, in shocked disbelief. Their voices cracked and they spoke in broken sentences as they commented on what they were seeing.

"... from a suite in the Palazzo hotel in Las Vegas, looking north. The explosion must have been at the Air Force Base ..."

There was mumbling in the background, then audible exclamations.

"Oh my!"

"Unbe-flippin'-lievable."

The camera zoomed in on the Stratosphere hotel as the dust cloud reached it quickly from behind. It started to shake and tip toward the camera.

"The Stratosphere is being shaken. There are large chunks of ... stuff ... in the cloud that's hitting it."

"Holy cow, what's crashing through the windows and walls?" the man asked.

"Look at the roller coaster on the roof!" the woman screamed.

The camera scanned to the roof in time to see the roller coaster leaving its track.

"It looks like there are people in some of the cars, but it's hard to tell from this distance." Terry knew that the Palazzo was almost two miles from the Stratosphere hotel, but the camera was able to follow the roller coaster all the way down, to where it disappeared into the boiling debris cloud.

As the camera zoomed back out, it showed the hotel beginning to collapse. The noise of the wind, the twisting metal, and debris crashing against buildings, miles away and behind the closed window, were now loud enough to drown out the words of the cameraman. Objects fell through windows that looked like furniture and bodies, as the exterior walls split open, broke apart, and fell into the cloud below. The building leaned across the street toward its neighbors, and then the entire edifice fell, structural steel screeching, twisting like wet noodles.

The sound from the video faded and a reporter from the television station started speaking.

"What we're seeing is the result of the explosion of a nuclear warhead at the Nellis Air Force Base, north of Las Vegas, Nevada, on July fourth. The viewer who sent us this video was in a suite, high in the Palazzo hotel, about two miles southwest of the Stratosphere hotel. He told us that he and his friends were using a telescopic lens to look around the city when they were attracted to the explosion by the bright light and noise. By the time they got to the room where they could see and record the explosion, the light had abated somewhat, or they surely would have been blinded by it. As it is, they witnessed the destruction of the Stratosphere, the mushroom cloud, and the leading edge of the pressure front that destroyed structures for several miles around the explosion. He told us that by the time the front reached the Palazzo, it felt like a strong earthquake, shaking the building, shattering windows, and pushing furniture against the wall. All three dropped to the floor when their window shattered, and they suffered only cuts and bruises. It could have been a lot worse."

The camera continued to zoom out, and the scene began to include other structures around the Stratosphere. The cameraman seemed to be trying to find the leading edge of the debris cloud. A multi-story parking terrace was blown sideways, chunks of concrete falling from upper floors to those below. Cars were crushed as they pushed through concrete barriers and into the air. Sparks flashed as power poles tipped and power lines stretched to their limit, then broke. Buildings collapsed and houses were blown away, flames exploding from inside, where gas lines were undoubtedly broken and the gas ignited by electrical sparks. As the debris cloud came closer to the Palazzo, people could be seen running from burning buildings, only to be overtaken by the fast-moving cloud. Then the window in front of the camera exploded and the camera fell to the floor, its lens pointed up toward the ceiling.

"Terry," Amos said, and Terry, who'd been mesmerized by the scene, turned to face the others. Becca, Emily, and Katie had laid their heads on their arms on the table, facing away from the TV. Mike had backed away from the table and put his head down. Lillie's head was on Amos's lap, and Amos rested one hand on her head, rubbing her neck and back with the other. The set of Amos's jaw convinced Terry that he was barely containing his emotions.

"I'm sorry, Amos," Terry said, realizing his own stomach was upset. "I should have been more sensitive."

"It's okay, Terry," Amos said, his anger probably the only thing keeping him from putting his head down like the others. "How much worse can this get? How about getting some water for everyone?"

"Sorry," Terry said again, as he turned the TV off, got up, and went to the office fridge. He brought back a pitcher of water, a stack of cups, and a bottle of antacid, which he set in the middle of the table. It took a few minutes before anyone's stomach settled enough even to attempt the antacid or the water.

"It's like a different world," Mike finally said. "Here we sit, in relative safety, while the world outside rips itself apart."

"We can't show that to the others," Becca said, her voice muffled because she was talking into her sleeve. "I'm not sure *we* should have watched it. Is all the news going to be like that from now on?"

"Maybe worse," Terry admitted. "The violence and crime were bad before the explosions. I can't imagine what it's like out there now. We've felt the earthquakes. The destruction could be worldwide. In fact, there's no way our country's leaders would sit back and not retaliate. What we've just seen, and worse, is happening all over the world, I'm sure."

"Terry," Amos said quietly, running his hand through his hair, "I take back what I said the other day. You and Michael don't need to monitor the news. In fact, I don't know if we even want to keep recording it."

"I think there's some value in recording it," Terry said, "if only as a historical record. Maybe to be shown at a war crimes tribunal someday."

As a doctor, Amos had thought he would be more clinical in his review of the death and destruction of war, but his stomach was roiling. His head, shoulders, and back ached. And his hands were stiff from being tightly fisted. He was supposed to be the strong one, the detached one.

He realized they weren't going to get anything else done for now, so he ended the meeting.

"How are you feeling?" he asked Mike after the others had left the room.

"I'll be okay, Dad. I just need to get my stomach under control. I've read about wars but, until seeing this, I really didn't understand." Mike walked gingerly toward the couch that sat against the wall. Abruptly, he changed direction and headed for the bathroom, his hand over his mouth.

As Amos watched, he thought about their decision to leave their former life behind and escape to another, safer one.

"Worlds in collision" he said pensively. Then he sat down at the table, lay his head on his arm, and closed his eyes.

Prime Situation Room

President McCormick sat quietly in his usual place at the midpoint of the conference table and rubbed the bags under his eyes. He considered the eight monitors on the wall in front of him, mostly oblivious to the people in the room with him. Only the sound of their crying seeped through his emotional shell.

When he'd heard that Chinese missiles had targeted five of the nine government bunkers, he hadn't been entirely surprised. He knew he had a traitor in the ranks. What frustrated him was that the U.S. missiles sent to intercept three of them had themselves been destroyed before they could prevent the disasters. Additional, retargeted missiles, also failed to intercept them.

Three bunkers—ENERGY, for the Secretary of Energy, JCS, for the chairman of the Joint Chiefs, and NDCP, for the director of National Drug Control Policy—now had less than ten minutes before the missiles would strike. Each bunker was full of people as important to the country as those who filled his Prime bunker, or any of the others. More importantly, they were filled with people who had spouses, children, and friends outside. They would never see their loved ones again.

The president had just been told that some of the occupants from each of the doomed bunkers had voluntarily and frantically left their bunkers in a desperate attempt to get far enough away to avoid the explosions and their aftermath, taking their chances on the outside. Others had gone to their quarters to be alone, or to try to contact family members in other parts of the country. A few had had to be sedated by medical personnel when they became hysterical. The rest now sat quietly—most of them with tears in their eyes, and some crying openly—in their respective situation rooms, facing the president.

In these final minutes, he had insisted that he be in Prime, talking with those in the doomed bunkers. He had debated giving an update on the terrorist attack on the CDC, but thought there would be a better time to bring that up.

"I feel inadequate to express sufficiently the debt of gratitude that we all owe you for your service to the people of the United States," he said.

"Speaking for all of us in the JCS bunker," Chairman of the Joint Chiefs, General Robert Peatross said, "we thank you for the opportunity to serve." The general sat stoically, his face serene, the consummate warrior.

The secretary of Energy and the director of National Drug Control Policy expressed similar sentiments, though not as calmly. They knew they were about to die, and there was nothing they could do but accept it.

The president choked up at the magnanimity of his people. It was all he could do not to cry. He didn't know if he could face death as bravely as they were. He was looking them in the eyes as the missiles struck.

ENERGY was the first to go. In a mountain valley north of Barstow, California, a hundred miles from Los Angeles, the scene on the monitor shook violently, the sound deafening. A huge crack appeared in the roof of the bunker, allowing heat and pressure to blast through the seam. The Secretary of Energy and his staff, seated at the table, disappeared in the flames, as the video and audio failed. President McCormick cried quietly, blinking tears out of his eyes.

Two minutes later, as General Peatross and his staff sat quietly in their bunker under a hill northwest of Fort Worth, Texas, the door to the room blew off its hinges, letting in a blast of immense heat that threw them forward, against the wall of monitors. Most were likely dead before they hit the wall and the power went out. The violence of the blast caused the president to jerk in surprise, tears streaking his cheeks as he wept.

Following the second blast, those in the NDCP bunker, in a hill west of Topeka, Kansas, rose and left the room, at first one or two, then gradually more, until the room was mostly empty. Greg suspected that they went to their quarters to be alone, perhaps to speak to their maker. The director stayed in his seat, his head moving back and forth as his people filed out. He waited for the inevitable, wincing involuntarily each time a door slammed. When the missile struck, a few minutes later, it must have been a direct hit. There was a blinding flash, then nothing—the screen was blank. This time, the president sobbed openly.

Through the entire episode, President McCormick thought about his discussion with SecDef Jim Seymour, about where to send each member of the NSC. It had not been arbitrary. They had decided, together, that the president's most trusted advisers would be placed in what they believed to be the most secret bunkers. As the president looked across the monitors now, he could see the results of that decision. Three of the eight monitors were now dark.

The other two bunkers that had been targeted, then rescued by missile intercepts, were the VEEP and SEC DEF bunkers. Vice President Art Klemp, in the VEEP bunker near Atlanta, Georgia, had been the president's lowest priority. Art was not a trusted advisor—he was not even highly regarded. It wasn't much of a consolation, but the four advisers he relied on the most had, so far, survived.

It took a few minutes for the president to collect himself emotionally. His heart ached, and he thought he could easily become despondent. During that time, only quiet sobbing could be heard. Feeling inadequate and helpless, he realized that he needed to say something.

"Jim, please have someone go to each of the bunkers and check for survivors. The rest of you, please take a few minutes to grieve, if you wish, then let's meet back here to take stock of where we are." He glanced at his watch. "Thirty minutes. Thank you."

The president rested his elbows on the table with his fists together, then rested his head on his hands and closed his eyes.

Vice President Art Klemp sat in the VEEP bunker, shaking with fear and panic. His thoughts flitted from one grisly scene to another, as he considered the destruction of the three bunkers and the deaths of their occupants. *That could have been me,* he thought each time. That was how Greg and Jim would get him out of the way, he decided. He was certain they wanted him dead and they would find some gruesome way to make it happen.

Art's overworked imagination ignored several facts inconsistent with his paranoid thesis: that the SEC DEF bunker had also been targeted, and that it was SecDef Jim Seymour's efforts that had ensured the missile targeted at the VEEP bunker had been stopped. Instead, he focused on the fact that the other four surviving bunkers, besides Prime, belonged to Greg's most favored advisers. Art was positive that Greg had arranged for them to be spared. He must have given them the best protected bunkers. But he knew he wasn't part of that clique—the VEEP bunker must not be safe. He had to get out. But where could he go?

Images of terrible deaths filled his head, his horror and paranoia driving him insane.

11

Don't tell me to be patient

The Wasatch Front, Utah, 9 July, 11:53 am, mountain daylight time
One of the last Russian missiles to elude U.S. defenses struck the military installation at Hill Air Force Base, southwest of Ogden, Utah. The explosion obliterated much of the medium-sized city and several surrounding towns, the intense heat driven by the wind in all directions.

When the energy from the explosion struck the Weber segment of the Wasatch Fault, the friction that had kept the fault stationary for hundreds of years was released. Twenty minutes after the explosion, the entire Wasatch Fault shifted, from Honeyville in the north to Nephi in the south, in a 7.4 magnitude earthquake. Natural gas lines that crossed the fault were automatically shut off by sensors, but not before setting off secondary fires.

Before the missile struck, hundreds of thousands of people had already left the valleys in response to government warnings. They went east and north into the Wasatch Mountains or south and west toward desert country. The remainder of the population of more than two million that lived along the Wasatch Front faced the full fury of the nuclear explosion and earthquake: flying debris, nuclear winds, and fire from the initial detonation, and further building collapse from the earthquake.

The shape of the mountain range, coupled with the wind direction and speed from the blast, channeled the fires up the canyons of the Wasatch Mountains and out across the Great Salt Lake and the desert. The waters of the Great Salt Lake boiled, rivers dried up, and people who stopped too soon were caught in the wind, smoke, and fast-moving fires.

The earthquake lifted the mountain range—or dropped the valleys, depending on one's perspective—as much as twelve vertical feet. Everything that could move—earth, homes, trees, cars, and people—slid off the mountainside, across the fault, and onto the adjacent land, becoming indistinguishable piles of debris several feet deep.

The shock waves from the explosion and earthquake were felt for hundreds of miles. The Hurricane and Washington faults near St. George, Utah, three hundred miles to the south, as well as previously unknown faults in southeastern Idaho and southwestern Wyoming, split the earth. Three hundred miles to the north, the calderas of Yellowstone National Park erupted in thermal activity.

The Preserve

"The radioactivity in the valley is still rising." Terry said, as Amos walked into the lab carrying a glass of lemonade.

"That makes sense," Amos said as he set his lemonade on the worktable and turned to look at the monitors. "The explosion in Las Vegas was five days ago. What we saw at first was probably the leading edge of the fallout cloud. The fallout is probably still being carried on the winds, headed this way. How about checking the weather conditions so we can confirm that?"

"Sure thing."

Terry had just begun to type at the keyboard when the table shifted violently to the side. Both men grabbed the edge of the table, as it continued to shift back and forth, as well as up and down, together forming a rolling motion, like a rowboat riding atop waves. Amos's glass of lemonade tipped over and bounced toward the edge of the table, spreading its contents in every direction. Amos tried to catch the glass, but missed, and it crashed to the floor, scattering glass fragments. He reached out and snagged a box of miniature video cameras as they started to fall off the edge. Tools and equipment rattled on shelves. A family photo fell off the wall, the glass face shattering on the floor. The shaking lasted nearly a minute.

"Dad," Mike called shakily from the couch in the office next door. He sounded disoriented and frightened.

The room stopped shaking, and Amos hurried to check on Mike after setting the box of video cameras on the floor and carefully avoiding broken glass. Mike was sitting up on the couch, wiping sleep from his eyes.

"Was that an earthquake?" he asked, his face mirroring the surprise in his voice.

"Sure felt like one," Amos said. "We need to go check on the others."

"Let's go," Mike replied as he stood shakily, then placed his hands on either side of his head and sat back down, as though his head had begun to swim from the sudden rise. Amos caught hold of his arm and helped him back up.

"Terry, get the Geiger counters and meet us in the community center," Amos called as he helped Mike step carefully along the corridor, wondering whether another tremor might strike at any moment.

When they reached the community center, Amos looked around quickly, observing the scene like a first responder. Emily was on the floor, moaning. Matt was kneeling beside her, talking to her quietly and trying to lift her onto the couch. She grabbed her left arm with her right and started screaming in agony, so he set her back down.

"Sydney! Sydney wake up!" Rylee wailed in panic as she knelt next to Sydney, one hand under her head. Sydney must have fallen, bumping her head on the table or floor. One leg of the table was bent, and the table leaned precariously to that side. Board game pieces lay scattered across the floor.

"She's dead!" Rylee screamed when her hand came away wet with blood. She scooted away, across the floor, frantically trying to wipe blood off her right hand with her left, then wiping both hands on her white blouse and blue jeans. A small pool of blood formed under Sydney's head on the floor.

Chris sat cross-legged in front of the TV monitor, staring blankly at the static on the screen.

"Michael, check the seals on the airlock," Amos said. Mike, fully alert now, hurried off.

Amos hurried over to Sydney as Brittany and Jason rushed into the room from the bedroom tunnel, likely in response to Rylee's screams. Their faces registered shock and panic as they looked around, then settled on their daughter, unmoving on the floor. The rest of the family entered behind them.

"Hi Rylee," Amos said calmly as he checked Sydney's vital signs, then her neck and head, without moving her. Satisfied that she was alive and had no other physical injuries, he rolled her onto her side carefully, supporting her head, to inspect the cut. Then he pressed a wad of tissue from a box on the table against it to stem the flow of blood. "Rylee, Sydney's going to be fine."

Rylee was still wiping her hands on her jeans when Lillie spit on a tissue and began calmly wiping at the blood. With one arm cradling Rylee's shoulders, Lillie used a fresh tissue to dry her tears. She relaxed almost immediately, but continued to cry quietly as she buried her face in her hands and leaned into Lillie, nearly knocking her over.

"Is she okay?" Jason asked.

"Just a sec, Jason," Amos replied as he continued his ministrations. The small cut on the back of Sydney's head had stopped bleeding, and he decided it probably wouldn't need stitches. Moments later, Sydney's eyes fluttered open. Amos breathed a sigh of relief and turned to Jason and Brittany.

"I think she'll be fine. I suggest you put her in bed with a cold pack on her forehead and a towel under her head. I'll come by and check on her in a few minutes." Brittany knelt immediately and spoke quietly to her daughter.

Amos moved over to help Emily, politely moving Matt, who appeared to be at a loss about what to do, out of the way. He kept his mood light, carefully assessing Emily's physical and emotional condition, focusing primarily on her left arm, which she favored.

"Hi Matt. Let me help. Hey Emily, got tired of sitting and decided to lie down for a while, did you?" Emily just moaned in response, but a smile played across her lips, briefly, in response to her dad's attempt at humor. Amos guessed that she had a broken arm.

"What's going on?" Jason asked from right behind Amos, surprising him. He'd assumed that Jason would be helping Brittany, who was struggling to lift Sydney, rather than standing threateningly over him. Sydney was now sitting on the floor holding the tissue to the back of her own head.

"I suspect that was an earthquake somewhere nearby," Amos said, as Terry came up to him with the Geiger counters. "Terry," Amos said, "will you run and get the small medical kit from the hospital? I need to stabilize Emily's arm before we move her. Thanks." Terry set down the Geiger counters and hurried out.

"Matt," Amos said, "try not to move her until Terry returns."

Matt nodded, and Amos started to rise. Jason grabbed his arm.

"Why didn't the Preserve protect us?" Jason yelled, drawing everyone's attention.

Amos tried to remain calm, but was sure the look on his face betrayed his surprise.

"Jason, if you'll be patient, we'll get the Preserve checked for leaks and get back to you. You can help by watching Sydney and checking on the others to make sure everyone's okay. Let Lillie know if anyone needs . . . "

"Don't tell me to be patient." Jason yelled, his face turning crimson. *"I'm sick of you telling me what to do. I want answers. Now!"* Brittany stood and grasped her husband's arm, trying to pull him away from Amos. Sydney began to cry as she watched the exchange. Jason pulled away from Brittany, pulling her over.

"Jason!" Brittany screamed. *"Stop it!"* Jason looked at Brittany in confusion, as if just waking from a dream. Amos had seen this reaction to shock before.

Amos took the opportunity to pull away from Jason, turning to Terry as he entered the room pushing a stretcher piled with medical supplies.

"Thanks Terry, I'll take those. Matt, will you help Terry?"

Matt was kneeling next to Emily again, helping her keep her left arm stationary and whispering to her. He looked up but didn't move, his pained expression showing his concern.

"I can help," Jason said, calmer now. "What can I do?"

Amos studied Jason for several seconds to see if he had recovered from his shock and was serious, deciding that he was.

"Okay, go with Terry. He'll show you what to do. But Jason, listen to me. If you seriously think that the Preserve could prevent the earth from shaking during an earthquake, I suggest you think a little harder. The Preserve is the safest place we can be right now, but we're still underground, and earthquakes affect things underground the same way they affect things above ground. I would appreciate it if you would think just a bit harder, before you scream at me in the future. Am I clear?"

Jason nodded, although he clearly hadn't really registered what Amos had said, then turned to Terry.

Terry had retrieved the Geiger counters, and now motioned with his head for Jason to follow him to a corner of the room, where he quietly showed him how to work the Geiger counter to sniff the air, focusing primarily on the welded joints in the corners.

Rachel hurried over to help Brittany and Sydney stand up. Together, they staggered awkwardly toward the bedroom wing. Lillie went over to help Amos with Emily, bringing Rylee with her. Rylee had her arms around Lillie's waist and was still crying softly.

Suddenly, the room started to shake again. Lillie, who was holding Emily's legs in an attempt to help Amos lift her onto the stretcher, fell down, dropping Emily and taking Rylee with her to the floor. Amos, holding Emily under the arms, fell against the stretcher. Luckily the wheels were locked, or the stretcher would have come out from under him and he would have fallen, too. Matt, who was just getting up from the floor, put steadying hands on Amos and Emily, which prevented him from dropping her. The whole scene turned to chaos as the frightened group twisted and turned with the violent shaking.

Amid the screams and shouts, Amos tried to understand what had just happened. A second earthquake? What would cause a second earthquake that powerful? An aftershock? Or was the first one a precursor? Many seconds later, the shaking stopped.

"Is everyone okay?" Amos asked as he looked around. No one was standing. Those who were near a wall were leaning against it. The others had all fallen to the floor.

"Was that another earthquake?" Chris Stephens asked from across the room. He was sitting on the couch holding on with both hands.

"Okay over here," Terry called, as he and Jason scrambled to pick up the Geiger counters.

"Okay here, too," Rachel called out, as she and Brittany stood awkwardly with Sydney and started moving again toward the bedroom tunnel.

"Are you all right?" he asked Lillie, as she tried, awkwardly, to stand. He leaned against the wall, holding Emily up by the armpits, trying not to drop her.

Lillie winced as she put weight on her right foot.

"I twisted my ankle," she said.

"Rylee," Amos said. Rylee looked up at him from the floor next to Lillie. "Will you help Lillie sit on the couch and keep an eye on her until I get back?" Rylee nodded mutely, tears running down her cheeks. "Thank you. Get her anything she asks for, okay?" Rylee nodded again, then held still as Lillie placed a hand on her shoulder and tried, unsuccessfully, to push herself to her feet.

"Becca, Katie, will you help over here?" he asked as they struggled to get their feet under them. They nodded and moved toward the stretcher.

"Katie, please help Rylee get Lillie to the hospital so we can check her ankle. We might as well get her over there instead of the couch. Becca, please take Emily's legs and help us get her onto the stretcher." Matt had one hand under Emily's backside and the other awkwardly holding up her left arm. Emily had passed out, likely from the pain of having her fractured arm jostled.

Terry and Jason headed toward the bedrooms, and Amos looked over at Chris, who was still in front of the TV, staring at the static.

"Chris, are you okay?" Amos asked.

Chris turned mechanically to look at Amos, shock on his face, his motions jerky.

"What *was* that?" Chris asked again.

"I think that was an earthquake." Amos had already concluded, from his knowledge of the Wasatch Fault, that the first disturbance might not have been an earthquake, but an explosion, one that caused an earthquake.

"Chris, turn the monitor off and back on again," Amos said. "If that doesn't fix it, find something else to do until Michael can look at it." Chris turned back to the TV, reached up, and flipped it off then back on again, but the static returned. He turned back to Amos and watched as people continued to file out of the room.

Becca had arrived to help, so Amos returned his attention to Emily. They lifted her onto the stretcher and he began to stabilize her arm.

"What can I do to help?" Matt asked self-consciously.

Matt's medical training should have kicked in automatically, Amos thought, and he decided he'd have to work with him on that. He could see Matt wanted to do something for Emily, but Amos didn't need him here. Besides, it wasn't a good idea for a doctor to work on someone they were so closely tied to emotionally—it could cloud his judgment. He wondered what that said about him, working on his own daughter.

"Good idea, Matt," he said. "I've got this under control. Why don't you go find where they've taken Sydney and check on her? See if she has a concussion or other injuries besides the one on the back of her head."

Matt nodded and headed off toward the bedroom tunnel, looking back at Emily with concern before leaving the room.

12

How many more people do we have to kill

Prime Situation Room, 9 July

The president must have fallen asleep, his head resting on his folded arms on the table, because he awoke to Eric shaking his shoulders.

"Mr. President, everyone's ready to continue."

Greg sat up straight, blinking the sleep out of his eyes. Jim was looking at him from the SEC DEF monitor with a sad smile.

"Right," he said to Eric, then looked back at the monitors. "Jim, what's the status of the bunkers?"

"There were no survivors, sir," Jim said, his voice tight with emotion.

"What about our arsenal?"

"We have twenty-four nuclear missiles. We also have a number of conventional weapons. All are yet to be targeted."

"What about the Russians?"

"No idea. They could have a few as well."

"Then let's not worry about the Russians. What else do we need to do?" He knew that most of the known military and other strategic sites in the Northern Hemisphere had been damaged by bombs or taken out of service by EMPs, aside from the hardened bunkers. If there was anything left to do, it was now a cleanup operation. At least, that's what he hoped.

"I think we should call it good," Jim said, shaking his head, "and focus on trying to rebuild."

"Tom, anything new on the attack at the CDC?"

"No, sir," Tom said. "The FBI lost him yesterday after he killed the suicide bomber and injured a mechanic, stole one car that broke down on him, then stole another. There's an APB out with a description of the car, but it hasn't been seen yet."

"Thanks, Tom."

"Mr. President," Chuck said, urgently, "I'm concerned about the CDC, and other research and storage facilities for biological, chemical, and other agents. If the containment facilities for any of them are compromised, we'll have an epidemic on our hands."

The president shook his head and chuckled sadly, thinking Chuck was suggesting dropping a bomb on the CDC. *The terrorists could have taken care of that for us,* he thought. But until the terrorists had attacked the CDC, he hadn't even considered the possibility of a viral or biological outbreak. He was glad someone else, with fewer distractions than he had, *had* thought about it.

"Tell me Chuck. How many more people do we have to kill before we can stop this madness?"

Chuck opened his mouth to respond, but the president held up a shaky hand to stop him.

"No, no. Forget I said that. Do we know the current status of the facilities?"

"I raised the concern because I spoke to the CDC director, Doctor Anne Lister, a few minutes ago. I wanted to assess their status following the attempted terrorist attack. The director told me that their power is out, but that they're currently contained because they're on generator power. She believes they can maintain for another thirty to thirty-six hours, but they need a more permanent solution. We checked with Fort Detrick and they're in slightly better condition. I hope the Level 4 facility in Russia and the Level 3 facilities around the world are also contained."

"What are their options?" the president asked.

"We either need to get them continuous power or more fuel to run the generators," Chuck said.

"You're already working with the power companies across the country to try to restore power, right?" the president asked. "How's that going?"

"Water management facilities—clean water supply and waste-water treatment—are our highest priority, but the available utility resources and spare parts aren't enough even for that task. There's no way we can interfere with the water and power company operations to help the CDC—not unless there are no other options."

"Are there other options?"

"We can't let those agents get out," SecDef Jim Seymour said emphatically. "The CDC is storing smallpox and who knows how many other deadly airborne pathogens. We've already lost half the country's population. These diseases could wipe out the rest."

"Well, then what do you propose, Jim?" the president said testily.

"Nuke 'em, now."

The president heard gasps and looked around the room, seeing shock on many faces.

"Would that kill the agents, Chuck?" The president was genuinely surprised at the suggestion.

"I believe so, sir," Chuck replied. "Even a small nuclear explosion should wipe out the agents completely."

"You believe so?" The question was asked by a familiar, whiny voice. The president looked at the VEEP monitor to see a visibly shaken and outraged Art Klemp. "You're going to drop a nuclear bomb on an occupied facility and you *think* it will work? Which are you, stupid or crazy?"

As much as the president wanted to discount Art's rant, he had a point. "I assume you made the suggestion, Jim," the president said, ignoring Art, "because you believe a nuclear weapon is the most likely way to destroy the agents? What about trying to get them more fuel?"

"It just delays the inevitable, and something could go wrong at any time. For example, we still have a terrorist on the loose. I think we need to destroy them while we still have the means to do it."

"What's the probability that it would work? And can we get the people out first?"

"Near one hundred percent, Mr. President. I'm confident the heat from a nuclear explosion would incinerate them. I think it's our best, possibly only, chance.

"The facilities should all have hazmat suits. If we have the researchers suit up and send military vehicles to pick them up, we can get them to the nearest shelters before we destroy the facilities."

"Then we need a list of all the Level 3 and 4 facilities around the world, and the public shelters nearest to those in the states."

"I have that information, sir," Chuck said.

"Have you sent me a copy?"

"I'll have it done immediately, sir."

"Thank you. Please send it to the other bunkers as well. We'll reconvene thirty minutes after receiving the list and consider what we need to do."

Art couldn't control his shaking. He staggered out of his conference room, wondering how Greg and Jim could use this latest crisis to get him out of the way. As he passed Senator Stenger, he was thinking out loud.

"They'll find a way. I know it," he said.

"Art, what are you talking about?" the senator asked, as he followed Art and his security team to Art's office.

"We have to get to a safer location," Art said, explaining what he suspected. His eyes darted around the room as he frantically searched for a solution.

The senator liked Art, but he didn't share his belief that the president would allow all the people in the VEEP bunker to die, just so he could kill Art. He'd been observing the president and believed that all of the man's actions reflected a genuine concern for the safety of his people. But he wasn't going to say that to Art, not when he appeared to be hanging on to his sanity by a thread. Instead, he nodded politely at Art's comments.

Art turned to his security detail, his eyes wild.

"Perry, you have to find a way to get me out of here."

"I'll check around, sir," Perry said, his normally expressionless face allowing the concern for his charge to reach his eyes.

The list of Level 4 research and storage facilities for contagious viral, biological, and other agents included the National Biodefense Analysis and Countermeasures Center (NBACC) at Fort Detrick in Frederick, Maryland, the Centers for Disease Control and Prevention (CDC) in Atlanta, Georgia, and the State Research Center of Virology and Biotechnology (VECTOR), in Koltsovo, Novosibirsk Oblast, Russia. The list of Level 3 facilities was longer, with facilities in the U.S., Russia, Europe, and other parts of the world.

"The CDC headquarters is actually in Druid Hills, northeast of Atlanta," Chuck explained when they reconvened. "It's about ten miles, as the crow flies, from the VEEP bunker in Norcross. Ft. Detrick, in Frederick, Maryland, is about the same distance from the SEC DEF bunker . . . "

"*Wait!*" Art Klemp shouted. The only fact that had registered with him was that the CDC headquarters—the target—was only ten miles from where he was right now. He knew in an instant that this was how Greg was going to kill him. He lost it.

"If you bomb the CDC, you could destroy my bunker like the others. I'm too close. I'm downwind. *I could get smallpox. I could die!*" Art stood as he worked himself up, banging his fists on the table and screaming into the camera. People near him in the bunker looked nervous and leaned away.

"Get a grip, Art," Jim said. "Weren't you listening? No virus is going to survive a nuclear explosion. Besides, my bunker is almost as close to Fort Detrick as yours is to the CDC. There's just as much risk to our bunker as there is to yours."

"*But . . . but . . . but . . . *" Art sputtered, trying to come up with a response.

"But nothing, Art," Jim continued. "Half the country is dead or dying. We've lost three of our nine bunkers already. Everyone has to die sometime. Grow a backbone."

What Art heard was *"everyone has to die"*. He finally caught his breath and focused his wrath on Jim.

"This is a conspiracy," he said through gritted teeth. "You want to destroy my bunker. You want me to die."

"There's a shelter in Johns Creek," HomeSec Chuck Dickson said, giving the president an option for Art, "a little over fifteen miles from the CDC. It's the closest one to the VEEP bunker that's out of the blast danger zone."

Fearing Art's panic would infect others in Art's bunker, the president appreciated Chuck's suggestion.

"That's enough. Art, you have two choices. One: you can stay in the bunker and hope it holds against the bomb targeted at the CDC. Two: you can put on a hazmat suit and relocate to Johns Creek. You have hardened vehicles, a security team, and everything else you need to survive outside long enough to get there. Jim has the same options. It's your choice."

"That's unacceptable!" he screamed. *"You know the air outside is already contaminated and the surviving population is hostile. This is just a death sentence for me and everyone else in my bunker. You've always had it out for me. You'd be happy if I died, wouldn't you?"*

Greg *did* think that it would be better for everyone if Art just disappeared, but he couldn't say that.

"Jim," the president said with a nod. He'd heard enough of Art's grating voice. He knew that Art, Bob Stenger, and six other people, from five of the bunkers, had attempted to communicate with the outside after he'd set up the monitoring system the day before. He'd had the others detained for questioning, but he believed that Art's or Bob's absence from the meetings would be too noticeable. So, now, he would do the next best thing.

Jim knew what the president wanted. They'd discussed the possibility before the meeting, when it appeared Art was becoming paranoid about his safety.

"Colonel Johnson," Jim said. "Mr. Klemp needs medical attention. Please take him to detention and have a doctor sedate him."

A large uniformed soldier with dark, closely-cropped hair stepped up behind Art, grasped his upper arms, and lifted him physically out of his chair. Art tried to resist, squirming and kicking and knocking his chair over, but the effort was wasted. Colonel Johnson was a hundred and twenty pounds heavier than Art and built like an NFL defensive tackle, which was what he'd been before joining the Army. Art was removed from the room, screaming obscenities at the president and his SecDef.

Greg knew he needed to pacify the other people in the VEEP bunker, who were now leaderless, certain that some were sympathetic to Art's position.

"Ambassador Porter," he said, looking at Daniel Porter, U.S. Ambassador to the United Nations, who had been sitting next to Art in the VEEP bunker. "Will you please provide leadership in the vice president's bunker during his absence?" The distinguished looking man in his fifties moved over to sit in Art's seat and nodded to the president.

"All of you, listen," the president said. "We have no choice in this. The viruses stored at Ft. Detrick and the CDC have to go. We'll consider all options before sending a missile, but we have to wipe out those contagions if we're to have any chance of surviving in the postwar world." The president paused and looked around his conference room, then back at the monitors on the wall. "We've had to make some tough decisions in the last few days, and this is one of the toughest. Rest assured that I'd make the same decision if it were me in the VEEP or SEC DEF bunker instead of you."

There was grumbling in the VEEP bunker and Ambassador Porter looked around before speaking.

"Mr. President, we will give everyone in the bunker the same options you outlined for Vice President Klemp and SecDef Seymour. Colonel Johnson has assured me that the military has the equipment required to rescue the occupants of the CDC and bring them here—or to the Johns Creek shelter. Their choice. He's also assured me that anyone who doesn't feel safe here will be given the opportunity to leave."

"Thank you, Mr. Ambassador. Okay people. The clock is ticking. You have twenty-four hours to make a decision.

"Chuck, I need you to organize this. Get the people where they need to be. How many shelters are in the Atlanta area that we need to relocate?"

"There are twenty-six inside a fifteen-mile radius," Chuck said, looking at the papers in front of him. "There are shelters outside the fifteen-mile radius, in every direction, but the one at Johns Creek is the closest to the VEEP Bunker."

The president whistled.

"How many near Ft. Detrick?"

"Twenty-two," Chuck said.

"Okay, contact them all and coordinate the transfers. Let's see how fast we can move them.

"Jim, retarget the missiles and be prepared to launch in twenty-four hours, pending my authorization. Let's make sure the people in those shelters have a chance to relocate.

"Cy, try to contact the countries on the Level 3 and 4 lists. Let them know what we're doing and our deadline. If you can't get them, keep trying until we reach the deadline.

"Anything else?" he asked, looking around the room, then at the monitors. "That's it then. Contact Eric if you have any other questions or suggestions. Chuck, Jim, and Cy, get those tasks started, then meet back here in thirty minutes. Tom, join us then."

The president got up and walked out.

The Wasatch Mountains

The Blunds' neighbors back in Logan, Patrick and Kathy McKensie, were in their seventies. Amos had given them the chance to join the family in the Preserve, but they'd decided it wasn't worth the inconvenience of living underground just to add a few years to their lives. If things got bad, they could go to the local shelter for a few days. Over the past few hours, Patrick had begun to regret their decision.

The only TV station still broadcasting, following the explosion at Hill Air Force Base, and the earthquake that had followed, showed video of the mushroom cloud, fires, and destruction from a distance. The lone reporter suggested that anyone able to evacuate should fill their car with whatever food, water, clothing, and other supplies they could manage, and leave the area immediately.

"Both Interstate 15, north, and Interstates 80 and 84, east, are impassible," he said. "If you can get to Interstate 80 west, or Interstate 15 or Redwood Road south, you can still get out of Salt Lake City, but we don't know for how long. There's major destruction between Salt Lake and Ogden, and we have no reports on what's going on north of Ogden. We're told the military is overflying the area and we'll try to get a report from them." A banner began running at the bottom of the TV screen, repeating the following message, while a buzzer beeped in the background:

EMERGENCY BROADCAST—Most TV, radio, and cell towers in your area are out of service. Please tune your radio to AM 1260 for the latest emergency broadcast information. Fires are racing up the canyons of the Wasatch Front on severe winds. Stand by for further updates.

"Da ya' thin' we should go ta' a shelte, Kitty?" Patrick asked his wife, Kathy.

"I don't know, Patrick. Do you think we're safe here?"

"Doan know. Lots o' folks is leavin', But ah can't 'magin da fiar gittin dis fa'."

While they were talking, the TV station went off the air. Patrick turned on an old radio sitting on a shelf. The announcer was in the middle of a report on shelter-in-place instructions. She explained that evacuation routes and other information, pertinent to the Salt Lake City and Wasatch Front area, would follow.

Patrick stood and walked to the door, glancing back at his wife before stepping outside. He needed to release some nervous energy, but what he saw didn't give him any relief. Clouds of dark, billowing smoke were rising from the canyon to the southwest— the direction of Ogden and Salt Lake City—and appeared to be moving quickly toward them. As he watched, fire erupted from the mouth of the canyon, as though from a dragon's snout, and began devouring the dry hay fields. He stood watching for several seconds before realizing that their neighborhood was directly in the path of the fire.

He no longer believed that the fire would burn out before it reached their home, so he hurried back inside to tell Kitty they had to leave.

"Les git sum thins," Patrick said. "We shud leave now."

"I'll pack us a lunch," Kathy replied as she rose awkwardly from the couch, using a cane for support.

"No tiam. Jus git yer purz and sweata." When Kathy gave him a questioning look, he added, "Hurra Kitty. Doan hav much tiam."

Patrick made several trips to the garage to load the car, while Kathy instructed him on things she thought they would need for a short stay away from home. Each time he returned from the garage he looked out the living room window to check the progress of the fire. When he could see flames behind the Blund and Carlsen homes across the street, he decided they had enough.

"Tiam ta go, Kitty," he said.

"Just a few more things," she said as she hobbled down the hallway away from him.

Patrick watched out the window restlessly. He could feel the heat from the fire and wondered how that could be so. Then he noticed that the wind had whipped the flames across the street and his front porch was on fire.

"Gotta go, Kitty, *naow!*" Patrick said as he rushed down the hall toward Kathy. He took the bag from her hand, took her by the arm, and helped her toward the garage. They could hear the popping and crackling as the flames burned into the attic. Smoke quickly seeped into the room through the ceiling, hanging in the air. They both started to cough.

Patrick led Kathy to the garage door and felt the handle: it was hot. *Fire in the garage,* he thought. *Gotta go out the back way.*

"Com' on," he said, changing direction suddenly, nearly pulling Kathy off her feet. The smoke was getting thicker quickly. They had to stoop to stay under it, which was difficult for Kathy, who had started coughing.

As Patrick opened the back door, the opening provided an outlet for the pressure that had been building up from the flames at the front of the house. The fire exploded toward them, throwing them through the open doorway onto the back porch. The explosion was so powerful that the door, portions of the wall, and the roof over the door, exploded out with them, crushing them. Kathy was dead before the flames arrived, but Patrick, still barely cognizant of his surroundings, died painfully as the fire engulfed his wrecked body.

The wind's intensity diminished as it crossed the Cache Valley, but it was strong enough to push the flames up Logan canyon toward Aspen Valley and Bear Lake. The fire, and the gales driving it, weakened as they passed through each of the small mountain valleys, but still reached almost to Garden City on the shore of Bear Lake. As the flames passed through Aspen Valley, the video cameras in the valley recorded first smoke, and then fire, the latter igniting the dry deadfall. The heat from the fire dried out the green trees and bushes, which then caught fire in turn, damaging the video and audio sensors attached to the trees.

Prime Situation Room

"It's a slow process," HomeSec Chuck Dickson said, responding to Greg's question about progress getting the country running again. "Every commercial satellite is dead from the EMPs. The milsats are still working, but we're overloading them as it is. With most communications out, plus localized damage and the huge loss of life—not to mention the impact of losing much of our leadership team—we're finding it difficult just to coordinate relief activities. Part of the problem is that a lot of the relief workers have abandoned their posts to be with their families. The ones we can find have to be convinced to leave their shelters so they can assess needs and reconnect with each other."

"Understandable," Greg said. "What are you getting so far?"

"Travel's at a standstill across major portions of the country. Any aircraft that weren't grounded by EMPs have been confiscated by the military for relief efforts.

"At the borders with Mexico and Canada, people who managed to get that far before the allied offensive are still leaving from the United States toward what they assume will be a safer location. They're on foot, since their cars and trucks are now dead and blocking the roads. No one's trying to stop them, and there are now large refugee camps along the south side of the Rio Grande in Mexico, and farther south.

"The reports that we're getting are alarming," he continued, looking at his notes. "Volcanoes that have been quiet for hundreds or thousands of years, all along the west coast, have become active, sending tons of volcanic ash into the air. The lava flows are downright scary. Satellite pictures of the Hawaiian Islands show a similar situation with the Mauna Loa and Kilauea volcanoes."

"Come on, Chuck," Greg said. "Volcanic eruptions? Is there evidence to support that?"

"Greg, we've never experienced nuclear war. We know what one or two nuclear explosions can do in a controlled environment. But with the number and distribution of explosions in such a short period of time, we've had to extrapolate—a lot—from the experimental data to a major war in the real world."

Greg shook his head, but encouraged Chuck to continue.

"Our geologists are confident that the earthquakes we've seen in the western states and other places were caused by nearby explosions. After considering the facts, they now believe that the volcanic eruptions were caused by a combination of the explosions and the quakes.

"And there's more. Huge clouds of ash cover much of the Northern Hemisphere, and the worry is that temperatures will drop to disruptive levels, causing other problems. The most confusing thing, though, is a report that the Mississippi River has changed course."

DNI Tom Mitchell was about to say something, but Chuck held up a hand to stop him.

"Tom, I know you're from Tennessee, but this is not the meandering of the river following severe spring floods that you're familiar with. Nuclear explosions between Chicago and Saint Louis have apparently dammed the river so that it's spreading out instead of following its normal channel. Most of Chicago has been submerged in Lake Michigan. And according to reports, the Missouri River is backing up at St. Louis, creating a new lake— dubbed Lake Missouri in the report—that *could* eventually cover much of northern Missouri and Illinois."

"Doesn't the Missouri River drain most of the north-central states?" Greg asked.

"Yes, it does," Chuck said. "The Missouri supplies almost half the waters of the Mississippi. That's a lot of water being backed up and diverted."

"Will the water eventually go back to its original channel?" Tom asked.

"I spoke with the Army Corps of Engineers," SecDef Seymour said. "They believe the water will eventually either overflow the temporary dam or flow around it. They've drained dams before, mostly those caused by the mudslides that sometimes back up mountain streams, and it takes time and planning to avoid a catastrophic collapse and downstream flooding. In this case, with the amount of water being backed up here, I think the water will overflow the dam before they can manage it.

"Currently it's flooding a lot of geography, and could be some of the worst flooding the area has ever seen, but if it overflows, with all the water that's backed up now, there could still be a lot of flooding downstream."

"Should we just blow up the dam?" Greg asked in frustration.

"Well, Greg, we can either give it to the Corps and see what they can do, or we can make a decision and move forward."

"Okay, Jim. Let's see what the Corps can do, but keep me informed. Anything else?"

"We've been reestablishing military chains of command," Jim said. "We're only able to reconnect with teams as they check in using hardened communications. It's a slow process. As Chuck said, we've confiscated every vehicle we can find that hasn't been affected by the EMPs."

Greg wondered how many vehicles Amos Blund had at the Preserve that were still operational. Then he wondered how many other people were out there like Amos, hiding in hardened bunkers, with working vehicles.

"We've lost nearly two-thirds of our military aircraft," Jim continued, "either because they didn't get off the ground or because they flew into an EMP. We're unable to recover a lot of airmen because we don't have enough working vessels to recover those who fell out of the sky over water. We've got one submarine dead in the water, because it surfaced to help with the rescue efforts and got hit by an EMP. And," he paused to take a deep breath, "we lost three bunkers full of our people."

The president sighed. He didn't know what to say. *I'm sorry* sounded so inadequate, and *thank you* didn't seem to fit the situation. He turned to his Secretary of State. "Cy?"

"We've finally been able to contact our allies in Europe by prioritizing traffic on the military satellites," Cy said. "They report similar damage and chaos throughout Europe. London and Paris have been destroyed, as have several other large cities in Western Europe. Israel took several direct hits, including at Jerusalem.

"We're still unable to get a response from our allies in the Pacific. Most of the Japanese and Pacific Rim islands are in ruins from explosions and tsunamis.

"No one has been able to connect with Eastern Bloc or Asian countries. Either their communications are out or they just aren't responding.

"The changes that Chuck talked about—earthquakes, in particular—also affected most countries in the Southern Hemisphere. Looks like no one got a free pass. But we've been in contact with many of the countries in Central and South America, Australia, and New Zealand. They're dealing with it better than we are since they have less destruction to deal with overall. Tom provided information from milsat feeds and earthquake centers that helped us identify the most heavily impacted areas."

"Excuse me, Cy," DNI Tom Mitchell said, interrupting. "Can I add to your report?"

"Of course," Cy said and nodded.

"Greg, the national electrical power grid was severely damaged by the explosions and EMPs, with power knocked out in an estimated eighty-five percent of the country. Large sections of transmission and distribution lines are gone. Major electrical components, like transformers, have been fried. We've instructed those communities that have power to prioritize its distribution, with water management being the highest priority and medical facilities second. That leaves very little power for anything else, and some of the local leaders are having trouble accepting it. They think medical facilities should be first."

"What are you telling them?" Greg asked.

"Without medical facilities, a few people die. Without drinking water and wastewater treatment, everybody dies."

"I imagine electrical transformers are the critical components needed to get the power grid back up, aren't they?" Greg asked and Tom nodded. "I presume you're contacting the manufacturers to get replacements?"

"They absolutely *are* the critical components," Tom said. "That's why I mentioned them. Unfortunately for us, in the nineties many companies implemented what was called, back then, *just-in-time* manufacturing. It meant that they didn't start manufacturing parts—like those large, expensive transformers—until they received an order.

"It's an idea that started in Japan after World War II, where they didn't have space to store inventory," Tom explained. "Following on that experience, companies worldwide realized that just-in-time manufacturing saved processing time and handling costs. Some U.S. companies even sold their existing raw materials inventories for pennies on the dollar, just to get rid of them."

"How long would it take to build new transformers?" the president asked.

"Before the power outage, it took months. Now, we have a Catch-22 situation. We can't get power to the manufacturers without having transformers and power lines, and we can't get the transformers until the manufacturers have power to run their operations."

The president didn't know how to respond to the circular logic.

"And that's just one of the problems we're up against," Tom continued. "An even bigger one is the issue of all the electronics that were taken out by the EMPs. Even if we could get the power to the manufacturers, there are dozens of choke points in every manufacturing process and supply system that require electronic switches and other controls in order to operate. We need to get power to the electronics manufacturers to build the parts. But even if we could, there are electronics that control their own processes and no one to manufacture those."

"What a nightmare," Greg said, shaking his head in disbelief. "What do we do? We can't just sit here and do nothing."

"What we've been *trying* to do," Tom replied, "is identify manufacturers in other countries that might be able to supply parts." The president's eyes lit up at the simplicity of that solution. "But don't get your hopes up. Most of the manufacturers are in Southeast Asia, and we haven't been able to contact them. And if they still have any manufacturing capability, I'm pretty sure they're not going to be interested in supplying parts to *us*.

"What we *are* doing," Tom continued, "is working with utility companies and state agencies to link local communications with our *milsats*. The military satellites can't supply electric power, but they *can* help us with communications, which we also need. We're getting the suppliers and users talking to each other to try to solve the problem. With your prior consent, we've started releasing the government's supply of hardened communications equipment to local agencies to fill gaps in the network."

The president nodded to acknowledge that he had, indeed, agreed to this part of the plan.

"There are thousands of agencies and companies to be contacted. Some networks are in such bad shape—power lines down, or missing key components like transformers—that it would be a waste of our resources to give them anything. But if we can get just one supplier of each critical part operational, we can work from there to get others online. We're hoping the suppliers and users can help identify priorities, then we can help by moving useable parts from other locations. In some cases, we've had difficulty locating business owners. In those instances, we're nationalizing their operations, per your executive order, so we can keep moving, but it's slow and tedious."

"Thanks, Tom. Keep it up." Greg said, tiredly. Tom gritted his teeth and nodded. "What else?" Greg asked.

"Greg," Chuck spoke up again, "there've been more aftershocks around the Pacific Rim. There have also been earthquakes across the United States, in most of the countries in the Northern Hemisphere, and in many countries in the south, too."

"Across the United States?" Greg asked.

"Mostly in locations where there was an explosion near an active fault. I'm sure you've felt some of them," he said.

"Yes, I suppose I have. It just didn't register that that's what they were."

"They're not all large ones, so maybe there wasn't much impact where you are. I can have the NEIC send you a report if you'd like."

"Yes," Greg said distractedly, "do that. Wait, wasn't Denver bombed?"

"It was," Chuck said, "but the NEIC is in Golden, which is about twelve miles west of Denver, in rolling hills, so the damage was minimal. There's also the impact to the population. Would you like me to summarize the reports?"

Greg straightened up in his chair, trying to focus on what Chuck was saying. This was what he really needed to hear.

"Go ahead," he said.

"As reports filter in from the various agencies," Chuck said, "initial estimates are that as much as half of the U.S. population—a hundred and fifty million people—are already dead or dying, as a result of the explosions and natural disasters. Most of the rest are running out of food and water, or are suffering from radiation poisoning, disease, or violence."

"A hundred and fifty million?" Greg asked, frowning.

"Well, it's only a statistical estimate, based on the reports we have so far. We're spread pretty thin at the moment, so we're focusing on large population centers. We've had to guess on the rest of the country, based on known events . . . "

"I get the picture," Greg said, interrupting Chuck angrily. "What are we doing to help, Chuck? I want details." They spent the next several hours discussing the details.

13

What the family needs is a celebration

The Preserve, 9 July

Matt appeared at the hospital a few minutes after the others, having quickly checked to ensure that Brittany had Sydney resting, as instructed.

"Since you're here, you can take a look a Lillie's foot," Amos said. Matt didn't move, but looked from Emily to Lillie and back again, obviously torn.

"I'm okay for now, Matt," Lillie said. "You better sit there by Emily and hold her hand."

Amos watched Matt's expression change from distressed to relieved as he moved toward Emily.

"Why don't you sit there," Amos told Matt, pointing to a chair near Emily's head on her right side. "You can monitor Emily's vital signs." He smiled inwardly, amazed and amused at Lillie's ability to read people's feelings.

Amos had already x-rayed the arm and confirmed that the humerus bone was fractured just above the elbow. He didn't know initially what else might be damaged, so he'd hooked Emily up with an IV to give her fluids and pain killers intravenously while he checked, just in case.

Emily was awake again, and Matt took her right hand in his. She smiled weakly at him and squeezed his hand.

"Do you hurt anywhere else?" Amos asked.

"No, just the arm," Emily said, wincing with pain each time Amos touched it.

Amos checked her for other possible skeletal damage, watching her face as he did so. She didn't seem bothered by his ministrations. He helped her roll over on her right side, careful to keep her left arm from moving, and checked her spine. Then he rolled her back onto her back.

"Well," Amos said, "other than the stiffness in your neck, back, and shoulder, I don't see any other problems. We'll put your arm in a cast and sling, and give you some pain meds, then have Matt take you home."

"Take her home?" Matt asked, startled. Amos thought Matt looked lost.

"It's a joke, Matt," Emily said. "You'll have to get used to Dad's humor."

Terry arrived while they were talking, removed Lillie's shoe, and used his hands to check for broken bones in her foot and ankle.

Amos smiled at Emily and Matt, then turned toward Lillie and Terry, to see what was causing Lillie to moan.

"Quit your bellyaching, Lillie," Terry laughed. "I'm sure it's only sprained, not broken. We'll take an x-ray to confirm my diagnosis and wrap your foot to keep the swelling down. As your doctor, I'm telling you to stay off your feet—or at least use the crutches."

Amos chuckled at Lillie's defiant expression. He knew Lillie wouldn't stay off her feet for long.

"You two are hilarious," Lillie said, then moaned again when Terry moved the table she was sitting on over to the x-ray machine.

☢

Amos and Mike walked to the office, Mike reporting that he hadn't found any radiation leaks in the Preserve. They found Terry rewinding a video recording in the office.

"Are you ready for this?" he asked Amos as he hit *stop*.

"Let's see it," Amos replied, concerned at Terry's tone of voice.

Terry showed them a news report confirming the explosion at Hill Air Force Base and the subsequent earthquake along the Wasatch Front. Then he showed them a recording from one of the monitors in Aspen Valley, overhead. Through the smoke, they could vaguely see fire consuming their beautiful valley. They could hear the howling of the wind and crackling of the fire.

Within moments, the sky darkened, as the fire continued to consume the trees and bushes. The video clouded up, was interrupted by static, then went out completely.

"All of the monitors went out?" Amos asked.

"All except one, high on the cliff face," Terry replied, showing them feeds from several others.

"Not good," Amos said, shaking his head and running his hand through his hair. He could see, in the feed from the monitor that had survived, that the fire was moving on without completely consuming the trees. Even so, the majority of the trees looked like smoking skeletons, and smoke also rose from the bushes on the ground, blowing eerily, like a night mist in a bog.

"At least we have one monitor left," Terry said. "I got here just before the rest of the video monitors went out. The environmental sensors registered increased radioactivity, as well" he said, walking over to the wall of monitors and tapping on one of the gauges. "They're frozen at the last reading."

Amos knew that this type of gauge registered its highest reading until the reset button was depressed.

"The fact that they malfunctioned means we won't know how

bad it really is out there until we go out with portable units," Amos said.

"I don't think we'll be able to go out and check the sensors until next spring," Terry replied.

"That's much longer than I'd intended," Amos said, "but I agree. I don't think we should let anyone go out there until the radiation has a chance to dissipate. The way the trees have burned, I don't know if any of the sensors and cameras can be salvaged."

"That's it then," Terry said, heading for the door. "Nothing else we can do. Let's go get something to eat."

"Come on, Mike," Amos said, thinking that they were now almost blind.

Mike sighed and followed his dad out.

When Amos returned to the Hospital, Lillie tried to stand.

"I can't sit here not knowing what's going on with the family," she said, "but it gave me time to think"

"Then the sprained ankle was a good thing?" he asked.

"No, it definitely *was not*," she said, "but it made me realize that we need something to take our minds off what's happening outside. What the family needs is a party. Surely someone has a birthday coming up."

While Lillie talked, Amos watched her, amused and amazed by her resilience. He laughed out loud, startling her.

"What's so funny?" she asked.

Amos hugged her to him, awkwardly because of her wrapped foot.

"You are the sunshine of my life," he said, quoting a line from one of his favorite old love songs. It made her smile.

Everyone gathered in the community center at Lillie's request. She entered on crutches and sat down hard on a chair at the front of the room, where Becca had set a cushion. Emily entered in a wheelchair, pushed by Matt. Sydney, still looking a little dazed, was helped to a chair by her mother. Amos had determined that she needed three stitches after all, so the wound was now bandaged and she wore a scarf on her head.

When everyone was seated, Becca helped Lillie stand and lean on her crutches.

"This is the first of what we're going to call *family council* meetings," Lillie said breathlessly. "Since we're one big happy family now, we want to provide a nonthreatening environment where each family member can feel free to express themselves."

Chris Stephens snickered and whispered something to Rachel, who was sitting next to him. Rachel, who was accustomed to and appreciated the family meetings, smacked Chris on the shoulder—affectionately, though, and she smiled as she did it.

"Take this seriously," she whispered. Lillie stared at Chris for a moment before going on.

"We appreciate everyone remaining calm while we assessed the impact of the earthquake. Terry confirmed that what we felt was an explosion at Hill Air Force Base, followed twenty minutes later by an earthquake on the Wasatch Front."

Suddenly Lillie was confronted by a deluge of questions.

"Whoa," she said, holding up both hands, in a gesture that gently held them at bay.

Amos could see Lillie was struggling to stay on her feet, so he encouraged her to sit. He placed a cushion on a second chair and rested her injured foot on the cushion. Then he stood and faced the family.

"More on the explosion and earthquake in a minute," Amos said. "First, we want you to know that Mike and Terry checked out the Preserve, and it's secure. All life support systems are at one hundred percent."

"Beam me up, Scotty," Chris said, laughing. Becca looked at him sternly. He slapped a hand over his mouth, but continued laughing into his hand. Rachel whispered something to him, frowning this time, and he laughed harder.

"Thanks, Chris." Amos thought Chris's joke was funny, but didn't know how the others would react if he started laughing. "I guess that comment sounded a little too *Trekkie*. But we really *do* have life support systems. We have a closed environment, just like the *Starship Enterprise*. You can think of everything outside the Preserve as outer space, and we don't want to go there.

"As I was saying, the support systems all check out. But, just in case, we're going to run routine checks on all systems, daily for a while, then weekly thereafter. So, don't be surprised or alarmed if you see us with Geiger counters or other measuring instruments."

"Don't start worrying until you see us wearing hazmat suits indoors," Mike joked.

"Michael," Amos said sternly. "He's joking. If we have a problem, we'll do something about it long before it's that serious."

"What can you tell us about what's going on in *outer space* right now?" Chris asked, looking like he was ready to start laughing at any provocation.

Amos thought about the news report they'd watched that morning—and Mike's comment about sanitizing the news. His stomach lurched and he suddenly had a sour taste in his mouth. He wondered what he should tell them.

"I'm sure that's on everyone's mind," he said. "We know there was an earthquake on the Wasatch front. We don't have any details about magnitude or damage. We believe the earthquake was initiated by an explosion nearby, probably at Hill Air Force Base, and probably nuclear."

"Why do you say nuclear?" Jason asked.

"Our instruments started recording increased radiation just before they stopped working. We also saw fire in the valley."

"What do you mean *the instruments stopped working?*" Jason demanded, alarmed.

"Aspen Valley caught fire?" Emily asked at the same time.

"I'm kind of guessing, Jason" Amos said, "but if the winds from the explosion were strong enough, they could carry the heat from the explosion up the canyon, eventually reaching Aspen Valley."

"You *do* realize how far we are from Ogden, and how many other valleys are between here and there—including Cache Valley—right?" Jason said in a challenging tone.

"I already said that I'm only guessing, Jason," Amos said, trying to control his frustration. "Like you, I would've thought our distance from Hill Air Force Base would prevent the fire from reaching us. But there was fire in the valley above us, so either the winds were very strong, or the explosion was closer to us than Hill. We can't tell any more than that."

"You said strong winds. How strong?" Matt asked.

"I believe the reporter said the Washington D.C. explosion caused winds in excess of five hundred miles per hour."

"Freakin' unbelievable!" Chris exclaimed. "A Category 5 hurricane only has winds around a hundred and sixty miles an hour, and we've seen what they can do."

Jason stared at Chris for a moment, then turned back to Amos.

"What do you mean, the instruments stopped working?" he asked again.

"While we were in here helping Emily and Sydney, Terry was recording what was going on in the valley."

"And?" Jason pressed.

"We watched some of the recordings a few minutes ago. There was smoke, then fire, then the instruments malfunctioned."

"Then, how do we know we're safe?" Jason asked.

"Oh, there's no question about our being safe. That was never an issue after we confirmed the integrity of our support systems. What it means is that we have to wait a while before we can leave the Preserve safely and repair or replace the sensors."

"And how long is a while?" Jason asked.

These were exactly the types of questions Amos had expected. But, coming from Jason, they made him suspicious, then angry. He controlled his expression with some difficulty and answered truthfully.

"The Board will decide when it's safe to go out."

"Then we can all go out?" Jason asked excitedly. "It will be safe?"

"No, Jason," Amos replied angrily. Lillie placed a hand on his arm, and he looked at her—knowing she would want him to calm down—then took a breath and continued. "To begin with, two people will be selected by the Board to go out and inspect the sensors. That's two people who have the ability to make repairs and have been trained to work in hazmat suits."

"How much training can that take?" Jason asked dismissively.

"You'd be surprised," Amos said. "I was certified by professionals during a three-day course and I *still* get claustrophobic when I work in one. You have to learn to breathe canned air, and you have to pace yourself or you can get sick to the stomach."

Jason smiled, but there was no humor in it.

"Since the hazmat suits don't stop radiation," Amos said, ignoring the strange look he saw in Jason's eyes, "anyone going outside will be taking a health risk. So, we need to be sure that the radiation level has decreased to an acceptable level before anyone goes. The dosimeters only verify the actual dosage received—they can't tell us anything in advance."

Jason opened his mouth to ask another question.

"The answer is *no*, Jason," Amos said.

Jason shut his mouth and frowned, but only for a moment.

"How long will it take before the radiation has dropped to a safe level?" he asked.

Amos looked over at Terry and raised an eyebrow. *Why do you think Jason's asking that?* he wanted to ask.

"Because the sensors malfunctioned," Terry said, "we don't know how high the radiation level is, nor do we know how the fallout is distributed. We'll run some calculations, based on what we know, and make an educated guess. Then we'll err on the side of caution."

"Does it bother you that now you're blind in here?" Jason asked sarcastically, looking at Amos.

More bullshit, Jason was thinking while he asked his questions. Nuclear bombs, earthquakes, five-hundred-mile-an-hour wind. Where did they get this stuff? He couldn't figure out how they were making the Preserve shake as if it were in an earthquake— maybe whatever experiment they were conducting in their lab had blown up. If that was the case, then all the injuries were a result of *their* stupidity. It wouldn't surprise him.

Maybe there actually were one or two earthquakes, but he doubted it.

And now they were saying they were blind and couldn't see what was going on outside? He wondered what they were getting out of this new lie. Did they really think he was that stupid? Did they think he would stop asking questions? Maybe they could fool the others, but not him. He was going to find a way to get answers.

From Jason's voice and expression, Amos was sure the man was making fun of him. *He thinks we can't handle not knowing what's going on outside,* Amos thought. Was he right, or was it Jason who couldn't handle it? Either way, Amos wasn't going to tell him they had one working camera left on the cliff face. Amos was still trying to think of an answer that didn't bring them to another confrontation when Lillie saved him from having to answer.

"Enough questions from the adults," Lillie said from her chair, with a disarming smile. Looking around at the others, she asked, "Any questions from the younger members of the family?"

"What's for dinner," Chris asked, making his mother laugh. His question broke the tension in the room better than anything Amos could have thought of. "Hey, that's a valid question. It's getting late and I'm hungry."

"You just had lunch," Becca replied, still laughing. "Dinner will be at the usual time."

"Trust a teenager," Lillie said, touching Becca's arm. Turning to Chris, she added, "We'll get to dinner as soon as we've given everyone a chance to ask their questions."

Amos raised his eyebrows, a sure sign that he was inviting

questions.

"Did you see people in the canyon before the monitors went out?" Rachel asked.

"There was a lot of traffic on the highway earlier," Terry answered, "headed toward Garden City, but none since the fire started."

Chris asked about the video and VR games, and Amos asked Mike to check into it. There were a few more questions, mostly about work assignments, but nothing more related to the earthquake.

"For the last item of family business," Lillie said, "we need to know everyone's birth dates."

"Is that *really* more important than dinner?" Chris asked.

"It definitely is," Lillie said, laughing. "Let's go around the room and get everyone's birthday. Becca, will you write them down?"

They discovered that Sydney Carlsen had turned fifteen on July second, and Katie Stephens was turning twenty-two on the thirteenth.

"Thank you. Here's what we're going to do. Next Friday, the thirteenth, we're holding a birthday party for Katie and Sydney after lunch. Maybe Brittany and Becca can meet with me tomorrow to help plan it. Would that be okay?"

"Awesome," Sydney said excitedly to Rylee, who was sitting next to her. "I thought we'd given up on birthdays and I'd have to stay fourteen forever." Several people laughed as the meeting came to an end.

The Preserve, 10 July

After breakfast, Amos invited the adults into the office to watch recorded video footage. Terry had pre-selected several recordings he thought were the most pertinent, while avoiding the ones that were most overwhelming.

"This recording is a satellite view of missiles being launched around the world," Terry said. On the night side of the world, all that was visible was the bright arc of flames trailing the missiles. The scene changed to a reporter behind a desk, talking, but Terry had the volume turned down.

"The stars shall fall from heaven, and the powers of the heavens shall be shaken," Brittany said.

"What was that?" Becca asked as everyone turned to look at Brittany.

"Since all this started," Jason said indifferently before Brittany could answer, "Brittany's been reading scriptures about the end of the world. She quotes them at me whenever something happens. Thinks it'll make me a better person or something."

Brittany glared at him.

"And the missiles made you think of stars falling from the sky?" Becca asked.

"Book of Matthew," Brittany said, nodding and continuing to stare at Jason.

"They do look a little like falling stars," Katie Stephens said.

"Or comets," Mike said.

"After the missile strikes," Terry continued, when there were no more comments, "debris from the explosions filled the air. Here's a satellite view of the northeast, showing the fallout cloud from the explosion in Washington, D.C." The scene showed the eastern coastline, mostly visible, with dark clouds spreading out from the capital to the northeast, covering a large portion of New England.

"And here's a view of the west coast." The satellite view showed dark masses of clouds, starting at the sites of the missile strikes and spreading out, generally toward the northeast. "San Diego, Los Angeles, San Francisco, and Seattle," Terry said, pointing to the location of each city on the screen. "This is the Hanford nuclear reactor site in southeastern Washington State, and this is Las Vegas," he added, pointing to two additional clouds away from the coast. "Hawaii was also hit, but it's off the screen to the west of this image. I think this cloud at the edge of the screen is the fallout plume." The clouds were already covering a large portion of the coast, spreading out into neighboring states.

They watched several more video segments, all of them dark and taken from the ground, showing grim clouds covering much of the sky.

"These videos were taken later, after dark, in major metropolitan areas of the country. Besides the cloud cover, you'll notice the absence of any kind of light—no street lights, no lights on in houses, nothing. There's obviously been major damage to the power grid over much of the country."

In the next video, the clouds parted and Amos could see a reddish-orange disc, vaguely, through the shifting clouds. The others must have noticed, too.

"Is that the moon or the sun?" Brittany asked.

"The moon," Terry said. "We can only see it because the clouds parted briefly."

"But it's red," Matt said, sounding alarmed.

"That's caused by all the particulates in the air, like dust particles, water droplets, and mist, or, in this case, nuclear fallout. In recent years it's happened often enough that meteorologists have started calling it a *blood moon,* primarily because of verses in the Bible that refer to the sun going dark and the moon turning red."

"Don't you have another quote for us?" Jason asked Brittany, his voice mocking.

Brittany's eyes started to water, and she clenched her teeth.

"The sun shall be turned into darkness," she finally said, "and the moon into blood, before the great and terrible day of the Lord come. The book of Joel."

"So, this is the second coming?" Jason asked, laughing.

"Who says it's not?" Terry asked, before Amos could decide how to respond.

"Oh brother," Jason said, brushing away Terry's comment with a wave of his hand. "Go ahead and defend her dumb ideas." He started to chuckle defensively. No one else joined in. "Oh, come on people, lighten up," he added.

"There's really nothing funny about any of this, Jason," Lillie said. "Millions of people are dead or dying out there. Before this is over, it may be in the billions."

"I don't see millions of people *dying out there*," Jason said. "All I see are some bright lights and a bunch of clouds. You're telling us they represent nuclear explosions, but I'm not buying it."

"What do you want, Jason?" Amos asked.

"What?"

"What do you want? Why are you acting so obtuse?"

Jason balled his fists. His face turned red.

"You've seen lots of evidence that there's a nuclear war in progress," Amos continued. "You've felt the tremors from the explosions and earthquakes. Do you want to see the bloody bodies and bomb craters?"

"Huh?" Jason was clearly surprised by Amos's newly confrontational attitude and seemed not to know what to say.

"What's it going to take for you to realize that this world may actually be dying?" Amos watched the stream of emotions cross Jason's face. *Is he angry, frustrated, confused, or just stupid?* he wondered.

☢

Jason was taken aback that they were all taking Brittany seriously. But it fit with what Amos wanted everyone to believe, so of course *he* would defend her stupid ideas. In fact, it helped his story.

Was there really a nuclear war in progress? Hell no! But he had to say something quickly to shift the focus away from him so they wouldn't start wondering what he was up to. He didn't want them to realize that he was looking for the lab so he could find whatever it was that they were hiding.

"All right," Jason finally said, putting his hand out in front of him defensively. "I'm sorry. I don't know what I was expecting. I'm sorry for making light of the situation."

Amos nodded once, but didn't speak.

Terry showed a few more recordings. One, he said, was of missile silos opening in Wyoming to retaliate on North Korea and Russia for starting the war. He also played recordings from newsrooms in Boston and Seattle, with the news anchors leaving their desks. He said they were giving instructions for everyone to find shelter, but he had the volume down on the TV, so they could have been saying anything. Jason tried to imagine what Amos was trying to accomplish by showing these videos.

"Can we see the explosion at Hill Air Force Base?" Matt asked.

"I haven't found any video of that," Terry said. "Maybe someone will come forward in a few days with a recording."

Finally, Terry showed them video he said was from one of the cameras in the Valley. Cars, trucks, and campers flowed past in a steady stream, bumper to bumper, headed up the canyon, supposedly toward Garden City. Then smoke and fire entered the valley. He let the video run until the camera went dead and the feed cut out. Jason heard Emily crying when the fire passed through the valley—she was pretty convincing.

Jason tried to figure out how they'd made such a convincing

video of something that had never happened. It looked like it had been professionally compiled from other events. Maybe he could call their bluff and get them to confess.

"So, the trees weren't totally burned, or blown over?" Jason asked.

"That's how it appears," Terry replied. "It looks like the wind blew the flames through the valley too quickly for the trees to burn completely."

"But the wind must have died down or it would have blown the trees over, right?"

"Umm," Terry looked over at Amos, and Jason thought he was getting close to an answer.

"So, there's a good chance Garden City may have been spared both the fire and the wind, right?" Jason continued.

Now everyone was looking at Jason questioningly. He didn't care. He decided he was going to find a way to escape the Preserve and prove they were lying.

"I don't know, Jason. I guess that's possible," Terry said, then turned to see if anyone else had questions.

There were a few more questions about what they'd seen in the videos. Amos and Terry were careful not to share information that would make them curious about the events they weren't being shown.

They avoided one other topic, too: before the meeting, Amos had been very specific with Terry and Mike—since they were the only ones who knew—that they had to exclude any mention of the one remaining camera that still worked.

"I'm not sure why I want that to be a secret," Amos had said.

"It's just a gut feeling."

"I respect that, Amos," Terry had replied. Mike had nodded his understanding.

Now, as they were leaving the office, Becca asked Brittany about the biblical passages, and Brittany agreed to show Becca where they were in her Bible. The smirk on Jason's face showed what he thought of Brittany's little excerpts.

When everyone else had left the office, Amos turned to Terry and Mike.

"Maybe we need to put tighter controls on the external door locks, keys, and equipment," Amos said. "Let's make certain each of the Board members keeps a close eye on their keys."

Terry and Mike nodded their agreement.

Amos remembered Chris's earlier *Star Trek* comment, bringing a tight smile to his lips.

"We need to keep the Starship Enterprise secure," he said.

"That, we do, Amos." Terry snorted a laugh and patted Amos on the back.

After the adults left for the office that morning, Rylee stood to leave.

"Where are you going?" Sydney asked.

"To my room," she said. She didn't want Sydney to know this was the day she planned to get Nathan to notice her.

"Fine. I'll come along so we can talk."

"No!" Rylee said, then realized she'd spoken too quickly. "I want to be alone for a while. I'm not feeling well. Thanks anyway."

Sydney looked at her curiously, then shrugged.

"Okay. I guess I'll go to the community center and play a video game. Come and join me if you get feeling better."

"Thanks. I will." Rylee hurried off, feeling a little guilty. As she walked down the tunnel toward her bedroom wing, she turned to see Sydney walking in the opposite direction. In her room, she pulled out tight-fitting exercise pants and a short, tight top that her mother hadn't known she'd brought. The thought of her mother at that moment nearly brought her to tears, but she quickly purged her mind. She dressed quickly, then went to the weight room.

Nathan had made everyone feel so uncomfortable, whenever they tried to share the weight room with him that Mike had moved some of the free weights into the exercise room. He'd also moved the bikes and treadmills, so they could be used without interacting with Nathan. Rylee had studied Nathan's schedule and knew he would be in the weight room at this hour.

When she entered the room, Nathan was lying on his back on a bench, pressing weights so large that Rylee thought they would crush him. He ignored her, as he always had, and continued working out. After twenty minutes, Rylee gave up and left.

Nathan noticed when Rylee entered and sat on a bench against the wall. He'd realized days before that she watched him whenever he was around. It irritated him that she could possibly imagine that he'd be interested in her. She was what, fifteen? Two years younger than him. What did she want? He didn't know anything about her, but as he thought more about it, he realized that maybe he and Rylee had some things in common. They'd both lost family, and neither of them had paired off with anyone else here. He glanced at her out of the corner of his eye—she looked pretty hot in that outfit.

And he was a little flattered by her interest. *I bet she likes looking at my chest when I don't have a shirt on,* he thought. He wasn't as buff as Aaron had been—the thought choked him up unexpectedly. He hadn't realized how much he'd idolized Aaron until his brother had died. No, he wasn't as buff as Aaron, but he was getting there. He pushed himself harder as he thought about it.

Maybe he should take a chance with Rylee. He decided he would think about it. But by the time he'd finished his routine she'd already left, and he focused on other things.

14

We're on backup power

The VEEP Bunker, 10 July

Vice President Art Klemp was scared. He was convinced that someone in the government—probably the president himself—wanted him dead, and would use the bombing of the CDC as a way to destroy the VEEP bunker, with him inside. Having witnessed the violent deaths of his associates, he did *not* want his life to end that way.

"Perry," Art said quietly, his eyes as big as saucers, "you've got to get me out of here." He was in the detention cell in the VEEP bunker, where he'd been since his emotional meltdown. "Not a good idea," Perry said. He was sitting outside the cell, keeping a protective eye on his charge. "The CDC scientists arrived a few minutes ago. They're being briefed about . . . "

"I don't care about the CDC scientists, Perry. Greg's trying to kill me."

"Then I suggest we leave the bunker and go to the shelter. It's farther away and reinforced like a bunker. And the president's not there."

Art's darting eyes finally focused on Perry. His lips curved up in a sly smile.

"Yes," he whispered.

"I'll let them know what you've decided."

"*No!* I mean, yes, do that."

Perry nodded to one of his team members, who was sitting at the end of the hallway.

The CDC

CDC Director Anne Lister had asked her deputy director, Dr. Thomas Strang, to gather the other twenty-two staff members into the lunchroom. It was a skeleton crew—mostly management and senior scientists—just enough to monitor safety and security in the facility. All of the contractors and most of the staff had been evacuated earlier, after the discovery of the terrorist plot to bomb the facility. When they were all there, Strang nodded to the director.

"Thank you for gathering on short notice," Director Lister said solemnly, her eyes bloodshot and worried. Her weak smile did little to ease the tension in the room. She sighed before continuing. "As you know, we're on backup power. We'll run out of fuel in about six hours unless more fuel is delivered before then. I don't need to tell you what will happen if we run out of power." She told them anyway, still having to convince herself that it had really come to this. "All of our containment systems will be compromised." She paused dramatically, looking around for a moment, then continued.

"As a precaution, we're going to evacuate the facility, while the Army comes in to assess our situation and decide what would be best for us. I need each of you to gather all of your personal belongings, put on your hazmat suits, and report back here in thirty minutes."

"Can I ask a question, Director?" Strang asked.

Anne smiled at him.

"Go ahead, doctor."

"What, exactly, is the Army going to do? *We* are responsible for the contents of this facility. We can't delegate our responsibility to the military." Dr. Strang was responsible for the smallpox virus experimental samples, and the director knew he would be reluctant to release them to anyone. Anne had always felt there was something a little off about Dr. Strang, but his work had been impeccable. And the question was reasonable—she had wondered about the very same thing.

"I asked that question," the director replied. "Besides dealing with the power problem, nothing's been mentioned. I think they would have told me if they had something else in mind. But they assured me the Army has medical personnel who will be responsible for safety and security while we're gone. They said we can return as soon as they have the situation resolved—before our fuel supply is depleted, they said. Any other questions? No? Okay. Be ready to leave in thirty minutes. We'll meet in the lunchroom. Thanks."

Within thirty minutes, all twenty-four people were standing in the lunchroom, each wearing an identical hazmat suit. A few had their hoods attached. They were all carrying boxes or backpacks containing their personal belongings.

"Okay," the director explained, "we will be leaving in two military personnel carriers. The Army is waiting outside the front doors. They'll attach a radiation dosimeter to each of our suits as we leave the building, and take us to a hardened bunker in Norcross, where they'll give us additional information. I'll go in the first carrier."

"I'll lock up and go in the second carrier," Dr. Strang volunteered.

"Thank you Dr. Strang," she said with a smile. "I'll give the

Army captain in charge the security passcodes so they can get in after we're gone. Let's go." The director attached her hood, picked up her box awkwardly, and headed down the corridor toward the lobby, followed by the others.

"Go now, while everyone's attention is focused on Anne," Strang said quietly to the doctor next to him, who then snuck back into the depths of the facility. Strang attached his hood and followed the others across the room toward the corridor. Everyone looked alike in their hazmat suits, so no one would notice that he and his associate weren't following until it was too late. At the exit to the room, he turned and put his back against the wall.

When his associate returned several minutes later, he was holding a small, insulated container, and his hood was attached.

"Good," Strang said, as he stashed the container in his backpack. They slowly moved toward the lobby, verified that both carriers had departed, then locked up and walked toward the parking lot on the far side of the complex.

The Preserve

"Emily and Matthew, do you have a few minutes?" Lillie called as they were leaving the dining room, holding hands. Emily was on her feet today, having escaped the wheelchair that "limited her mobility."

"Sure, Mom. What's up?" she asked.

"Dad wants to talk to you," Lillie said. Emily shot a questioning look at Matt, who shrugged. Lillie led them to the office, hobbling on her crutches. They found Amos leaning against his desk, with his arms folded and legs crossed, laughing about something with Terry. He smiled as they entered the room.

"How are you two getting along?" he asked.

This time, when Emily looked at Matt, his face mirrored her

concern.

"We're fine Dad. Why?"

Lillie had told Amos it was time Emily and Matt should get married. There'd been comments from family members about their behavior. Lillie had heard jokes that the two lovebirds should "get a room." Amos had laughed, and suggested that Lillie should go ahead and handle it, as keeper of the house and family.

"Well, I think you need to be the one to explain that *you* will be performing the wedding," she'd replied.

He'd agreed, so now the young couple was here, wondering what he wanted.

"We're just concerned about your welfare," Amos said. "With more people stuffed in here than we designed for, the Preserve is like an anthill. There are people everywhere you go, so there's no privacy."

"We agree," Emily said hesitantly. "There's no place to go to be alone. Whenever we put our heads together to talk, someone interrupts."

"I'm not surprised."

Emily and Matt looked at each other, then at Amos again. Emily looked like she might start crying.

"What would you like us to do about it?" Amos finally asked.

"What we'd like . . . " Emily looked at Matt for help, but he was speechless.

"Yes?" Lillie asked.

Emily and Matt looked at each other again, with longing, but couldn't—or wouldn't—say what Lillie knew was on their minds and in their hearts. It was Lillie who finally said it.

"I think you should get married."

Emily started to cry. She clung to Matt, who choked back tears of his own.

"That's what we really want, but how can we do that here—I mean, legally?"

Lillie smiled and turned to Amos, who was also smiling.

"What if I told you I can perform the wedding?" Amos asked. "Legally."

"How?" Emily asked through her tears.

Amos explained how he'd anticipated the need for a minister, had organized a church online, and had named it *The Church of Aspen Valley*.

As he explained, Emily squeezed Matt tighter, with her one good arm, bouncing on the balls of her feet. Amos looked over at Lillie and, seeing her smile, returned it.

"So, you're the minister of *The Church of Aspen Valley?*" Matt asked, chuckling.

"And you can perform our marriage?" Emily asked, a quiver in her voice.

"Correct, and correct" Amos replied.

Emily leaped into her father's arms, almost knocking him over onto the table.

"Thank you, Daddy. Thank you," Emily said, hugging him around the neck with her good arm and kissing him on the cheek while he laughed a bit uncomfortably.

Lillie came over and Emily hugged her mother, too.

"Thank you, Mom," she said. Then she turned and kissed Matt—a long, passionate kiss that was clearly embarrassing for him. Lillie was amused at Emily's enthusiasm—and Matt's effort to look dignified. She noticed Terry, standing quiet and motionless off to the side—it must have been awkward watching this private family moment.

"Congratulations Matt," Amos said, giving Matt a slap on the back.

"Thank you, sir," Matt said. "I mean, Amos."

"When?" Lillie asked. Emily backed up a step and looked at her.

"When what?" she asked.

"When do you want to get married?"

"Right now?" Emily asked, her face glowing as she looked at Matt.

"We should give it some thought, don't you think?" Lillie asked, laughing. "What kind of wedding would you like? What do you want to wear? Who do you want to invite?"

Emily became thoughtful as her mother asked each question. When she got to the last one, Emily was startled. Of course, everyone would be involved.

"Okay, we'll talk about it this afternoon," Emily finally said, sharing a look with Matt.

"Great. Let's share our thoughts about wedding plans this evening. We'll announce it at the birthday party on Friday. Let's keep it our secret until then, okay?"

Emily went to her dad and gave him another hug.

"Thanks, Dad. You've made us very happy."

"I'm sorry we're in the middle of a war," he said, turning serious.

"We always envisioned a big, special wedding for you," Lillie added, coming over and placing her hand on Emily's arm. "Hundreds of people, lots of decorations and presents."

"It's okay, Mom," Emily said, smiling. "All the people who really matter are here with us. It *will* be special. Thank you."

15

This place is crowded

Johns Creek shelter, 10 July

The Johns Creek shelter had been built in the basement of a public building and had been designed for this specific purpose. The thick walls and ceiling were reinforced concrete. The single entrance consisted of steel inner and outer doors, separated by several feet, to form an airlock for decontaminating people and supplies entering the shelter. There were no windows, but there was a sophisticated monitoring system at the entrance to the facility so that anyone approaching from the outside could be both seen and heard.

The military personnel carrier from the VEEP bunker arrived at about mid-day, delivering two doctors from the CDC, along with Vice President Art Klemp, his four-man security detail, and ten others. Army Sergeant Lerner, inside the shelter, had been notified of their arrival. The newcomers were each disinfected before being allowed to remove their hazmat suits and enter the shelter.

Those already in the overcrowded shelter were unhappy at having to share space with seventeen more people, but when the vice president entered the shelter there were gasps of recognition, and he became an instant celebrity. As he moved across the room, surrounded by his security team, several people approached.

"I'm so glad you're here," one said. "I hope you can get us more information about what's going on."

"You should be the president. I bet you'd handle this crisis better than McCormick," another said.

At first surprised, then encouraged, by the mostly warm welcome, the vice president's repressed emotions were released. He relaxed, the comments making him smile and think to himself, *yes, I bet I could have.* He unconsciously puffed out his chest with pride.

As he took stock of the people around him, it seemed that most of them were glad to see him—they looked hopeful. One young woman was holding an infant in her arms and had a small child holding onto her skirt. She looked worn out, but had a smile on her face. There didn't seem to be a man with her.

There were other family groups: men and women standing close together; parents with teenagers or small children. Some looked like they were here by themselves, or with a friend.

One pretty young woman in a flowered blouse and pink capris looked like she was restraining herself, like she would throw herself at him given the invitation—at least that's what he told himself. He noticed the large man behind her, frowning, his eyes on the young woman, possessive. *Her father?* he wondered.

"This place is crowded," Perry, the head of his security detail, said in his ear. "I don't like the looks of some of these people. We need to get you somewhere that's less public."

"Find a place, Perry," the vice president replied indifferently. He was enjoying his sudden popularity. "Move anyone who's in the way," he said without malice. It was his right, as vice president of the greatest superpower in history, to have his own space, and he was certain everyone would understand.

Perry turned to the three other men in his detail and whispered instructions. As the men dispersed to various parts of the shelter, some onlookers appeared curious, others concerned.

"Come with me," the vice president said to Perry as he moved into the crowd and began shaking hands, answering questions with greater confidence, and in more detail, than he really had. He knew he was giving the illusion that he had come to help them—and that was the plan. These people needed to believe he was in charge, even if he wasn't.

When Sergeant Lerner approached several minutes later, Perry tried to block him, even though Lerner outweighed Perry by at least fifty pounds, all muscle. Perry stood his ground, backed by his training and the 9 mm Beretta handgun in his shoulder holster.

"Mr. Klemp," Sergeant Lerner said, "I'm receiving complaints that your security detail is being disruptive. What are . . . "

"Sergeant?" Art interrupted him, raising his eyebrows in question.

"Lerner. Sergeant Lerner, sir. I'm responsible . . . "

"Sergeant Lerner," Art interrupted him again. Lerner didn't have a quick temper, but Art could see he was pushing the big man's buttons. "It's *Vice President* Klemp." Art's smile was pasted on and suddenly turned malevolent. "I'm now the senior government official in the shelter. I will take the space my team identifies for our use and delegate the rest of the space and people to your supervision, until I decide otherwise."

"Technically, Mr. Vice President, I report through the chairman of the Joint Chiefs to the president. You're not in my chain of command."

Art let Lerner get out an entire sentence, because he wanted to know where Lerner was going with his explanation.

"Then I relieve you of your command. I'll assign someone else to manage the shelter."

"The doctor and nurse run the shelter, not me," Lerner said in frustration. "I handle security, which includes disputes."

"In that case, my security detail will take over security. Now I'll ask you and anyone else in the shelter who has a gun to hand it over to Perry," he said as he pointed to his head of security.

Lerner began to object, when movement to his right drew his attention. Perry had just drawn his Beretta and pointed it at Lerner's chest, his finger on the trigger. Lerner lifted his gun out of his holster with two fingers and held it out for Perry. Perry took the weapon, flashing a smile that lasted about half a second and looked menacing, and tucked it into his waistband. Art noticed another member of his security detail relieve another soldier of his gun—a soldier he recognized from the VEEP bunker, who had arrived with him, today.

"Is that all the weapons in the shelter?" Art asked the group of people now staring at him with a mixture of concern, contempt, and fear. No one responded.

"If I find out later that someone was holding back, it will not go well for them. Now, I'll ask one more time. Are there any more guns in the shelter?"

Two more men came forward, reluctantly handing over handguns to Perry, looking angry enough to chew nails. Perry gave each of them another half-second smile.

"Thank you," Art said, insincerely.

Sergeant Lerner hadn't moved—he was still standing where he'd been during his conversation with the vice president, who'd moved to the side to have a better view of the group. Now Art turned back to Lerner, who'd balled his fists at his side.

Art smiled at Lerner's discomfort. *Have to keep an eye on this one,* he thought, and turned back to the group.

"Just a misunderstanding about who's in charge." He smiled disarmingly and continued. "We'll have to make some adjustments in the living spaces to accommodate the new people. If anyone has a question or concern, please bring it to a member of my security detail."

CDC facility, Druid Hills, northeast of Atlanta, Georgia

The ultra-secure CDC facility had been evacuated by the military several hours earlier, the occupants taken to the VEEP bunker. When the bomb dropped in Druid Hills, the CDC and its surroundings were vaporized. Every structure within a five-mile radius was completely demolished or severely damaged. Beyond that, there was structural damage to buildings and homes out to a twenty-mile radius. Above the explosion, a mushroom cloud rose several miles into the air, then dispersed downwind to drop its fallout for hundreds of miles.

VEEP and SEC DEF bunkers

To the occupants of the VEEP bunker, ten miles away, the explosion at the CDC felt like a powerful earthquake, but the bunker held, structurally. The occupants breathed a sigh of relief when no leaks were found. The CDC researchers wouldn't be as comfortable in the crowded bunker, but they would survive for now.

The occupants of the SEC DEF bunker, which had survived the explosion at Ft. Detrick, felt the same way.

Johns Creek shelter

The ground shook, furniture and dishes rattled, and there were loud noises upstairs, above ground, but that was the extent of the damage from the CDC explosion.

Still, some people were concerned. They approached the shelter doctor, Beth Byron, a plain-looking woman in her early thirties, who was in conversation with her nurse, Ben Schick, and two CDC researchers.

Dr. Byron had responded to the government's request for volunteers to work in the shelters when it appeared that the terrorist threat was real. Nurse Schick, in his late twenties, had also volunteered to help. Together, they'd been providing healthcare for the other seventy-six men, women, and children who'd been frightened into seeking shelter in the overcrowded Johns Creek shelter.

Dr. Evelyn Schumann, along with her friend and associate Dr. Melissa Gibbons, were CDC scientists—PhDs, not medical practitioners—who had been evacuated from the CDC. Convinced by Vice President Art Klemp's argument that the VEEP bunker wasn't safe, they'd decided to go to the Johns Creek shelter with the others. They were surprised when they'd learned that the CDC would be nuked, considering the viruses, bacteria, and other pathogens stored there, but as they'd discussed it, calmness had replaced their initial worry.

"The most virulent of the viruses," Evelyn had said, "is—was— smallpox. Anthrax and some flu pandemic viruses were stored there as well, any one of which would be trouble by itself. The military evacuated us before we found out that they were going to drop a bomb on the facility. We were told that the nuclear explosion would destroy them all—it'd be the ultimate antiseptic."

"Does that bother you?" Beth had asked. "You've spent years studying viruses, getting to know them, so to speak. Does it trouble you that they've been wiped out—that they won't be available for research any longer?"

Evelyn had had to think about that for a minute before responding.

"I see where you're coming from, but the only thing that

bothered me was that they didn't tell us in the beginning what they were planning to do. Really, it's better this way. We had only enough power to contain the viruses for another few hours. If any of them had ever gotten out, in this postwar environment, it could have been a disaster."

"Like this isn't already a disaster?" Beth had asked with a mirthless chuckle.

Now, as the shelter occupants approached, the doctors stopped talking about deadly viruses.

"That shaking we felt, was it the bomb going off at the CDC?" a middle-aged woman asked.

"I'm sure it was," Dr. Shumann said with a sympathetic smile. "They told us it would probably feel like an earthquake."

"Will there be any more explosions?" a white-haired woman in a bright housedress asked. "I don't think my heart can handle another surprise."

"Come by later today and we'll check your heart," Dr. Byron said with a smile.

There's a story behind that housedress, Evelyn thought,

A large man, accompanied by a smaller woman and a young woman in brightly colored blouse and capris, approached.

"Dr. Byron," the woman said, "Our space has been taken over by the vice president and his entourage." She said it like she was referring to a rock star and his touring companions. "Can you tell me where we should put our things now? Where we should sleep?"

Evelyn recognized the young woman as the pretty one Vice President Klemp had been eyeing, and she thought Klemp would have a suggestion for *her,* as long as her parents didn't come along.

Dr. Byron looked around the room, visualizing where everyone had been located and where the new occupants should settle down. But it was nearly *standing room only* now.

"Come with me, Raquel," Beth said, as she reached out and took the mother by the arm. "I think I know just the place for your family."

"There were eight people in our room," Raquel said, shaking her head.

"We'll take care of it," Beth reassured her with a pat on her arm.

Northeast of Atlanta

The blinding light and strong wind hit him at the same moment, coming from the passenger side of the car as he drove. The windows shattered, showering him with glass—again. The car bounced up onto two wheels but continued rolling forward, threatening at every moment to tip over.

Saleh struggled not to panic. He was thrown against the car door because he hadn't bothered to fasten his seatbelt, and was temporarily blinded by light, but he held the steering wheel steady, reflexively, and the car finally dropped back onto all four tires, then ran into a metal power pole. The sudden stop threw him forcefully against the steering wheel, setting off the airbag and injuring his chest.

As his vision returned, he looked over the hood of the car, through the broken windshield. He quickly realized he wouldn't be going any farther unless he found another ride. The pole, now tilting badly, stood right where the radiator should be and steam rose from under the hood.

Saleh cursed, then realized that he should be grateful that Allah had protected him from hitting the pole harder. His foot had slipped off the gas pedal and the car had slowed considerably before impact.

He looked around, surprised at the damage. Everything—homes, cars, trees, bushes, even flowers and grass—had been *pushed* sideways by the powerful wind. The sky, which had been clear moments earlier, was filled with dark billowing clouds, rising from the south and spreading out in all directions, blocking out the midday light. The wind still blew through the car's shattered windows, bringing with it a nauseating smell of burnt wood, paint, and chemicals.

His nausea and near-blindness threatened to overwhelm him. But as he struggled through the fog in his mind, he eventually remembered why he was in Atlanta. He once again thanked Allah that he was still alive to finish his mission.

16

Look at all the refugees

Colorado, 11 July

Denver, Colorado, had been struck by one of several missiles that had been aimed at NORAD's underground missile defense management headquarters, the Cheyenne Mountain Air Force Station under Cheyenne Mountain, which was in Colorado Springs, fifty miles to the south. Many who'd survived the destruction in Denver, but suffered from radiation burns and other injuries, began to migrate toward the Pueblo Reservoir and Arkansas River, about fifty miles south of Colorado Springs, on Interstate 25.

A steady stream of refugees flooded the interstate. White flakes fell on and around them from dark clouds. For most, the desire for water outweighed the dangers of travel. Besides, the government had said the fallout was survivable.

The refugees walked, alone or in small groups, but as part of the larger body of survivors. Most carried what they could on their backs, in wagons, in wheelbarrows, or using whatever they could find. Some had bicycles, horses, or other means of non-motorized transportation. A rare few had cars that still worked, ones built before the mid-1960s, when manufacturers started adding electronic control systems.

"Look at all the refugees," the farmer said to his wife, as they looked out the front window of their small home at the steady stream of southbound travelers.

The living room was dark, except for the candles set up on the hearth and the battery powered lantern shining into the room from the kitchen. They had no lights or refrigeration, so they'd been eating food from the fridge as fast as they could and keeping the freezer closed as much as possible, to preserve the food they couldn't eat or dry fast enough. They had no heat or air conditioning, but thankfully it had been a warm summer so far. And they had no phones or electronics of any kind.

"It's a good thing we have some food storage in the cellar and corn in the fields. I hope it's enough to last until the government gets the power back on," the farmer said, as he continued watching the refugees pass by. "Those poor people must be carrying everything they have of value on their backs."

He had gone to the store the day before for supplies and found it closed, with the lights out. Through the windows, which had been smashed in, he could see that the shelves were empty. And the stench of decomposing bodies that filled the air had overwhelmed his senses, information which he hadn't shared with his wife and never would.

"They must be headed for the reservoir," his wife said. "Didn't you say our pump is pressure fed?" He nodded. "Then we should be fine."

He'd tried to get information on what was happening in Denver and across the country on his emergency radio, but most of the radio stations were off the air. Those that were still broadcasting had very little information and none of it good.

As they watched, an old flatbed truck rumbled past on the highway, honking at people, likely trying to get them to move out of the way. A tarp covered a pile of stuff on the bed, probably possessions they thought they would need or didn't want to leave behind.

"Why is that truck working, Kevin?" she asked.

"I heard a report on the radio, speculating that older model cars might work because they didn't have all the electronic components that newer cars have. Something about EMPs. I guess they were right. They said that even a few newer cars, if they've been stored in metal or concrete buildings, might also work. That truck obviously works, but if they're planning to go very far, they may have trouble finding more gas."

"What do you mean?"

"No electricity to run the gas pumps."

"Look, Kevin," she said, directing his attention back to the highway. The truck had passed, but two cars approached, also honking their horns. When a group of the refugees stood in front of the cars, holding up their arms to stop them, the lead car continued, eventually bumping into one of the refugees. Suddenly, several of the refugees swarmed the cars with rocks and other objects, smashing windows, reaching through and fighting the occupants. The driver of the first car was dragged from his seat, thrown to the ground, and kicked until he stopped moving. The other occupants were also physically removed from both cars, by force if they wouldn't go willingly, and pushed out of the way. Then the refugees fought each other to get into the cars or hang on to the sides.

Kevin and his wife watched from the farmhouse as the cars, with their new drivers and passengers, sped away, running over one woman who stood in the way and losing others who didn't have a good enough grip.

Before either of them could comment, a group of four men turned and walked down the ramp toward the farmhouse.

"Kevin," his wife said, suddenly concerned. "What if they're coming here?"

"I'll turn them away. Why don't you check on Amy and Ian? Make sure they're in the house."

Kevin wondered if Amos had been right once again—he had always been right when they'd disagreed, ever since they were kids. A knock pulled him from his thoughts.

"Mr. Blund?" a voice called from outside the front door.

"Do I know you?" Kevin asked, as he opened the door a crack to see the man.

"The name's on the mailbox, Mr. Blund. We don't have food or water. Can you share a little?" The man pleaded.

"We don't have enough to share," Kevin said, anxiously. Seeing the angry red rashes on each man's face and neck, he felt sorry for them, but he could see others on the highway across the fields, walking past. He was afraid that word would spread and they would be inundated with pleas for help. "We'll run out shortly ourselves."

The man looked at the fields of corn all around the house.

"It looks like you have plenty. Can't you share just a little—enough to get us to the next town?"

Kevin's wife, Mandy, spoke from behind him.

"There's a pump behind the house. You can fill your water jugs there. Help yourself to some corn on your way back to the highway."

Kevin frowned at Mandy as the men turned away and walked off the porch. He closed the door and locked it. Mandy sidled up next to him and, together, they peered out the window, watching the men walk to the edge of the field, then pluck ears of corn with abandon. Behind them, a steady stream of refugees approached the small farm.

"Dang," Kevin said. "More refugees. Mandy, take the kids to

the fields without being seen. Make sure there's nobody out there first. I'm going to get my rifle."

"Amy!"

Kevin could hear the worry in his wife's voice as she called their fourteen-year-old daughter.

"Get Ian and come to the back door. Hurry."

"What is it, mom?" Amy asked, carrying an unhappy six-year-old Ian under one arm. He was holding a plastic toy truck in one hand, swinging it at Amy, who fended it off with her other hand.

"Let me go!" he shouted.

"Ian, baby, we need to go out to the field, quietly. Can you pretend we're hiding from pirates, and be very quiet?"

"What is it, mom?" Amy asked again, panic edging into her voice.

"Kevin, they're not out back," Mandy called, looking out the window by the back door.

"A whole bunch of them are coming to the front door now," Kevin called back. "They're talking to another group in the yard and pointing toward the back of the house. You gotta' go now."

"I won't leave you to face them alone, Kevin."

"We don't know what they're capable of. Now go!" Kevin turned away from his family while Mandy spoke to the kids.

"The highway's full of refugees from up north," Mandy told her daughter as she put on her coat. "Your dad's worried they could get difficult. He wants us to hide in the corn field." Kevin turned back to see Mandy take Ian from Amy and hand Amy her coat. Then Mandy opened the back door and pushed Amy out in front of her. "Run," she said.

A knock at the front door made Kevin turn back. He took one last look at the back of the house and watched for a moment as Mandy and the kids sprinted toward the back fields. He let out a breath.

"Who's there?" he called through the door. He didn't dare open it this time. The group was getting larger, and he didn't have much faith in his ability to fight back a stampede into his house.

"Please sir, share some food and water with us."

"We don't have anything to share," Kevin replied.

"That's not what we heard. We know there's water out back. We just want a little, same as you gave them. You need to share."

"Help yourselves to the water, but we only have enough food for our own needs. You can take some corn from the fields behind you, if you want. Maybe the next farm will have more. Now, be on your way."

As Mandy crossed the back yard, she heard a gunshot, a grunt, then struggling. She was torn between going to help Kevin and following Amy, who was probably nearing the center of the corn field. She made a quick decision, gritted her teeth, and followed her daughter into the field. The cornstalks slapped against her arms and face as she ran. She pulled Ian down into her shoulder to protect him from the lashing. Tears began to form in her eyes as she considered the possible result of her choice. As she ran, she heard someone behind her shout.

"There's more of them. Get 'em!"

Mandy took a quick look back and saw five men rounding the corner of the house. It was hard to see them through the cornstalks that separated her from the men, but they had obviously seen her. She searched frantically for her daughter. She had to reach Amy and get to safety.

Within moments, she heard the creaking and swishing of

cornstalks behind her. The men were close. *Where's Amy?*

"Hurry Mom," she heard Amy say from somewhere deeper in the field.

She searched frantically for her daughter, then saw the bright red jacket the girl was wearing. Amy was moving back toward the house.

"Amy," Mandy hissed, "go back. I see you. I'm following. Get to the creek!" She wondered, as she followed her daughter, holding Ian close to her chest, what they would be doing right now if they'd gone to Logan to be with Amos and Lillie.

Mandy had reached the middle of the field when an arm grabbed her around the waist, bringing her to an abrupt halt. The man twisted Mandy around just as another man ran past, chasing Amy. The quick, unexpected spin caused Mandy to drop Ian. He fell to the ground, hard, and began to cry. But he would have to wait.

Mandy withdrew a .22 caliber handgun from her coat pocket, aimed it at the man's face with her now-free, shaky hand and fired. The bullet entered the man's cheek, leaving a small hole. He got a dazed look on his face, let go of Mandy, and collapsed to the ground. His body twitched for a moment, then lay still.

The other three men stopped, now only a few yards away. Their frightened eyes moved back and forth between their travelling companion, lying on the ground, and Mandy. She returned their stare, afraid to move.

When Amy screamed, Mandy scooped up Ian, turned, and ran toward the terrified sound. Within moments, Mandy reached her daughter. She was on her knees, and had both hands up trying to dislodge her attacker, a twentyish man, who held her by her long hair.

Mandy stopped five yards from them, and the attacker turned

to look at her. She brought the gun up and fired, hitting him in the chest. He looked at his chest, then back at Mandy, his face contorted in disbelief. He let go of Amy's hair and clutched his chest with both hands, trying to stop the blood pumping from the wound. He wobbled, then fell sideways, still pressing his hands desperately against the spot where he'd been shot.

Amy looked fearfully up at her mom, who was holding the gun loosely in her extended hand. "There's more," she whispered, nodding behind her mother.

"Take Ian and run!" Mandy said. She handed Ian to his older sister, then turned toward the three remaining men. They were advancing cautiously, spreading out through the rows of corn. Not knowing how to handle the situation, she fired a shot at one of the men, then turned and ran after Amy. It soon became painfully obvious that her shot had missed. She could hear the sound of pursuit from behind and to both sides. The men were flanking her and her kids.

She didn't know what to do, but what she did know was that she couldn't let them get her kids. A moment later she was grabbed from behind, spun, and tripped to the ground. The movement caused her to drop her gun, and when she looked up it was in the hands of one of the men, trained on her face. As Mandy struggled to determine her next move, Amy screamed again. Her mother twisted toward the sound, which was behind her as she lay on the ground. Through the cornstalks, she could see that another of the men had tackled her daughter. The man struggled to hold on to Amy, while the girl swung at the man with her fists and kicked with both feet. The struggle was intense, and the man with the gun smiled, apparently amused by what he must have perceived as a futile effort by the young girl to escape the grasp of his friend.

"Tell her to stop struggling," the man with the gun finally said.

"Fight him, Amy," Mandy yelled, as she looked around for Ian.

The pistol fired and dirt kicked up at Mandy's feet. She stopped, and so did Amy. Quiet rustling came from the corn farther away, and Mandy hoped it was Ian, running for his life.

Within moments, the third man arrived. He grabbed onto one of Amy's arms and, together, the two men roughly hauled her to her feet and dragged her back toward the house. As they passed, the man with the gun motioned Mandy toward the house as well. She stood slowly and followed.

When they arrived, the house was full of people, who were busy clearing out the freezer and cupboards of all their contents and bringing boxes of food up from the cellar. They were all in a good mood, cheering and shouting about what they'd found. It was clear that they represented several different groups of refugees, and some of them were arguing over who should get what. Those who'd arrived last thought the food should be divided evenly, while those with their arms full said they would keep what they had. As Mandy watched, a fist was thrown and a fight began across the room.

Mandy, Amy, and their captors had stopped just inside the back door, staring at the scene around them. Mandy started to cry. She looked toward the front room, searching for Kevin in the moving mass of bodies, but couldn't see him.

The man holding the gun on her stepped forward and fired into the air, causing sheetrock dust to fall from the ceiling. Everyone stopped moving.

"We were here first," he said. "You will all drop the food and leave."

"You're dreamin' pal," a large man carrying a case of canned fruit said as he turned toward the front of the house. Mandy heard a quiet click. The big man must have heard it too, because he paused mid-stride. Before the man could turn around, a bullet pierced his back. The .22 caliber bullet didn't bring him down, but he dropped the case of food, turned back toward the gunman, and charged.

Mandy moved out of the way while the gunman was distracted. He fired two more shots before the large man could reach him—one hit his target in the head and one hit him in the chest—and still the man charged. When he reached the gunman, he fell on top of him, knocking the shooter to the floor. Then, finally, the large man stopped moving. The gunman rolled the dead man off of him and stood. Most of the people had fled out the front door, taking with them whatever they could carry, and the rest were right behind them, fighting each other to get out.

The house was a disaster. Cupboard doors were off their hinges. The fridge and freezer doors stood open with spilled food dripping on the floor. Cans and packages of food were scattered across the floor. Furniture was broken. There were holes in walls. It looked to Mandy like a bull had fought its way through the house. She sobbed.

"Pick up anything they left behind," the gunman said to his two travelling companions, as he grabbed Mandy by the arm. Then he led the way, walking around, looking through doorways, and holding the empty gun as though it still gave him power. "Check the cellar, too."

As he moved into the living room, the others followed, dragging Mandy and Amy with them. Mandy finally saw what had happened to Kevin. He lay in a crumpled heap to the side of the front door—pushed aside by an angry and indifferent mob. Mandy struggled ineffectually against her captor. Amy screamed and tore away from the man holding her, then knelt by her dad and tried to straighten him out on the floor; but the man grabbed her again and dragged her away, pushing her onto the coach.

"Stay there," he said.

The gunman finally turned back to Mandy. "It's your fault we missed out on the free-for-all," he said with a sneer. "But we still have you." Then he started to unbuckle his belt.

"Noooo," Mandy cried, struggling frantically to break free and praying that Ian was far from the house.

Amy screamed and tried to stand, but the man watching her slapped her hard across the face and pushed her back down, forcefully.

"Shut up," he said.

Similar scenes unfolded all along the hundred miles of highway between Denver and Pueblo, and across the nation. While many refugees were kind and patient, others behaved in ways they never would have, prior to the bombs. When they didn't get what they wanted, they stole from each other. They became belligerent, threatening, violent. They consumed what food and water they could find, even if it was already contaminated. Farms were ravaged, animals slaughtered, and wells were drained and unwittingly contaminated. Many people trying to hold out against the refugees were violated, or outright murdered.

As time progressed, survival went to the meanest, or the most violent, not necessarily the strongest or healthiest. Those who were alone, or in small groups, gradually joined up with other like-minded refugees for protection. The sickness spread throughout the Northern Hemisphere. It wasn't a virus, but any observer would have been forgiven for thinking it was—it was just as contagious.

Official reports of what was going on dwindled, then disappeared, as reporters and their management quit trying, focusing on their own survival. Eventually, only government-issued reports were available. Finally, even those stopped.

Johns Creek shelter, 12 July

Two days after the vice president arrived from the VEEP bunker, a family of three approached the Johns Creek shelter. It was easy enough for anyone to recognize, if they passed by it, by a large sign attached to the front of the building that read: "Johns Creek Central Emergency Shelter."

Dr. Beth Byron became aware of the family when she heard banging on the outer door and a desperate woman's voice pleading into the intercom.

"Help us, please. We need water and food. Please."

"We don't have any," a member of the vice president's security detail, posted near the door to monitor movement—both inside and outside the shelter—said into the intercom. "Go away."

"You can't do that," Beth called, storming across the room. "We need to help anyone who approaches us."

"Don't let them in." The vice president's voice stopped Dr. Byron in her tracks. "They'll let in outside contamination. They could be contagious. They could have smallpox."

Beth spun around to face him.

"They can't have smallpox. The CDC was bombed. There *are* no more viruses. They're probably suffering from radiation exposure. The president said to take them in and make them comfortable."

"Besides that," Evelyn said, coming up to stand by Beth and handing her disposable protective clothing, "the CDC was bombed two days ago and the incubation period for smallpox is twelve days. And they couldn't have contracted it from the explosion."

"Then they have some other contagious disease," the vice president said as he sauntered across the room to face Beth and Evelyn, while they each donned a plastic lab coat, nitrile gloves, and a mask that covered their nose and mouth. "I'm overruling you, virus or not."

"You may be a political *bigwig*," Beth said loudly, "but I'm still in charge of caring for the sick. I say we need to let them in and treat their radiation burns."

Throughout the argument, Beth could hear the people outside, still banging on the door and pleading for help. Others in the shelter cautiously came forward, by ones and twos, to stand behind the doctors and face down the vice president.

Perry came alongside the vice president and whispered in his ear, making him jerk.

"Are you willing to take on the whole shelter over this?" he asked. "Do you really believe the bomb didn't wipe out the viruses?"

The vice president looked at Perry, a surprised look on his face. Beth knew that the security detail was hired to defend the vice president, with their lives if needed. So, apparently, Perry's comment was unexpected. She wondered if he had the will to fight, if his own people didn't back him. His next comment convinced her that she had guessed correctly.

"Okay, doctor, it's your show this time," he said with venom in his voice. "Everyone else back away. We'll let the doctor have a look." He turned back to Beth. "You know the difference between radiation burns and smallpox, or other contagious diseases, I presume?"

She nodded with confidence.

"If there's any indication that they have anything other than radiation burns, they, *and you*, go out the door," he threatened.

She nodded again, a little intimidated by the vice president's anger.

The security guard unlocked the inner and outer doors and backed away.

Beth entered the airlock and opened the outer door a crack to look out. The visitors looked like a family of three. The man's arms were draped over the woman's shoulders and she held onto a young girl's hand. All three had rashes on their exposed skin—faces, hands, and the woman's bare legs—that looked like radiation burns. They also had minor injuries that could have been caused by flying debris from the explosion. She was sure they were suffering from radiation exposure. Then she started to doubt herself. Was there any way they might have some contagious disease, like smallpox?

"Please help us," the mother said. The daughter cried, great tears rolling down her cheeks. It tore at Beth's heart to see them in this condition. She had to do what she could for them.

"Check their mouths," Evelyn said quietly from right behind her, and handed her a flashlight.

Evelyn's support reassured her. As unlikely as it was, if the visitors had smallpox, the first positive sign would be visible lesions in the mouth.

"We'll take care of you," Beth said nervously. "I'm a doctor. My name's Beth. First, please open your mouths for a quick checkup." The mother looked confused, but mother and daughter opened their mouths. Beth shined her flashlight into their mouths in turn, trying to keep the light out of their eyes. No lesions. She started to relax.

When Beth turned to the father, whose face was in shadow, he was unresponsive. He appeared to be leaning on his wife, rather than supporting her, as Beth had supposed. The wife must have seen the look of concern in Beth's expression, because she turned toward her husband and placed her fingers between his lips, forcing his mouth open.

"He threw himself on top of us when this powerful wind knocked down buildings and threw things at us," the mother said apologetically, in a raspy voice. "He was hurt, and we haven't found water in the two days since then."

Beth confirmed that there were no lesions in the father's mouth, clicked off the flashlight, and pushed the door open wider to let them in. Then she quickly closed the door behind them.

"We need to disinfect you as best we can before you enter the shelter," Beth said, apologetically, thinking how embarrassing it could be for them if she asked them to undress before entering. "The shelter is full of people who haven't been exposed to the radiation."

"You need us to undress, don't you?" the mother asked, her voice hoarse.

"That would be best. Just the outer layer."

Evelyn entered the airlock with protective clothing for the family, similar to what she and Beth were wearing. Ben followed, dressed the same way, and handed bottled water to the mother and daughter.

"Evelyn's also a doctor," Beth said, feeling guilty about stretching the truth, but needing Evelyn's help, "and Ben's a nurse. They'll help us. Okay?"

The mother nodded, so Ben took the man from her. He was unresponsive, so Ben undressed him, wiped down his arms, hands, and head with disinfectant, and put the lab coat on him.

When they had all three of them disinfected, and their discarded clothing stuffed into a trash bag, Evelyn pushed open the inner door and spoke to the others in the shelter. "Will some of you give us a hand?" she asked.

Reluctantly, two men and a woman stepped forward to help.

"What do you need?" the woman asked.

"Radiation sickness isn't contagious, and we've washed our visitors, so don't be afraid of touching them. You two," she said, pointing to the two men, "will you help Nurse Schick get his visitor into the medical observation room and put him on the bed in the middle? You," she said to the woman, "go to the medical office and ask Doctor Gibbons to bring cotton sheets, food, and drink to the medical observation room."

"You're sure we won't get contaminated?" the woman asked.

"As I said, we've already disinfected them, so you shouldn't get any radioactive fallout on your skin or clothes," Beth said. "If you're concerned about it when we're through here, you can change clothes and wash. I'll have nurse Schick gather any discarded clothing and destroy it. Trust me, you'll feel so good about helping that you won't care about the clothes." She tried to sound positive for the benefit of those who were watching and listening, including the mother and daughter.

Later, as Nurse Schick followed up with the volunteers, Beth, Evelyn and Melissa tried to make the visitors comfortable, treating their injuries and irritated skin and giving them food and water. The father was still unresponsive, so Beth hooked him up to a saline drip IV. As tired as his wife was, she insisted on helping. Eventually Beth insisted that they get some rest. The medical team would keep watch through the observation window.

They were asleep in minutes.

17

I think I know what happened

Johns Creek shelter, 13 July

Dr. Byron entered the room to relieve Nurse Schick, who had the early morning watch. She'd decided that their three patients—she'd called them *visitors* in front of the other shelter occupants, to minimize the emotional impact of their condition on everyone—needed to be monitored until the father recovered from his injuries. In the dim light of a night-light, Beth could see that Ben was asleep, his head resting on his arm on the table, snoring softly. She smiled kindly—she'd really grown to love Ben's gentle, caring manner. He was the best nurse she'd ever worked with.

So that she wouldn't wake anyone, Beth left the light off and retrieved a flashlight from a shelf near the door, then donned her protective clothing and went into the observation room next door to check on their patients. In the dim light, it appeared to Beth that the rashes on the mother's exposed skin were no better, but it had only been a few hours. The mother was shaking and moaning. Maybe she was having a nightmare, reliving the explosion and two days of torture, and wondering where they would find relief.

The mother didn't react to Beth's light. Beth would have spoken her name, but she didn't know it, hadn't asked for it in the rush of the previous day's activity. She felt the mother's forehead with her gloved hand and could tell that her temperature was high—possibly with an infection. Her pulse was high, too. She raised the mother's eyelid and shined the light in her eye, noting that her response time was slow.

Beth was beginning to worry that the woman suffered from something more serious than radiation sickness. Out of curiosity, she shined her light inside the mother's mouth and saw lesions on her tongue. Really? She had to make sure, so she backed off, blinked her eyes a couple of times to ensure she was seeing clearly, then looked again. A brighter light would give her a better view, but it definitely looked like there were lesions all over the woman's mouth, not just on the tongue. But it couldn't be, could it?

Beth stood up and looked back through the window at Ben, considering waking him to get a second opinion. She was saved from making a decision when Dr. Schumann opened the office door and walked in, carrying a cup of coffee.

"What's up?" she asked quietly through the intercom on the wall, then yawned. Nodding toward Ben, she added. "Not him, I see." When Beth just looked at her, she turned to look at their three visitors. "You've been checking our patients and you're not pleased with the prognosis," she guessed.

"Get some gloves and a mask and take a look."

Evelyn studied Beth as she set down her cup and took the two steps to the cupboard—the office was that small.

"That serious?" she asked, as she donned her protective clothing.

"You tell me."

Evelyn took the light and shined it in each patient's mouth.

"Oh my!" she exclaimed quietly. When she was done, she turned back to Beth and whistled quietly. "Not good. Not good at all."

"How could they have smallpox?" Beth asked. "It's only been three days. It has to be something else."

"Let's not jump to conclusions," Evelyn said. "Turn on a light and let's look again. This is definitely more than radiation poisoning, but smallpox has a twelve-day incubation period. Unless . . . "

Evelyn looked into a far corner of the room, thinking for a moment.

"I thought it might be an infection from injuries, because of the fever," Beth said, turning on the overhead light.

Evelyn felt the father's forehead with her gloved hand, then drew it away quickly, in surprise. She checked their mouths again.

"It's an infection alright. It's smallpox. I can't think of anything else it could be. But how?" Evelyn looked back at Beth. "I told the vice president yesterday that there was no way the virus could have escaped the CDC. How could I have been wrong?"

"I need to call this in," Beth said, interrupting her thoughts.

"My supervisor at the CDC is Dr. Julie Headrick," Evelyn said. "She's in the VEEP bunker. Make sure she's told as well. You place the call and I'll try to keep a lid on this."

They disposed of their protective clothing as they left the observation room. Beth pulled out her phone and moved to a corner of the office to place her call. Evelyn went to Ben and shook his shoulder gently. He came awake instantly, his arms flying out to the sides.

"Wha . . . ?"

"Shush," Evelyn whispered. "Get Melissa in here without waking anyone else. We need to talk—quietly."

"Something wrong?" Ben whispered as he looked around, focusing on Beth in the corner, talking on the phone.

"We'll talk about it when you get back with Melissa."

While she waited for the others, Evelyn thought about the events of the previous day, trying to determine how they had misdiagnosed the family's symptoms.

President Gregory McCormick - Prime Bunker

President McCormick sat at the conference table in his secure bunker, holding a cup of coffee. Three of the eight monitors on the wall were now blank, reminding him of the explosions and deaths of the previous day. His heart skipped a beat, and his hands shook as he set his coffee cup on the table.

His advisers were alone in their respective bunkers. Sitting next to Ambassador Porter in the VEEP bunker was CDC Director Anne Lister and a young woman the president hadn't met.

"Mr. President," HomeSec Chuck Dickson said. He had requested this meeting. "Director Lister, from the CDC, and one of her supervisors, are with Ambassador Porter in the VEEP bunker. You need to hear what they have to say."

When Ambassador Porter heard the introduction, he turned to the camera. "Mr. President," he began, "You've met Director Lister. This is Dr. Julie Headrick." Dr. Headrick nodded at the president. "She received a disturbing message from the Johns Creek shelter this morning."

"That's where Art is now, right?"

"It is, sir. Dr. Headrick, please tell the president what you told me."

The president watched as Dr. Headrick tried to compose herself. He'd seen this before—people nervous about speaking directly to the president of the United States. He smiled reassuringly, and Dr. Headrick began, explaining the situation at the shelter. He listened calmly—the tapping of his fingers on the table top was the only indication that he was disturbed by her news.

"How sure are you that this is smallpox?" he asked calmly when she was finished.

"Dr. Byron's diagnosis was confirmed," Dr. Headrick said. "One of my scientists from the CDC, who's familiar with the virus, checked the patients before we called Mr. Dickson. I'm afraid there's no doubt."

"Let's not be hasty," Director Lister said, defensively.

The president ignored the director's comment, speaking to Dr. Headrick instead.

"What instructions have you given Dr. Byron?"

"She's to isolate herself and the other three medical people, along with the three civilians who helped care for the victims. She's to give the remainder of the shelter occupants explicit instructions on what symptoms to watch for and to let the medical team know immediately if any symptoms appear. She's also to report to me daily."

"Wait just a minute," Director Lister said. "It could be something else."

"Dr. Headrick, please keep Ambassador Porter and Chuck—Director Dickson—updated on the situation at the shelter."

"Yes, sir."

"Mr. President," Director Lister said.

"What is it, director?"

"It could be something else."

"No, it couldn't, Anne," Dr. Headrick said quietly. "There's nothing else we were working with that has those specific symptoms."

Lister just stared at her subordinate.

"Thank you, Dr. Headrick," the president said.

Dr. Headrick and Director Lister stood to leave.

"Director, please stay," the president said. A concerned look passed between the two women, then Director Lister sat back down.

"What do you want to do, Greg?" Chuck asked.

"I don't know, Chuck," Greg said and banged the tabletop with a fist, startling Lister. Then he turned back to the VEEP monitor. "Director, how do you think smallpox escaped the CDC facility? We dropped a nuclear weapon on it."

Lister squirmed a little, making it look like she was settling into her chair, then looked up at the president.

"I'm still not convinced—" she started to say, but he cut her off.

"I'm not accusing you, Director. I just want to know how it could have happened. We need answers and solutions." He had ample testimony that it *was* smallpox. He didn't need Lister taking it personally, trying to defend herself.

Lister took a deep breath before answering.

"If it really *is* smallpox, I would say there are two possibilities. The first would be an accidental leak. Our employees were in a hurry to leave. We follow strict procedures, but if our doctors failed to follow procedure, that might have allowed the virus to escape."

"What's the likelihood of that happening?" Chuck asked.

"Very low. It takes two doctors, together, to access any active, contagious virus. That means that two doctors would have to make serious mistakes simultaneously, or—and this brings me to the other possibility—that they conspired to intentionally remove the virus from the secure facility, to prevent it from being destroyed."

"Can you think of any one—or two—doctors who would want to prevent us from destroying the virus?" the president asked.

"I can tell you that most of our doctors are passionate about their research. Whether or not any of them would intentionally—"

"Director," the president interrupted, "can you provide a list of names of those authorized to access the smallpox virus?"

"Yes. That's easy. There are only six besides me."

"Will you please supply those names to Director Dickson?"

"Of course, sir. If there's anything . . . " Lister said proudly.

"I'd like you to assess the situation in the shelter and give Dr. Byron as much help as possible. She's about to have a lot of people very angry with her for not identifying the disease before it was allowed into the shelter." *And Art's one of them,* he thought, realizing that the vice president could become too difficult for the doctors to handle.

"Yes, of course. I'll . . . " the director was slightly cowed by the president's demanding demeanor.

"What I'd like you to do is work directly with Dr. Headrick, on call twenty-four seven, until this situation is resolved. You and Dr. Headrick will report daily to Director Dickson, and he'll keep me informed. Any questions?"

"No, sir," the director replied quietly.

"Thank you. Now, is there anything else we need to know about this virus? For instance, why was the incubation period three days instead of twelve?"

"Sir?" Director Lister asked in surprise. "Three days?" She was suddenly flustered. In the confusion of the move from the CDC to the bunker, she hadn't thought about the incubation period.

"Yes, it was only three days from the time we bombed the CDC to the moment the doctors positively identified this as smallpox. How do you explain that?"

Director Lister suddenly knew exactly what had happened, and who was responsible. President McCormick was staring at her, waiting for an answer. How much should she tell him? She realized that she couldn't lie to him and she couldn't withhold information that he needed in order to deal with this latest crisis.

"Mr. President," she said, then had to stop and swallow to relieve her dry throat. It didn't help much. "I think I know what happened."

She paused, so the president prompted her by motioning with his hand.

"Some . . . a few of our senior scientists do research on viruses, attempting to understand them better. Two of our doctors were working with smallpox, to see if they could modify it."

"What were they trying to modify?"

"They wanted to make it less virulent. Or, alternatively, of shorter duration."

"It sounds like they succeeded."

"Yes, and no."

The president waited for her to go on.

"In a Prelim—that's a preliminary report—they said they thought they had succeeded in shortening the incubation period."

"And?"

"I was waiting for their next report when we were evacuated. I'm sorry."

"Ok, let's get them in here and have them tell us what they found."

"I'm sorry sir, but those two scientists are missing."

"*They're what?*" The president shouted, then lowered his voice, but his pulse raced. "Explain that, please."

Lister cringed, then straightened up.

"They didn't get on either of the trucks when we evacuated the CDC," she said, trying to regain her dignity. She'd told herself a hundred times that it wasn't her fault.

The president sat quietly, staring at the director, as he digested this new information. He had shared a short phone call with Amos Blund a few days earlier. It was no big deal, he had thought at the time. He had merely wanted to know how Amos and his family were doing so he could briefly take his mind off global problems. But they had talked, briefly, about the plan to nuke the CDC and similar facilities. Amos had said; *"You're talking about medical professionals—PhDs—who've spent most of their career babying those agents. They may try to take their samples with them."*

"What were you expecting in their next report, Director?" the president asked.

"They were supposed to tell me if they were successful in reducing its virulence. They were also supposed to report on any other changes they saw—any side effects of the initial alteration."

"So, you're telling us," the president said, "that you have information confirming that the incubation period is shorter. But you don't know if the virus is less virulent, the same as it was, or more potent than before. Nor do you know if there are other side effects of the change. Is that right?"

"Can you give us any other information to help shed light on what's happening?" Chuck asked before she could answer.

"Well, we should have their lab notes on the server. I can find them and get back to you."

"Is there any reason they would want to hide what they were doing?" Chuck asked.

"None that I can think of. They gave me a Prelim. That means something is on the server."

"Thank you," the president said, concealing his fury and his frustration. "I'll look forward to hearing what you find."

Lister nodded, then rose and left the room. The president nodded to the ambassador, who turned off his connection, and the VEEP screen went dark.

"Amos warned me about this very thing. What are we going to do?" Greg banged his fist on the table again, startling Chuck.

"You spoke to Amos about the virus?" Chuck asked, sounding upset.

"Yes, kind of," he said, realizing he had just spoken without considering the effect it would have on his advisors. They might think his talking to Amos was a breach of national security. "I wanted another opinion about nuking the CDC. He assured me it would work, but only if someone on the inside didn't sabotage it. He actually suggested that someone might try to take their research with them. I can't believe he was right—again."

Greg studied his advisors, clearly sensing their displeasure. He thought about how important these people were to him, and how valuable they were to the country. He'd served with Jim Seymour in the Gulf War and had recommended him for the SecDef position. Tom Mitchell had managed Greg's successful campaigns for the Senate and the presidency. Cy Hutchison had served with him in the Senate. And although he hadn't met Chuck Dickson before his name appeared on a shortlist of candidates for the HomeSec position, Greg had come to respect his skills and abilities as much as he did the others.

"We could always nuke the shelter," Chuck said angrily, breaking into the president's thoughts.

"That would certainly solve a couple of my problems," Greg replied.

"You're referring to Art, I suppose."

"Can you imagine how Art would respond if he found out

about a plan to nuke his shelter?"

"It wouldn't be pretty, but if we succeeded, he'd be dead."

Greg half-smiled, then frowned. It was a solution, but a costly one.

18

What's happened is impossible

Johns Creek shelter, 13 July

Evelyn called the three volunteers into the medical office, while Beth spoke to Dr. Headrick on the phone. When Beth eventually turned to face them, she saw five concerned people standing close together, though Evelyn was a little apart from the others, probably because she'd been in proximity to the patients and didn't know if she was now contagious herself.

"I want to thank each of you," Beth said, "for your help yesterday with our visitors. Unfortunately, I have bad news."

The three volunteers turned their heads to look through the window at the patients.

"Are they dead?" the woman asked.

"No," Beth replied, "but in a few days, they may wish they were. You may, too."

They looked at Beth with confusion on their faces.

"What do you mean?" one of the men asked.

"What I'm going to tell you will be disturbing. I want you to think about it before you do or say anything. We'll answer all your questions, but I don't want you to get upset or leave this room before I have a chance to talk it out with you. Will you do that for me?" They all looked at her curiously but nodded their agreement. Only Evelyn knew the truth—her grimace turned to an encouraging smile when Beth looked at her.

"Promise?" she asked again, and they all nodded, again. "Ok. I don't know how, but our visitors have smallpox."

Everyone started moving and talking at once, one in shock— or maybe denial—the others moving toward the door. Beth had anticipated this and put both hands in front of her, moving in front of them.

"Wait. You said you'd listen. Please wait."

"You can't be serious," one said.

"You lied to us," another said.

"I can't believe this!" a third said.

But they stayed, and the two who didn't have their faces in their hands stared at Beth.

"Here's the thing. What's happened is supposed to be impossible. Smallpox has an incubation period of twelve days, and the explosion was only three days ago."

"That doesn't make sense," one man said angrily, his voice rising with each successive word.

"You're right, it doesn't. We don't have an answer. But here's the other thing. The smallpox virus isn't contagious until lesions appear in the mouth. We checked their mouths before we let them in the shelter and there weren't any, so you shouldn't be exposed."

"You mean the lesions are there now?" The woman asked, raising her head from her hands. She started to collapse and had to be helped to a chair by a couple of others.

"Can they be cured—vaccinated?" a man asked.

"Yes, the lesions are there now. We found them this morning. And yes, the patients . . . the visitors can be vaccinated, and so can you, if we can get some vaccine here." Anticipating the next question, she continued. "We've notified the authorities and they're going to help us. What we need you to do now is to stay calm and agree to a short isolation, until we get the help we need. Will you all agree to that?"

There were slow, cautious nods around the room.

"What about you and the other doctors?" one of the men asked.

"We have to be quarantined, too. All of us, just like our visitors. Except we'll stay in the office, instead of in the observation room. In case we're not contaminated, we don't want to become contaminated by being in the room with them. We'll tell the others what we're doing and ask them to cooperate. They'll have to take over some of our responsibilities, but that should be a minor inconvenience."

The woman who'd been helped to a chair, started to cry.

"What can we do to make this easier for you?" Evelyn asked.

The woman looked up at Evelyn, then stared at Beth, with tears in her eyes.

"What will my husband and daughter do after I'm dead?"

Shocked at the question, Beth stammered before getting herself under control.

"You're not going to die if I can help it, Raquel. You'll be back with Jim and Callie in a matter of days."

Evelyn realized that this was the mother of the girl in the brightly colored clothes. Callie was the girl, and Jim was the large man who'd been sheltering Callie from Vice President Klemp's attention.

Beth had told Evelyn that the family had been here since the government had started warning citizens to go to the shelters.

Evelyn didn't have children of her own—she hadn't had time—and she vowed to keep an eye on the girl if anything happened to the mother.

"How old is Callie, Raquel?" Evelyn asked, in an effort to get Raquel's mind off her situation.

"Eighteen," Raquel sobbed.

"She's a beautiful, sweet girl. I bet you're very proud of her."

Talking to Raquel about Callie was helping a little. Raquel sniffled and straightened up.

"Thank you, Doctor," she said. "That's very kind of you to say."

"Please, call me Evelyn," she said and smiled. Raquel tried to return the smile, but it was a little sad.

President McCormick - Prime Bunker

"What are the names of the missing CDC doctors?" The president asked Director Anne Lister.

Anne hung her head as she answered.

"One is . . . was my Deputy Director, Dr. Thomas Strang. The other was a close friend of his," she said quietly. She couldn't look at the president—she was too ashamed.

President McCormick must have guessed what was going through Anne's mind.

"You're not surprised, are you?" he asked.

Anne shook her head, then looked up at the president.

"I should have seen this coming. They were so outspoken about the need to keep the samples for research." She looked down again. Her mind was flying over everything she knew about Strang, his associate, and the virus.

"Explain, please," he demanded.

Anne took a deep breath and let it out.

"The World Health Organization recommended destruction of the virus stocks as early as 1986. Due to resistance from the United States and Russia, the WHO agreed to allow them to be kept temporarily for specific research purposes. In 2010, the WHO concluded that there was no public health purpose being served by continuing to retain them. But some scientists maintained that the research was essential for *knowledge,* as pure research."

"So, how did they get the samples out of the facility?" Chuck asked.

Anne explained what she suspected: that Dr. Strang had offered to lock up the CDC so he could intentionally miss his ride and leave separately with the samples.

"What did you find on the server?" the president asked. "Did Strang leave any notes that will help us understand what we're up against?"

"Yes and no," Anne replied.

The president felt like telling her to knock it off with the *yes and no* responses, but remembered that President Richard Nixon was famous for needing only the time it took to say "let me say this about that" to come up with a response to almost any question posed. That was likely what the director was doing, giving herself a moment to process the question, so he waited, though impatiently.

"What did you find, Director?" Chuck asked.

"Their notes are incomplete. They made a list of all the possible side effects they could think of, everything they needed to test. They have a few notes on the list, mostly the word *negative.* But the notes aren't complete."

"Will you please give a copy of the report to Director Dickson so he can have his people look at it?" the president asked, even though it was an order.

"We can help . . . " Anne began, but the president cut her off.

"I'd like you to summarize your thoughts on what we need to know. I'd also like an independent report from Director Dickson's people. Thank you, Director," he said finally, dismissing Anne.

Before she could leave, Chuck spoke.

"Director Lister, I want to be sure I'm not missing anything you've told us so far. You're saying that the samples were removed from the facility the day of the evacuation, which was also the day of the bombing. Then, two days later, a family appeared at the shelter, already infected with a mutated virus that normally has a twelve-day incubation period?"

Anne shrugged and nodded. Chuck and Greg stared at each other, as if they were trying to read each other's minds. Finally, Greg turned to Anne.

"What about the vaccine?"

"It's being prepared as we speak. Enough doses should be delivered today."

"Triple the number of doses, please, Director," Greg said. He added, "thank you," dismissing Anne and the ambassador.

"Can anything else go wrong?" the president asked, once Director Lister and the ambassador were gone.

"Greg, we need to find out if this conspiracy to remove the virus samples extended to Ft. Detrick and Russia," Chuck said quietly. His remarks caught the attention of the rest of group, who had been quietly listening, likely considering the improbable circumstances that might now doom the remainder of the population.

"I still say we're better off to bomb the shelter," Jim said.

"Should we send out a team to search for other contaminated people between the CDC facility and the Johns Creek shelter?" Tom asked.

Greg stirred and looked at his team.

"Jim, you're closest to Ft. Detrick. Send out a team to see if they can identify anyone with smallpox."

"I'd send out an entire battalion if I had one," Jim muttered.

"Send another team to find those CDC doctors. They should be easy to spot—they'll be the first people who contracted small-pox, so they'll be farthest along. Once we know where they ended up, we can expand our search from there to find other contaminated people."

"I'll send one of the doctors from each facility with the search teams. That should help."

"Good idea. Next priority: prepare to send a team to the Johns Creek shelter to eliminate everyone there," Greg continued sadly.

"Don't you think we should wait to see if the vaccine is effective in controlling the virus?" Tom asked.

"We're talking about a virus that's mutated into who-knows-what," Jim said indignantly. "We may have the fate of the world in our hands. Greg, I'll have them ready before the end of the day." Almost to himself, he added, "Maybe we should carpet bomb the entire area."

"Jim," Greg said, "let's try it this way first. I'm really struggling with the idea of the collateral damage we're creating. Tomorrow is soon enough to take care of Johns Creek. No one's leaving the shelter today. They'll all be afraid of what's waiting for them out-side. Art is probably wetting his pants. He thought being in the bunker was bad.

"Cy, try to contact Russia. If you can't raise them, find a way to leave them a message. They need to find out if the virus escaped their Level 4 facility. They can contact us if they have questions or need help."

"Greg," Tom said as the president stood to leave. "I'm uncom-fortable with your decision to kill everyone in the shelter."

Greg frowned. He didn't like his decisions being questioned, but he allowed a little latitude with these men. He would listen to what Tom had to say.

"We could gain valuable information from observing the infected people," Tom went on. "I'm sure that's what Director Lister would say. We could let her monitor the people to see if there are other differences between a normal smallpox virus and this mutated version. She would see it as completing the research that her people were doing at the CDC and Ft. Detrick. We could keep it contained inside the Johns Creek shelter and better understand what we're dealing with."

"Greg, we can't let that virus out of the shelter," Jim cautioned.

"I agree," Greg replied. "And I want Art and his security team contained. Okay, here's what we'll do. We'll send the vaccinations and let the doctors vaccinate everyone. Then you'll send a team of soldiers to neutralize Art, his security team, and anyone else who appears to be hostile. Anyone who's left, we'll make available to Director Lister to study. But nobody—and I mean *nobody*—leaves that shelter. Are you satisfied with that, Tom?"

"Yes, sir. Thank you."

"Jim?"

"Fine, sir. What about the other shelters around the CDC and Ft. Detrick?"

"You mean, could what's happening at Johns Creek be happening elsewhere?"

"Yes sir."

"Okay Jim, check the other shelters. Any questions?" Greg asked. "Or suggestions?" He added with a pointed look at Tom.

When no one spoke, Greg continued.

"Okay, Tom, what's the latest on the terrorist?"

"Last report we had," Tom said, "he'd switched cars again,

north of Atlanta, just before the explosion at the CDC. We pulled the FBI out of the area right after that for their own protection. I can't explain why he was still hanging around Atlanta."

"Maybe we got him when we nuked the CDC," Jim suggested.

"Take care of two problems with one bomb? Is that what you're thinking?" Greg asked.

"I'll send some men to his last known location and see if they can spot the car," Jim suggested.

"Great," Greg said with a nod of approval, "you have your assignments. Let's do it."

Greg stared at one of the now-dark monitors. He had failed to prevent a war that had wiped out as much as half the U.S. population—no, half the Northern Hemisphere, maybe even half the world. And now he had to contend with an out-of-control virus that could wipe out the remainder of the planet's population and try to track down a slippery renegade terrorist.

Northeast of Atlanta

"Bloody phone's buggered," Saleh thought out loud. He'd spent the first couple of days after the failed attack trying to stay ahead of the FBI. He'd purchased food from an all-night market—he had plenty of money and didn't want to attract any more attention than necessary—but was surprised by the clerk's comment.

"You're going to *pay*, instead of just taking it like everyone else?" the clerk had asked, sarcastically.

"Why shouldn't I pay?" Saleh had asked.

"I'd appreciate it if you *would* pay. But everyone's worried there won't be any more food after this is gone, and maybe there won't. The war, you know."

Saleh had noticed that the shelves were almost empty and had thought it was unusual. The clerk's explanation helped him understand why. So he had gone around and picked up as much food as he could carry.

That had been before the explosion and car crash.

He wanted to arrange more explosives to finish the mission, but when he'd tried to phone Ahmed in Syria, there had been no service. He'd considered trying to get back to the drop in Virginia, or finding an internet café to place a post, but when he'd tried to get on the internet using his phone he'd had the same problem. He'd tried to walk, thinking he would look for another car to steal, but he had shooting pains in his left leg and it wouldn't hold him up without crippling back pain.

So he'd stayed with the car, sleeping in the back seat, using his backpack as a pillow, and read his Koran. And since the rashes had appeared on his skin, he hadn't felt well enough to do anything.

He'd heard about the nuclear exchange—Armageddon, they'd called it—on the car radio, before the radio stations had stopped broadcasting, and the damage it had caused to cities around the world.

Now he forced himself to consider the possibility that Ahmed's hideout had been destroyed and Ahmed killed. He began to wonder if it was actually possible that Allah had allowed the infidels to find and destroy Ahmed's village. It was hard to believe, but he didn't have anyone else to contact for verification. Maybe Allah had decided that the Al-Qaeda leadership needed to be humbled for some reason. Or maybe Ahmed had lost the faith.

Was it possible that Ahmed had been punished for Saleh's failure at the CDC? He was surprised at the direction his thoughts were taking him. Doubts about his own worthiness entered his mind for the first time in his life.

"But we've lost leaders in the past and we've always come back stronger, wiser, and more determined," he said in an effort to convince himself that he could still succeed. Hearing the words aloud comforted him and strengthened his resolve.

Johns Creek shelter

Ben handed out protective clothing to the newly quarantined group. He showed them where to dispose of used clothing and where to get more. Then Beth opened the door and looked out. The others were starting to move around the common room, bringing food from the kitchen and sitting in small groups at tables or on couches. A few looked concerned, possibly because of the protective clothing, but they had seen her dressed this way when the visitors had arrived.

Beth knocked on the door she was holding, to get everyone's attention. It took a few moments, but she didn't want to shout. When she had the attention of most of them, she spoke.

"May I have your attention?" she asked. "I need you to get everyone out into the common room so I can share some information with you."

"Can't you tell us," one man asked, "and we'll pass it along?"

"I'd rather only have to say it once. Please?" Beth looked to her left and saw one of Art's security agents sitting in front of the door to Art's room. "Would you please tell Vice President Klemp that we need to have all of you join us for this announcement?"

The agent didn't speak, but knocked on the door and entered. A few minutes later—they took their time, with everyone standing around impatiently—Art and his agents walked out, looking crisp and professional. The rest of the shelter's occupants looked like peasants by comparison.

"What can I do for you, Doctor?" Art asked politely, in contrast to his previous demeanor. He still hadn't bothered to learn her name, as far as she knew. Beth took a deep breath.

"You will surely remember that we told you yesterday's visitors could not have smallpox, because smallpox has a twelve-day incubation period. I've been in contact with the director of the CDC and she assured me that all of the smallpox samples were accounted for, the day before the evacuation, three days . . . "

"Those three have smallpox!" Art shouted angrily. "I knew it! You lied to us, you stupid woman!"

Beth already felt terrible—the stress of the situation threatening to immobilize her. Now, Art's abrasive, insulting behavior tipped her over the edge. Her face crumpled. She put her face in her hands and started to cry. Evelyn came up behind her and put an arm around her sympathetically.

Evelyn looked at Art, with his hands balled into fists and his face a mask of hatred.

"She didn't lie," Evelyn said.

Art turned his wrath on Evelyn.

"What do you know about it?"

Had he forgotten that she was a scientist at the CDC? Or was he just so self-absorbed that he couldn't see beyond his own pointy nose?

"I happen to work for the CDC, if you've forgotten," Evelyn said defiantly.

"Of course. I know that," Art said defensively, but his manner softened slightly.

"Then you also know that we've been telling the truth. If you were listening, you would know that what we're seeing is impossible."

"Obviously not impossible," Art said angrily, cutting her off, "just above your pay grade to understand."

"Oh, very clever, Mr. Vice President," Evelyn replied, her anger beginning to show through. "*We* have three sick patients, but *you're* in the midst of losing an entire country."

Art started toward Evelyn, his hand raised with the palm out flat, as if he would slap her. To her credit, Evelyn stood her ground, didn't flinch. Perry caught up with Art and whispered into his ear.

"I advise caution, sir," Perry said quietly.

Art stopped short of Evelyn and lowered his hand. He was a couple of inches taller and looked down into her face with clenched teeth.

"You go too far, *doctor*. You should remember your place or you'll regret it."

Without acknowledging Art's comment, Evelyn handed a still sobbing Beth off to Melissa and faced the group again, ready to finish Beth's explanation.

"Get the contaminated *visitors* out of here," Art said to Perry with a sneer. "Put them on the street."

Evelyn turned back to Art and Perry.

"You'll do no such thing. Those three are now contagious. If you touch them, you risk being contaminated yourselves. You will leave them where they are." Turning to the group again, Evelyn added, "The four of us, and the three others who assisted us yesterday, will be quarantined as well. The rest of you will take over food preparation and cleaning until we get out of quarantine. Any questions?" she asked, looking directly at the vice president, then turning back to the group. Art seethed, although he and Perry had backed up a little when Evelyn had used the word *contagious*. No one spoke up—likely not wanting to draw attention to themselves. Finally, the large man, Jim, raised a hand.

"Yes?" Evelyn asked. "You're Jim, aren't you?" When the man

nodded, Evelyn asked, "What can I do for you?"

"How's my wife?" Jim asked, softly for a man his size.

"She's fine, Jim. She's worried about *you*." Then Evelyn spoke to all of them again. She noticed that Art and Perry had moved away and were talking quietly by themselves.

"All of you, listen. We don't know if any of us have been contaminated by our casual exposure to the patients. We're taking every precaution possible to confine the disease. We're told vaccinations are on the way and should be here later today. We will inoculate everyone, including the patients, to further reduce the possibility of catching the disease and the severity of any illness from it. If you have questions, please feel free to use the speaker on the wall next to the door and one of us will answer as best we can.

"Don't be afraid, stay calm, and take care of each other. Thank you." Evelyn turned, noting that Melissa had taken Beth into the medical office. She and Ben joined them and closed the door behind them.

Evelyn didn't look at Art after she finished her explanation. But Art was watching her, thinking about how he would get back at her for her insults and insubordination.

He'd ruined Greg's chance to kill him in the bunker, and clearly now Greg was trying again with this virus. He knew the president would keep trying to kill him until either he succeeded or he was stopped, so Art would have to find a way of stopping him.

19

I have all the air I need

The Preserve, 13 July

After dinner had been cleared away, the family stayed in the dining room to celebrate.

Brittany Carlsen entered the room carrying a cake decorated with yellow daffodils—Sydney's favorite flower—and fifteen lit candles. Brittany started singing "Happy Birthday," and the others joined in, all except Jason and Nathan, who were in the room but didn't participate. Rylee divided her attention between what was going on with Sydney and the cake, and Nathan, who was sitting in the far corner of the room. She caught him looking at her and a little thrill ran up her spine. She'd been back to the weight room every day, and Nathan had yet to talk to her, but he was noticing her now.

"Before you blow out the candles," Brittany said, "you need to make a wish."

Without hesitation, Sydney blurted out, "I wish Lillie were my grandma!"

Ever since they'd met that day in the Carlsens' living room, she'd been clear that she admired Lillie, and she'd found excuses to spend time with her once they'd arrived at the Preserve. Even so, Lillie looked surprised—though delighted—at the revelation.

"If you say it out loud, it won't come true," Rylee scolded, focused on Sydney for the moment.

Sydney frowned as Brittany set the cake down on the table and looked at Lillie, pleadingly.

Resting her elbows on the table and her chin on her hands, Lillie smiled broadly at Sydney from across the table.

"You can call me Grandma anytime you want. But just remember, I'm not *that* old." When Lillie winked, Sydney grinned ear to ear.

"And you can call Amos, Grandpa," Lillie added, as she took Amos's hand. "He *is* that old."

Sydney looked at Amos uncertainly, then smiled when he did.

"I don't mind being a grandpa," Amos said cheerfully, "but being married to a grandma makes me feel *sooo* ancient." Lillie smacked him on the chest with her open palm, then leaned over and gave him a kiss on the cheek.

After Sydney blew out the candles, they sang "Happy Birthday" again, this time for Katie, then cut the cake.

When everyone had finished eating, Lillie ushered everyone into the community center.

Johns Creek shelter

When the vaccinations arrived, Beth was notified by phone. She was still suffering from powerful feelings of guilt and self-doubt, and was on the verge of losing it again at any provocation. Wearing protective clothing, she opened the office door carefully so that her appearance wouldn't scare anyone. Even so, several people looked up as she stood in the doorway, concerned expressions on their faces.

"I'm dressed this way for your protection," she said. "The vaccinations are here and I need two volunteers to go get them and bring them to me."

When no one volunteered—probably worrying about smallpox coming in from outside—Beth turned back to the office.

"Ben, will you help me?" she asked.

Ben and Evelyn quickly joined Beth, dressed similarly, and together they walked through the common room to the airlock door, spreading the other occupants like Moses parting the Red Sea. One of the vice president's security agents unlocked the door and backed away before they arrived.

"They're here," Ben said, when the military truck appeared on the intercom monitor.

Beth, who'd been watching the concerned, fearful, angry faces of the people in the room, gratefully followed Ben into the airlock, leaving Evelyn to stay by the door in case Art tried to lock them out. She knew her concern was irrational, because Art might well be sealing his own fate if he didn't get a vaccination, but he hadn't been acting rationally since he'd arrived.

While Beth and Ben were getting the vaccinations, Melissa came out of the office, dressed the same way as the previous three, and placed a small table next to the office door, where Beth and Ben placed two boxes and opened them. Melissa removed three syringes from one of the boxes and took them to the observation room to vaccinate the patients.

"Ok, who'd like to be first?" Beth asked, taking a deep breath.

"I will," a voice behind her said quietly. Beth turned to see Raquel standing in the doorway of the quarantine room, wearing protective clothing like the others. Beth smiled beneath her mask, the corners of her eyes crinkling, and motioned Raquel to come forward. Evelyn wiped Raquel's upper arm with a disinfectant, vaccinated her, and placed the used syringe in a sharps container. That was all it took for others to come forward for their vaccination.

"So, this will prevent us from getting smallpox?" one man asked, while holding the hand of a woman next to him.

Beth was pleased with the question and was about to answer when Evelyn spoke up.

"Would you like me to answer that?"

"Oh, yes. Please do," Beth said.

"Historically," Evelyn said loudly so everyone could hear, "vaccinating people who haven't been exposed to infection has significantly reduced the number of people who acquire the disease. It's also reduced the severity of the symptoms for those who *did* get it."

"How many die after getting the shot?"

"It reduces the mortality rate from about thirty percent to near zero. The symptoms turn out to be more like those of chickenpox."

That seemed to satisfy the man.

What Evelyn didn't say, but what she'd explained to Beth and Ben, was that since the virus had mutated, she really had no idea what the vaccinations would do. "We might all be dead by morning," she'd admitted.

When only the vice president, his security agents, and the doctors were left to be vaccinated, Evelyn turned to the vice president, who was as far away as he could get and still be in the same room.

"Are you ready?" she asked

"How do I know you won't try to poison me?"

"Have you given us a reason to want to poison you?" Evelyn asked snidely. "We've just vaccinated eighty-nine other people from these boxes. You decide."

Then she turned to Ben and started prepping him for his vaccination, but her thoughts were on the mutated virus and possible consequences. If the president were as smart as she thought he was, he would try to eliminate the virus anywhere he encountered it, even it if meant killing everyone in the Johns Creek shelter.

The vice president glared at Evelyn's back. He was getting tired of losing arguments to these women, but he'd get payback when the chance came. He looked at Perry, who just stared back—his face unreadable—then went to get his shot.

The Preserve

Lillie asked everyone to form a rough oval with their chairs—the community center was the wrong shape for a circle—so they could continue the party. When everyone was sitting, Brittany picked up a heavy, gift-wrapped box from the table behind her.

"This is from your father and me," she said, handing it to Sydney, who set it on the floor and carefully peeled the tape back to save the pretty wrapping paper. Inside was a deluxe art set, including markers, colored pencils, crayons, oil pastels, pencils, and sharpeners.

"They're wonderful" Sydney gushed, giving her mother a broad grin.

"I bought them when you started taking art lessons a few months ago," Brittany said, more to the adults than to Sydney. "I wanted to give them to you for your birthday, so I brought them with us."

"Thanks, Mom."

"She's very artistic, you know," Brittany explained to Lillie and Becca. "I just wish we had someone here who could continue teaching her."

"Actually," Becca said, looking at Katie. "Katie's very artistic. Some of her students' parents commented on how much their children loved her art lessons."

"I'd be happy to give her some lessons," Katie said.

"That would be awesome!" Sydney exclaimed.

Brittany and Becca shared a smile over Sydney's excitement, and then Brittany handed Sydney another package that contained art books, sketchpads, construction paper, watercolor paper, and other art supplies.

Sydney and Rylee sat cross-legged on the floor, in the middle of the room, scattering the art supplies in front of them as they chattered excitedly.

"There are a couple of easels in the classrooms that we can use," Katie told Brittany, "and you can help me if you'd like."

"I'd like that," Brittany said, as she watched the girls pick up each item in turn and comment on it.

With the girls distracted, Becca handed Katie a large, gift-wrapped box. Katie's mouth fell open as she lifted out a beautiful, pastel blue party dress.

"I bought it before all this started," Becca explained, "but there wasn't a good time to give it to you."

"Oh Mom!" Katie exclaimed. "It's beautiful. I'm so glad you thought to bring it. Thank you." Katie reached over and gave each of her parents a hug, careful not to step on the dress.

"Happy birthday, Katie-girl," Terry said. "Try it on. Let's see how it looks."

"Where are you going to wear it?" Mike asked, as Katie turned toward the bedroom tunnel.

Becca frowned, having already thought about the social limitations imposed by the Preserve, and hoping no one would say anything to spoil Katie's special day. She was sure Mike meant no harm, but wished he'd kept his comment to himself.

"We'll have a dance," Lillie said, coming to the rescue.

Katie, who'd looked disappointed by the prospect of the dress being wasted, brightened up immediately.

"Then, can I have the first dance?" Mike asked, smiling.

"Oh yes!" Katie exclaimed, bouncing lightly over to Mike to plant a quick kiss on his forehead. "You can have them all." Then she hurried out of the room, not noticing Mike's blush or her mother's smile.

Katie returned shortly wearing her new dress and a bright smile. The dress had a modest neckline, short, puffy sleeves, and fell to just below her knees. She floated to the middle of the room, then twirled so everyone could see the full skirt. There were hoots and whistles of appreciation from the men. Mike looked especially pleased.

Katie gave each of her parents another hug, then sat by her mother and whispered excitedly.

"Emily has an announcement," Lillie said when she could get everyone's attention again.

Emily and Matt had been sitting quietly on one of the couches, holding hands. Now, Emily took Matt's arm and led him between the chairs to the middle of the oval. She looked around the room, her eyes bright and her smile as wide as Lillie had ever seen it—clinging to Matt, light on her feet, and obviously madly in love. Matt looked genuinely happy as well. For once he didn't look embarrassed or lost.

"Matt and I are engaged to be married," she announced without hesitation.

The small group cheered and congratulated them, and Lillie heard Chris call out "About time!"

"Who's going to perform the wedding?" Rachel asked when the room quieted, stopping everyone except Emily.

"Daddy," she said.

Everyone who didn't already know about the Church of Aspen Valley, looked at Amos questioningly, so he explained. Emily's beautiful, beaming face stilled any doubts and forestalled further questions.

Rachel moved first. Standing, she went to Emily and gave her a hug.

"I'm so happy for you," she said with a smile.

"I hope Chris will make you as happy as Matt's made me," Emily whispered as she hugged her back. Rachel stiffened, possibly worried that Chris might be listening, then recovered quickly. She gave Emily another smile and hug, then gave Matt a hug as well. After that, most everyone else took it in turn to congratulate the couple.

"When will the wedding be?" Rachel eventually asked.

"We have a few details to work out," Lillie said, clapping her hands to get everyone's attention. "I suggest we have the wedding two weeks from today. What do you think?"

"Today is the thirteenth," Emily said. "July twenty-seventh sounds good to me." With a loving look at Matt, she added, "What do you think, Matt?"

"Let me check my calen . . . " Matt started to say until Emily frowned and hit him playfully on the shoulder. "Excellent plan," he said, shifting gears quickly and hugging her.

Lillie laughed. In her experience, that was always the right reaction when in doubt, and the others joined in.

While Lillie and the others were preoccupied with the couple, Amos had moved over to a spot where he could sit and observe. The party had been exactly what everyone needed, just as Lillie had known it would be.

The girls had moved their art supplies to a table at Brittany's urging. Rachel looked through one of the art books with them while Chris looked on, all of them oblivious to what was going on with the others. Mike and Katie sat on a couch, Katie still in her birthday dress, talking animatedly, and obviously enjoying Mike's attention, while Mike picked at one of the puffy sleeves and laughed.

The odd man out was Nathan, who appeared to be sulking in a corner.

Amos noticed that, aside from himself, Jason was the only adult not talking to anyone. Jason's focus, as usual, was somewhere else, as if he were contemplating his next move.

His gaze settled back on Nathan. He didn't know Nathan well, and hadn't paid much attention to him since their arrival, but whenever he saw the boy, he was always alone. Amos knew he'd spent a lot of time with his brother, Aaron, who'd died in the car accident, and suspected that he—and maybe Jason—blamed the Blunds for Aaron's death.

Nathan was gazing in the general direction of Rachel and Chris, who were talking with Sydney and Rylee. If Nathan believed that the Blunds were responsible for Aaron's death, it was possible that his sour expression was showing his contempt for Rachel. But that didn't fit. If Nathan blamed anyone, it wouldn't be Rachel. *Maybe,* Amos suddenly realized, *Nathan wants what*

Chris has—Rachel's attention—and he sees Chris as competition.

As if he sensed Amos looking at him, Nathan turned and made eye contact. Amos didn't look away, and Nathan stood up suddenly and left the room, his expression never changing.

Lillie took Amos's hand and smiled. It filled him with love to see her smiling face.

"What's troubling you, big boy?" she whispered, as she handed him her crutches and sat next to him. He noticed that the party had broken up while he'd been watching Nathan. Almost everyone else had left the room. He smiled back and whispered, even though no one could hear them.

"Am I spoiling the party?"

"We're together. We're safe. Why the long face?"

"You're right. And the party was just what we needed."

"Of course it was," she said matter-of-factly, which made him laugh.

"I just can't shake the feeling that we're not out of trouble yet."

"It's Friday the thirteenth. Are you superstitious?" She smiled when Amos shook his head. "You're concerned about Jason." She made it a statement.

"And Nathan," he added.

She looked around.

"He left a little while ago. Have you noticed Nathan spending time with anyone else?"

"No. Why?" she asked, after thinking about it for a few moments.

"He was glaring at Chris and Rachel." He told her what he thought it might mean.

"I've noticed the way Nathan looks at Rachel," she agreed, nodding in understanding. "It concerns me some, since we don't know his background. But it didn't cross my mind that he might . . . do you think he might try to hurt Chris?"

"He *was* part of the plot to follow us to the Preserve and rob us," Amos reminded her with a shrug. "It didn't work, but he was involved in it all the same. I haven't given it much thought, but it's possible that he and Aaron and their friends thought we had something of value and wanted it."

"Do you think they caused the accident on purpose?"

"No, I think the accident was an accident. But they *did* fire the gun that killed Tyler and Megan Parker."

"And Joshua. Do you think we need to search Nathan's room for weapons?"

"I'm not ready to go that far—yet. If we didn't find anything, it would create some serious hard feelings. Best to just keep an eye on him."

"Tell you what," she said. "I have more access to people on a daily basis, so I'll keep an eye on the four of them."

"Four?"

"Rylee's still infatuated with Nathan."

"Oh. Have you talked to Rylee about that?"

"Not yet. But I'm watching her."

"Thanks. I love you."

"I love you, too." She kissed him.

While Amos and Lillie talked, Brittany and Becca encouraged the girls to pack up the art supplies, then ushered them off to bed. Amos helped Lillie stand and tried to give her the crutches, but she shook her head and leaned on him, limping over to a couch, where they could be more comfortable.

This was their favorite time of day, when parents were busy encouraging children to go to bed, and everyone was settling down for the night. They could be alone for a few minutes before they, too, had to get some rest. Since their group had become like an extended and expanded family, they needed more energy than they once had to get through the day.

They sat together in companionable silence for a few minutes. Lillie rested her hand on Amos's thigh while Amos massaged the back of Lillie's neck.

"Are you sorry?" Amos asked finally.

"About what?" Lillie asked dreamily.

"About leaving so much of our life behind. We're living underground, and we can't find out what's going on in the outside world. We can't even see the sky."

Lillie smiled.

"The most important part of our life came with us—our family. And what is there to see outside, anyway?"

"There is that." Amos chuckled.

"Didn't you say we could go out in a few weeks to fix the monitors?"

He didn't respond right away, and she looked at him.

"That was what I thought originally," he said with a sigh. "But, with the explosion in Ogden and the earthquake, I think next spring would be a better estimate. It could be a long time before we can go out and breath the air."

"I have all the air I need right here." She gave him another quick kiss.

"I liked that," he said. "Let's do it again." She obliged, then stood and led him off to the bedroom, leaving the crutches behind in the community center.

20

We're in uncharted territory

Johns Creek shelter, 14 July

Evelyn woke feeling cold. *No,* she realized, *I have chills.* She put a hand to her forehead, finding it hot. She started to get up to get a thermometer, but had to lie back down. She ached all over and felt nauseated. She heard a moan a couple of feet away, and turned slowly to see Beth holding her head and stomach.

"Beth," Evelyn whispered. Beth turned her head to look at Evelyn. "You too?"

"Yes," Beth moaned. "Head and muscle ache, fever, chills, malaise and stomach ache—we've got it."

"We better find out if anyone else is sick," Evelyn said.

"I don't want to," Beth responded, then started to roll over in an attempt to rise.

Evelyn matched her, step by slow step, until they were both standing, bent over and moaning. After quick visual inspections of each other, and after taking their temperatures—101.2 and 101.3 degrees Fahrenheit—they inspected each other's mouths. Neither had lesions, but each was beginning to show evidence of skin rashes on their arms, legs, and heads. Evelyn knew these were all classic symptoms of the prodrome, or pre-eruptive, stage of smallpox, at two to four days. She and Beth were now suffering from the same symptoms as their three patients—the symptoms they had previously diagnosed as radiation exposure.

"I've got to call this in," Beth said. "Can you find out about the others here in the office?"

"Better idea," Evelyn replied, "let's check first, then you can give them the whole story."

"Course, right. That makes more sense. I can't think clearly."

They checked the other people in quarantine. Every one of them had similar symptoms.

Beth found Ben lying on his side, shivering under a thick blanket.

"Ben!" Beth exclaimed, then gasped when Ben turned his head and she saw his flushed face and chattering teeth. Evelyn, who was right behind her, handed her the thermal strip to take his temperature.

"No wonder he's shivering," Beth said, reading the thermal strip on his forehead. "One-oh-two point four. Open your mouth, Ben."

He did, but couldn't stop shaking.

"He has lesions on his tongue," she whispered, looking at Evelyn. "How can that be? We were only exposed two days ago and he's already in the prodrome stage."

"Remember, he had to carry the male patient across the shelter when they first arrived. That must have speeded up the process."

"Speaking of our patients, we'd better check them." After the woman had started shivering the day before, Beth had checked their vital signs and had decided to use IV drips to keep all three hydrated—and to keep them mildly sedated.

"Beth," Evelyn said with a gasp, "you won't believe this." Beth turned away from Ben to see Evelyn looking through the observation window at the patients.

"Help me, please," Ben whispered hoarsely, grasping Beth's arm weakly. "I can't take this. I want to die."

Tears welled up in Beth's eyes. She'd only known Ben for a couple of weeks, but in that time, she'd grown to love the big, sweet guy. To see him in such pain and misery broke her heart.

"It's ok, Ben. We'll fix you right up," she lied, patting his arm and pulling away in the process. She didn't know what she could do—she might be in the same shape before the end of the day.

Beth moved slowly over to Evelyn, to look at the patients, and gasped.

"It's hemorrhagic, isn't it?"

"Classic symptoms of hemorrhagic smallpox," Evelyn replied. "Bleeding under the epidermis, making the skin look charred or blackened. Red eyes, smooth skin, fatal within seven days."

"Let's go check," Evelyn said. "They look like they've been thrashing around." All three patients were tangled in their cotton sheets, darkened limbs spread at odd angles, and it looked like the mother had pulled over her IV stand.

"Is that significant?"

"Hemorrhagic smallpox causes internal organs to shut down, leading to death. If they've been convulsing, it means they were in a lot of pain. If not for the sedative you gave them, we might have heard them screaming."

"I didn't hear a thing."

"Neither did I, but I was pretty wiped out from the stress of the day."

As they talked, they donned fresh protective clothing and entered the observation room. They checked their patients for pulse and breathing, but there was nothing. All three were dead.

"But it's only been four days," Beth said, tearfully.

"Now you should report," Evelyn said. "I'll hook Ben up with an IV."

Beth stared at Evelyn, wondering if she thought Ben might have hemorrhagic smallpox. But she couldn't ask—she was too afraid to hear the answer. Instead, she went back into the office to place her call.

"Doctor, I don't feel good," a sweet, young voice said from the intercom box on the wall.

Beth looked out the window in the door and saw Callie, her flushed face almost as bright as her clothes, holding her head.

Not Callie, Beth thought. She wanted to cry. She had a shelter full of sick people, and she was too sick to help those who were too weak to protect themselves.

"I need to make a call, Callie," Beth replied through the intercom. "Why don't you sit there by the door? I'll only be a minute." She heard a noise that sounded like Callie leaning against the door, then sliding down until she was sitting on the floor. Beth went to a corner and made her call.

Northeast of Atlanta

Saleh shook uncontrollably. His head hurt, his skin itched, and his whole body ached, inside and out. He had previously struggled to get his warm coat from his backpack—every movement was difficult—and put it on. He'd thought it would help, but it hadn't. He felt his forehead and was shocked at how hot it seemed. He located his water bottle where he'd tucked it after his previous drink and tipped it to his lips, hoping it would satisfy his thirst, but the bottle was empty. He threw it away from him with what little strength he had, but it bounced off the window and hit him in the chin, then fell onto the floor. He thought he had another one, but he didn't have the strength to lift his head and open the backpack again. He tried to recite the prophet's words from the Koran, but the pain in his head made it difficult to think—or sleep. All he could do was lie still, wide awake, and pray. He thought that even death would be a relief.

President McCormick - Prime Bunker

CDC Director Anne Lister had just completed her report to the president, explaining in detail the confirmed contamination of the caregivers and the suspected spread to the other shelter occupants.

"So now, everyone who came in contact with the contaminated family has smallpox. And some of the others may have it too. Is that what you're telling us?"

Anne nodded.

"Thoughts, anyone?" the president asked, as he looked from one to another of his advisers.

"Sir, if I may?" Anne asked.

"Go ahead, Director," the president said, trying to control his frustration.

"I've been thinking about this a lot since our meeting yesterday. With this new development, it's obvious that the virus has evolved. Something has caused it to act atypically. The incubation period should be twelve days, not two to four days. The three patients shouldn't have died nearly that quickly, especially after receiving the injections. The people in the shelter who had no direct, physical contact with the patients shouldn't be getting sick at the same time as the ones who had physical contact."

"What do you think happened?" Chuck asked.

"I don't know what to say," Anne answered. "But it seems apparent that Dr. Strang's manipulations of the virus shortened the incubation period and made the virus more virulent. What we've seen so far is impossible with the old strains. What might happen from here on is a mystery. We're in uncharted territory."

"What was normal with the old strains?" the president asked.

"Normal prognosis is, or was, thirty percent fatality in the un-vaccinated. That rose to fifty to seventy-five percent in severe cases and near one hundred percent in the case of hemorrhagic small-pox. Where all of these folks have now been vaccinated, based upon all previous infections, that *should* drop to near zero—say, less than five percent. They should probably all be sick for a few days or weeks, then get better."

"But now, with the mutation?" Chuck asked.

"With the mutated virus, I have no idea. They could all be dead by morning," Anne replied sadly.

The president sensed her mood. He felt bad for thinking it, but their deaths might be the best thing.

"Tell me about hemorrhagic smallpox," he said, lightly shaking his head to clear the unpleasant thoughts.

"Well, historically, in about two percent of infections, mostly in adults, the patient suffers extensive bleeding into the skin, mucous membranes, and gastrointestinal tract. The whites of the eyes turn red, and bleeding under the skin makes it look black. Hemorrhag-ing in the spleen, kidneys, muscles, and other parts of the body, causes organ failure and results in death, often between the fifth and seventh days of illness, but certainly by the tenth day. Keep in mind, though, that we're talking about a twelve-day incubation period, and then five to seven more days after beginning to feel sick. With this mutated virus, with a three-day incubation period instead of twelve, I don't' know what to expect. It progresses un-believably fast."

"What can we do to help?"

"You've done all you can do, unless you want to go to the shel-ter and get contaminated yourself." The president gave Anne a stern look. "Sorry, sir. No disrespect intended . . . sir."

"Fine," the president said. "Have we figured out what happened to the missing doctors?"

"Just what I told you before, sir. They must have hidden until the transports were gone, then left the area on their own."

"My conclusion exactly," SecDef Seymour said. "They probably didn't get far enough away, before the explosion, to avoid flying debris. Maybe their car broke down, or they stopped for a drink, and thought they were in the clear. They didn't know we were going to bomb the facility."

"That family showed up at the shelter two days later," Jim continued. "My guess is that the missing doctors got within a two day walk of the shelter before stopping. The samples probably got damaged then."

"Director Lister," the president said. "Do we know if anything similar happened at the Ft. Detrick or Russian facilities?"

The president had directed Jim and Secretary of State Cy Hutchison to check on the other sites, but maybe the director could get better information through her own channels.

"No one's contacted me," Anne said.

"Will you please contact them, if you can, and see if you can determine their status?"

"Yes, sir. Right away. Anything else?"

"Keep tabs on the shelter. I want to know immediately if anything else unusual happens. Thank you, Director." Anne nodded and left.

Johns Creek shelter

More than half the shelter's occupants woke with flu-like symptoms similar to Callie's, including one of the vice president's security agents, but no one believed it was flu.

"Get him out of here before he contaminates all of us," the vice president told Perry, pointing at his own sick agent.

"It's probably too late for that," Perry said, though he began moving toward the sick agent.

"Do it anyway. And find out what those doctors are doing to protect us. Let them know that their number one priority is to keep me from getting sick."

Perry shrugged inwardly, thinking that his boss was losing it. But he'd sworn to defend the man's life, and he would keep that oath. He returned, wearing surgical gloves and a mask, and brought enough extras to supply the vice president and the other members of his team.

"What's this?" Art demanded.

"This is what the doctors are doing to protect us. They want everyone to wear gloves and masks from now on until they say it's safe to take them off."

"This is asinine," Art said, as the rest of the security team donned their gloves and masks. He stood, watching his agents for a few more moments, then swore again and put on the mask and gloves.

By the end of the day, everyone was sick and miserable, with rashes, high fever, malaise and headaches. Most of them had macules—small, round, flat, discolored areas—on their foreheads, arms, and legs. Many were suffering from nausea, vomiting, and backache.

In the case of all three doctors, Ben, and the three volunteers, the macules had spread to all parts of the body and had begun to turn into papules—hard, round, elevated lesions that itched.

Beth cautioned everyone to resist the urge to scratch, which could cause severe scarring and infection, especially in the crusted scab stage. That would come later, in about two weeks—at least with a normal disease progression, but it might happen any day with this mutated version. The next few days would be especially difficult on the children. As miserable as the adults were, it would be almost impossible to keep the children from scratching the "itchy spots".

Beth called Director Lister and reported on conditions in the shelter.

"I'm at the end of my rope, Director. I don't think we can keep this up. It's almost impossible for the four of us, sick as we are, to take care of ninety-one other sick people. If we don't get some relief . . . " She left the sentence unfinished, just shook her head, which, of course, the director couldn't see.

"We're looking at options now, Dr. Byron," the director replied. "We could send a couple of medical people in hazmat suits, or we could move all of you to a facility where someone else could take care of you."

Beth started to cry. The only part of the message that registered in her mind were the words *someone else could take care of you.*

"Oh, that would be great," Beth said through her tears, though she didn't hold out much hope that it would actually happen.

"Can you give me a little more detail . . . " Director Lister started to say, then stopped. "What's that commotion, Dr. Byron?"

Beth cried even harder.

"It's another fight. This is taking its toll on everyone here. Vice President Klemp and some of the others have gotten violent. He's bullying everyone and picking fights. I don't know who he's picking on right now." Since his exposure, Art's paranoia and normally narcissistic personality had turned to aggression and violence.

"What's his security team doing?"

"Watching, mostly. When I asked Perry, the lead agent, if he would stop the vice president, he just said that he swore an oath to protect him, that the other people were my problem." Beth's crying turned into sobs and she hiccupped.

"Stay by the phone. I'll get right back to you."

Beth seemed not to have heard, and went on speaking through her sobs.

"He's battered several women and broken ribs of three men who tried to interfere. I don't know where he gets the strength. He's not that big. Everyone should be listless, but a lot of people have got their energy back. They may be even stronger than before. Now some of the men, and even a few of the women, have started picking on the ones who are weaker. I don't know what to do."

She broke down and barely registered Anne's last words.

"Okay, doctor. I'll get right back to you."

President McCormick - Prime Bunker

"What do you think is going on, Director?" Greg asked when Dr. Lister finished explaining what Beth had told her.

"I think these are part of the virus's mutation," she said. "First, the incubation period was cut short. Now we're seeing personality changes—enhancements, maybe even increased strength. The disease just isn't progressing normally, and everything that's happening is happening very fast. I wish we could study it."

"Jim, Chuck, what do you think?" Greg asked—then regretted it the moment the words had left his mouth. He'd asked his advisers not to mention eliminating people in the shelter in the presence of the director, and they might interpret the question he'd just posed as permission to discuss it now.

"I think we need to take out the entire shelter before this mutated disease escapes," Jim said.

"You can't do that," Anne gasped. "Those are people we know

in there."

"Not anymore, director," Chuck replied. Anne stared, open-mouthed, as Chuck continued. "This team," he said, waving his arm at the wall of monitors, "is responsible for what's left of this entire country. We can't allow a mutated virus to be released into the public when we don't know what it's capable of doing."

Anne sputtered, as if trying, unsuccessfully, to form an argument.

"All the people in the shelter have now been vaccinated," Jim said. "And they might survive. Very soon, they'll realize that they can just walk out of the shelter. Art, or one of his agents, has the key, no doubt. As angry as they are now, and possibly with increased physical capabilities, we don't know what will happen when they encounter people on the outside. If they've become violent, it could be both dangerous and ugly. We have to stop them, now."

"You told Dr. Byron you would call her back with a solution, right?" Greg asked. Anne looked at him with her mouth open, unable to speak, but she nodded mutely. "Alright, tell her we're sending a couple of doctors to help handle the sick. When Art finds out, he won't feel threatened by a couple of doctors—it sounds like he's already pushing the doctors around. But don't say anything about the fighting or Art or anything else. Can you do that, without mentioning anything we've discussed here?"

"What are you going to do?" Anne asked quietly, already suspecting that she knew the answer.

"We're going to neutralize the threat in the shelter," Greg said. "If that means immobilizing Art, his security team, and anyone else who gets aggressive, that's what we'll do."

"Can't you have someone call the security team and tell them to stop the vice president?" Anne asked.

"That would be the easiest solution, if it would work," Chuck said. "But I don't think it would, for two reasons. One, if we tell the security team their detail is being dissolved, they'll just become additional aggressors that we have to deal with—but *these* aggressors have guns. Two, if we try that approach, we'll tip off Art and lose the element of surprise. How good is your acting, Director?"

"I can try," Anne said.

"Thank you," Greg said, dismissing her, and she stood and left the meeting.

"Ambassador?" Greg asked, looking toward Ambassador Porter, who was in the VEEP bunker with Anne. "Will you please go with her and listen to their conversation?" The ambassador nodded and his screen went dark.

"Jim, I don't want any survivors. If Art suspects anything, he could become difficult."

"Understood," Jim said. "I'll get Colonel Johnson to set up a team that can pass as doctors. It shouldn't be too hard if they're wearing hazmat suits. We'll move tonight. The darkness should help."

"Thank you." Greg said, certain that Jim would know the best way to handle it.

Northeast of Atlanta

Saleh heard noises. It took a few moments to register that two men were having a conversation nearby. He opened his eyes but couldn't see them, so he tried to concentrate on what they were saying. They were far enough away that he only caught snatches.

" . . . injured or dead . . . food . . . need it . . . "

He was lying still because every time he moved, some part of his body screamed with pain.

The door handle rattled, then a hand reached through the window and snagged the strap of his backpack from under his head. Surprised and angry, Saleh reached out, grabbed the thief's arm, and twisted. He heard a crack and the thief was thrown off balance and fell, screaming. He released the arm and threw the car door open, hitting the thief in the face and knocking him unconscious. His partner, frozen in place until that moment, turned and ran. Saleh didn't take time to think; he picked up his gun where he'd set it on the car seat and shot the fleeing man in the back.

The incident over, he noticed something he hadn't before: the itching and pain he'd felt for so long had subsided to a dull ache, as if the adrenaline of the confrontation had supercharged him. Surprised, he took stock of his physical condition. The rashes, which had turned into sores, then scabs, and then discolored bumps on his skin, no longer itched. His left leg and lower back still hurt—probably nerve damage and would take time to repair itself—but overall he felt surprisingly healthy and strong. And somehow, where he'd felt on the verge of death before, he'd suddenly found the strength and speed to take on a pair of thieves.

Unaware that the CDC had been bombed, he thought that maybe now he could move ahead with his attack on the facility. He left the would-be thieves where they were and walked away from the scene, carrying his backpack, hobbling a little from the discomfort in his back and leg.

He didn't get far before he realized that he wouldn't be stealing another car in this direction. All around him, the buildings were damaged and the cars were overturned or smashed, many buried or crushed by garages that had caved in, homes that had collapsed, and telephone poles that had snapped or been thrown down. And the smell of death was getting stronger, too. He hobbled in another direction and found similar damage. When he began to wear out, he decided that he'd better stay close to the car.

The thieves were still lying where he'd left them. He considered trying to help the man with the broken arm, but decided against it. He'd come to America to kill infidels, after all. He shot him in the head instead, then painfully dragged each of the bodies to the nearest building and tossed them inside. He found a water bottle in his pack, took a long drink, and settled into the back seat, falling asleep as he considered his next move.

21

I would never choose those colors

The Preserve, 14 July

"What's up?" Amos asked, as he and Terry entered the lab. Mike was sitting at the Observer controls, with the gate open to the Smith's parking lot in Logan.

"Hi Dad, Terry. I'm taking the gate to all the places I think we'd be interested in visiting, so we'll have coordinates, in case we want to jump there in the future." When Amos didn't respond, Mike was sure his dad had figured out his real purpose: he was trying to find a good argument for letting him go through the gate, into what he was convinced was a parallel world. He needed to say something to dispel his dad's suspicions.

"I've been all the way down to Ogden, and up to the north end of Bear Lake, and I've found some differences. Wanna see?" He watched his dad's expression change from suspicious to curious as he looked at the gate.

"What have you seen?" Amos asked.

"Our neighborhood, for one." Mike turned the Observer off, plugged in new coordinates, then turned it back on. They were looking at Terry's house, but from twenty feet in the air.

"You did it again, Mike," Terry said proudly, "but I don't think we live there. I would never choose those colors."

The yard was green with life and well maintained. The afternoon sun shone brightly on the front of the house. But Mike had to agree: the house wasn't the same.

"I'm convinced I was right about this being a parallel world," Mike said, "and I agree with Terry. I don't think we live here in this world."

"Let's try our house, Michael," Amos said,

Mike moved the portal around the block and faced the Blunds' house, which was also different. There was no lab in the back yard, and the mailbox that Lillie had painted bright blue a couple of years earlier was back to being a dull gray.

"What does that tell us, Terry?" Amos asked.

"If Mike's right, and this is a parallel world, then possibly things have evolved differently in this version."

"Such as?" Amos asked. When he didn't get an answer, he went on. "So, some possibilities. We live somewhere else. We made different career decisions and never met. We married different women with different tastes."

When Amos paused, Terry took over.

"Or we never married? We died young? We're hallucinating again? Amos, this line of investigation won't get us anywhere. We want to know whether this is really a parallel world or not. How do we find that out?"

"I think the only way we can do that," Mike said, "is to find our parallel selves in this world and determine once and for all that that's what this is—a parallel world, but with differences in certain details."

Amos placed his elbows on the table and rested his chin on his fists as he stared at Mike.

"How do we do that, Michael?"

"One of us has to go there and do an internet search," Mike said seriously, staring back at his dad.

"Aren't you worried about introducing paradoxes that could

destroy the universe?"

"What do you mean?"

"Well, if we can believe the science fiction we've read—and this feels just like science fiction—every time we interact with something in this other world, we'll introduce a variable that changes something down the time stream. We talk to someone, and that influences a decision they make later. We say something, and discover that they speak a totally different language. We try to buy something, and find out their coinage is different. Maybe their customs or laws are different, and we inadvertently violate one. Someone asks for ID, and ours doesn't match . . . "

"I get the idea," Mike interrupted. "So, what do we do?"

"Terry?" Amos asked.

"No, no," Terry said, amused. "Leave me out of your little love fest. Amos, why are you so uptight?"

"You two want to go traipsing off through an unknown world without thinking through the possible consequences?"

"So, you admit it's a parallel world," Terry said.

"I said unknown world, not parallel world. And that's not the point."

"Okay, Amos. Granted, we can't just enter this world and start looking for our other selves. But you have to admit, it looks like Logan, the date is correct, the subdivision is even laid out the same way, despite the fact that we chose ugly houses to live in. Why couldn't it be a parallel world?"

"I have no answer, Terry. Do either of you want to hang around to see if your doppelganger shows up, or do we make a plan to answer some of our questions?"

"It's almost dinner time," Terry said, looking at his watch.

"Can we come back later?" Mike asked.

"Of course," Amos sighed.

"Then I've seen enough, for now."
"Me, too," Terry added.

22

We need to get out of here

Johns Creek shelter, 14 July

Beth left the office and went to the common room after speaking with Director Lister. They'd already determined there was no reason for anyone to stay isolated now. There'd been a mirror on the wall by the door before, but she'd removed it because she knew she looked as hideous as the others. The papules had already begun to spread and swell. Some had started to drain.

All around the common room, people tried to avoid looking at each other, though there was nearly nowhere they could rest their gaze without seeing someone else's face, swollen with ugly, dark papules. Broken furniture littered the room, along with shattered glass and shards of mirror, and the other areas of the facility looked just as bad. A few people moved around, walking stiffly, as though their clothes irritated their skin. Some had taken off shirts, cut off pant legs, or stripped down to underwear, and no one wore shoes or socks.

Suddenly there were angry words and a man pushed a woman off a couch, swearing angrily at her. She didn't fight back or cry, just curled up into a tight fetal position on the hard floor.

Beth realized she was becoming despondent. She tried to think happy thoughts, but her body told her there was absolutely nothing, no matter how small, about their situation that was positive. She found that she didn't care about the other people anymore.

She didn't even care that three decaying, stinking bodies lay in the observation room, covered with sheets. There was nothing she could do for anyone else. She had to get herself through this.

She had a fleeting thought about Director Lister sending medical help. Was she supposed to tell someone about that? She realized that she didn't care about the answer.

She leaned against the wall and watched as little disturbances broke out around the room. The people reminded her of monkeys. She remembered standing in front of the monkey enclosure at the zoo for hours. She'd watched a female monkey, sitting on the branch of a tree, grooming her baby. A large male had come along and swiped at the female, then poked her. But she hadn't defended herself—just wrapped her long arms around her infant, turned her back on the aggressor, and made herself as small as possible—as if she could hide her baby somehow. That's what she saw now in the common room: aggressive monkeys picking on passive ones, who did nothing to defend themselves except to turn away and make themselves small.

Someone came out of the room behind her—the medical office, she remembered. Her name was Evelyn—Dr. Shumann. She had to struggle to remember even that much. Evelyn's face was as ugly as everyone else's, covered with dark boils. Smallpox, she remembered, but not ordinary smallpox. This one was special. It was turning them all into monsters, both physically and emotionally. Heaven help the world if anyone got out of here alive.

"Have you told them?" Evelyn asked, distractedly.

"Told them what?"

"Hmmm . . . about the medical help coming tonight," Evelyn finally said.

Oh yeah, Beth remembered.

"Everyone, listen a minute," she said in a hoarse voice, as she pushed off from the wall. She had to swallow twice to get enough moisture in her throat to continue. A few people closest to her turned to listen. "They're sending a couple of doctors to help us." She had to think about it to remember why. "We're all dehydrated . . . and the medical staff is too weak to help anymore. They should be here tonight."

One of the vice president's agents got up and walked slowly into Art's room. He wore jockey shorts, with his gun belt strapped loosely around his waist, so that it hung down on one side. He returned a few moments later with the vice president and the rest of the security detail, all of them walking slowly—they looked like waddling ducks—in various stages of undress, and with pained expressions on their faces. Except the vice president. He wore slightly wrinkled slacks and a short-sleeved dress shirt.

When they headed toward the outside door, Beth called out to the vice president, without moving.

"I can handle this," she said. "I'm responsible for medical treatment in the shelter." Something about the vice president's presence seemed to quicken her pulse, and her head and her heart started to pound.

The vice president turned and walked slowly toward her, his men moving behind and to both sides of him. When he was about eighteen inches away, glaring at Beth with hatred in his eyes, he punched her in the midsection without warning. She doubled over and fell to the floor, moaning.

"Oh, that was satisfying," he said with a wicked grin. "I've wanted to do that since we arrived. Mind yourself, woman. This is obviously a trap. We'll take care of it."

He's paranoid, Beth thought through her pain.

"He's crazy," Evelyn whispered in Beth's ear, as she struggled to help Beth to her feet.

Several others called out to the vice president—mostly insults—as he walked toward the middle of the room, followed by his security team. He cast a malevolent glare around the room.

"Where's that cute little gal in the flowered blouse and capris?" he asked, when he couldn't see Callie—then someone moved and he caught a glimpse of her. She'd changed clothes, but those she wore now were still colorful enough to attract his attention. "Ah, there you are, hiding. Come out here where I can look at you."

The large man in front of her tried to block her way, but she spoke to him and he moved aside.

"It's okay Daddy. He'll hurt you again if you get in the way."

"That's right, sweetie. You don't want to see Daddy get hurt again, do you?" Big Jim had a large bandage around his midsection to minimize the pain from his broken ribs as much as possible.

Callie moved slowly, stiffly, into the middle of the room. She'd pulled her blouse up and tied it under her breasts, so her midsection was bare, and she'd cut her pant legs so most of her thighs were exposed. She wore no shoes or socks.

His eyes roamed her body. She'd look sexy if not for all the ugly bumps. But he'd wanted her since he'd first laid eyes on her. Besides, he would show that *female* doctor that he could have whatever he wanted—she was in no condition to stop him this time.

"How old are you, sweetie?" he asked wickedly. When she hesitated, he grabbed her arm, making her cry out. "I said, how old are you?" he asked again through clenched teeth, still holding her arm.

"Eighteen," Callie said quietly.

"Are you a virgin?" She hesitated again and he yanked on her arm, again. This time she started to cry. Jim, and several others, started to move toward them. Art turned to Perry and pointed at Jim with his free hand.

"If he moves again, shoot him."

Perry drew his gun and aimed it at Jim. Everyone froze, and Art grinned evilly. When he dropped Callie's arm, she backed up a step.

"I asked you a question."

Callie nodded slowly.

"That's good," Art said. "I've never had a virgin. Even my wife was second hand merchandise when we got married. Take your clothes off," he demanded, as he pulled his shirttail out of his pants.

There was a loud knock at the outer door and a loud voice came through the intercom.

"Dr. Beth Byron. We're doctors. We're here to help care for the sick."

Beth watched Art, from where she'd fallen to the floor, suddenly lose interest in Callie and turn to face the door, along with everyone else. Callie scrambled into her mother's arms, hiding her face against her mother's shoulder. They both slid to the floor, kneeling and crying, Raquel's arms around Callie—two monkeys hiding in plain sight, making themselves as small as possible.

Beth wondered if any of them would live to see morning.

"Check the camera," Art told his agent.

"Two people in hazmat suits," the agent replied. "Can't see anyone else."

Evelyn, who had reached Beth and was helping her stand, called in a hoarse voice—the loudest she could find.

"If you harm those doctors we'll all die of dehydration, you idiot."

"Shoot her," Art said to Perry. As Perry turned his gun on Evelyn, Art recanted. "On second thought, save your ammo for the soldiers who will be with the doctors. And try not to harm the doctors," he added with a sneer, aimed at Evelyn.

The agent unlocked both doors and spoke into the speaker by the door. "It's unlocked." The doctors entered the airlock, and took time to decontaminate their white hazmat suits before passing through the inner door into the common room.

The two men in hazmat suits weren't doctors, but Special Forces soldiers. The glare from their plastic faceplates partially hid their faces, and their utility belts concealed loaded guns, stun grenades, and other weapons.

They hoped the vice president and his agents would assume they were filled with medicines and bandages—things doctors needed to treat patients. They just needed to distract everyone long enough to get to them.

"Can we come in?" the lead soldier asked, as they entered the common room slowly, feigning awkwardness in their suits. "We were told to come and help Dr. Byron and Dr. Shumann with patient care."

"I'm Dr. Shumann and this is Dr. Byron," Evelyn said from across the room as she helped Beth, still holding her stomach, to stand.

The soldier had a moment of uncontrolled shock at the doctors' appearance.

"Dr. Shumann," he said, "we were told the disease was more advanced than it should be, but this is a surprise." He hoped his comment would cover the unprofessional lapse in his role as a doctor, and fool the vice president and his agents.

"I hope you don't mind if we leave the suits on," he continued, as he waved one hand from head to foot and looked around. There were close to a hundred people in the room, all of whom had ugly, dark bumps on their exposed flesh. He walked slowly toward the middle of the room, away from the vice president and his agents, followed by his partner.

Melissa took Beth from Evelyn and helped her into the medical office, so Evelyn could work with the soldiers.

"I'm sorry, doctors," Evelyn said, turning toward the medical office. "If you'll come with me, we can discuss the best approach for taking care of everyone."

"Of course, Dr. Shumann," the soldier replied without following her. "Is there anything we can do for these people now? We were told the virus is extremely contagious." He waved his arm toward those in front of him, the way a magician uses one hand to direct the eyes, while the other hand is performing *the trick*. He needed to distract the agents—Perry, who still had his gun at his side, and the others, who had their guns handy on their hips.

Evelyn was a little confused when the soldiers didn't follow her—it probably showed on her face—but she turned and walked slowly toward them, explaining that everyone had what appeared to be a modified form of smallpox.

"The disease is progressing at a staggering rate," she said, "but we've all been vaccinated. Our conclusion is that the virus has mutated in some way."

"The virus *has* mutated," the soldier confirmed, still trying to convince everyone that they were doctors. They opened the pouches on their utility belts as Evelyn caught up with them, but what they removed were weapons, not medical supplies.

Suddenly, both soldiers spun around, one throwing a stun grenade across the room at the agents while the other raised an automatic pistol and started firing. The grenade exploded in light and sound, blinding and deafening everyone except the two soldiers, who both wore vision and hearing protection inside their hazmat suits. Two of the vice president's agents went down quickly. The other two *fell* down from the shock of the exploding grenade, which prevented them from being shot immediately, but they were temporarily blinded and disoriented.

Art dropped behind his fallen agents, which shielded him from the full effect of the grenade. He pulled a handgun from the holster of the nearest agent and began firing wildly in the general direction of the soldiers, forcing them to seek cover. The noise from the grenade deafened him temporarily, so he didn't hear the screams of the people hit by his stray bullets.

The fact that the two doctors were actually soldiers didn't surprise him, but the timing of their attack did. Why had they walked *into* the group of people, instead of away from them, when soldiers would normally protect innocents from getting in harm's way? Then it dawned on him. Greg didn't consider any of them innocents. The soldiers' instructions must have been to kill everyone.

He didn't care about the others, but he wanted to walk away from this—he still had plans. He knew he wasn't the marksman the soldiers were, so he jumped behind a couch and fired indiscriminately into the crowd, hoping that even if he didn't hit the soldiers he might keep them pinned down. He didn't know the gun he wielded was Sergeant Lerner's Springfield XD 9mm handgun, which held sixteen rounds. After shooting what he thought was most of a clip, he started being more careful to aim before firing. When his two stunned agents regained their equilibrium a few seconds later, they joined him in taking shelter and firing at the soldiers, exchanging expended clips for full ones from their utility belts.

The lead soldier could see that most of the furniture was broken, so he and his partner fought off the occupants, who were diving in all directions and scrambling away from the action, to get behind the largest pieces. Then he communicated their situation to the other two members of their team, waiting outside in the truck, using the headset inside his suit.

What he didn't know was that he had an ally in Sergeant Lerner. He'd just decided to take the offensive, and was communicating this to his partner, when Lerner appeared on their left, in a t-shirt and jockey shorts, holding a thick wooden plank in front of him. The Sergeant charged the vice president, to the left of the center of the room, and the soldier quickly realized that the move was intended to take the hostiles' focus away from *them*.

Moments later, the security agents leaned out to get a better angle on the sergeant and the soldiers picked them off. But one of Art's bullets hit the second soldier in the neck, above his bulletproof vest, clipping a major artery.

"I'm hit," the soldier cried out in pain as he went down. Lerner was hit, too, and fell, writhing in pain.

The remaining soldier made the mistake of assuming that the only threat to him was from the vice president, certain that the vice president's agents would have confiscated any other weapons in the shelter.

Focused on Art, the soldier didn't notice the two men sneaking up on him, or hear the warning shouts. Suddenly, he was hit over the head and knocked unconscious. As Art watched, the two men dragged the unconscious soldier into the middle of the room, where they checked his utility belt for weapons and removed his hazmat suit.

Art used the distraction to check on his agents, all of whom were dead or dying. *Dammit,* he thought in frustration. Then he looked back at the two men working on the unconscious soldier. *Hardly a trained security detail, but I guess they'll have to do.*

He started to rise, intending to talk to the two men, when the outer door slammed open and two more people in hazmat suits burst in with automatic weapons blazing. The one on the left sprayed down that side of the room, dropping anyone who entered his line of sight, while the other did the same on the right—on the vice president's side of the room. It happened so quickly that the startled vice president slipped in a pool of blood and fell down, with bullets whistling over his head. As he fell, he fired two shots in desperation—one went wide, but the other hit one soldier in the arm, making him drop his weapon. Alerted, the second soldier turned his weapon in Art's direction.

Art was sure he was a dead man. He pointed his gun and fired, hitting the soldier in the head. He fired again, but only got a click.

The soldier screamed, trying to get his suit's helmet off. He kept firing in Art's direction, but Art had already scurried to another part of the room.

Adrenaline pumped in Art's veins, euphoria making him feel indestructible. He reached out and snagged another gun from the floor, next to one of his agents, then emptied it at both soldiers, still shooting long after they lay, unmoving, on the floor.

When he raised his head far enough to look around, he could see bodies sprawled all over the room in unnatural positions. Blood and tissue decorated the walls and ceiling. His vision was tinted red and his ears rang from the noise, but as his hearing returned, he could distinguish crying, moaning, sobbing, and calls to dying or dead loved ones. It all washed over him as if on a movie screen. He pictured himself as the *real* Terminator and smiled. Arnold Schwarzenegger was nothing compared to him. He felt like he could take on the entire world.

Seeing the downed soldiers, he wondered if there were more outside. He needed a better weapon—an automatic, like the soldiers had. Keeping an eye on the door, he hurried to the nearest one and picked up his fallen weapon. The soldier moaned and reached for him, so Art shot him to test the weapon. It worked just fine.

He quickly searched the pouches on the soldier, finding more ammunition and a grenade. He took them and went to the outer door.

He didn't think about the risk he was taking, didn't think about the fact that he was unexpectedly no longer in pain, and that his sores didn't itch anymore. He felt powerful, even invincible. He entered the airlock and, holding the gun up, opened the outer door and looked outside. *No one on the steps.* He hugged the wall of the stairwell, as he climbed quickly to the top of the steps and looked around.

It was dark—no moon, no stars, no lights of any kind except for the glow coming from the shelter itself, which cast his shadow across the stairwell entrance through dark mists. He blinked, trying to get his eyes to adjust to the lack of light, but it didn't help much. After long moments he was finally able to barely make out the dim silhouette of a military truck a few yards away, on his right. Its lights were out and it appeared to be unattended. Had they really sent only four soldiers? There might be others hiding, waiting in ambush. Probably not, though—that wouldn't be Greg's style—but more would undoubtedly be on the way. The second pair of soldiers probably sent word to the VEEP bunker. This was his only chance to get away.

He returned to the shelter and slammed the doors closed behind him. He noticed that a few of the occupants had ventured out of hiding, but that they hid again when he entered.

"It looks like the coast is clear, for now," he said. "I'm leaving. Anyone who wants to go with me has three minutes to get ready. The rest of you are on your own." A few people cautiously left their hiding places. There were whispers, then shouts. Art didn't wait to see who would join him, just crossed to his room, stepping over bloodied, obscenely contorted bodies, lying with limbs outstretched, careful only insofar as he wanted to avoid stepping in blood. None of it touched him emotionally—he was above caring about any of it.

In the room, he saw a backpack that belonged to one of his agents.

"That'll do," he said aloud, and grabbed the backpack, dumping it out and stuffing some of his own clothes into it. He'd been hoarding a little food, so he stuffed that in, too, and he knew where his agents stored their ammo, so it joined the food and clothes. Then he went back to the common room and collected his agents' guns, shoving them in as well.

As he crossed the common room toward the exit, once again stepping over the bodies and pools of dark, red blood, he looked around one last time. He noticed that the two men who'd snuck up on the soldier earlier were now lying in pools of blood in the middle of the room, casualties of the second shootout. When he went to the door, a few of the boldest men and women followed. One was hopping, hurriedly pulling on a shoe, not bothering to tie it. Some had backpacks, and some had weapons they had collected from the soldiers. One of them stood by the soldier who'd been knocked unconscious.

"What should I do with him?" he asked Art.

"I don't care," Art replied. "Shoot him if you want." With that, Art left. He heard the shot just as he reached the top step.

When Art got to the military truck, he didn't hesitate. He climbed into the driver's seat, found the keys in the ignition, and started the engine. The headlights came on automatically, and he shifted the truck into gear.

"Wait for me," came a cry from the direction of the shelter.

"Hurry it up, then," he snapped. Three people stumbled into the cab. Two more climbed into the open back as Art stepped on the gas. The truck jerked into motion and began to move through the swirling mist.

Art realized he hadn't decided where he wanted to go. Things had happened so quickly. But, as he thought about it now, the one thing he'd wanted to do—had been obsessed with for months—

was paying Greg back for the way he'd been treated. The president was holed up somewhere west of D.C. He didn't know where, but he was certain someone in the VEEP bunker *would* know. He turned left at the next intersection and headed toward his former hideout.

In the Johns Creek shelter, the few people who hadn't been killed or severely injured crept silently out of their hiding places. They were among the least aggressive and more easily frightened, who'd hidden at the first sign of trouble.

Beth came out from the medical office, where she'd taken cover and then hidden, and saw Evelyn, lying on her face on the floor. She had several bullet holes in her back. It was hard to believe, but Beth began to wonder whether maybe the soldiers had come to kill them all. If that was true, then they couldn't hope for any help from the government. In fact, other soldiers were probably already on their way. She wondered whether there was anything she could do about it, but the thought quickly evaporated.

Beth was numb, feeling nothing. Even the cries and moans around her didn't register.

"Maybe we should leave," she thought aloud. She shook her head, not understanding why she was having such a difficult time formulating a thought. She slapped herself across the cheek. It stung, but it awakened her mind.

"Hello," she said. No one reacted.

"*Hey* you people!" She felt frustrated as her thoughts began to take form. "*Hey!* Can you give me your attention please!"

She found a strength in her voice that hadn't been there before. The few people who were still able to move turned toward her.

When she had their attention, she spoke again.

"I know some of you have lost loved ones. There's nothing you can do for them now. What you *can* do is come with me and save yourselves. I believe we're being hunted by our own government."

One woman, who was cradling a dead man's head in her lap, challenged her.

"What for? I have nothing left!"

"For him," Beth said, emphatically. "Shake it off. Get some clothes, some food, some weapons—if there are any left—and come with me."

"Where?" another voice asked.

"I don't know. Away from here. We'll figure it out. But we have to go, now. I'm going to pack. I'm leaving in five minutes." As she went back to the office to pack, she noticed that some of the people in the common room had started to move. There was no joy left inside her, but she thought, *maybe, just maybe, I can make a difference.* That had always been her mantra. And at least she was thinking more clearly now.

Beth found Ben and Melissa in the office. Ben had been shot. The round had gone cleanly through the fleshy part of his left arm, and Melissa had already bandaged it. He grimaced in pain as he turned to look at Beth.

She told them what she had in mind, and Melissa nodded.

"We're already packed. I gave Ben some pain meds and we'll take more with us. My backpack is full of medication, bandages, and as many of the vaccinations as would fit." That explained why she was dressed in layers—there was probably no room for clothes in her pack.

When she returned to the common room, a few people were already there with bags in their arms filled with stuff, and others were arriving from the hallways. All eyes turned toward her.

She looked around at the carnage and noticed Callie, kneeling over her mother, who had been shot. The girl was sobbing.

"People," Beth said, "you need backpacks. You can't carry your things in your arms. You'll tire too quickly."

"I don't have a backpack," one woman whined.

"Get someone else's. They won't need it. Melissa, will you help them?"

"I'll help, too," Ben said, wincing and favoring his bandaged arm.

Beth went to Callie and knelt down across from her.

"Callie," she said. Callie didn't respond. Beth reached over and lightly touched Callie's forearm. Still, Callie didn't look up. Beth knew she would have to take a more aggressive approach, even though it was against her nature. She grasped Callie's upper arm and tried to get her to stand, but Callie resisted and cried out.

"Callie, she would want you to survive this. You have to let go. We'll mourn together, but when we have time, when we're safer. Right now, we need to go." Callie allowed herself to be raised to a standing position.

"Where are your things?" Beth asked. Callie pointed, and they went together. "Take a change of clothes, some food, and something from your mother and father if you want." When Callie was slow to decide what to take, Beth grabbed a few things for her—her mother's hairbrush, a framed photo of her parents—and filled her pack with clothes. Then she led Callie, still crying, back to the common room.

"Beth," Melissa whispered, "there are two people who are still alive, but injured too badly to go with us. They'll hold us up."

Beth shook her head sadly. "Do they have family members here?"

"Dead."

"I'm sorry, Melissa. We have to leave." Beth headed for the door, with the others following. They were leaving the seeming safety of the shelter and going to—what? She looked around the room one last time, seeing all the bodies, thinking how few of the occupants had survived the encounter with the soldiers.

You came close to eliminating us, Mr. President.

She waited with the others on the steps, noticing right away the absence of light. Melissa caught up after a few minutes, helping Ben and crying. Beth thought she knew why. There would be people alive in the shelter when the soldiers arrived, but they wouldn't survive the encounter.

They were a miserable lot. Three men, nine women and none of the children. Three of the survivors had been shot—they were in obvious pain and had to be helped by others.

Beth asked Melissa to close and lock the shelter door.

"Throw away the key," she said. "That might slow the soldiers down for a precious few minutes. It'll give us a bit more time to get away before they figure out we're gone."

Once the door closed, not even the light from the shelter helped them see their way. Beth held her hand in front of her face and only imagined that she could see it, since she knew what it looked like. Melissa switched on a flashlight and moved it around, so they had an idea of what they were facing.

The last of the survivors had just stumbled out of the stairwell when Beth heard a motor and saw headlights in the distance. A truck was coming from the southwest, from the direction of the VEEP bunker.

"Kill the light," Beth said, at the same time that Melissa turned it off. They'd have to travel in darkness for safety.

"Run!" Beth called out, turning to the north. The group ran awkwardly away from the lights and noise, unable to see obstacles in the way, but helping each other as best they could. They disappeared into the swirling mists immediately, the adrenaline of fear urging them on.

Beth knew the soldiers would figure out that people were missing, that some had escaped. The government knew how many people had been in the shelter before this all had started. That meant that the soldiers would come looking for them, which in turn meant they had to get far enough away that the soldiers couldn't find them.

A few minutes later, she heard automatic weapons firing behind them. It started suddenly and lasted only a few seconds. She knew, then, that the soldiers had taken over the tomb formerly known as the Johns Creek shelter.

She could hear Melissa sobbing a few feet away, but couldn't see her.

"Melissa?" Beth called, then waited to see if Melissa would say something.

The sobbing slowed, then stopped. Melissa spoke from the darkness, her voice shaky.

"I gave them a pain killer and told them someone would arrive soon to help," Melissa said through her tears. "I intentionally lied to them. Now they're . . . "

She couldn't continue, and she sobbed uncontrollably.

It occurred to Beth that she should console Melissa, but whatever it was that a person needed in order to give someone else consolation, she didn't have any of it left.

"They're coming this way," a woman whispered from nearby. Beth turned and saw the headlights coming toward them.

"Hide!" a young woman shouted, fear in her voice.

"Ouch! There are bushes here," a man said.

"Quick, back into the bushes," Beth said.

"Hands and knees, people," the man's voice came again. "Ouch, that's my hand. Give me a sec."

Beth dropped to the ground and belly-crawled backward, under the bushes, until someone grabbed her ankles and pulled.

The truck passed slowly, the soldiers shining floodlights on both sides of the road, through the mists. The light passed across their hiding place, first at chest level—which was over their heads because they were kneeling—then at their feet.

With the light provided by the floodlights, Beth could see her miserable companions crouching and kneeling all around her. She heard a gasp and looked to her right, seeing the light shining on blue jeans. She didn't think the noise was loud enough to give them away, but she realized after a moment that she was holding her breath, listening for any change in the sounds coming from the military truck.

After what seemed like an eternity, the lights and the truck continued down the road and around a corner.

Later, out of breath, Beth stumbled through the dark, helping an injured woman. She could sense, more than see, Melissa on her left, one step behind.

Beth thought about where she wanted to go, and where they should go, and what places they should avoid. She was surprised at the sharpness of her mind, and her increased energy level. It was as if adrenaline were supercharging her.

Vice president Art Klemp - southwest of Johns Creek

Shortly after leaving the shelter, Art had seen the headlights of a military truck approaching. He'd parked in the shadow of a damaged building and turned off his own truck's headlights.

"Duck," he said as the truck approached, passed, and continued on toward the shelter. They hadn't been seen.

Now he was in a race for time. He ground the ignition and punched the gas, causing everyone in the cab to jerk backward, then pushed the truck as hard as it would go. He wanted to get to the VEEP bunker before the soldiers returned from Johns Creek.

"Where're we goin'?" one man asked. Art didn't answer at first. He thought of these people as hangers-on, wanting a piece of his ultimate glory. But he needed them if his plan was to succeed, even if only as pawns, or decoys.

It started to rain, so he fumbled around with knobs until he found the windshield wipers.

"I have a debt to pay," he finally said. "We're going to a secret bunker where some government people are hiding. They kicked me out." He wasn't about to tell them that it had been his choice to leave the bunker. They'd never know that he'd had a panic attack and had had to be sedated—not if he had anything to say about it. These people needed to believe that they were pursuing a just, necessary revenge. It would make them more cooperative, given what they'd just gone through.

"They're responsible for what's happened to us." He had convinced himself that this was true. *They could have found another solution to the CDC virus problem,* he told himself. "Now we're going to pay them back."

"Ooh, I'd like to get my hands on the people responsible for this," one of the men seethed.

Art couldn't tell if it was the same man who'd asked the question or someone else. They all sounded about the same to him in the dark, noisy truck. Besides, he really didn't care which was which. They were here to help him get into the bunker and get the information he wanted—nothing more.

"You'll get your chance tonight," Art said.

They traveled on in silence, everyone bracing themselves

against Art's reckless driving through the dark streets. The only light came from the truck's headlights. The only sounds were the squelching of the tires on the rain-slick roads, the swishing of the wiper blades, and the occasional *thump* as they bounced over something in the road. Every so often, Art swerved to miss some large debris that had rained down during the nuclear explosion at the CDC. He had a fleeting thought that he should drive more slowly, but he didn't care. He took corners at high speed and raced through dark intersections without slowing or stopping.

After a while, Art decided to share part of his plan, just enough to hold the men's interest. He hadn't thought through the details anyway. "This bunker is hidden under a house in a cul-de-sac, with no other houses on the street. The government owns the entire street and the wooded acreage around it. The bunker is secured by . . ."

"What do you mean?" someone interrupted.

Art had a sudden urge to turn around and slug the person who'd interrupted him. He took a breath and spoke through gritted teeth.

"There are only two ways in. One is through a hidden door in a bedroom closet. The other is through a hidden door in an old shed in the back yard. I know the shed is monitored by outside cameras. I think the house is too, but we'll take a chance on the house, because of the rain and lack of light. There are two sets of doors with a space in between, like the airlock at the shelter. Once we get inside, we have to get through the airlock doors, which are built to withstand forced entry."

"That doesn't sound encouraging," someone said.

Art thought about the energy he'd felt during the gunfight in the shelter, as well as afterward. He didn't know why, but he felt like superman.

"How do you feel?" Art asked. "Like you could break through solid walls?"

"Well, yeah!" the man said. "That's exactly how I feel."

The others agreed excitedly.

"Then we don't have a problem," Art said, knowing he had them hooked. He just had to reel them in, he thought, and smiled wickedly in the dark.

23

That fat, old colonel was fast

VEEP bunker, 14 July

Art was still trying to determine the best way to gain access to the VEEP bunker when they arrived in the neighborhood. A hundred yards before the entrance to the street, he drove the truck into the trees and turned off the headlights.

"Everyone out," he said. "The street is just up ahead. We'll sneak through the woods and come up on the side of the house."

They clambered out hurriedly. It was raining harder and the wind had picked up. The two men who'd ridden in the back of the truck were dripping wet. Art could see the mist from their breath, but he didn't feel cold. He stared into the woods, but couldn't see a way through, so he went back to the truck and found a flashlight in the glove compartment.

They didn't sneak—they stumbled and tripped their way through the dense foliage, following Art's flashlight, which helped those closest to him see at least a little of what was in front of them. Those behind followed, stumbling and cursing. Each time someone moved a branch out of the way, then let go, the person behind them was showered by the wet vegetation.

Art didn't seem to notice how wet he got. He hurried in the direction he thought would take him to the side of the house. He couldn't imagine them keeping a guard outside in the fallout, with this rain, but then he had never understood what drove soldiers to do what they did. It didn't matter either way. He would take his chances. He moved as fast as he could, ignoring the obscenities coming from behind him.

He stopped suddenly, everyone behind him stumbling and running into one another. He pushed back on the person directly behind him who'd blundered into him.

"Sorry," came a man's voice.

Ahead of them was a house in the middle of a clearing. They were closest to a back corner. There was a porch light, but it had difficulty penetrating the mist and darkness at this corner of the house. He looked for cameras in the trees, and under the eaves of the house, but it was too dark to tell if there were any there.

"We're going to have to take a chance," he said excitedly.

Art studied the two-story house, trying to identify the best way in. The bunker was in the basement, behind reinforced concrete walls and steel doors. But from the outside, you couldn't tell there even was a basement—not unless you walked right up to the house and looked down into a window well. The building was brick, all the way to the eaves. He could vaguely see larger bricks spaced every three feet or so up the corner, protruding out from the rest of the wall—very decorative. There must have been a second-floor bathroom in the corner, because he could just make out a tall, narrow, rectangular irregularity in the brick near the corner on the side wall. There was a larger one below it on the first floor.

That was it. Art turned and took his first good look at his followers. He could only see the three closest to him, and in the dim light from the porch they looked like drowned rats. Two of them were wiping wet leaves and mud off their arms and legs. He picked the third—a tall, slender, attentive man, with short, curly, black hair—who looked to be in his late twenties or early thirties.

"What's your name?" Art asked.

"Dayron," the young man said, dragging out the first syllable. "Dayron Wilson," he said, standing straighter and puffing out his chest.

"Here's what I need you to do, Dayron. See that narrow window on the second floor?" Dayron squinted at the house, then nodded. "I need you to climb up there and force your way inside. Think you can do that?"

Dayron looked doubtful, then suddenly lit up. "I could climb up the corner, holdin' on to those bigger bricks."

"Great," Art replied. "When you get up there, see if the window's unlocked. If not, break the glass and climb through. Can you do that?"

Dayron nodded.

"You need a rock or something?"

Dayron shook his head.

Really? Art wondered.

"Do you have a weapon?"

"Just my hands and feet, but I'm an ultimate fighter, so I'm pretty good with 'em." When Dayron raised his hands to emphasize the point, Art noticed his muscled upper arms and shoulders.

"Should I go now?" Dayron asked.

"Not yet. When you get inside, listen for guards in the house. If one comes to investigate, take him out any way you can—quietly if possible." He tried to visualize this kid taking on an armed security guard, possibly Special Forces, with his bare hands. He couldn't see it, but he didn't know what ultimate fighters were capable of—or, for that matter, whether the invincibility they were all feeling might translate into increased capability. He was about to suggest that Dayron call out if he got into trouble, but realized he didn't have a backup plan. *Besides,* he thought with a smile, *we did okay back at the shelter.*

"If there's one guard," he continued, "there may be two. Take out the second one as well. When you get past the guards, open the downstairs window in this corner and let us in." He didn't want this kid to mess up his plan. At the same time, it didn't trouble him at all that he was sending Dayron into a situation that would likely get him killed.

Art turned to the rest of the group. They had all come forward to hear what was going on, so he didn't have to raise his voice much to be heard.

"We're going to wait here for Dayron to get in and open a window for us. Once that happens, the rest of you follow me, one at a time, to the window. Wait until the one ahead of you is against the house. You all heard the plan?"

There were nods of agreement.

"Now, Dayron," Art said.

Dayron raced across the lawn and pressed himself against the side of the house. No lights came on, and there were no audible alarms. Art didn't know why not—maybe the weather messed with the alarms and they'd turned them off. Or maybe the alarm would only be heard *inside* the facility. Outside it was quiet, with no sound apart from the rain and wind in the trees.

Dayron moved to the corner and tested his grip on the wet bricks, then started to climb. His shoe slipped off the first brick, so he removed his shoes, tied the laces together, and flung the shoes over his shoulder, then he started again. He moved quickly, reaching the second story within a few seconds. He braced his feet against the top of the lower brick and reached over, pushing on the window. It didn't budge. He climbed up to the next brick, hung by his fingertips, reached over with his bare foot and kicked the window in. The glass shattered, but there was little noise—at least from where Art stood.

Dayron reached through the hole he'd made, unlatched the window, and quickly climbed in. There was no sign of other activity inside the house. With every minute that passed, Art's confidence in Dayron's ability diminished and his frustration increased. He considered sending more of his followers to break in the first-floor window and attack that way. That approach would warn the security team, but Art had to get in there.

After about ten minutes, Art drew his gun, thinking he would have to attack. He turned toward his followers, about to speak, when he heard a whistle. His followers looked past him to the house, so Art turned, too. He could see Dayron's tall, lanky figure standing in the open first-floor window, waving them over. His silhouette was backlit by an inside light.

Art ran across the lawn and climbed through the window. The others followed, one at a time, as instructed.

"I did what you said . . . " Dayron started anxiously, but Art cut him off.

"Later, Dayron. We need to keep moving."

"What do I do with these?"

Art turned to see that Dayron was holding two automatic handguns.

"Where did you get those?" Art was amazed. He hadn't heard a shot fired.

"Hid behind the bathroom door for the first guard. Used my favorite move. Surprised the second one comin' up the stairs."

Art smiled. "I knew you could do it." The truth was that he was shocked and genuinely impressed by the young man. Dayron lifted his chin a little higher and looked around, as if to see if everyone else was as impressed as was the vice president of the United States.

"What do we do now?" someone asked, bringing Art back to

the task at hand.

"We see if my old passcode gets us through the security doors," Art replied. "Everyone who has a weapon, get it ready. We may encounter resistance on the other side of the doors. Who has guns? Raise them so I can see." Two of the men had guns from the shelter. Art made sure Dayron and the other two, both women, each had a gun. The two men, who held the guns as though they had experience, helped the others refill the magazines. Art watched, checking and loading his own gun, following their instructions.

"Follow me," Art said, when they were ready. Then he moved rapidly down a hallway without turning on lights. Their wet shoes squelched on the linoleum floor and rainwater dripped from their clothes.

In a windowless basement bedroom, Art opened the closet door and pushed the clothing—an assortment of men's and women's clothes—to the side, revealing a metal door with a numbered pushbutton pad.

"We'll go in, in waves. You and you," Art said pointing to the two men who had experience with handguns, "you'll go in first. Toss these flash grenades in ahead of you." Remembering the experience in the shelter he added, "Uhh, make sure you cover your ears and close your eyes for a second. Then, shoot anyone who raises a gun. You two," Art said, pointing to the women. "You'll go in next and move to the sides. If they continue to resist, keep shooting. Stop when they drop their weapons and put their hands up. Dayron and I will cover the rear. We'll watch for the soldiers returning from the shelter." Art looked at his team, one at a time, to gauge their attitudes. He was again surprised by the look he saw in their eyes. They were ready, and they looked mad. But then, he felt the same way.

"Ready?" Art asked. Everyone nodded. The first two men

waved their guns and bounced on the balls of their feet in apparent anticipation.

"Okay," Art said and punched in a passcode. The door started to open. Art, then the rest, rushed into the airlock. Art shot out the camera above the door. He knew someone on the other side of the door was aware of their entry and would be surprised by the lack of visual confirmation.

"Identify, please," a female voice said. "Was that a gunshot?" Art ignored the request and punched his passcode into the second door control panel. He moved aside as the first wave came up to the door, threw the flash grenades, and rushed into the smoke-filled room. The shooting started. Art closed the first door and fired a shot at the control panel, hoping that would disable the door. It worked in the movies.

"Go," Art said to the two women, who rushed through the door and fanned out to the sides. The shooting stopped as quickly as it had started. Art entered the room, followed by Dayron. There was a young woman in uniform—a corporal, with a nametag that read "Prettyman"—at a desk to the left, her hands in the air. One of the men had a gun aimed at her. Farther back in the room, the second man was standing over two bodies, picking up handguns from the floor.

On the right there was an older soldier, a captain, sitting at a desk, scowling at Art. He held his right arm with his left hand, blood oozing out between his fingers where he'd been shot. One of the women in the second wave had a gun on him.

"Art Klemp," the captain said, "I didn't recognize you at first. That's a new look for you."

Art knew he was referring to his disfigured face and arms, which were now covered with dark pustules. His hair was also plastered down on his head and water formed a puddle at his feet.

"We didn't expect to see you back here, not after your chicken fit . . ."

Art couldn't allow his followers to hear about his departure from the bunker. He raised his gun and shot the captain in the face. Blood splattered everywhere and the captain fell backward in his chair, then sideways onto the floor. The woman holding a gun on him squeaked and jumped back in surprise.

Art turned around and looked at the corporal, who still had her hands in the air.

"Do *you* have anything to say?" he asked. She shook her head slowly, but he could see in her eyes that she was calculating her options. "Don't try it," he said.

Her eyes went blank and she looked down.

"Is the Ambassador still in charge here?" he asked and she nodded. "What are the security words of the day?" He was referring to the fact that the military had established a security procedure for the bunkers which included two keywords, one a color, and the other an object. Both were changed every day. If Art were to ask her to contact someone, and she were to use either of the keywords in a sentence, it would alert the person being contacted that there was an emergency situation, like the one the young corporal was currently facing. They would know to send help.

"Don't even think about giving me the wrong words," Art added, seeing the look in her eyes. She could call for help, but now she had been warned that her life was forfeit if Art survived.

"Yellow and swing," the corporal said.

Art turned to one of his followers—one of the women—who was on the side closest to the corporal. "You stand behind this one and watch her. She's going to call Ambassador Daniel Porter and ask him to come out here. If she uses either of the words *yellow* or *swing* in a sentence, kill her." The woman nodded, walked behind the corporal and aimed the gun at her back.

Relieved of his responsibility for the corporal, the man who'd been watching her turned toward Art for instructions. "You two," Art pointed to the two men of the first wave, "stand on either side of that door, out of sight, where you can shoot and not get shot. If anyone comes through the door with a gun out, shoot 'em."

Art looked at the other woman follower and said, "take shelter behind a desk on that side of the room and wait for my instructions."

"What should I do?" Dayron asked.

"Stay by me," Art said, as he moved to where the older soldier lay on the floor. Before they ducked down behind the desk, Art pointed his gun across the room at the corporal.

"Call him now," he said.

Ambassador Porter was surprised at the call from the security desk. He was just finishing up a report for the president's Daily before getting ready for bed. Corporal Prettyman hadn't said why he was needed, just that he was. As he walked down the hallway toward security, Colonel Johnson called to him from an office on his left.

"What's up, Ambassador?"

"You're working late, Colonel. Call from security. Said they needed me."

"Strange," the colonel said. Standing, he went with the ambassador. As they pushed open the double doors and entered Security, their attention was focused on the desk, where Corporal Prettyman had her hands folded in her lap.

"Don't go for your gun, Colonel," a voice on their left said. Looking toward the voice, it took a moment for the colonel to recognize the vice president because of his disfigurement. He looked around and assessed their situation—three dead on the floor, the corporal and the ambassador, who needed his protection, Art and his partner, plus two very wet bad guys with guns. He realized he needed time to put together a strategy.

"What do you want Mr. Vice President?" he asked politely.

"Good of you to join us, Colonel. You're actually more likely to have the information I need than the ambassador. Give me what I want and we leave, and no one else gets hurt."

The colonel knew it wouldn't be that easy, but he needed to stall for time, to get his soldiers back here and get Art in a cross fire. The problem was the ambassador. How could Johnson protect him? He was sure he could take Art and his friends, even by himself, if he just had a distraction.

Suddenly, the gun was lifted out of his holster. He hadn't recognized the quiet squelching noise as being a bad guy sneaking up on him. *Hmm,* he thought, turning around slowly and seeing two men with guns behind him, *that changed things.* Maybe he'd better listen to what Art had to say.

"What do you want?" he asked again.

"The exact location of the president's bunker."

"We don't know where he is," the ambassador said, too quickly.

"Where do you want me to place the first bullet," Art said as he pointed his handgun at Corporal Prettyman. "I've been practicing. I should be able to hit within two inches at this range."

Art actually had no idea if he could hit the corporal at this range, especially if she moved, but he thought the threat alone would get the colonel to come up with what he wanted. Besides, he had a follower behind her who would follow through for him, he was sure.

The ambassador had gone pale.

"That won't be necessary," Colonel Johnson said confidently. "I'll give you the information."

The ambassador looked at him with relief on his face.

"Do you want it written down, see it on a map, both? What?"

Art thought about the truck they had come in. It had GPS, but they might not be able to take it all the way.

"I want it loaded on a GPS device and printed route instructions."

"That's good. That's what I would have asked for," the colonel said, appearing to be impressed. "Can I get a tech in here to prepare that for you?"

"No, I think our young corporal here," he pointed to her again with his gun, just to make a point that she was still in danger, "can do that for us. Just give her permission to load the coordinates."

"Corporal Prettyman?" the colonel said, looking at the soldier.

The corporal raised both hands into the air to show she had nothing in them.

"I need to get a GPS unit out of this drawer," she said.

Art could see his follower behind the corporal, while the others couldn't. He waved with his gun for her to come forward to watch, which she did.

"Clever," Colonel Johnson said. He was talking to keep Art calm, to see if he could get Art to relax enough that it would improve the odds, just as he had done in numerous hostage situations in the past. He didn't know how stable Art was now—he hadn't been all that well balanced in the first place. "There will be no surprises. We're doing what you asked."

"No tracers on the GPS, Colonel," Art said.

"No tracers. Corporal, make sure you have a clean one." Johnson wasn't really too worried about giving Art an untraceable GPS unit. They would track him down long before he got near the president. Everything in the room was being recorded on video and audio, and they could direct a satellite to watch the truck Art was using as soon as it started to move.

When Prettyman finished loading the GPS coordinates, she set it on the desk in front of her.

"You want a printout of the route instructions?" she asked.

"Yes," the colonel and Art said at the same time. Then Art motioned to his follower.

"Watch her," he said. The corporal typed something into her computer and a printer started up behind her. When it stopped chattering, the follower picked up the printout and looked at it.

"Looks the same as what was on her screen," she said.

Art walked over to the desk and picked up the GPS unit, then turned back to the colonel. "I guess you know I can't let you follow us or alert anyone, Colonel."

"I thought as much," he said, as his arm shot out behind him. He grabbed Art's follower, dragging him to the front, fighting for control of his gun. Art's shot hit his own follower in the chest. Then the colonel had the follower's gun up and aimed at Art, who ducked to one side. The colonel swung the follower around one hundred and eighty degrees and fired at the other follower behind him, hitting him in the chest. The man fell backward with a surprised look on his face.

Prettyman swung around, grabbed the woman behind her, and pulled her onto her lap with the gun under her chin. The colonel grabbed the ambassador and threw him through the doorway, back the way they'd come, at the same time bringing the dead man in his arms back around between him and Art.

Art and Dayron were hiding behind the desk again, as was Art's one other remaining follower. That fat, old colonel was fast. Art was shocked at how quickly the situation had changed.

"Stalemate, Art. You let the corporal leave the room, we let you go out the way you came in."

Art knew that he needed to get away, but he'd disabled the doors. Then he heard the outer doors opening. The colonel bellowed. "Soldiers in the airlock, can you hear me?"

Someone yelled back from inside the airlock.

"We hear you, Colonel."

"*Do not* open the doors," Johnson said. "We have a situation here. You will get back in your truck and drive back out to the highway. You will wait fifteen minutes, then drive back in. No questions, is that clear?"

"Clear, sir. The door controls are damaged, so we're leaving the outer doors open. Complying now, sir."

"Ok, Art, what'll it be? You can use the fifteen minutes to get out of here, or we can stay at stalemate until they come back."

Art turned to the corporal.

"Get out of here," he said.

Prettyman got up, keeping Art's follower in front of her, and backed all the way across the room to the exit. As she passed the colonel, she looked into his eyes. He smiled briefly to show his concern for her safety. Prettyman pushed the woman out into the room and rushed past the colonel, who backed into the hallway, closing the doors as he passed, keeping the dead man in front of him in case Art took one last cheap shot. He paused partway down the hallway and listened. He could hear Art giving instructions to his remaining followers, rapidly retreating footsteps, then the shush of the airlock doors closing. Even so, he didn't let his guard down until he was well down the hallway.

"Here come reinforcements," Prettyman said from behind him.

"Hazmat suits, men," he said as he dropped the body that had protected him and headed for the shower.

Colonel Johnson, Corporal Prettyman, and Ambassador Porter were vaccinated against smallpox minutes later, then quarantined.

24

He saw the name of the McCormick advisor

The Preserve, 14 July

Mike turned on the Observer and sat with his face inches from the gate, which he'd opened just enough for him to read a few words at a time. He had to move the opening back and forth horizontally to read the newspaper headings, but when he shifted to a single column, he could follow the text straight down the page to the fold.

He'd promised his dad he wouldn't go through the gate, but he was determined to learn as much as he could about the twin world. So, here he was, after midnight, reading the front page of a newspaper next to the courtesy counter inside the Smith's market, illuminated by the poor backlighting from the lab.

He blinked, yawned and shook his head. It had been a long day, and he struggled to stay awake, but the headline intrigued him: **MCCORMICK ADVISOR NEGOTIATES UNPRECEDENTED BI-PARTISAN AGREEMENT IN CONGRESS**. He'd just about given up trying to stay awake, when he saw the name of the McCormick advisor: Amos Blund.

25

Do you have any good news for a change?

President McCormick - Prime bunker, 14 July

"Do you have any *good* news for a change?" Greg asked cynically, looking at Jim in his SEC DEF bunker situation room. Jim had requested this meeting, saying he had urgent information for the president.

"Actually, I think I do," Jim said with a cautious smile.

"Well, spill it!"

"When our teams were driving around Johns Creek, one of the soldiers noticed a car that matched the description of the one the terrorist was last driving. The team called to confirm the license plate—it was a match."

"And?" Greg asked, sitting up straighter in his chair.

"They thought there was someone inside the car, but they were just passing by at the time. When they called it in, they were told not to go back in case it *was* the terrorist. Going back they might spook him into running. Not that he could drive away—the car had plowed into a power pole. But they thought he might leave on foot."

"So, maybe he died in the accident?" Greg asked hopefully.

"They didn't know, so we thought we better set up surveillance before approaching the vehicle."

"I think the agents who stopped the attack on the CDC should be the ones to approach him," DNI Thomas Mitchell said, interrupting Jim. "We could get valuable information from him if we take him alive."

"Sorry Tom, but I disagree," Jim said, shaking his head. "Your boys are used to negotiating, but terrorists don't negotiate and they don't give themselves up to their enemies. You saw what he did at the CDC, killing his suicide bomber rather than letting him be captured."

Greg watched Tom fume. He probably realized that Jim was right and it frustrated him.

"What's your plan, Jim?" Greg asked.

"We waited until after dark, then sent in a team for surveillance—backed up by snipers. They're setting up right now. We should have video and audio capability, so we can watch and listen. I'm just waiting for word that they're ready."

"Are you going to just shoot him and be done with it?" Tom asked.

"No. We want to capture him as much as you do. But we want to be prepared for any eventuality. I don't want any of our guys to get hurt."

An aide approached Jim and whispered in his ear.

"We're ready. I'm turning my monitor over to the broadcast."

The street was dark. With no power, there were no lights. The camera used an infrared lens, making everything appear spectral, in shades of green and grey. Jim described the scene for Greg as it changed, pointing out the car, centered in the image—it looked like the power pole had grown out of the car's engine, leaning at about a five-degree angle—then the locations where soldiers were standing and snipers lying, awaiting word to move forward.

As Greg watched, he could vaguely see one group of soldiers, wearing night vision goggles, moving toward the car from behind. Then he saw what the approaching soldiers were seeing, from an infrared helmet cam. At least four soldiers were leapfrogging from one doorway to another along the street, starting from about fifty yards away.

Then he saw the car from another angle, as another group approached from a side street on the left. They stopped about thirty yards away, across an open street.

The view changed again, to show what one of the snipers saw. He was about three stories above and across the street. He had a clear shot through a shattered car window at the person sitting in the back seat.

A penlight shone on what appeared to be a book. The light reflected off the pages and lit up the person's face, vaguely. Then, abruptly, he turned his head, closed the book, turned off the light, and disappeared in the darkness.

Northeast of Atlanta

A scraping noise outside the car drew Saleh's attention. It seemed out of place, sounding more like a booted foot than a nocturnal animal. It could have been another victim of the earlier explosion, but he couldn't afford to take any chances. It could be the FBI again, and he still had a mission to complete.

He closed his Koran and shut off the light, thanking Allah for his miraculous recovery and excellent hearing. In the darkness, he located his gun, ducked, and listened, trying to pinpoint the direction and distance of the intruder. Hearing nothing more, he raised his head slowly and peered out the window, looking as far as he could in each direction.

He heard the noise again and this time he was certain: it was the sound a boot makes scraping on gravel, in this case on the debris from the damaged buildings that littered the sidewalk. He looked intently to the rear of the car and thought he saw movement, but couldn't be sure. Should he wait to see if the person passed without stopping, or should he take the offensive?

The person was trying to be stealthy, that was clear, and that meant it was probably the FBI.

In his head, he heard the words of one of his trainers from his youth camp. "Always have an escape plan," the trainer had said. He realized that, while he had survived this long by following his training, he had now allowed himself to become trapped—cornered in the back of this car.

He opened the car door, slid out, and lay prone on the sidewalk. The dome light failed to turn on, as he'd expected, since nothing else in the car worked anymore. Now he could see the stealthy movements of at least two people a few yards away. If he stopped those two, would there be more behind them? And if so, could he take out all of them before they got him? He knew that as soon as he fired a shot, he would give away his location, so he looked around quickly for another hiding place. There was a doorway across the sidewalk where he'd carried the bodies of the assailants earlier. It would have to do.

President McCormick - Prime bunker

"We've lost the target," the voice of the sniper said. "It looks like he opened the door and slipped out."

The image changed to the helmet cam from the team making the rear approach. The soldiers had stopped moving.

"He's hiding in the shadows."

Suddenly two shots rang out, the flashes coming from ground

level next to the car. The shooter could be seen for an instant, moving on the ground, and then was lost again in the shadows.

"Augh . . . " one of the soldiers cried out, then fell in front of the soldier with the helmet cam. There was a flurry of motion as one of the soldiers came from behind and stooped to check on the fallen man. Meanwhile, the others moved forward quickly, the helmet cam staying close to the buildings and two more stopping at the rear of the car.

Another shot came, this time from a doorway across the sidewalk from the car, and behind the vehicle a soldier fell backward with a grunt.

The view returned to the sniper cam, focused on a doorway where the shooter appeared to be hiding. There was someone in the deep shadows, an extended arm visible through the night vision lens.

"What's going on," Greg asked, concerned.

"The team across the street is going to cross to the car and approach around the front and back," Jim said. "The sniper is on standby."

"But the sniper has the best chance of stopping the terrorist."

"Do you want him alive?"

Greg weighed the options quickly and made his decision.

"Take him out, now, before anyone else gets hurt."

Northeast of Atlanta

Saleh heard the men crossing the street. He stood up from where he had crouched, low in the shadows of the doorway. Now he could see a team of four or more dark shadows moving quickly toward him. He didn't know if there was a back door to this building, but he remembered the debris he'd seen earlier, which would probably block any exit out the back.

Today he would be in paradise.

He aimed over the top of the car and began firing at the shadows.

President McCormick - Prime bunker

The view changed to the helmet cam of one of the soldiers running across the street, zigzagging to present a more difficult target. Then shots were fired from beyond the car. One soldier went down, then another, in quick succession. Then the helmet cam soldier dropped.

The view returned to the sniper cam, focused on the doorway where the flashes from the shots lit up the target. The sniper fired once, and the shooting stopped, the extended arm disappearing into the shadows.

Soldiers voices came over the intercom, nervous and excited at the same time.

"Target is down! Teams report!"

"Team Alpha! Three men down! Send medics and transport, STAT!"

"Team Bravo! Three men down! Send medics and transport, STAT!"

"Team Alpha, approach target, carefully, and confirm."

The view changed back to the rear-approach team, where the helmet cam and another soldier continued to leap-frog, arriving on either side of the doorway, peeking into the doorway, then charging in, firing.

Preview:

World in Chaos

(Book 3 of the Gemini Gate series)

The Preserve, Aspen Valley

Mike stepped through the gate into the deserted parking lot in front of the Smiths grocery store. He turned to remind Katie to keep an eye on him, when a deep voice spoke from his right.

"Well, what do we have here?"

Mike spun around to face three men about his age, sitting cross-legged on the ground and leaning against the building, about fifteen feet away. They wore sleeveless t-shirts and had long, dirty hair, tattoos, and multiple piercings. Smoke from whatever they were smoking—something that smelled unfamiliar—wafted past him.

There shouldn't have been anyone there. He'd checked out this location thoroughly, just fifteen minutes earlier.

He glanced around to see if he could spot the gate, but it had closed behind him there was no sign of it.

"Katie," he called quietly in case she could see him, even though he couldn't see her.

"The name's Eli," the deep-voiced man said, chuckling, "not Katie. You have a friend with you, do you? A gal? Bring her out here so we can get to know her."

His voice suggested what he had in mind. The speaker stood slowly and moved casually toward him, the other two following and moving to either side of him.

Mike looked around again, this time for a way out, and saw that the few cars in the dark lot were spread out, with no one around them. He considered running, but didn't want to turn his back on them.

His mind raced. What had happened to the gate? Had Katie accidentally closed it? When it didn't reappear immediately, he wondered if she'd forgotten her instructions. Would she remember how to reopen it? Did she know he was in trouble? How had he missed seeing these guys, and how dangerous were they? *Come on Katie, get me out of here,* he thought.

He looked back at the three men. They had cut the distance to him in half and had spread out, trying to cut off any escape.

Back in the lab, the last thing Katie heard as the gate shut down, was a deep male voice say, "Well, what do we have here?" She realized immediately that Mike was in trouble.

"Mike," she called, but he didn't respond. "Mike! *Michael!*" she called again, frantically looking at the controls, and around the room, trying to figure out what had happened to the gate. Mike had shown her exactly what to do to minimize the portal without closing it completely, so she could monitor what he was doing and then open it again if he had to return quickly.

She tried to remember exactly what he'd said and shown her, but now she couldn't think clearly. She realized she was panicking.

"That won't help Mike," she thought out loud. "Get control of yourself."

She took several slow, deep breaths to steady her nerves, shook both hands in the air, and tried to think. Turn this knob to the left, but not all the way to the zero. She'd done that, and it still wasn't on the zero. To get it back, she had to turn it to the right. The larger the number, the larger the opening. She turned the knob, but nothing happened.

Had she accidentally turned it all the way to zero without noticing? She turned the knob back and forth several times with no result.

She made a frustrated sound and stomped her foot. She didn't know what to do. Mike had told his dad he wouldn't try this on his own. And he wasn't on his own—she was here—but instead of helping, she was messing it up and didn't know how to fix it. She started to cry.

"Mike, I'm so sorry."

Maybe she had accidentally kicked a plug or something. She looked around for a power cord and soon found one that came from the Observer. She followed it to the outlet on the floor, under the work table. It looked okay. She got down on her hands and knees and crawled under the table, then wiggled it to see if it was plugged in all the way, which it was.

What else? She'd watched Mike input coordinates, but she didn't know enough about that to try it. Besides, she didn't want to change the coordinates—he'd told her to leave them where they were.

She couldn't think of anything else to try.

Mike had told her they were doing this at night because he didn't want their parents to accidentally walk in and stop them, the way they had the last time. She realized she really wanted her dad or Amos to walk in right now, but they were probably sound asleep.

Why did Michael insist on doing this on his own and after midnight? She realized, with tears streaming down her cheeks, that if she didn't get help, she might lose Mike forever—and she was wasting time.

"I'm sorry Mike," she cried as she ran from the room.

About the Story

The Gemini Gate series combines real-world geopolitics, including a detailed, behind-the-scenes look at the White House and the possibility of a global thermonuclear Armageddon, with a fictional technological discovery that just might hold the secret to saving the human race. It takes a component of science fiction—a hypothetical, fictional technology—and embeds it in a realistic, present-day world.

Background

The Three Mile Island Nuclear Generating Station, reactor number 2 (TMI-2) in Pennsylvania, suffered a radiation leak and partial meltdown on March 28, 1979. It was said to be 'the most significant accident in U.S. commercial nuclear power plant history'.

At that time, I worked as a project engineer at a nuclear power plant construction site in Washington State. Eventually, four of the five power plants that were under construction in Washington were cancelled, due to spiraling construction costs that resulted from safety concerns and a labor dispute, at the same time that energy consumption declined in the northwest. The Washington Public Power Supply System (WPPSS, or Whoops, as it became known in the media and on TV in the eighties) was forced to default on $2.25 billion worth of municipal bonds—a humiliation for the financial industry. You can read about it on my website, www.stevenewilde.com.

The failure of the nuclear industry to provide reliable, safe, low-cost energy to the public made me wonder what would happen if an accidental or—heaven forbid—intentional nuclear accident occurred in the western United States, and my story about the Gemini Gate was born; but it took a few years for it to mature into a five-book series. It led me to speculate on the ability—or inability—of government leaders to work together to prevent thermonuclear war, and what it would take to survive the resulting chaos.

The premise of the Gemini Gate series is: faced with the prospect of nuclear weapons in the hands of madmen—what we see in today's headlines would have us believe that there are radical ideologies in the world that would welcome another world war—the U.S. government feels compelled to confront the perpetrators and defend itself; while the people of the world suffer as a result of global political decisions, with the exception of a few, like the Blunds and Stephenses, who anticipate and prepare in advance to survive the chaos.

When the idea for the story came to me, Aspen Valley existed, but only in my mind. Having travelled extensively throughout Utah over the years, visiting the beautiful and unique natural treasures of Utah's State and National Parks and forests, I tried for years to match up what was in my head with a specific location. Driving up Logan Canyon to a family vacation at Bear Lake a few years ago, I realized that we were in the right canyon. I just needed to find Aspen Valley. It's there, a little different than I've described it in the story, but close enough to recognize it. If you're ever in Logan Canyon and spot it, send me an email to let me know.

I've been to and love many of the places I've written about in the series. Many of my characters are reflections of people I know and care about; I hope you see yourself in one of them.

One of my goals in writing this story was to give each character a unique and believable personality. So, many of the characters in the series are patterned after people that I know or have known. Just to be sure that I don't offend anyone, let's just say that if you identify with one of the characters, he or she was meant to resemble you—except for Jason, who is a composite of all the bad character traits I could think of.

This story is a work of fiction. All of the characters in the book are from the author's imagination and any resemblance to known persons is purely coincidental. Location names, government organizations and functions and the effects of man-caused and natural disasters mentioned in the story are accurate to the best of my ability to determine.

Acknowledgments

I need to thank the people who've helped me develop, edit and publish the first three books in the Gemini Gate series. Steve Brown, Kevin Cook, Dan Duvall, David Noble, Felicia Osborn, Chris Palmer and Dan Wilde reviewed one or more of the volumes and provided valuable feedback on content and grammar. The people at IndieBookLauncher.com: Nas Hedron for editing the first two books and educating me on writing styles; and Saul Bottcher, for painting the first three book covers, setting up the books for publication, and putting up with all my questions. I couldn't have gotten this far without all of you pitching in to make me look good.

Most of all, I need to thank Marilyn for putting up with my obsession to tell this story. She's been my best critic and greatest supporter through the long hours at the computer. For your patience at all my interruptions, to run my latest idea past you, and each time I jump out of bed to finish a scene that has suddenly come to me, I love you.

About the Author

I grew up in Salt Lake City and graduated from the University of Utah in Civil Engineering. My wife, Marilyn, and I have five children and fifteen grandchildren. My life revolves around my family and most of my spare time is spent with them. Together we enjoy camping, hiking, travel and get-togethers with friends and extended family. In my quiet time, I enjoy gardening, family history, emergency preparedness, home remodeling, reading and now, writing.

I've traveled to six continents, either for pleasure or business. I survived two floods in Rio de Janeiro and a drenching rain forest in Costa Rica. I've been stung by a Ray on a California beach, I managed the construction of a graphite composite America's Cup race boat and watched it compete and win off the coast of San Diego. I also managed the construction of a graphite composite prototype of the V-22 Tiltrotor aircraft. I managed the construction of five large steel wind turbines, which were installed in Washington, Wyoming and California. I managed and coached project managers in the U.S. and Canada and helped several of them earn their Project Management Professional certification.

Like many people, I had a story in me that wanted to be told, but life got in the way of actually writing the story until recently. My career as an engineer and project manager has led me through multiple industries and specialties, including electric utilities, nuclear power plant construction, water management, global mining and aerospace. Each of those experiences contributed to the broad perspective needed and the interest to research and write about the potential effects of global thermonuclear war on the infrastructure, on people and on the world, itself.

The premise of this story is that, faced with the prospect of nuclear weapons in the hands of madmen, the U.S. government chooses to confront the perpetrators and fight back, rather than sit idly and be abused.

Like you, I hope we never see nuclear war. However, what we see in today's headlines led me to speculate on the ability—or inability—of government leaders to control the radical ideologies that threaten to engulf us in world war.

Feel free to contact me with questions and suggestions.

This story about worlds in collision is meant to entertain. I hope you enjoyed it. Don't miss the sequel *World in Chaos* (Book 3 in the Gemini Gate series), and be sure to check out my website www.stevenewilde.com for background information about the story, characters, locations, facts behind the fiction, and other relevant information.

Thank you.

Steven E. Wilde
Facebook: StevenEWilde_GG
Email: StevenEWilde@gmail.com
Website: www.stevenewilde.com

www.ingramcontent.com/pod-product-compliance
Lightning Source LLC
Chambersburg PA
CBHW051606100726
47898CB00001B/251